KENTUCKY CHOIRBOY

The life and times of a Confederate
raider from his escape from Camp Douglas
to the raid on St. Albans, the extradition
trial in Montreal, and the pursuit of justice
against the Ku Klux Klan

NICHOLAS KINSEY

Printed on acid-free paper

First Printing, February 2025
ISBN 978-1-998600-01-4

Cinegrafica Films & Publishing
820 Rougemont
Quebec, QC G1X 2M5
Canada
Tel. 418-652-3345

In memory of my mother
Winifred Mary Pryce

AUTHOR'S NOTE

This novel is an imaginative re-creation of the life and times of a Confederate raider from his escape from the Camp Douglas prison camp in 1864 to the raid on St. Albans, Vermont, the extradition trial in Montreal, and the pursuit of justice against the Ku Klux Klan for the ex-slave, George Dinning. Solid historical research went into writing this novel, which was inspired by several remarkable books: Adam Mayers' *Dixie and the Dominion*, Michelle A. Sherburne's *The St. Albans Raid*, Linda Richards' *Reminiscences of America's First Trained Nurse*, and Ben Montgomery's *A Shot in the Moonlight*. The novel is closely based on the historical record. The events and even the names of the characters are accurate. Of course, when the facts are not available, the writer's job is to invent. This book remains a work of historical fiction.

Bennett H. Young

PREFACE

"The bouquet of flowers thou gavest to me
I'll keep to the last in remembrance of thee
Its beauty may wither, its fragrance depart
But the donor shall not cease to live in this heart."
A poem by Armistead Barksdale
to his sister Bettie, September 1863

During the Civil War in America, thousands of poems about the conflict were written by ordinary people. They appeared in newspapers, periodicals, and broadsheets. Poetry was ubiquitous during the 19th century. Children recited poems at school. Soldiers died with poems on scraps of paper in their pockets that they intended to send home to their loved ones.

Soldiers were lonely and bored most of their waking hours and were deeply affected by their separation from their families. Poems were a source of inspiration on both sides of the conflict and helped memorialize the dead. They were often intimate works intended for an audience of one.

TABLE OF CONTENTS

30. Arrival in Quebec City
31. Bennett & Eliza head for New Brunswick
Map of St. John River
32. Snowstorm in Maine
33. Wood launches attack
34. Colonel Ermatinger arrests Bennett and friends

Going home: 1865-69
35. Dublin
36. Elder's Hotel meeting & harvest
37. Eliza invites Iris to St. Albans
38. Byron's phantom limb pain
39. Ezra's murder
40. Byron suspects a bayonet was murder weapon
41. Byron and Eliza visit the regimental office
42. Byron and Eliza are attacked
43. Trinity College rugby match
44. The Millers reveal the truth to Byron
45. Eliza races to town to save Byron
46. Marriage vows & wait for pardon
47. Bennett trails Lord Gordon to Montreal
48. Bennett spots Jefferson Davis at hotel
49. Overnight train ride to Toronto
50. Train stalled in blizzard arrives in Toronto
51. The return home

Nursing School, Boston: 1872-73
52. Iris trains as a nurse
53. Long days and longer nights
54. Iris treats Codman daughter at home
55. Bennett & Eliza visit Boston
56. A case of diphtheria
57. Bloody flux and patient notes
58. Iris & Ida set a trap for Polly
59. Outbreak of puerperal fever
60. Iris suffers from severe depression

Map of Western Kentucky

Yellow Jack & Hickman, Kentucky: 1878-79

George Dinning trial: 1897-99

Historical Notes
Acknowledgments
Picture Credits
Other books by the Author

PROLOGUE

May, 1899
Louisville, Kentucky

"There was a great rejoicing in hell this morning," said Bennett H. Young standing in front of the white jury in a Louisville courtroom. "When men of intelligence and high standing like the two lawyers who have spoken for the defendants in this case, stand in a court of justice and condone assassination and argue that a man may be murdered or driven from his home and his family by a self-constituted mob that may elect to take his life and destroy his property, all the demons smiled and applauded."

He paused for a moment to let the words work their magic. The courtroom was packed with reporters from every major newspaper in the country. The old Confederate soldier was delivering his closing statement in the civil trial of some thirty whitecappers accused of burning down the home of the ex-slave George Dinning. He looked back at Dinning, his wife Mollie, and his daughter Eva in the audience, whose lives had been turned upside down by the mob.

"We may in view of the brutality towards this man, his wife, and children, want to cry out. 'Is God dead?'"

The silence in the courtroom was complete. Even the usual coughing and clearing of throats from the gallery had stopped. Bennett Young was a prominent lawyer in Louisville and one of the finest orators of his generation. He was fifty-six years old with a handlebar mustache and white hair and spoke with great authority. He had the full attention of the jury, who were hanging on his every word.

"The counties of Logan and Simpson are named in honor of noble Kentuckians. Benjamin Logan defended himself against Indian attacks and Captain John Simpson was involved in the Northwest Indian War and the War of 1812."

"From these two counties, named for distinguished and heroic Kentuckians, came the men who are guilty of the cowardly and brutal conduct towards this poor, helpless negro man and his innocent family. If they are fair representations of the present type of man Kentucky is producing, we must confess that we are the degenerate sons of noble sires."

"Far down in Simpson County on the edge of Logan and close to the Tennessee line, lived the humble, untutored negro who appears as the plaintiff in this case. By dint of industry and hard, unceasing toil, he had secured 125 acres of land for himself. It met all his wants and there in a rude, uncomfortable log cabin he had lived with his wife and eight children."

The old Confederate soldier was suing the mob of KKK for an amount of fifty thousand dollars to pay for the damages to George Dinning whose home had been burned to the ground and whose family chased off the land. The decision was in the hands of the jury: twelve white men, all solid Louisville citizens. No one could have predicted the outcome of the case.

One

July 5, 1863
Tebb's Bend, Kentucky

They waited in the waist-high weeds for the order to charge. No one said a word. They were all young cavalrymen in their twenties. Some were praying, some were chewing tobacco, and everyone was swatting away the mosquitoes and horseflies. The sun beat down mercilessly on them. Their officers stood among them and looked forward to an engagement that would bring them great honor on the battlefield. They had left their horses in the rear and advanced on foot to within striking distance of the fortified railroad depot which defended the bridge over the Green River. The men felt uneasy and awkward attacking on foot with muskets and would have much preferred to attack on horseback, blazing away with their pistols, but they had been told this would be an easy victory for them.

A small force of 250 Union soldiers from the 25th Michigan Infantry was solidly entrenched in the narrow neck of land east of the bridge on a knoll. The only access to the bend was through the Narrows, an opening barely 100 yards wide, flanked on both sides by the river. Union Colonel Orlando Moore knew he was in a strong position. The Confederates would have to attack on a narrow front that would not allow them to use their superior numbers to their advantage. He improved the fortifications by installing rifle pits in front of the main position and using felled trees to build a breastwork with sharpened spikes in two zigzag rows in front of the abatis. He was ready and waiting for the Confederate charge.

General John Hunt Morgan had left Sparta, Tennessee, on June 11 with 2,500 Confederate soldiers and four artillery cannons, bringing the terror of war to the Union forces. He was convinced his cavalry could easily break through the Union defenses at the bridge, so he launched three regiments in a direct assault. After the long wait, the officers of the 8th Kentucky Cavalry ordered their men to charge. Private Bennett Young was among the young men caught up in the frontal assault. They ran across the field carrying their minié rifles with fixed bayonets. When they were within a hundred feet of the enemy fortification, they were ordered to throw themselves on the ground as a barrage of bullets whizzed over their heads. Bennett dropped to the ground and turned to look at his friend, who had been hit by a ball that had passed clean through his neck. He was suffering horribly from the wound and was barely conscious when he begged Young to take him off the field.

No one could survive the withering fire coming from the Union side until suddenly an opportunity revealed itself. The 2nd Kentucky Regiment launched an attack on the south side, firing on the Union soldiers with their pistols. Young stood up, lifted his friend on his back, and ran as fast as he could through his comrades to the field hospital set up behind the Confederate line. A medical officer approached as he arrived with his friend on the grassy embankment near the surgeons' tent.

"Put him down over there," ordered the officer. "We'll get to him as soon as possible."

Bennett laid his friend on the grass and the officer came over to get a closer look.

"He's dead, I'm afraid," concluded the officer after he had touched the wounded man's neck for a pulse.

Bennett collapsed on the grass near his friend as the officer moved away to triage the wounded men. He was in a state of shock. He had run through a hail of bullets to save a friend, and it was all for naught. He sat near the body for a time and said a silent prayer for his friend as the embankment started to fill up with wounded men. He stood up and returned to join his unit.

The battle raged on as the Rebels reached within feet of the Union line. At times, they occupied one side of the fallen timber while the Union soldiers occupied the other side. It was almost hand-to-hand fighting as the Rebels fell back, regrouped, and charged again. It was after ten o'clock in the morning when General Morgan decided to call it quits. He flew a flag of truce so that his men could collect their dead. It had been a costly battle with 36 dead, 45 wounded and some 20 officers captured.

For Private Young, it had been an unforgettable day. It was his first experience in combat under deadly enemy fire, and the death of his friend had shaken him to the core. The young man had been a cattle drover from Somerset in Eastern Kentucky and Bennett knew his life story. He had never understood why his friend had signed up. He had no property and no relatives in the Confederacy. He was thirty-two years old and lovesick for a woman who had refused his attention and married another man. With nothing left to live for, he mounted his horse and rode off to war. The story of his friend would haunt Bennett for the rest of his life.

Two

May 1864
Camp Douglas, Chicago

"There was no end to the sounds in the camp. The shouts of the guards, Freddy's voice as he recited his favorite poems, the sound of rotten meat hissing and popping over makeshift fires, the banging of pots and pans in the camp kitchen, the wind blowing off Lake Michigan, the dull clank of shovels and pickaxes as men dug graves, the bird song during funerals and the pitter-patter of the rain on the windowsill as I read the bible I carry in my vest pocket."

Bennett Young was one of 12,000 greybacks crammed together in a miserable POW camp on the shores of Lake Michigan. The camp had been designed for half as many men. It was called 'the eighty acres of hell' by its inmates. It was a dangerous place for men, worse than any battlefield. Poor sanitation and overcrowding spread dysentery, smallpox, typhoid fever, and tuberculosis. One in five soldiers was dying from some disease or another in the camp.

Corporal Young was a twenty-one-year-old veteran cavalryman with collar-length brown hair and a scraggly beard. He had fought with the 8th Kentucky Cavalry under General Morgan and gone on the thousand-mile raid through Indiana and Ohio in July 1863. Morgan's Raiders had destroyed railroad and telegraph lines, seized supplies, and taken prisoners, wreaking havoc in the Union rear. After three weeks of hot pursuit by Union troops and local militias, the Raiders had been forced to surrender at New Lisbon, Ohio. They were sent to Camp Douglas to wait out the end of the war.

Bennett was working in the cemetery one day with a dozen young men dressed in the ragged grey pants and shirts of the Confederate Army. Bennett was digging a grave with a pickaxe and shovel near his friend Reuben. Together, they worked the earth as they listened to Freddy, a chubby-cheeked poet, who tirelessly recited lines of poetry while he dug a hole. Freddy recited Henry Timrod's *A Common Thought*.

> *"Somewhere on this earthly planet*
> *In the dust of flowers to be,*
> *In the dewdrop, in the sunshine,*
> *Sleeps a solemn day for me."*

> *"At this wakeful hour of midnight*
> *I behold it dawn in mist,*
> *And I hear a sound of sobbing*
> *Through the darkness - hist! oh, hist!"*

Freddy had lost an eye after a head injury at the Battle of Shiloh in 1862 when Union forces had overrun the Confederate line. He had spent months in a Union hospital and found respite from the tedium of daily life by reciting lines of poetry. The men put up with Freddy as long as he kept his voice down around the guards. They were often so incensed by his behavior that they threatened to smash his head with their rifle butts.

Freddy felt the warmth of the sun on his face and smiled as he recited the rest of the poem.

> *"In a dim and musky chamber,*
> *I am breathing life away,*
> *Someone draws a curtain softly,*
> *And I watch the broadening day."*

> *"As it purples in the zenith,*
> *As it brightens on the lawn,*
> *There's a hush of death about me,*
> *And a whisper, "He is gone!"*

Freddy was deep in a hole when the men heard a commotion over by the railroad tracks. The Union soldier guarding them suddenly took off on horseback as they heard screams coming from the railhead. From the desperate sounds, Bennett surmised that a man had been run over by a wagon and was probably looking down at a severed leg or arm. Accidents happened all the time at Camp Douglas.

Bennett and the other gravediggers instantly threw down their shovels and ran for the shoreline of Lake Michigan. Bennett grabbed his grey forage cap and hauled Freddy out of the grave, shoving him along.

"Freddy, it's time to go!" yelled Bennett as he followed his friend Reuben in a mad dash for the lake.

Reuben was barely nineteen years old and looked sickly. He feared the war; he feared the guards, and he feared the food. He had lost thirty pounds on his small frame after six months in the camp. He hurried after the men as Bennett kept an eye on the guards congregating at the Illinois Central railhead about half a mile away. The men raced for the shoreline, feet pounding on the swampy grass near Lake Michigan. Some men fell into the bays and inlets but quickly scrambled out. A shot was fired at the railhead and several guards climbed into the saddle to cut off the escaped prisoners.

"We gotta find a boat," cried Reuben in desperation.

The horsemen were approaching at a fast clip. A Union guard closed on Bennett, who dived into the lake at the last moment. The horseman whipped past him and went after Reuben, slashing him in the neck with his saber. Reuben dropped like a stone into the marsh water with a bloody ear and neck as the horseman pursued another man, shooting him dead with his pistol. The prisoners quickly gave up, raising their hands. Bennett saw Reuben lying in the water, bleeding out. With his arms raised, he dashed into the marsh to help his friend.

"Reuben!" Bennett cried. "Reuben!"

Bennett dropped to his knees, cradling his friend in his arms. There was a terrible gash in his neck. Bennett struggled to lift him clear when he felt a brutal shove from behind and pitched face-first into the water. When he looked up, he saw a bearded Union soldier standing over him.

"Leave him," the man snarled. "He ain't gonna make it."

As the soldier turned his attention to the others, Bennett dragged Reuben over to the shore so he wouldn't drown in the shallow water. He noticed the glint of a metal object on the bottom and plunged his free hand into the lake water. He grasped Reuben's miraculous medal that his grandmother had given him on the day he had gone off to war. It was an antique silver medallion of Mary with open arms, standing on a globe, crushing a serpent beneath her feet. Reuben had been a very religious young man, and he had this in common with Bennett. They had often prayed together. Reuben had been a firm believer in Mary, the Lady of Graces, who dispensed God's grace, and whose immaculate soul made her uniquely powerful with God. But Mary was nowhere to be seen in the barren landscape of the camp. By the time Bennett had laid Reuben out on the shore, the young man had bled out.

In the distance, the prisoners could just make out a small fishing boat a mile out, heading away from the shore. They knew that a lot of the boats were friendly to Confederate prisoners and sometimes carried them across the bay to safe havens on the eastern shore. From there, they could sail north to the safety of Canada.

The camp commander waited in Garrison Square for the escapees to arrive. The guards on horseback followed the prisoners and the wagon containing the bodies of the dead men. Bennett and his friends stumbled along after the wagon. The guard who had killed Reuben was a keen young Union soldier named Corporal Keeley. He had planned to fight the Rebels on the battlefield but had been reprimanded for theft during training and sent to work in the POW camp. Keeley dismounted with a swagger and stood to attention opposite the commanding officer sitting on the porch of the HQ building.

"Corporal, what are you doing with that fuckin' sword?" asked the officer. "Ain't nobody got a sword in this camp. I thought I told you to get rid of it."

"It ain't no sword, sir," said Keeley with pride. "It's a saber."

"OK, let's see it. Show it here."

The corporal pulled the saber from its guard and held it up so the officer could see the blood on the blade.

"You used it just now on one of them prisoners?"

"Yes, sir. It keeps down the vermin, sir," Keeley said with a sly smile.

"I'm sure it does. How many are dead?"

"Three, sir. They were all troublemakers."

"Good work, corporal. We gotta make an example. Put the others in the pit."

"Yes, sir. Thank you, sir."

After saluting, Corporal Keeley did an about-face and led the surviving men over to the camp's fearsome 'White Oak dungeon'. The dungeon was a dark underground pit, six feet by eight feet, with a small barred window high up on the wall and entry through a hatch in the ceiling. The tiny space had a damp floor and a bucket of urine and feces in the corner. Bennett and his friends descended a ladder into the pit until a cry was heard from the men below.

"We got a dead one down here," screamed a man who had stepped on the body.

The new arrivals grabbed the dead man and lifted him through the hatch so the guards could dispose of his body. They took no time removing the ladder and slamming the hatch back down. The ten men in the pit barely had sufficient room to stand up because the space was so small. There was little or no air, and the pit stank of fear, sweat, and urine.

Corporal Young turned toward three cadaverous-looking men who had been locked up for days.

"How long you fellas been in here?" he asked.

"A week," said a white beard wearing a forage cap. "The dead one was here when we arrived."

"So, you think we're gonna be dead in a week or two?"

"Yep," nodded Forage Cap. "That'd be about right."

Freddy has been unusually quiet and now he launched into his favorite poem, *Shiloh: A Requiem,* by Herman Melville.

> *"Skimming lightly, wheeling still,*
> *The swallows fly low*
> *Over the field in clouded days,*
> *The forest-field of Shiloh.*
> *Over the field where April rain*
> *Solaced the parched ones stretched in pain*
> *Through the pause of night,*
> *That followed the Sunday fight*
> *Around the church of Shiloh..."*

"Can you tell the poet to shut the fuck up?" asked a bald prisoner in dirty clothes.

Bennett turned to Freddy, whose face was lit up with cheerful exuberance as the words filled his head. He seemed to be living on another planet, totally unaware of their predicament.

"Hey, Freddy," cautioned Bennett.

Freddy lowered his voice and continued in a whisper. After a while, he fell asleep leaning against the wall.

Several hours later, in the dungeon's silence, Bennett heard muffled voices.

"Hey, fellas. Where are those voices comin' from?" asked Bennett of his closest neighbor.

"The hospital," said Forage Cap.

Bennett turned his attention to the tiny barred window, which threw a pale glow into the pit. They could just make out the voices of sick soldiers and nurses talking in the smallpox ward in the hospital basement.

"Yeah, they're always talkin'," said Forage Cap. "Ain't nothin' new, Corporal. They talkin' at all hours."

Bennett pushed his way to get closer to the wall with the window as a prisoner jostled him for space.

"Fuck you, man. This is my place," complained a fat greyback.

"Step back," ordered Bennett. "I only want to have a look at the window, soldier."

"Ain't no way to get up there, Corporal," said the fat inmate as he let Bennett pass in front of him.

Bennett looked at the iron bars on the window. The bars looked solid enough, but the window was very dirty and no one had been up there to clean it in years.

"Hey, Freddy," said Bennett, "give me a hand here."

Freddy pushed his way through the men and Bennett climbed on his shoulders. He removed a spoon from his pocket and started working it into the soft mortar around the window. He scraped away the crumbling mortar and, after a moment, he succeeded in releasing a cement block that fell to the floor. The prisoners soon focused their attention on Bennett's work on the window. He managed to release a second cement block, which came tumbling down.

"Hey, corporal," said Forage Cap. "Let me have a go at it."

Bennett climbed down and Freddy lifted Forage Cap on his shoulders. Forage Cap had a metal shank which he worked into the harder sections of mortar. Slowly, small chunks of mortar came away, and the bars were loosened.

"Where's this window go?" asked Bennett.

"The basement on the south side," said Forage Cap.

"They're gonna put us in front of a firing squad if we ever get out of here," said a prisoner with bad teeth.

"It's better to die in the open air any day than to suffocate like a rat in a hole," said Freddy, smiling at the man.

"Amen. We get outta here. I got a buddy on the far shore," said a man with untreated burns on half his face.

"He better have a boat," said Forage Cap.

"Sure, he does. We juss gotta send him a signal."

The work went on for hours. The men relayed one another, chipping away at the mortar.

In the early morning hours, the last man crawled through the tight window frame into a room in the hospital basement. They waited as Corporal Young searched a bin and came up with a dirty, blood-stained lab coat.

"We're gonna need a disguise to get out of here," said Bennett, putting on the coat. "There will be a guard at the front desk."

Forage Cap collected a second lab coat and put it on just as Freddy launched into another whispered rendition of the Shiloh poem.

"Tell this asshole to shut the fuck up or I'm gonna stuff a rag down his throat," said Burned Face.

Freddy stopped in mid-sentence and looked at Bennett.

"Please, Freddy," whispered Bennett.

Freddy closed his eyes and recited the poem silently in his head.

"Let's go find a gurney," said Bennett.

Forage Cap nodded, and they left the other men near the stairs. After a moment, Forage Cap returned and signaled for the others to follow him.

In the long corridor leading to the front door, Bennett put a man on a gurney and covered him with a sheet before heading down towards the front desk. Luckily, there was no one at the desk as they passed by. Bennett sent Forage Cap and the man on the gurney out the front door and hurried back to the basement to collect Freddy and the remaining men.

An hour later, Bennett and his fellow prisoners had found their way to the shore of Lake Michigan. It was two o'clock in the morning and a chill, off-shore breeze was blowing off the lake. Forage Cap had stolen an oil lamp from the hospital and lit its wick. With his hand covering the flame, he signaled the international distress signal in Morse code: dot-dot-dot, dash-dash-dash, dot-dot-dot.

"You think they saw it?" asked Bennett.

"Maybe they did, maybe they didn't. We wait ten minutes and start again," said the man.

The men laid down on the sandy beach and waited. No one moved. It could be hours before a boat came for them, but that was their only hope of rescue. Bennett closed his eyes and whispered a prayer. He was joined by Freddy and another man.

"Our Father in heaven, hallowed be your name," murmured the men.

"Ah, shut up," said Forage Cap. "Ain't no God gonna save us on this damn beach."

"Leave 'em be," said Burned Face. "Let 'em pray. You don't know nothin'."

"Your kingdom come, your will be done, on earth as it is in heaven," murmured Bennett and the other men.

Three

It was an hour before dawn when a Union patrol passed along the shore with a lantern looking for escaped prisoners. There were five soldiers on the patrol, telling stories and joking among themselves.

Bennett and the others lay motionless in the reeds along the marsh, hoping to avoid a confrontation with the soldiers who had stopped only yards away, to light up their cigarettes and help themselves to whiskey from a flask.

"What's the difference between a bedbug and a man sleeping with snakes under his bed?" asked one soldier before he took a slug of whiskey.

"No more of your jokes, Johnny," said a bearded corporal.

Johnny smirked and looked at his buddies.

"One of 'em creeps over the sleepers... and the other sleeps over the creepers," said Johnny.

There was laughter all around before the men moved on along the shore. Five minutes later, Bennett and his fellow prisoners were back on the beach, watching for movement in the fog on the lake. As time passed, the lake fog got thicker until it was almost impossible to see anything on the water.

A whispered voice called across the water.

"Hey, you Rebs?"

Bennett sat up to listen to the sound, as did Forage Cap, Burned Face, and the others.

"How many you got?" came the voice.

"Ten," whispered Bennett.

"Walk out into the water so we can see you," ordered the voice.

Bennett and the men stepped into the cold lake water and headed out. When they got a hundred yards from the beach with the water up to their chests, a small skiff accosted them. They were hauled one by one into the skiff by two large men and told where to sit. One man had a pistol and kept it pointed at them until they were all seated. For a moment, Bennett wondered whether they had just been recaptured by Union forces.

"No worries, fellas. We're friends, Johnny Rebs, just like you. You're gonna be free soon."

A sailor raised the mainsail, and the skiff moved east through the fog. The dawn came up, and the boat sailed on, arriving at Benton Harbor on the other side of the lake around noon. As they came near the mouth of the St. Joseph River, a fishing boat appeared and joined them. Bennett and the men thanked the crew and transferred over to the fishing boat, which quickly headed north to South Haven.

Two days later, the men climbed onto the Detroit train in Kalamazoo. They had ditched their tattered Confederate kepis and gray uniforms, shaved off their beards, and wore old clothes and hats. They sat in small groups on the train and disembarked in Detroit. There they found their way to the address of a known Confederate sympathizer. The next day, the man took them in a wagon north to Sarnia on the border, where they crossed the St. Clair River into Canada.

July 1864
Toronto, Ontario

Bennett, Freddy, and two friends from Camp Douglas walked through the crowds in the market stalls along Front Street towards the Queen's Hotel, opposite the main railway station. As was his custom, Freddy was reciting a new poem as he followed his friends through the crowd. The market was a popular spot for Americans to get together and exchange information about the war. The boys had been in Toronto for over a month and were living hand-to-mouth in a barn behind the house of a Confederate sympathizer. They were penniless and spent their days looking for work or begging for food. After several weeks of misery, they decided to see what the Confederate Secret Service could do for them.

They entered the luxurious lobby of the hotel and asked for Jacob Thompson at the front desk. The boys looked scruffy in their rough clothes and long hair, among the well-dressed customers and the hotel staff in their elegant uniforms. There was a telegraph office off the main floor and a shop that sold the latest American newspapers. As the men waited in the lobby, Bennett went into the shop and bought a copy of the Chicago Tribune. The front page announced General Robert E. Lee's victory at Cold Harbor against a superior force of Union soldiers under the command of General Ulysses S. Grant.

Bennett passed the newspaper around to his friends, who were elated by the news. A young man in a dark frock coat and top hat arrived at their table and introduced himself as Captain Thomas Hines, military attaché to Colonel Jacob Thompson. He had short black hair, a thin face, and a bushy mustache. After the men had discussed the Cold Harbor victory and made small talk, Hines invited Young to join him and Thompson in the dining room.

"Wait here a moment, Corporal," said Hines as he went off in search of appropriate clothes for Bennett, who was still wearing a threadbare Confederate Army coat with missing buttons. He returned with a black frock coat loaned for the occasion by a friendly hotel porter. Bennett removed his coat, which he left with Freddy, and put on the black frock coat.

"Good," said Hines. "That fits you well. Let's go, Corporal."

At Thompson's table in the richly decorated dining room, Hines made the presentations and Bennett was introduced to Colonel Thompson, who was clean-shaven with patrician good looks and wore an impeccable frock coat and vest. He was having lunch with an older man and an attractive young woman. They had just finished their meal and Thompson's guests stood up as Hines and Young sat down. They shook hands and said their goodbyes to Colonel Thompson in the accent of the deep South. Toronto was full of rich Southerners who had come north to avoid the vicissitudes of war.

"Corporal Young, what have you been up to in this lovely city?" asked Thompson as a waiter arrived and refilled his wineglass.

"I was thinking of studying law at the university, sir."

"The law. Excellent idea, young man. You know I was a congressman for many years, so I can recommend a career in law. We need well-trained lawyers in the South."

"Corporal Young and his friends fought with John Hunt Morgan, sir," said Hines in a whisper to his boss.

"Perhaps I misunderstood your interest," said the colonel, looking flustered. "We're looking for men with your kind of experience."

Bennett Young later learned from Hines about the colonel's military background. Thompson had a horse shot out from under him at the Battle of Shiloh and later joined General Pemberton when he took over as commander in the West. The colonel had been promoted to Inspector General and had taken part in the Battle of Vicksburg. The loss of Vicksburg had been a major blow to the Confederacy, cutting off the lifeline of goods and supplies traveling by steamboat up the Mississippi River.

The following day, Corporal Young was invited to a meeting with Thompson's associates at the Queen's Hotel. He met Thompson's partner, Clement Clay, who was a friendly lawyer with long hair and a full beard from Alabama. He had served as a U.S. senator but felt that he was not cut out for the life of a Confederate agent in Canada. He missed his wife and family, and his life back home.

Captain Hines invited Bennett to examine a map of Johnson's Island near Sandusky in Lake Erie. There was a drawing of the prison camp on the island which housed 2,500 men, mostly officers in the Confederate Army. The fourth man at the meeting was John Beall, who was to be responsible for the attack on the prison.

"Tom and I want your opinion, Corporal," said Clay. "We thought you might have some useful insights with your experience at Camp Douglas."

"Well, thank you, sir," said Bennett, happy to be invited to the meeting.

Bennett looked at the camp drawing and the map. There were twelve prison barracks inside a wooden stockade that ran along the water's edge where boats could come in to deliver prisoners or remove them.

"What do you want to know, Captain?" asked Bennett.

"How high would you estimate the stockade walls to be, Corporal?"

"See the barracks over there and then look at the second floor of this building? They are about the same height. The stockade wall must be at least fifteen feet high. You won't be able to climb over it easily."

Hines looked up at the young corporal and then at Beall.

"We estimate eight to ten feet, Corporal," said Beall.

"With all due respect, sir," said Bennett. "Prison camps are built to keep people inside their walls. You can jump over an eight-foot wall, but not over a fifteen-foot wall."

"How high were the walls at Camp Douglas?" asked Clay.

"It was a fence, sir. I would say about 12-feet high."

Beall was still not convinced his estimate was wrong. He looked disapprovingly at the corporal, who had neither the rank nor the experience in his view, to be at the meeting.

"Have you talked to Major Winston and Captain Davis, sir?" asked Bennett. "They would know."

"Pardon me," said Clay. "Who are these men?"

"Well, sir. They were POWs at Johnson's Island until they escaped back in January. There were four of them who made it out. I met them here when I arrived in May."

"This is the first time I've heard of an escape," said Hines.

"The story goes that they were able to climb the stockade wall during a change of the guard and set out across the ice to the peninsula north of the island."

Bennett pointed to the area on the map.

"From there, they went on to Port Clinton and then to Detroit. They crossed the river into Canada by jumping from ice floe to ice floe."

"What an amazing story! Thank you, Corporal," said Clay. "We must find those men, Captain."

"I hope they're still in town, sir," said Hines.

"How far is the Marblehead Peninsula from the island?" asked Beall.

"Less than a mile," said Hines, "but the problem is how to get our prisoners across that stretch of water? That's why we need a boat."

"Even with the best of plans, sir, you won't be able to release a lot of prisoners," said Bennett.

"Why is that?" asked Clay.

"Many will have amputated limbs," said Bennett, "and will be suffering from dysentery just like we did at Camp Douglas."

"He's right," said Hines. "We can only remove the fittest."

"If you could release a thousand men and get them across to

Marblehead," said Bennett, "you could arm them and they would become an unstoppable force. You could seize Toledo or Detroit."

Hines and Beall smiled at one another.

"Thank you, Corporal," said Clay. "You've been most helpful."

"Course, I remember Cynthiana," said the old British soldier of fortune. Colonel George St. Leger Grenfell stood six feet tall in a dirty red shirt and forage cap. He had blue eyes and a beard with shoulder-length hair.

It was a lovely summer day, and the men were having drinks at an open-air café on the wharf near several wooden lake schooners.

"We charged the railroad depot, which was the last enemy stronghold in the town. We had it surrounded and Morgan was blasting away with two cannons, but the Union forces wouldn't give up. Lt. Colonel Landram was holed up inside, so I was ordered to lead the cavalry charge and exterminate the bastard. It could have gone either way. They had a lot of firepower."

"They say you were shot eleven times, you and your horse," said Godfrey Hyams, an impoverished Englishman who served as Thompson's courier.

"They talk a lot of rubbish. It wasn't too bad for me. The horse got the worst of it," said 'St. Lege' as he was called by his friends.

There was laughter all around, and a man brought over a bottle of scotch to refresh the old warrior's drink. St. Lege was a mythic character, having fought in Morocco, Algeria, India, Crimea, and even South America before coming to the United States in 1862 and enrolling in the Confederate Army under John Hunt Morgan. He later served under Braxton Bragg and J.E.B. Stuart.

Colonel Thompson had convened the commissioners, Clement Clay and James Holborne, and their Confederate friends to the informal meeting at the lakeside café. Holborne was a law professor at the University of Virginia. The only man absent from the meeting was George Nicholas Sanders, a political fixer who had once served as the U.S. Consul to Britain during the Pierce presidency. He was known as a man who got things done. He was away at Niagara Falls attempting to put together peace talks with the U.S. government.

It was this group of Confederate politicos, lawyers, and fixers whose job was to bring the war to an end either by peace negotiations, by a revolt in the Northwest combined with attacks on military prisons, or any other means at their disposal. Unfortunately, none of them had any experience in organizing clandestine wartime operations. Along with the commissioners were Captain Thomas Hines, Captain John Castleman, and Lt. George Eastin, who would soon be involved in several Confederate Secret Service operations in the US.

Corporal Young sat quietly in a corner with Godfrey Hyams, listening to the war stories. After the men tired of the idle chatter, Thompson took over and explained the details of his plan to free 5,000 prisoners at Camp Douglas and recruit the Copperhead groups in the Midwest. The Copperheads, known as the 'Peace Democrats', were opposed to the war and wanted an immediate peace settlement. They were ripe for rebellion against the Union and Thompson believed they could be used to bring an end to the war. The operation would be staged in Chicago.

"What do you think?" asked Clement Clay at the end of the long evening. The men were back to telling tall tales about their victories on the battlefields, and most of them were drunk.

"Sounds like a plan, sir," said Bennett, who wasn't impressed by Thompson's optimistic assessment of the forces at play in Chicago.

"You don't drink, Corporal?" asked Clay.

"No, sir. I'm not much of a drinker."

"How'd you get mixed up with John Hunt Morgan and his men?"

"I joined up after some friends of mine were attacked by Union troops near our home," said Bennett. "I thought it was time to teach the Yankees a lesson."

"Why don't you join us?" asked Clay, who seemed to be taken with the young corporal.

"I don't know, sir. I was thinking of going to Richmond to get a commission and returning to the fight, but I have no money."

"I understand it is hard to live on a corporal's pay in Canada."

"Eleven dollars a month is nothing in this country, sir. If I get the commission as lieutenant, I will earn almost ten times as much."

"You're not married, are you?"

"No, sir."

"Then go to Richmond, get the commission, and come back to us. We'll pay your travel expenses, Corporal."

"Well, thank you, sir."

The following day, Bennett set off for Richmond by way of Halifax. Clay drove him to the train station on Front Street and they sat in a café for a while before it was time to board the train for Montreal.

"Are you returning to St. Catharines, sir?" Bennett asked.

"Yes, I like it there. Sanders is in Niagara Falls, so we talk quite often. When was the last time you saw your parents, Corporal?"

"It's been two years now, sir. I write to them often."

"Do you have any brothers and sisters?"

"Yes, sir. I have an older sister and three brothers."

"I will pray for your safe return, Corporal," said Clay.

"Thank you, sir," said Bennett as the train conductor called for boarding.

Clay followed Bennett along the platform to the passenger car and shook his hand before he climbed on board.

Four

"Days passed and nights, and then the
beautiful Bermudas rose out of the sea, we entered
the tortuous channel, steamed hither and thither
among the bright summer islands, and rested at last
under the flag of England and were welcome...
Bermuda was a paradise, but one had
to go through hell to get there." Mark Twain

St. George's Island, Bermuda

It took Bennett two days to get to Bermuda from Halifax. He lodged in a boarding house in St. George's Town at the Eastern point of the archipelago. He was strolling along the boardwalk when the blockade runner *Condor* steamed into the port. An admiring crowd appeared out of nowhere as the ship came up the channel. It was a sleek vessel built for stealth and speed to slip past naval blockades. It was over 200 feet long with a shallow draft and could do up to 16 knots on a good day. It had a distinctive appearance, with its three funnels and two paddle wheels amidships designed for clandestine river operations. The steamer had been built on the Clyde River in Glasgow and was on its maiden voyage to North America. It would take Bennett to Wilmington, North Carolina, where he would take the train on to Richmond.

Wilmington was the main port of entry for supplies into the Confederacy during the war. It traded cotton and tobacco for munitions, clothing, and foodstuffs. British steamers came and went loaded down with war materiel for General Robert E. Lee's forces in Virginia. The ships sailed from the British colonies in Bermuda, the Bahamas, and Nova Scotia, and had to be fast enough to avoid the Union's gauntlet of blockading ships.

Suddenly, a large group of well-dressed ladies and gentlemen arrived on the boardwalk in buggies and carriages and cheered the arrival of the *Condor*. Among them was an elegant fifty-year-old Washington socialite named Rose O'Neal Greenhow, the famous 'Wild Rose' as she was called in the Confederacy. She had been a spy in Washington during the early years of the war and provided invaluable intelligence on Union troop movements. She had been arrested and imprisoned along with her daughter and later exchanged. She was returning from London with dispatches for the Confederate cause after having spent a year overseas. The Confederate States had strong commercial ties with Britain and France.

While in London, Greenhow had had an audience with Queen Victoria and had become engaged to a British diplomat. She had been invited to the court of Napoleon III in France and had discussed the commercial interests of the country. She had published a prison diary entitled *My Imprisonment and the First Year of Abolition Rule at Washington,* which sold throughout the British Isles.

An older gentleman joined the festive group on the boardwalk with a bottle of champagne and glasses. He popped the cork and poured drinks for Rose and her friends as the *Condor* put into port.

The following morning, Bennett followed Rose Greenhow and several porters loaded down with luggage up the gangway to the *Condor*. The ship steward was waiting to greet Mrs. Greenhow and take her to her cabin when a crowd of passengers on the deck surged forward to get a look at the famous Washington socialite. It was not long before she was comfortably installed in the dining room, drinking tea and surrounded by admirers.

"What about Bull Run?" asked an older man.

"Well, there was a time back in 1862," said Rose, "when we had intelligence coming in from all kinds of sources. It's not so easy now, gentlemen."

"I heard that the Rebel commander, General Beauregard, had a copy of the Union commander's orders to his troops before the battle."

"Our people gave us great intelligence," added Rose quietly.

"I heard that you were thanked by Jefferson Davis himself," said one woman.

"Yes, that's true, my dear."

As the ship was leaving the port, Bennett left the dining room and retired to his third-class berth in the bowels of the ship. It wasn't until much later in the evening that he was to meet the famous spy.

After dinner was served, Bennett was invited by Captain Hampden to sit at his table for a brandy along with several diplomats and their wives, the Wild Rose, and her admirers. It wasn't long before Rose interrupted the questions of her admirers by asking the young corporal a question.

"So, Mr. Young, where are you going?"

The group of admirers turned to have a look at the young corporal, who hadn't said a word all evening.

"Well, ma'am. It's no secret. I'm from Kentucky. I fought with Morgan's Raiders in '63 and was imprisoned at Camp Douglas. I'm on my way to Richmond."

"How did you get out of that hellhole? I've heard it is one of the worst prisons in the Union."

"I escaped, ma'am, and made my way to Canada."

"Good for you, young man."

"So why are you returning now?"

"I'm going to Richmond to get my commission, ma'am, as a lieutenant in the Confederate Army."

"They need good officers, Mr. Young. I'm sure they'll be happy to have you."

A richly dressed gentleman asked Rose about her own time in prison.

"You were arrested and locked up in the old Capitol prison and still you were able to send out coded messages?" asked the man, enthralled.

"I was exchanged in a prisoner swap in June 1862 and was reunited with my daughter in Richmond. But now, ladies and gentlemen, it's getting late," said Rose, standing up. "It's been a long day. Time for bed."

It was not until two days later, as the *Condor* was fighting a storm, that Bennett saw Rose briefly in the dining room as the ship was being hammered by the waves. Captain Hampden had come below to announce to the frightened passengers that they would soon be in the Cape Fear River.

Bennett stood on the deck with several passengers whipped by the wind and spray, watching as two Yankee ships pursued them into the mouth of the river. It was a close-run thing as the ship was tossed about on the waves. They had almost arrived at Fort Fisher and the protection of the Confederate guns when the ship ran aground on a sandbar two hundred yards from the beach.

"We've run aground, ladies and gentlemen," announced the British captain as he assembled the passengers in the dining room.

"Are we safe here?" asked a gentleman who feared falling into the hands of the Union soldiers.

"For the moment," said the captain.

"I need to get ashore," said Rose. "Can you lower a boat for me, captain?"

The captain looked at the woman as if she were mad.

"No, ma'am. It's way too dangerous. No one should be out in this storm."

The captain consulted with a crew member and then returned his attention to the passengers.

"Put on your life vests and stay inside. That's an order."

Rose Greenhow was not having any of it. She stood up and went over to talk to the captain.

"Captain, I must insist. I cannot stay on board and run the risk of a Yankee ship taking me hostage. Please, sir. I beg of you."

"Madam, I would be sending you to your death if I put you out in a boat in this weather."

"I'll take that risk, captain, but I must go."

Cape Fear River, North Carolina

Half an hour later, as the ship was being pushed and pulled by the waves, the captain agreed to put out a boat for Rose. Bennett offered to join her along with four sailors to man the oars. It was touch and go for the first hundred yards, but it looked like the tiny boat was almost at the beach when a huge wave lifted it high into the air and flipped it over. Bennett fought his way to the surface and clung to the overturned boat, as did the four sailors, but the Wild Rose had disappeared. The sailors and Bennett plunged again and again into the murky water to try to locate their illustrious passenger but to no avail. The boat drifted slowly toward the shore and the men were saved.

It was several hours later, after the wind had slackened, that the sailors found the body of Rose Greenhow. She had hidden a small notebook on her person, along with a copy of her memoir. Inside the book, there was a note to her daughter. The rumor had it that Rose drowned because she had sewn $2,000 worth of gold coins into her underclothes and around her neck. Her body was taken to Wilmington, where she was honored with a military funeral.

The next day, after attending the funeral, Bennett bought a ticket on the Wilmington & Weldon Railway, which ran through Goldsboro and Petersburg on its way to Richmond, Virginia. The trains in the South rarely arrived on time, because the steam locomotives ran out of fuel and had to send out work crews to cut firewood. Nevertheless, Bennett was happy to be on dry land again after the frightening ordeal in the Cape Fear River.

Five

Richmond, Virginia

Bennett Young left his rooming house and crossed the street to avoid a dozen amputated veterans demanding money from the passersby. There were drunks asleep in the back streets near the whiskey shops and furloughed soldiers sprawled out on the wooden sidewalks. Women were selling themselves from doorways and youngsters were engaged in every criminal act imaginable. He had never thought the Confederate capital could be in such dire straits. Bennett came from a small town in Kentucky where he had never seen such misery.

In the summer of 1864, the outlook for the Confederacy was very bleak indeed. Of the eleven states that had seceded from the Union in 1861, only six remained relatively intact. The Confederacy had given up hope that Britain and France would provide diplomatic recognition for the independent country. General Ulysses S. Grant was putting pressure on Richmond from the North while in the South, General William Tecumseh Sherman was getting ready to march through Georgia. The Union victories at Gettysburg in the East and Vicksburg in the West seemed to have sealed the fate of the Confederacy.

Richmond was a gloomy place as the Union brought its forces to bear in a total war. Lincoln planned to grind down their spirit and break their will to fight. In April 1863, there was a bread riot in the streets of Richmond because of the rising cost of food and other necessities. The rioters had looted the shops for two hours before the military authorities had put a stop to it. The citizens of Richmond were suffering and were desperate for the necessities of life. Throughout the war, Richmond had been the medical front line for wounded soldiers arriving from the battlefields. As he walked along the street, he could see the largest hospital of the Confederacy on a hill in the eastern part of the city. The Chimborazo tended to the wounded and had one of the lowest mortality rates in the South. It was overflowing with some of the 20,000 wounded men from the Gettysburg disaster.

Bennett noticed the large numbers of black workers cleaning the streets, hauling supplies, and doing grunt work. He wasn't aware that Virginia had the largest number of slaves in any southern state. They were the backbone of the Confederate workforce. They worked on cotton and tobacco plantations, in iron works, in field hospitals, and in the building of fortifications while the whites went off to war. He passed the Virginia State Capitol with its Corinthian marble columns, where both the Confederate Congress and the Virginia State Legislature met. It was a magnificent building, and Bennett was mightily impressed. This was where Jefferson Davis and his ministers voted on the laws that governed the Confederate States. He walked around the building twice before he made his way to an obscure office building behind the capitol.

The Secretary of War James Seddon was in his office handling urgent business when the young Kentucky corporal climbed the wooden stairs in the old building. Surprisingly, Seddon was in good spirits when he greeted Bennett.

"Corporal Young. I've been looking forward to meeting you. Clement Clay has written to me about your projects," said Seddon. "Please come into my office. We have a lot to discuss."

They sat down in leather armchairs before a wide bay window overlooking the street.

"You've heard about Rose Greenhow, I suppose," said Seddon. "Everyone is talking about her."

"Yes, sir. I was on the *Condor*."

"So you just arrived from Wilmington? How was she?"

"I hardly knew her, sir, but I think she was an amazing woman. I was in the lifeboat with her when it flipped over."

"My God. You are lucky to be alive, Corporal."

"She was very brave to risk going out in a lifeboat in a storm like that."

"You know the Wild Rose was the public face of the Confederacy for quite some time. She was an invaluable asset. We're sorry to see her gone. What is this plan of yours for raiding the Northern towns?"

"Well, sir. I only mentioned it briefly to Mr. Clay, but the plan would be to recruit a small Confederate force in Canada to attack the border towns, sack and burn them to the ground."

"It is right that the people of New England should feel the pain of war. Their officers and troops are responsible for some of the worst atrocities committed in recent months."

"I would need money and resources to do such a thing, sir. My Confederate friends in Canada are living hand to mouth. They want to help, but..."

"Of course, Corporal. You will have it, but first, you will need to visit each of the border towns you wish to attack and make a report to Thompson and Clay."

"Yes, sir."

After an hour, Bennett emerged from Seddon's office with papers signed and full support of the Secretary of War for the raids against the Northern cities. The trip had been a success. He would be returning to Canada as a new lieutenant in the Confederate Army.

Wilmington, North Carolina

Bennett couldn't wait to get out of Richmond. The misery of the people was just too much for him. He went directly to the train station and was soon traveling south in relative comfort. It took him less than two days to make the journey back to Wilmington, even after a layover of five hours, while the chief engineer sent out a crew of woodcutters to feed the boiler. He arrived on the coast just in time to book passage on the *Thistle*, a fast blockade runner going to Bermuda with a heavy load of cotton on board.

Among the passengers, there were diplomats, businessmen, sales agents, and even a few families heading to Europe. The ship left Wilmington in the evening and descended the Cape Fear River as far as Fort Fisher, where it waited for several hours in the shadow of the fort for a Confederate naval ship to arrive. In the early morning, the *Thistle* followed in the wake of a Confederate ironclad ram, which took it out through the new inlet into the open sea. The ironclad had armor-plated casemates with sloping sides to deflect enemy fire, and its bow was fitted with a massive iron ram, enabling it to smash through the Union cruisers. The ironclad acted as a decoy, engaging with the enemy ships of the blockade while the *Thistle* raced north, parallel to the shore before heading east to Bermuda.

When the boom of distant guns was heard, the passengers were sent below. The muzzle flashes lit up the sky but did little damage to the Confederate ironclad, which fired back at the enemy ships while the *Thistle* threaded her way north through the blockade. After an hour or two, the *Thistle* found herself alone on an open sea, heading east at a fast clip.

The passage to Bermuda went smoothly, and Bennett soon caught a ship on its way to Halifax. He was happy to return to a peaceful life in Canada. It was a lovely summer day when he arrived at the port and looked up at the stone fortress of Fort George on the top of Citadel Hill. Halifax had ruled over British North America for over 100 years and the town was home to Britain's North American and West Indian naval squadrons. With the war on, Halifax was a busy place for trade and war materiel. Ships from England bound for New York and Boston often stopped in Halifax for fuel and provisions, as did other vessels heading east.

Bennett walked around the town watching happy families strolling along the streets without a care in the world. Husbands weren't rushing off to the front and abandoning their wives and children. No amputated veterans were begging in the streets. It was refreshing to see people enjoying their lives and living for the moment. The next day, Bennett left Halifax by coach for the Bay of Fundy, where he would take another boat to St. John, New Brunswick. From there, he would travel up the St. John River valley to Rivière-du-Loup before taking a train to Montreal. The only fast rail link for points west at the time went through Portland, Maine, and was denied him.

Montreal

In a cabaret on St. Catherine Street, a soprano was singing *Beautiful Dreamer* by Stephen Foster, accompanied by a pianist. The new lieutenant entered the smoke-filled room and stopped near the stage to listen.

"Beautiful Dreamer, wake unto me,
Starlight and dewdrops are waiting for thee;
Sounds of the rude world heard in the day,
Lull'd by the moonlight have all passed away!
Beautiful Dreamer, queen of my song,
List while I woo thee with soft melody;
Gone are the cares of life's busy throng,
Beautiful Dreamer, awake unto me!
Beautiful Dreamer, awake unto me!"

The entire room was captivated by the singer. At the back of the room, a tall, sun-burned man surrounded by several attractive women stood up to applaud the singer. Lt. Bennett Young soon spotted his contact among the men at the table. They were all expat Confederate soldiers, working for Clement Clay and having a good time.

Bennett went over to them and shook hands with Clay and the Confederate agent George Sanders, a squat man with a goatee. Clay invited the lieutenant to join them in a private room away from the crowd. The piano player launched into *When Johnny Comes Marching Home.*

"When Johnny comes marching home again
Hurrah! Hurrah!
We'll give him a hearty welcome then
Hurrah! Hurrah!
The men will cheer, and the boys will shout
The ladies they will all turn out
And we'll all feel gay
When Johnny comes marching home."

In the private room behind the bar, George Sanders wanted to know everything about Bennett's trip to Richmond.

"I was only there for three days, sir, but the situation is critical," Bennett told him. "People are starving and beggars fill the streets."

"I've heard the same things, George," said Clay.

"So, Lieutenant, you came back here," said Sanders with a sly grin, "to lead an attack on the northern cities."

"Yes, sir. Secretary Seddon approved my plan."

"Your plan?" asked Sanders.

"Sorry, sir. Our plan."

"You will be under my command, Lieutenant. I'll be running this operation," Sanders said. "We don't want you going off and doing something foolish, now do we?"

With that said, Sanders set off on a long tirade, telling the young lieutenant what needed to be done and how to do it. Clay remained silent as Sander's droning voice sucked all the air out of the room.

Six

October 25, 1864
Saint- Jean, Quebec

Six weeks later, Lt. Bennett Young was under arrest in a rooming house in a small Canadian city located on the Richelieu River some twenty-five miles southeast of Montreal. A constable stood by the parlor door while forty-year-old John Abbott, QC of Montreal, conducted an interview with the lieutenant. Abbott was a clean-shaven lawyer with a dour expression and immaculate clothes. He sat opposite the lieutenant in his muddy civilian clothes.

"What's Colonel Thompson like?"

"He's a big talker, sir. Jefferson Davis chose him to lead the Confederate mission in Canada. He was a big shot back in Mississippi, a rich landowner and a congressman. I heard he worked for President Buchanan as Secretary of the Interior before he resigned."

"Clay promised you a position when you returned from Richmond?" asked Abbott.

"Yes, and no. I wanted to be back in the fight and Clay paid my expenses to go to Richmond as a courier."

"You carried documents to Richmond?" asked Abbott.

"Yes, sir. I carried letters for the Secretary of War from Thompson and Clay, supporting my request for a commission."

"What is Mr. Sanders' role?"

"He's a fixer, sir. He has spent most of the summer working on a peace initiative at the International Hotel in Niagara Falls. He's had talks with William Jewitt and Horace Greeley, the editor of the New York Tribune, and the occasional emissary for President Lincoln."

"I never heard anything in the newspapers about a peace initiative," said Abbott.

"Well, they didn't get far before Lincoln shut it down. Clay told me that President Lincoln wrote a letter to Jewitt and Greeley on July 18 inviting the commissioners and Jefferson Davis to come to Washington to discuss any peace agreement that would maintain the integrity of the union and abandon slavery. Of course, Davis was not willing to accept any proposition without full independence for the Southern states."

"So the peace initiative was a complete failure?"

"Yes, it was, but the commissioners still hold out hope that President Lincoln's refusal to negotiate will have a negative influence on his chances of re-election."

"Well, we'll see about that soon enough, won't we?"

"Yes, sir."

"What was your first mission for the Secret Service?"

"Clay sent me south to Columbus, Ohio, to try to organize a prisoner escape from Camp Chase?"

"How did you get across the border?"

"That was the easy part, sir. I took a boat across Lake Erie to Cleveland and then a train to Columbus. No one was watching the border."

August 1864
Columbus, Ohio

Ohio was a Union stronghold. There were Confederate prisoner-of-war camps at Camp Chase in Columbus and Johnson's Island on Lake Erie. Bennett had not been back to the state since he had been captured at the Battle of Buffington Island on the Ohio River with Morgan's Raiders. A number of his compatriots were still imprisoned at Camp Chase, and the plan was to reconnoiter the town and prison to organize a revolt.

Clay and Sanders had given Bennett a cover identity and papers to go with it. He had been sent on his way with $100 and a pistol for protection. He'd bought a change of clothes—a dark frock coat, baggy trousers, and a wide-brimmed felt hat—to give himself the appearance of a successful businessman. He had sewed his real identity papers into his new clothes along with his Confederate commission papers, identifying him as a lieutenant in the army. His fake papers were only good for casual scrutiny and would not prevent him from being hanged as a Confederate spy. If he could prove he was a lieutenant in the Confederate Army operating behind Union lines, he would not risk the gallows or the firing squad.

Clay saw him off at the train station in Montreal and wished him well. Bennett thanked Clay for his trust and friendship, and as the train pulled out of the station, he realized that he had absolutely no idea how to organize an attack on a prison. He had been given only one local contact in Columbus: a Methodist minister who was close to the Confederate sympathizers in the city. He arrived in Columbus at midday on a Friday and made his way to the church in the western part of the city. He sat in a pew for over an hour and prayed before he was approached by the reverend himself.

"Can I help you with something, young man?" asked the old greybeard.

"Hello," said Bennett, standing up. "You are Reverend Stiles, are you not?"

"Yes, I am."

The two men looked at each other and not a word was spoken for a long minute.

"Come with me, sir?" asked the reverend, who led Bennett to the vestry and shut the door.

"You've come from Colonel Thompson?" asked the reverend.

"Yes, sir."

The following day, Bennett walked four miles west of the city to have a look at the perimeter fence at Camp Chase. The camp had started as a training facility for army volunteers and only later became a prison. In the summer of 1864, there were eight thousand Confederate prisoners in the camp. Bennett had been imprisoned there for a short time back in 1863 before he was moved to Camp Douglas near Chicago. The two prison camps were laid out in a similar manner. He quickly identified the guardhouse, the hospital, the commissary, the officers' quarters, and the barracks. The camp was located on the National Road leading west to Springfield.

It was all very well to find a way to free the prisoners, but he also had to keep them from being re-captured. As soon as the cry of alarm went out, Union soldiers would be converging on Columbus from Zanesville in the east and Springfield in the west. Ohio was a fortress with more Ohio men serving in the Union Army than any other state.

As Bennett walked around the perimeter fence, he found numerous weak spots that could be breached or scaled with ladders. He concluded that it would not be too hard to liberate the prisoners, but where would he hide so many men in open country as they were moved north under the cover of darkness to the Canadian border?

Bennett saw a delivery wagon heading to the camp and stopped the driver.

"You going to the camp?" asked Bennett.

"The commissary, mister," said the baker's assistant, wearing a white cowl. "I gotta deliver all this bread."

Bennett looked at the fresh loaves of bread in the wagon.

"Mind giving me a lift?" asked Bennett.

The man nodded and Bennett jumped up on the seat next to him. It was a hot day and Bennett removed his dark coat and sat in shirtsleeves next to the driver as they were waved through the front gate. They took the long road into the camp, past the guardhouse. Security was tight, but a bread wagon was not something to raise the suspicion of the guards. They arrived at the commissary and the baker's assistant went to work unloading the bread while Bennett casually drifted off to have a look around. He didn't get very far before a Union soldier waved him back into the commissary, where he finished helping the baker's assistant unload the wagon. The man offered Bennett a ride back to town.

After they left the prison camp, the boy had a question for Bennett.

"You ain't no Union man, are you, sir?"

"Me?" exclaimed Bennett.

"Yeah, your accent, sir. You're from Kentucky, just like my ma. She's from Lexington, and you speak just like her."

"Yeah, I'm from Kentucky."

"So whatcha doin' so far north?"

"Looking for work."

"You ain't no Confederate spy, are you?"

"Me, no, never."

The boy laughed, saying he was only joking.

"My mom's 'secesh'," said the boy, grinning at Bennett, who smiled back at him. He had gotten off easy.

Late in the day, Bennett returned to the church and met with a dozen Confederate sympathizers in the basement. Some men could hardly walk and others had appalling wounds from the war. They had survived as best they could in Camp Chase and been released early. They formed a circle around the lieutenant and the reverend.

"The lieutenant is here to learn about your time in the camp," said the reverend. "He knows it quite well, having spent time there in '63. He wants to know what it's like today. Any volunteers?"

The men shifted in their chairs, reluctant to be the first to speak. Finally, a man stood up. He had a terrible facial wound from a bullet that had taken out most of his lower jaw. Bennett had seen worse but tried to keep his expression neutral and look the man in the eyes.

"It's a terrible place, sir. They treat you like cattle," whispered the man. "They put us in these shanties with leaky roofs. We couldn't sleep on the beds without getting soaked. The guards thought it was funny."

The man then sat down. He had opened the floodgates and another man quickly stood up to take his place.

"They say they are Christians," the man said bitterly, "but they treated us like animals."

"The food was horrible," said another. "It wasn't fit for humans. I wouldn't feed pigs the kind of slops they served us."

The next speaker didn't try to stand. A pair of crutches rested across his thighs and he was missing a leg.

"We didn't have enough wood for cooking," he said. "They gave us only five small sticks of wood per day for a mess of twenty-five men, and even that wasn't delivered until late at night for men who hadn't eaten a thing for an entire day. By that time, most of us didn't have the strength to build a fire."

The men recognized Bennett as one of their own, a man who had lived through much of what they had experienced on the battlefield and in the camps. *There is a big difference*, reflected Bennett. *I've been lucky. I'm still in one piece, but these poor fellas will never be the same again.*

He felt humbled and a little ashamed. The men deserved his

attention and respect, so he sat there and let them talk. They told him the conditions in Camp Chase were abominable, similar to those he had experienced personally at Camp Douglas. The litany of horror went on for the better part of an hour before Bennett stood up.

"Thank you for inviting me here, Reverend. It's a pleasure to meet you all. The Confederate Service is looking for able-bodied men to launch an attack on Camp Chase and free the prisoners. How many men do you think we can find here in town?"

"I don't know that you can," said the reverend. "Most of our veterans have gone south and returned to the fight."

"There are thousands of prisoners in that camp, Lieutenant," said a man in a wheelchair. "Ain't no way to get in there without a large force."

"You'd need several hundred armed men to create a diversion while you breach the perimeter, sir," whispered the man with the missing jaw.

Bennett nodded at the ex-soldier, realizing that the man might be disfigured, but he had not lost any of his reasoning powers. These men had solid military experience, but today they were out of the war and their only priority was trying to feed themselves and stay alive.

It had been a mistake to come here, thought Bennett. *What were Thompson and Clay thinking? He'd been dispatched on a fool's errand. He would have to be mad to try to liberate the prisoners from Camp Chase. You could make a case for Johnson's Island in Lake Erie, but Camp Chase was in the middle of the state, surrounded by Union forces.*

Seven

August 29, 1864
Chicago, Illinois

The train journey had taken two days, south to Cincinnati and then on to Indianapolis and Chicago. The rail cars had been crowded, but as always Bennett kept to himself, avoiding making conversation with his fellow passengers. That became increasingly difficult on the last leg of his journey when more people had come on the train. It was only then that Bennett remembered that his arrival in Chicago would coincide with the beginning of the Democratic National Convention. That would put him squarely in the belly of the beast, surrounded by northerners of every stripe. Bennett realized that the huge crowd of people converging on Chicago would also be the perfect cover for his mission in the city.

The rail cars had been crowded, but the train station in Chicago was utter madness. Bennett stopped and stared, wondering if he had ever seen so many people gathered together in one place. He forced himself to start walking, ignoring a small boy hawking newspapers near a shoeshine stand. From his reading of the newspapers in Ohio, he understood that the convention would be the arena for a major political confrontation between two different factions of the Democratic Party — the War Democrats, led by Major General George B. McClellan, and the Peace Democrats led by Horatio Seymour, the former governor of New York. McClellan was the acknowledged front-runner and his supporters wanted to keep the war going and restore the Union. On the other hand, Seymour's Peace Democrats and a faction called the 'Copperheads' had had enough of the war. They thought it had been a huge mistake from the start, and they favored an immediate cessation of hostilities. It would be a struggle to get a consensus behind any candidate to go forward against the incumbent Lincoln in the November election.

Bennett had no idea why Thompson and Hines wanted him in Chicago at the same time as the convention, but he suspected there must be some scheme afoot to influence the Democratic convention in favor of Seymour and the Peace Democrats. He stepped out of the train station and into the street. It was dark already, and he didn't have much time. He fished out a folded sheet of paper in his breast pocket to check the address. He was instructed to go to a certain safe house in the city where he was to meet Thompson's people. Bennett knew better than to take a hansom cab or to ask the passersby for directions, so his journey from the station took much longer than it should have. He squinted at the city map again and looked for landmarks. He eventually rounded a corner and froze in his tracks.

He could hear shouts coming from the safe house. His first thought was that the place had been raided by the Chicago police or a detachment of Union soldiers. The racket was coming from a nondescript building, sitting diagonally across the street and perhaps twenty yards from where he stood. It looked like an old warehouse or a meeting hall. He moved on, affecting the casual gait of a gentleman out for an evening stroll. He remained on his side of the street long enough to assure himself there were no signs of a military or police presence in the area, and then cautiously crossed the street to the building itself. He opened the side door, fearing a trap, but all he saw was an empty vestibule with a stairway leading upstairs and another going down. The shouting was coming from downstairs and was much louder now that he was inside. He listened long enough to discern that a meeting was in progress. He went downstairs. The scene had more in common with a comic opera than a clandestine meeting. There were some twenty men in the room, all shouting and gesturing at the same time. Bennett could have been a troop of Union soldiers for all the attention they paid him. He recognized many of his fellow prisoners from his days in Camp Douglas. Bennett tapped the nearest man on the shoulder and his eyes widened in surprise when he saw who it was.

"Good to see you again, Lt. Young," said the man. "I heard you made lieutenant."

"Hey, Turner. Good to see you too," said Bennett with a grim expression. "We're gonna need lookouts on the first floor. One to cover each side of the building."

"I'll handle it, Lieutenant."

Turner quickly recruited two Camp Douglas men who filed past Bennett on their way upstairs. He looked up to realize that the men's departure, quiet as it had been, had drawn attention to where he was standing near the stairwell. Captain Hines had stopped talking and was staring at him.

"Lieutenant Young," he said sternly. "You favor us with your presence."

Bennett simply inclined his head. He was in no mood to explain or apologize. He could tell that Captain Hines was using his late arrival both to put him in his place and as a device to regain control of the room.

"As I was saying," Hines said pointedly, "our initial plan was for our men and the Copperheads to take control of the city. They were to cut all the telegraph wires coming in and going out of Chicago and then to move in and capture the federal arsenal to enable Colonel Grenfell to attack Camp Douglas and free the prisoners there."

Hines paused for effect.

"However," he continued, just the right tinge of regret in his voice, "it is not to be. Colonel Thompson and I thought the Copperheads would come through for us, but they have not. They've gone home."

The Copperheads were part of the Peace faction for a reason. They were farmers who wanted no part in the Civil War. They had little or no military training. It was ridiculous to believe that they would suddenly decide to sign on for a risky assault on a heavily guarded federal prison. Bennett was surprised that a man like Colonel Grenfell with his military experience had bought into it. *You can dress it up any way you want*, Bennett thought, *but bad planning is bad planning. Based on what he'd seen of their plans for Camp Chase, and from what little he knew of the Copperheads, the whole exercise had been doomed to failure from the start.*

The room had gone silent at Hines' words—whether from disappointment or relief. It was difficult to tell. Hines looked around the room before speaking again.

"I must warn you," he said, "that Chicago is no longer safe for us. I have received word that there will soon be some three thousand federal troops converging on the city, and we are in danger of being discovered.

I'm sorry it has turned out this way."

"Discretion is the better part of valor," said Colonel Grenfell, trying to calm the men. "Sometimes it is better to step away and put off your plans for another day."

"I can offer rail tickets," said Captain Hines, "to those of you who wish to travel with me and Captain Castleman through Indiana and Ohio. I would advise the rest of you to return to Kentucky and rejoin the fight from there."

The meeting was over. The room slowly coalesced into two groups, one of them consisting mainly of Captain Hines and Colonel Grenfell. The other was a group of Camp Douglas veterans who gathered around Bennett just as the two lookouts came downstairs.

"It looks like our mission here is over, sir?" Turner said.

"Yes, it is. It's time to get out of town," said Bennett.

"Tonight, sir?"

"Yeah, it's late, but the streets are full of people. No one will notice us. I'm heading north, back to Canada. You boys can come with me if you like. I want to be on the early train for Detroit."

October 25, 1864
Saint-Jean, Quebec

A servant brought in a tea tray and left. John Abbott poured the tea and waited while Bennett put milk and a lump of sugar in his cup.

"So the Chicago assault was a fiasco?"

"Yes, sir."

"How did you get away?"

"We scattered. We left the same night in small groups and caught the early train for Detroit. A few days later, we crossed the St. Clair River into Canada."

There was a knock on the door of the parlor and the constable outside stepped inside to have a word with Abbott.

"Mr. Abbott, sir," said the constable. "There's a Mr. Carter here who wants a word with the prisoner."

"Constable, tell that man that he'll have to wait. Defense counsel has priority," said Abbott.

"Yes, sir. I'll tell him."

The constable nodded and retired.

"What did Colonel Thompson have to say about the failed mission?"

"I first went to see Clement Clay in St. Catharines to make my report. He was not surprised by my view of the assault on Camp Chase. Clay is a realist. He told me that Thompson had sent him a letter about the failed Chicago uprising. He was livid that the attack had failed after he had given $25,000 to Hines and Castleman to organize it and it had come to nothing."

"Where did you go after meeting Clay?"

"I went on to Toronto to talk to Colonel Thompson, but he wouldn't see me. His adjutant ordered me to return to Kentucky and join up, but I refused. Finally, Colonel Thompson agreed to meet me and he treated me in the worst possible way. He called me a 'deserter' and a good-for-nothing and told me to go away. So I picked up my things and went to Montreal with the money Clay had given me to organize the attack on the northern cities."

"This was after the fall of Atlanta on the 2nd of September?"

"Yes, sir. The Confederacy needed our help and nothing we had done had given them any relief on the battlefield. Thompson had a new man working with him named Charles Cole, who was planning the attack on the prison at Johnson's Island. I wished him well, but I had a mission of my own to complete."

"Well, thank you for the background, Lieutenant. Judge Coursol of the Montreal district court has set a hearing for November 2. As your legal counsel, I must inform you that the trial in Montreal will be a very public event and a political bombshell. The government will be pushing hard for your extradition. They are already under intense pressure from Washington, and I hear that this man nosing around town is a clerk sent by the Attorney General in Quebec City to investigate the case. I would be very wary of him, Lieutenant, and say as little as possible."

"Yes, sir."

"So why did you choose St. Albans?"

"I visited several border towns in New York and Vermont in September and early October. St. Albans was a large market town and had several banks. The plan was to organize a scare party to put fear into the minds of Northerners by robbing their banks and burning down their towns."

"This was the plan submitted to Clay and Thompson?"

"Yes, sir. I was to recruit ex-soldiers for the attack and pay them with money provided by Clay. We called ourselves the 'Retributors'. Just retribution for the burning and killing going on in the Shenandoah Valley by General Sheridan and the men of the Vermont regiments."

Under rainy skies, Colonel Edward Ermatinger, resplendent in the red serge and shako hat of the Saint-Jean military detachment, watched his men load the prisoners into an open wagon. Lt. Bennett Young was led out of the house in shackles by several armed men, followed by his lawyer John Abbott, and Carter, the pesky Crown clerk that Abbott had warned him about. The soldiers pushed the lieutenant into the wagon and chained him to the floor with six other men.

"Well, sir. I hope the Crown got what it wanted," said Abbott to Carter as they watched the men being loaded.

"We did, sir. This case is pretty well cut and dried. They'll be extradited back to where they came from before you can say Jack Robinson."

"I wouldn't be too sure about that, sir. Tell your boss, Monsieur Cartier, that we'll give him a good fight."

"George-Étienne said you don't give up easily, Mr. Abbott. But I think some battles can't be won. Good day, sir."

With this, the clerk climbed into a buggy and his driver drove him to the railway station. He would be taking the train to Quebec City to report to the Attorney General of Canada, Georges-Étienne Cartier, on the goings on in Saint-Jean. Abbott stayed behind to watch the prisoners depart for Montreal under armed escort.

Eight

September 1864
St. Albans, Vermont

Lt. Young rode up Main Street and dismounted opposite the American House. He wore a dark frock coat, vest, and baggy trousers while sporting a new bowler hat. He entered the hotel and took a room before returning to the streets. He walked around the town, making sketches of the banks and other buildings in a leather journal. He made a detailed plan of the town, noting the location of the banks, livery stables, hotels, and other sites.

After hours of walking, Bennett entered a tea shop on Main Street and sat down. A waitress arrived and served him while he added some notes to his observations about the town. Bennett tried not to stare as an attractive young woman came in and sat down at a nearby table. She was in her twenties and dressed in a white blouse, dark skirt, and bodice under a threadbare coat. She appeared nervous and uneasy under her light blue bonnet.

Bennett averted his gaze and pretended to be engrossed in his notes, but he couldn't help himself. He dared another glance and found himself looking into the most arresting green eyes he had ever seen.

"Hello, miss," he stammered, embarrassed. "I was wondering whether you might know how many people work at the foundry here in town."

"What an odd question," she said, smiling.

A waitress brought over a pot of tea and placed it in front of her. The young woman thanked her and then looked back at Bennett.

"I'm afraid not, sir. I've just come from there. I'm looking for a job."

"So, they don't need more workers at the foundry or the mill?"

"They are not hiring, sir. That's all I know. It's not easy to find work now. Where are you from?"

"I'm from Montreal. I'm a theology student."

The woman nodded and drank her tea in silence. She then stood up and put on her coat.

"Good day to you, sir."

In the afternoon, Bennett rode out to get a look at Governor Smith's magnificent mansion called the 'Towers' on the corner of Congress and Smith Streets. He knocked on the door and then chatted with the doorman. An older woman appeared in the foyer and struck up a conversation with Bennett. She turned out to be the Governor's wife and would have introduced Bennett to the man himself if he had been in town. She showed him around the house and stables. She was particularly proud of her horses, which had been bred for racing and needed great care.

Bennett's casual walk around the mansion was to determine whether their plan to burn down the Governor's mansion was feasible and should be part of the retribution campaign. He didn't know it, but a year earlier, in November 1863, Governor Smith had requested 5,000 muskets, ammunition, and horses from the War Office in Washington to protect the town in case they were attacked by Confederate forces in Canada. His demand for military assistance was refused.

As Bennett left the Governor's mansion and headed back to town, he ran into the young woman from the tea shop in a buggy coming his way on the road.

"Hello, sir. What a surprise! What are you doing here?" asked the young woman.

"I've just come from the Governor's house, miss," said Bennett. "Are you on your way home?"

"Yes, I am."

"How far are you going? Perhaps I can accompany you."

"That's very gallant of you, sir. Thank you."

"Fine, then. I'll join you."

Bennett dismounted and tied his horse to the buggy. He climbed in next to the woman who smiled at him as the buggy headed off.

"My name's Bennett, miss, Bennett Young. What's your name?"

"Eliza, Eliza Miller. I would prefer that my father not see us together, Mr. Young."

"I understand, miss. I'll leave well before we get there."

"What's a theology student from Montreal doing in St. Albans?"

"That's a very good question, Miss Eliza," said Bennett as he noticed her green eyes again and the slender strands of gold dancing in her irises. Bennett was smitten. He had gone for over a year with no feminine presence in his life, and he missed the female touch.

October 10, 1864
Quebec City, Quebec

A large group of distinguished politicians, business leaders, and bureaucrats gathered in a conference room of the Château Louis to thrash out a constitutional agreement for the new Canadian Union. They represented most of the British colonies in North America, and each had come to protect their political and commercial interests in the new confederation. They were seated around a long table strewn with the proposals under consideration, various law books, and other documents. The discussions were often contentious, the arguments heated, but the men would pause from time to time to look out the bay window at the majestic St. Lawrence River below them and feel the calming effect of the old river on their nerves. The view was extraordinary. The broad reach of the river was dotted with tiny ferry boats working their way against the current to the town of Levis on the south shore, *goélettes* sailing around the island to the east and paddle-wheelers belching black smoke as they sailed west against the strong current.

The first conference for a new Canadian Union had been held in early September in Charlottetown on Prince Edward Island and had led to this second conference in Quebec City. With the war going on south of the border, Canadian politicians were convinced that a union of the province of Canada with the colonies of New Brunswick, Nova Scotia, and Prince Edward Island would be an effective tool to protect them against annexation by the United States. After the annexation of Texas in 1845, lots of Americans believed that it was their 'manifest destiny' to expand across all of North America. It was this belief that had allowed Washington to justify their war with Mexico. There were ongoing disputes over the Oregon boundary and the Northern Maine boundary after the Aroostook War, or what was called 'the Pork and Beans War'. The boundary disputes could easily have led to war with Britain, but they were eventually settled by the Webster-Ashburton Treaty of 1842 and the Oregon Treaty in 1846. Canadian politicians were well aware that it would only take a minor land dispute along the ill-defined border for the Americans to attempt to seize one or several British colonies in North America.

There were 33 delegates at the conference. The British government had merged Upper and Lower Canada into the Province of Canada in 1841 with Kingston as the capital. Upper Canada became Canada West and Lower Canada, Canada East. The prime minister at the time was Étienne-Paschal Taché, who shared power with his deputy, a clean-shaven, curly-haired Scot by the name of John A. Macdonald. Macdonald was one of the leading voices at the conference, along with the founder of the Toronto Globe and leader of the Reform Party, George Brown, and the Attorney General of Canada, George-Étienne Cartier. Another key player was Alexander Galt, the financial wizard, who had been a finance minister in a previous government under MacDonald and Cartier. Macdonald stood up and read aloud from the 17th resolution:

"Representation in the House of Commons shall be based on population, as determined by the Official Census every ten years. The number of members at first shall be 194, distributed as follows: Upper Canada: 82, Lower Canada: 65, Nova Scotia: 19."

Macdonald smiled at the delegates from Nova Scotia and then

continued.

"New Brunswick: 15, Newfoundland: 8, Prince Edward Island: 5."

There was a long pause as the men reflected on the fairness of what was to be the division of power in the new nation.

MAP OF QUEBEC

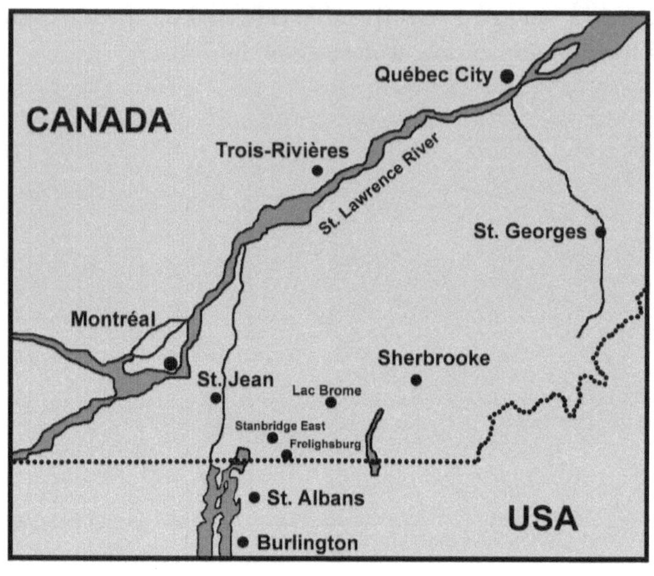

Nine

October 19, 1864
St. Albans, Vermont

After he visited St. Albans, Bennett returned to Montreal to consult with Clay and Sanders. They approved the plan and Bennett received an amount of $1,400 from Clay to launch the attack. He was ordered to recruit thirty soldiers for the Fifth Company C.S.A. Retributors, but the number was later reduced to twenty-three. They were all former prisoners of war who had escaped to Canada and were struggling to survive in the city. Young and his men jokingly referred to the raid as the 'Vairmont Yankee Scare Party'.

The raiders traveled by train to St. Albans in groups of two or three from Montreal and Saint-Jean and others arrived indirectly by carriage from Burlington in the south. Bennett and two of his men set foot in the town on October 10 and stayed at the Tremont Hotel, while the others lodged at the St. Albans House, the American House, and the Willard Boardinghouse. The men were conscious that their Southern accents might give them away, so they spoke as little as possible to strangers and posed as hunters, horse traders, tourists, and itinerant laborers. They walked around the town to have a look at the livery stables, the gun shops, and the restaurants to get a feel for the local gossip.

Although St. Albans looked like a peaceful oasis far away from the battles raging in the South, the war impacted the lives of numerous people in the town. There were funerals every week for local boys who had gone off to war and had been buried anonymously in mass graves. The trains coming north carried more and more sick and wounded men. The local factories manufactured muskets, while the woolen mills produced large numbers of blankets, uniforms, and other items for the army. While the men were away fighting the war, the workforce consisted mainly of women, the young, and the elderly. Bennett had planned the attack for Tuesday, October 18th, but decided to delay a day because Tuesday was a market day. He learned that the streets would be packed with farmers selling their wares. Bennett feared that his men wouldn't be able to control the crowds.

It was just after three o'clock in the afternoon on Wednesday, October 19, and the wait was over. It had rained during the night and the roads were muddy. Bennett led five of his men down Main Street to the American House. He had done this sort of thing dozens of times with John Hunt Morgan's cavalry, taking possession of enemy towns across Kentucky, Indiana, and Ohio. The plan was to scare the unarmed citizens, not to ambush them, and to use the element of surprise to the utmost. He stood before a group of people gathered on the verandah of the American House and fired two 36-caliber Colt Navy revolvers in the air.

"Gentlemen, I am an officer in the Confederate Service. I have been sent here to take this town and I'm going to do just that. If any man offers resistance, I'm going to shoot him."

Samuel Lackey came up behind the shocked onlookers, who turned to see a man holding a gun on them.

"Gentlemen," he said cheerfully. "You heard the lieutenant. We're all going to head quietly over to the village green."

Lackey and William Teavis led the frightened local men over to the park, forcing other citizens to join them on the way. Meanwhile, James Doty rode his horse down Main Street, stopping ordinary citizens from coming into town. In other parts of town, Charles Swager and his men threatened the locals at gunpoint, took their horses, and sent them over to join their fellow citizens in the park. Not all the townspeople were so cooperative. Bennett noticed a well-dressed man hurriedly lock up the jewelry store and head down the street.

"Sir!" Bennett hailed him. "You are ordered to go over to the village green!"

Inexplicably, the man ignored him.

"Listen to me, sir," said Bennett, losing patience. "If you do not follow my order, I will shoot you. Go to the village green now!"

Collin Huntington was the owner of the jewelry shop and had no idea who Bennett was. He stared at Bennett and suddenly broke into a run, going in the wrong direction.

Bennett didn't want to shoot the man, but he had no choice. The whole plan rested on keeping control of the local citizens. He aimed and fired. The man pitched forward into the mud.

"Good shot, Lieutenant!"

Bennett turned around to see Samuel Gregg and Dudley Moore grinning at him. They were on horseback and coming from the Tremont Hotel, on their way to their second assignment, which was to cordon off the railway station and the foundry. There were telegraph lines at the railway station, but more importantly, the foundry employed over four hundred men, too many for Bennett's small force to handle.

The raiders surrounded the wounded man. He was moving a little now and in obvious pain. Bennett came over to help.

"You boys better get up there and block off the road," said Bennett to Greg and Moore. "I'll get someone else to take care of him."

Gregg and Moore left to block the road as several raiders joined Bennett and helped him take Huntington across the street to the park. Already there were some twenty hostages on the village green guarded by Lackey.

"Try to find a doctor for him," Bennett said to Lackey.

St. Albans was a prosperous regional town and had three banks. The raiders planned to attack all three and make Vermont pay for Union transgressions in the Shenandoah Valley. Two raiders, Thomas Collins and Marcus Spurr, entered the St. Albans Bank and threatened the teller, Cyrus Bishop, with their revolvers. When Bishop ran towards the director's room and attempted to close the door behind him, Collins and Spurr jumped over the counter and forced the door open, hitting the teller in the head.

"Do that again and I'll blow your brains out," yelled Collins, pointing his revolver at the teller.

"What's going on, fellas?" protested Bishop.

"We're Confederate soldiers and we're robbing your bank," said Spurr. "Where's the gold?"

"We ain't got none," said Bishop.

At that moment, Louis Price and Squire Teavis burst in, joining Collins and Spurr at the bank. They pointed their guns at the other clerk, Martin Seymour.

"What about silver?" demanded Spurr.

"Yeah, we've got that," Bishop admitted. "What are you men doing here in Vermont?"

"We're robbing and plundering under orders from General Early, just like the Yankee army is doing in the Shenandoah Valley," said Collins. "Where you keepin' your silver?"

"In the safe," said Seymour.

"Open it. That's an order," said Spurr.

The men were putting the stolen banknotes in their leather army haversacks as Bishop opened the safe and showed the raiders three bags of silver worth $1,400. They added the silver to the banknotes.

"We can't carry so much," said Teavis. "Let's break up the bags."

They divvied up the silver between them, stuffing bank bills and US greenbacks into their bags. Collins approached the two bank employees.

"OK, fellas, it's time to take the oath," said Collins. "Raise your right hand and repeat after me: I do solemnly swear..."

Bishop and Seymour glanced at each other but obediently raised their hands. They repeated Collins' words:

"I do solemnly swear that I will not fire upon Confederate soldiers and not raise the alarm, for said soldiers are here to retaliate against the barbarous atrocities of the Yankee General Sheridan in the Shenandoah Valley."

Collins grinned at Spurr as he realized just how easy it was to get these ordinary civilians to submit to their demands. A man appeared at the door to the bank, knocking to gain admittance. Spurr opened the door to a local merchant named Samuel Breck and yanked him inside. He shoved him up against the wall and pointed a revolver at his head. He rifled through his jacket pockets with his free hand and discovered a thick envelope stuffed with bills.

"Hey!" protested Breck. "That's 393 dollars to pay off a loan. You can't take it. It's private property."

"That makes it the bank's money," Spurr grinned, "and we're robbing the bank."

He spun Breck around and sent him off to join the bank employees in the director's room, where the other raiders were busy stuffing bills into their haversacks. He had barely reached the door when a young man blundered into the bank, his eyes widening when he saw the gun in Spurr's hand. The raider quickly grabbed the youngster and put him in with the others before he locked the door.

Collins and Price steered Bishop into the next room, leaving Teavis to keep an eye on the captives. The room was almost empty except for a small desk, a chair, and a large safe for keeping bank bills and other currency.

"Open it up," ordered Collins, gesturing at the safe.

"I don't have the combination, sir," stammered Bishop.

"Mr. Bishop," said Collins, pushing the muzzle of his revolver hard into Bishop's chin. "How much do they pay you to work in the bank? I'm sure it's not enough to die for."

Bishop's shoulders sagged, and he removed a scrap of paper stuck underneath the desk. He dialed in the combination and pulled the heavy door open. Collins and Price gasped when they saw what was inside. There was more money in there than they'd ever seen before in their lives.

Ten

Down the street, Charles Higbee was busy saddling horses for the raiders in Field's livery stable. He was a small man with sharp features and mutton chops, wearing the same black fedora with a feather in it that he had worn when he marched into Lawrence, Kansas. Higbee was a veteran of Quantrill's Raiders who had run wild that August day in 1863, slaughtering over 150 civilians during the infamous attack. He had been Quantrill's adjutant and had handled all the stolen money. Higbee was no saint, but it was not what he had signed on for, and he left Quantrill not long afterward for Canada.

His current assignment was to procure horses for the men. He led out a string of saddled horses when a shout stopped him. A big, heavyset man was furious and coming at him, waving his arms.

"Stop that," protested Sylvester Field. "Those are my horses. What do you think you are doing?"

Higbee ignored the man and pulled his pistol. He fired a shot at the man; the bullet passing through his top hat. Field ran for cover as Higbee mounted a horse and led the string out onto Main Street.

A raider by the name of William Hutchinson with bushy side whiskers entered the Franklin County Bank and went up to the counter where Marcus Beardsley was working as a cashier.

"Do you deal in gold, sir?" asked Hutchinson.

"No, I'm afraid not, but you might want to ask Mr. Armington over there about gold."

Mr. James Armington was a prosperous St. Albans merchant who was standing near the teller's window. Hutchinson approached him.

"I have some Liberty head gold eagles, sir?"

Armington turned to look at the stranger.

"How many you got?"

"Six," said Hutchinson.

Armington bought six gold eagles worth $10 each from Hutchinson and left the bank with a colleague who was waiting for him by the wood stove.

Moments later, Daniel Butterworth, Dudley Moore, and John Moss stormed into the bank, drawing their pistols.

"OK, ladies and gentlemen, we are Confederate soldiers and we've come to rob the bank," announced Butterworth from the doorway.

Moss herded the customers to one side while Hutchinson grabbed Beardsley by the arm and dragged him into the director's room. Hutchinson gave out a low whistle when he saw the safe. It had a massive door, and he prodded Beardsley in the back with the muzzle of his revolver.

"Open it," he ordered.

Beardsley did what he was told. He could do nothing but watch as Moore and Butterworth looted the contents. As soon as they had finished, the raiders seized Beardsley and locked him inside.

Erasmus Fuller rode into town and stopped when he recognized several of his horses on the street behind the Tremont Hotel. He owned the Fuller Livery Stable and possessed dozens of horses. He drew his pistol and waved it about as he approached Bennett on Main Street.

"Hey, those are my horses," yelled Fuller.

"Put down that gun, sir, and go to the village green. That's an order," replied Bennett.

Fuller was furious to be ordered about and tried to take a shot at Bennett, but his pistol wouldn't fire. The lieutenant laughed as Fuller rode away. He ordered his men to continue herding the local citizens over to the park.

At the First National Bank, similar mischief was happening. Caleb Wallace, James Doty, Alamanda Bruce, and Joseph McGrorty were robbing the bank. Wallace pointed his pistol at the head of the cashier, Albert Sowles.

"If you offer any resistance, I'll shoot you dead," said Wallace. "You are my prisoner."

As Wallace watched Sowles, the others went into the bank vault and filled their haversacks with banknotes. On the floor, there were numerous bags full of coins.

"Those bags are full of small change, sir," said Sowles to the men.

McGrorty pulled a knife and cut into a few bags to see whether Sowles was telling the truth. The men collected as much loot as they could carry and left Wallace in the bank with the cashier.

"Now, Mr. Sowles," said Wallace. "I want you to lock the door and stay put. If you come out, my men will shoot you."

Sowles nodded and locked the front door as Wallace took leave of him. In the lobby, an old military man, General John Nason, was reading the local newspaper, unaware that a bank heist had just occurred under his nose.

As Wallace descended the stairs to the wooden sidewalk outside the bank, he ran into a local man named William Blaisdale in a hurry to get to the bank before closing time.

"The bank's closed, sir," said Wallace.

"No, it ain't. Not yet," retorted Blaisdale.

"The bank's just been robbed, sir. You are to go over to the village green with the other men."

It had been a bad day for Blaisdale. He made it worse by grabbing Wallace by the neck and throwing him down the steps. The next thing he knew, Joseph McGrorty was grinning at him over the barrel of a gun. That ended the fight and Blaisdale was led away.

Erasmus Fuller, still smarting from his ignominious encounter with Bennett, had wasted no time replacing his weapon and rounding up help. He approached the raiders at the head of a group of armed men through the alley near Miss Beattie's millinery shop. Fuller opened fire on the raiders who returned fire and one of Fuller's party, Elinus Morrison, dropped to the ground grievously wounded. The other men dropped their guns, turned tail, and ran. A seamstress in the shop witnessed the scene and saw the raiders move down the street, allowing Fuller and another man to carry Morrison to the doctor's office. Across the street, Leonard Cross stepped out of his photography studio to question Bennett and the raiders milling about in front.

"What's going on?" asked Cross. "What are you celebrating?"

"I'll tell you, but you must first come across the street," said Bennett.

A moment later, Bennett gave an order to Sam Lackey, who was carrying several glass bottles in his bag.

"Sam, throw a bottle of Greek fire at that building."

Lackey's bottle of incendiary chemicals struck the sign on the Atwood store and it burst into flames. Greek fire or *ignis graecus* was an incendiary concoction little changed since Roman times, but no less effective. The Romans had used it to burn enemy ships. It was a mixture of sulfur, naphtha, and quicklime and could not be extinguished with water. Cross gaped as fire engulfed his building, then turned and ran through the growing crowd of onlookers. Bennett looked around and didn't like what he saw. The crowd would soon be too big to control.

"Boys," said Bennett to his men. "March up the street and chase those people away."

The raiders headed up the street, firing their guns in the air to clear a path for themselves while the lieutenant on horseback covered their rear.

A buggy appeared out of nowhere and started up Main Street. Eliza Miller had driven her mother to the shops, and they were on their way home after buying provisions. As they arrived at the corner of the American House and the First National Bank, Eliza pulled up at the sight of her new friend, the young theology student from Montreal, sitting on a horse in the middle of the street and brandishing two pistols. Bennett was busy directing people over to the village green and stopped what he was doing when he caught sight of Eliza.

"What are you doing here, Bennett?" she asked.

"I don't have time to explain, Eliza," said Bennett, "but you need to get out of town. It's dangerous for you and your mother."

Eliza and her mother were dumbfounded as they watched the raiders leading people over to the green park.

"Go, Eliza, go."

"Are you going to be all right?"

"I'm fine, Eliza. Please, go now," pleaded Bennett.

Eliza whipped the horse, and the buggy trotted off along Main Street.

Captain George Conger jumped down from his wagon and walked

down Main Street to find out what was going on. He met Lt. Young coming around the corner.

"Sir, we are Confederate soldiers conducting a raid on your fair city," said Young. "You are my prisoner. You must go over the village green."

Bennett ordered one of his men to take Conger across the street to the park when the man suddenly broke away, running off towards the American House. The raider fired a shot at the man but missed. Conger ran into the building and slipped out through the back alley. He quickly spread the alarm. He sent several men home to get their guns. The men soon returned carrying hunting rifles and shotguns. Conger led the group onto Main Street near the American House. The raiders were down around the Tremont Hotel and were throwing bottles of Greek fire at various businesses.

Higbee arrived on Main Street with a long string of horses for the raiders just as Bennett noticed the armed group of townspeople coming down the street. He had no idea who Captain Conger was, but this group looked like a serious threat. They were holding their fire until they got close enough to do some real damage. It wouldn't be long before there would be a volley of shots coming their way. Bennett watched impatiently as his men converged on the horses. Higbee secured the last of the heavy bags of loot on a pack horse while the raiders mounted up.

"Keep cool, boys, keep cool," said Bennett as the armed mob behind George Conger started firing their guns in the air in the hope of chasing off the raiders. Bennett raised his right hand.

"Are we met?" he yelled, a grin on his face.

"We are met, Lieutenant!" bellowed the raiders in unison as Bennett gave the signal.

The raiders took off at the gallop, going north along Main Street, firing their pistols to scare off the locals. A resident, Wilder Gilson, had a good eye and a loaded musket in his room overlooking the street. He aimed at the fleeing raiders.

Bennett had waved his men on but reined in his horse to cover their escape. The raiders thundered past with Higbee bringing up the rear, slowed down by the heavily laden pack horse. Bennett was just starting back for him when Higbee cried out suddenly and swayed in the saddle. Bennett got to him just in time and grabbed the reins of the pack horse.

"Go on," Bennett yelled.

Higbee kicked his horse into motion and was followed by Bennett with the pack horse in tow. Bennett noticed the blood spreading across the back of Higbee's shirt and realized that his friend wouldn't be able to remain in the saddle for long. Pulling hard on the reins of the pack horse, Bennett leaned down low on the neck of his horse and they raced out of town.

Eleven

The raiders headed northeast, taking the road to Sheldon instead of going west to Swanton along the shore of Lake Champlain. Young and Higbee tried to keep up but were eventually left far behind in the mad dash north. Halfway to Sheldon, Young and Higbee pulled off the main road and headed for a ramshackle farmhouse hidden in the trees. Young dismounted quickly and helped Higbee off his horse. They hid the horses behind the barn and watched the road.

At the main house, they found Eliza Miller standing in the doorway with her hands on her hips, observing them with a look of pure hatred.

"What are you doing here, Bennett Young? You're secesh! The whole town is out looking for you."

"I need some help, Eliza," said Bennett. "My friend is wounded."

"I've got nothing to say to you. Go away."

"Hear me out, Eliza. It will only take a few minutes of your time, please."

"One minute, then you leave."

Eliza opened the door and the two men entered the kitchen where her aging father and mother were sitting quietly near the stove drinking tea. The Miller house was barely habitable, full of old furniture with peeling wallpaper and windows patched up with cardboard and wood shingles. Bennett sat Higbee down on a wooden chair while Eliza's parents watched them.

"We need to clean his wound, Eliza," said Mrs. Miller, getting out of her chair. "We don't want it to get infected."

Eliza, flabbergasted, watched her mother step outside with a bucket to pump water from the well. She turned to Bennett and glared at him.

"He needs a doctor, Bennett. You can't leave him here."

"We need your help, Eliza. I'll pay you well if you can hide my friend here and get him some medical help."

"What's he done?"

"Nothing much. He stole some horses in town, that's all."

The furious look on Eliza's face told him that she thought stealing horses was serious enough. She was about to tell him so when her mother returned with a pan of water and put it on the hob. Without a word, her father went outside to fetch more wood for the fire.

"Do you know a doctor, Eliza?" asked Bennett.

"Your uncle Carl lives down the road, Eliza," said Mrs. Miller. "He's a vet and handy with a knife. He might be able to remove the ball."

"Mother, I don't want these men around. For God's sake, they're Johnny Rebs."

Stunned, her mother dropped into a chair as the door opened and Mr. Miller returned with the wood.

"Johnny Rebs?" she asked incredulously.

"There ain't no Johnny Rebs this far north, Eliza," said her father, feeding wood into the fire.

"They're Johnny Rebs, Pa. I can assure you. You can hear it in their voices."

Eliza turned to Bennett.

"You boys stopped at the wrong place. My brother Eric is fighting with the 8th Vermont Infantry Regiment. No way we're gonna help you."

Higbee collapsed on the floor and Bennett rushed over to help him up.

"Put him on the table," sighed Eliza's mother, resigned to providing aid. "We better have a look at the wound. Get his shirt off."

"Ma!" screamed Eliza.

"Do it, Eliza."

Eliza shook her head in frustration but did what she was told. She grabbed a cloth and wiped down the table while Bennett helped his friend out of the chair.

"We're just goin' to have a look, Bennett," Eliza said briskly as they settled Higbee on the table. "Then you better be on your way."

Bennett nodded as Eliza's mother went to fetch a bottle of whiskey and a glass from the cupboard.

"Give the man a drink, Eliza," she ordered, handing Eliza the bottle.

"This is gonna be mighty painful."

Back in town, Captain Conger had raised a posse of some fifty citizens, young and old, some on horseback and others in wagons. They had muskets, shotguns, and pistols and were all keen to engage with the enemy. They raced out of town, following the fresh tracks in the mud, and slowed only to collect the occasional banknotes scattered along the roadside. The posse turned east on Plank Road, so intent on their pursuit of the raiders that they galloped right past the Miller farmhouse.

The raiders were a good ten minutes ahead of the posse. They were approaching the town of Sheldon when Wallace, lagging behind the others, spotted a farmer on horseback in a nearby field. With his horse about to collapse from exhaustion, he made a split-second decision. He reined his horse in and turned off the road into the field. He trotted over to the man and jumped down from his mount.

"I must have your horse, sir."

The farmer's horse looked a lot fresher than his own mount. Wallace pulled $500 of banknotes from his pocket and held it out so the man could see the money. The farmer looked at him, speechless.

"Please, sir," Wallace implored the man.

He was desperate and close to pulling out his gun to force the issue, but at the last minute decided against it. The astonished farmer just nodded and dismounted. He gave Wallace the horse and saddle in exchange for the wad of banknotes. Wallace transferred his haversack to the fresh mount before swinging himself up into the saddle. Neither man said another word. Wallace nodded his thanks again and trotted off with the horse before launching into a full gallop, cutting diagonally across the field back to the road.

Five minutes later, the posse arrived on the scene and the farmer took fright. He ran away on foot across the field, dragging Wallace's exhausted mount along with him. He was convinced that the posse was out to rob him. A member of the posse recognized the horse from the livery stable in town and gave chase, mistaking the farmer for a raider.

As the raiders galloped through Sheldon, Collins in the lead noticed a hay wagon parked near the bridge. He reined in his horse on the other side of the bridge and waved the raiders to a halt. The men looked at Collins as if he'd lost his mind.

"Let's get that wagon on the bridge, fellas," he yelled.

The men caught on to his plan and jumped down off their horses. They ran back across the bridge. Lackey was about to join them when Collins grabbed his arm.

"You got any more of that Greek fire, Samuel?"

"As a matter of fact, I do," said Lackey, smiling.

Lackey returned to his horse as Collins observed the men's efforts to move the wagon. It had been parked close to the bridge, but there was a sharp incline leading to the bridge entrance. It was a struggle to keep the wagon moving, even with the men pushing and pulling together. More men ran across the bridge to help. One of them stopped in the middle of the bridge and waved his arms.

"Rider coming," he yelled.

Collins squinted across the bridge but couldn't identify the rider. Whoever it was, he was coming fast, reins whipping from one side to the other as he urged his horse on. The man on the bridge waved his arms again.

"It's Wallace!" he said.

Collins swore as he saw the wagon pause just before the bridge entrance, the men struggling to hold it in place on the incline. A moment later, Wallace slowed his horse and trotted across the bridge. The men at the wagon gave it a mighty shove and rolled it up onto the bridge. Holding a bottle of Greek fire, Lackey walked across the wooden bridge to the wagon and tossed it on the load of hay, which almost instantly erupted in flames.

"Where the hell have you been?" Collins asked Wallace.

"I had to stop and buy a horse."

"We steal horses," Collins growled. "We don't buy 'em."

"Well, I bought this one," said Wallace, leaning over and patting the horse's lathered neck. "Best money I ever spent."

By the time the posse arrived, the hay was blazing away, and the raiders were long gone. Conger and his men could do nothing but watch the fire burn, consuming part of the bridge.

At the Miller house, a big, burly man in his forties named Carl with a large mustache and straggly beard went to work on the wounded raider. He was an unlikely surgeon as he probed the wound with a surgical knife and steel forceps. He was surprisingly gentle for such a big man, careful to stop probing each time Higbee screamed with pain.

"Give him some more whiskey, Eliza. We ain't in no hurry."

Eliza stood up and poured another glass of whiskey for Higbee, who quickly emptied it. As the patient settled down again, Carl probed the wound under the watchful eye of the lieutenant, Eliza, and her parents.

Later, after Carl had removed the ball and Higbee had lost consciousness, Bennett and Eliza stepped out of the kitchen and walked over to the barn.

"I can't stay for long, Eliza. As soon as it gets dark, I must be on my way."

"You can't leave him here, Bennett."

"Let me make you an offer, Eliza. I'll pay you one thousand dollars if you take care of Charlie and bring him over the border to Frelighsburg in a couple of weeks."

Eliza was astonished. She could hardly believe such a generous offer. Her parents were barely getting by with the war on. There was little or no work in the town, and what work there was paid a pittance.

"You must be joking, Bennett. Where you gonna get money like that?"

Eliza suddenly noticed the pack horse and its heavy bags.

"You robbed the banks, didn't you?" she exclaimed.

"You need the money, Eliza. Your ma and pa need the money, but you've got to be real careful. You don't want the neighbors giving you away."

Twelve

Quebec City, Quebec

It was raining hard as a hansom cab pulled up at the door of the Spencer Wood Estate late at night. A man in a frock coat and top hat got out and opened an umbrella as he ran towards the entrance to Government House. He knocked on the door and was immediately admitted by the butler. As he waited in the hall, the bearded Governor-General, Lord Charles Monck, descended the stairs in his dressing gown to where John A. Macdonald, dripping wet, sat waiting for him.

"I'm sorry to disturb you at such an unholy hour, Charles," said Macdonald.

"That's quite all right, John," said Monck. "What a horrible night to be out and about."

"I couldn't get away any earlier."

"I have some news to share with you. Please come into the study."

The two men stepped into Monck's study and sat down in leather club chairs surrounded by oak panels displaying the portraits of illustrious British military men and previous colonial administrators. They had scarcely settled into their chairs before the butler appeared with a bottle of brandy and two glasses. He poured one for Monck and the other for Macdonald and then left the two men to their business.

"How are Lady Elizabeth and the children?" asked Macdonald.

"She's fine, John, and so are the children," said Monck with a smile. "How's the conference going?"

"The usual rows over the legislative union and the division of power, Charles. It's to be expected. We're making progress, but it's all very exhausting. I'll be up half the night writing new resolutions for the meetings tomorrow."

"Well, that's something."

"I've brought a copy of the Boston Evening Transcript. The raid is in all the American papers. They're starting to organize militias to defend their borders from future attacks. I'm worried it could escalate."

"The chief of police has sent constables to scour the countryside looking for the men. I'm having them brought to Montreal for trial."

"The timing of this raid couldn't be worse, Charles. We could be at war with Washington again if we don't play our cards right. I'm thinking of calling out our Canadian militia to prevent any further incidents on the border."

Stanbridge East, Quebec

It was very late at night as a bailiff named Edmund Knight raced up the back stairs of Elder's Hotel accompanied by a local justice of the peace, Henry Whitman, and two armed men. They followed the hotel barman, who was carrying an oil lamp to illuminate the stairs. They stopped at a room on the second floor and waited silently as they listened for sounds. Nothing. Not a sound was coming from the room.

Knight silently opened the unlocked door and slipped inside to find two men fast asleep in the same bed. He gave the bed a hard kick to wake up the men.

"You're under arrest," he shouted. "Get up!"

Marcus Spurr and Alamanda Bruce, still groggy with sleep, had no chance to escape as Whitman and the others crowded into the room.

"Why are you arresting us, sir?" asked Spurr.

"For robbing the banks in St. Albans," Knight told him.

"Are you a British officer, sir?"

"No, I'm a bailiff. Get dressed."

Knight and the others kept a watchful eye on the men while they put on clothes caked in mud.

"You boys have been riding hard," said Knight with a grin. "The road from St. Albans is in worse condition than I thought."

Spurr and Bruce knew better than to reply. They stood quietly while Knight handcuffed them. One of Knight's men began rummaging through the bags on the floor. He let out a low whistle.

"Look what I found, Mr. Knight," he said, removing a large bundle of bank bills. He handed the bills to the bailiff and then removed the four Colt Navy revolvers hidden in the bottom of the bags.

The arrest was the start of a lucky streak for Knight and his men. The same evening, after they'd locked up Spurr and Bruce, they arrested Thomas Collins as he entered Henry Bacon's Hotel and Samuel Lackey on the sidewalk nearby. Their successful run of arrests continued the following night. James Doty and Joseph McGrorty were rudely awakened at gunpoint in a barn nearby.

Knight and his men made a total of six arrests and confiscated thousands of dollars in bank bills, US greenbacks, and treasury notes — all without firing a shot. The next day Knight dutifully handed the loot and his report to Guillaume Lamothe, the chief of police in Montreal, by order of the judge of sessions.

St. Albans, Vermont

It was about two hours until sunup and Carl was long gone, after promising to visit the patient in the morning. Eliza's parents had gone to bed and Charles Higbee was asleep on the daybed in the sitting room. The lieutenant was in the kitchen eating a plate of eggs, ham, and toast as Eliza brought him a cup of tea.

"Careful, it's hot."

"Thank you, Eliza. I can't thank you enough for your help."

"I still don't understand why you Rebs attacked our town. The people of St. Albans are innocent of all the crimes you mentioned. It's not our fault that there is a war on."

"Nobody is innocent, Eliza. We are all responsible for the killings and loss of life. I'm sick and tired of the war myself. I can't wait for peace to come."

"Where are you from, Bennett?"

"I grew up near Lexington, Kentucky. I enlisted with the 8th Kentucky Cavalry. All I've seen is death and destruction for the last two years."

"What are you going to do when you get to Canada?"

"I'm sure the Confederate Service will find other work for me, but I've lost all interest in the war. I want to get away, maybe go to Europe to study until the war is over."

"Europe? You mean London, Paris?" asked Eliza, her eyes sparkling.

"Why not? I've done all I can for the Rebel cause. I need to move on."

Eliza returned to the stove and began to murmur a line of poetry as she poured herself a cup of coffee.

> *"Success is counted sweetest*
> *By those who ne'er succeed.*
> *To comprehend a nectar*
> *Requires sorest need."*

From behind her, Eliza heard the lieutenant join in, reciting the same lines in perfect unison.

"That's a wonderful poem, Eliza."

"You know it? Success is counted sweetest?" asked Eliza, delighted.

"Of course I do, Eliza. You think people from Kentucky live in another world. We love Emily Dickinson's poems just as much as you do."

Eliza smiled at the lieutenant and went into the sitting room to find a book of poems by Walt Whitman, Herman Melville, Henry Timrod, and George Henry Boker.

"We had a fella in Camp Douglas in Chicago who'd recite poems all day long. I know most of Dickinson's poems."

The lieutenant picked up the book and flipped through the poems of George Henry Boker. He looked up at Eliza and started to read from *The Wilderness*.

> *"Mangled, uncared for, suffering thro' the night*
> *With heavenly patience, the poor boy had lain;*
> *Under the dreary shadows, left and right,*
> *Groaned on the wounded, stiffened out the slain.*
> *What faith sustained his lone,*
> *Brave heart to make no moan,*
> *To send no cry from that blood-sprinkled sod,*
> *Is a close mystery with him and God."*

> *"But when the light came, and the morning dew*
> *Glittered around him, like a golden lake,*

And every dripping flower with deepened hue
Looked through its tears for very pity's sake,
He moved his aching head
Upon his rugged bed,
And smiled as a blue violet, virgin-meek,
Laid her pure kiss upon his withered cheek."

"What a lovely reading!" said Eliza as she marveled at Bennett's deep baritone. The man had a way with words.

"It's a great poem, Eliza," said Bennett quietly, moved by the reading.

There followed an uneasy silence. Bennett would have loved to go on talking to Eliza, but it was getting late. He smiled at her and then stood up. It was time to go.

"Will you write to me, Bennett?" Eliza blurted, blushing at her temerity.

"Yes, of course I will," Bennett promised. "You'll take good care of Higbee?"

Eliza nodded and led him out of the kitchen into the cool air of the morning.

Thirteen

Montreal

Long lines of carriages moved slowly down Craig Street toward the portico of the St. Lawrence Hall. Under the yellow gas lamps, distinguished-looking men and women disembarked in evening dress and went inside. The Quebec Conference delegates were arriving to celebrate their work on the seventy-two resolutions adopted for the new constitution. A huge banquet had been organized in their honor, with hundreds of guests drinking champagne and listening to heartfelt speeches. John A. Macdonald was on the podium, finishing up his address.

"If we are not blind to our present position, we must see the hazardous situation in which all the great interests of Canada stand in respect to the United States. I am no alarmist. I do not believe in the prospect of immediate war. I believe that the common sense of the two nations will prevent a war; still, we cannot trust to probabilities. The government and legislature would be wanting in their duty to the people if they ran any risk. We know that the United States at this moment is engaged in a war of enormous dimensions, that the occasion of a war with Great Britain has again and again arisen, and may at any time in the future again arise. We cannot foresee what may be the result; we cannot say but that the two nations may drift into a war as other nations have done before. It would then be too late when war had commenced to think of measures for strengthening ourselves or to begin negotiations for a union with the sister provinces. Thank you, ladies and gentlemen."

Macdonald stepped down to great applause from the crowd and joined his political rival George Brown, and his friend George-Etienne Cartier, who had been co-premier of Canada East, while Macdonald represented Canada West from 1857 to 1862. Brown stood up and went to the podium.

"One hundred years have passed away since the conquest of Quebec, but here sit the children of the victor and the vanquished, all avowing hearty attachment to the British Crown, all earnestly deliberating how we shall best extend the blessings of British institutions, how a great people may be established on this continent in close and hearty connection with Great Britain."

"No constitution ever framed was without defect; no act of human wisdom was ever free from imperfection; no amount of talent and wisdom and integrity combined in preparing such a scheme could have placed it beyond the reach of criticism. And the framers of this scheme had immense difficulties to overcome. We had prejudices of race and language, and religion to deal with, and we had to encounter all the rivalries of trade and commerce, and all the jealousies of diversified local interests."

"To assert, then, that our scheme is without fault would be folly. It was necessarily the work of concession; not one of the thirty-three framers but had, on some points, to yield his opinions; and, for myself, I freely admit that I struggled earnestly for days to have portions of the scheme amended. But admitting all this, admitting all the difficulties that beset us, admitting frankly that defects in the measure exist, I say that, taking the scheme as a whole, it has my cordial, enthusiastic support, without hesitation or reservation. I believe that it will accomplish all, and more than all, that we, who have so long fought the battle of parliamentary reform, ever hoped to see accomplished."

Frelighsburg, Quebec

It was dawn as Lt. Young reached the outskirts of a tiny village that sat just five miles north of the Vermont border. Near an isolated farm, he turned off the road onto a dirt track and headed for a copse of trees. He led Higbee's mare and the pack horse with its load of bank bills and silver into the woods and dismounted.

An hour later, Bennett knocked on the door of the farmhouse. A ten-year-old girl with a dirty face and short, closely cropped blonde hair opened the door.

"Hello, miss. Is your dad around?" asked Bennett.

The girl said nothing for a long minute, looking Bennett up and down warily. She looked more like a boy than a girl. There was something wild and rough about her, like a homeless orphan who had lived without a lot of maternal care.

"Who are you?"

"My name is Bennett, miss. I'm from Farnham."

"My uncle went to town to help out," said the girl. "He took his gun with him. They're trying to catch a bunch of bad guys."

"Where's your aunt?"

"She ain't up yet, sir. Would you like a cup of tea, sir? I just made it."

"Thank you, miss. I would love a cup of tea. What's your name?"

"Iris, sir. *Tatie* Dorothée, don't get up 'til late."

Bennett entered the kitchen and took off his coat. He sat down at the table near the wood stove.

"That's a very nice name, Iris. The name of a goddess, or is it a flower?"

"A goddess, I think. My *maman* gave me the name, sir."

"The goddess of the sea and the sky."

Iris nodded as she admired the silver medal attached by a leather cord to Bennett's neck. He noticed her interest.

"It's a miraculous medal, Iris. A medal of Our Lady of Graces. It belonged to a friend of mine."

Bennett showed it to Iris who ran her finger over the figure of Mary crushing the serpent.

"It's a heavenly gift from Mary. If you wear it, you will receive graces, Iris. Graces are God's gifts that are free and undeserved."

Bennett heard a voice from the bedroom.

"Ris? Who you talkin' to, girl?" asked *Tatie* Dorothée.

"There was a man at the door, *Tatie*. I invited him in and I'm giving him a cup of tea."

Iris poured the tea from a pot on the hob and brought it over to Bennett.

"What man?" said the voice.

The aunt stumbled out of the bedroom, pulling a robe over her nightdress and rubbing her eyes.

"Morning, ma'am," said Bennett.

"Where you comin' from, sir?" asked Dorothée.

"Farnham, ma'am."

"Go on, Ris. Get me a cup. My husband's out looking for those damned Americans who escaped from Vermont."

Erasmus Fuller and George Beals were searching the outskirts of Frelighsburg in their wagon when they saw three horses parked behind a barn on the road south to the border. Fuller went to have a look and recognized the horses from his livery stable in St. Albans. There was no sign of the raiders, so he signaled to Beals and the two men in the wagon to head up to the house.

In the kitchen, *Tatie* Dorothée was standing at the stove frying bacon and eggs for her visitor as Iris sat on a stool, watching the lieutenant.

"What's your name, young man?" asked Dorothée.

"Bennett Young, ma'am."

"I don't know anyone with that name in Farnham, sir."

Suddenly, the front door flew open. Fuller stood tall in the doorway for a fraction of a second before he threw himself at the lieutenant. Bennett twisted out of his chair and went for his pistol before he was clubbed to the floor by Fuller. Bennett was younger and faster than the older man and quickly got to his feet, gaining the upper hand, but it was short-lived as Beals and his men came in through the back door. The men seized Bennett and hauled him out of the farmhouse to their wagon.

Iris watched the scuffle, and her heart went out to the young lieutenant. He seemed to be such a nice man while these other men were uncouth louts who were beating on him. She spotted the lieutenant's miraculous medal lying on the floor and picked it up.

"Sorry to bother you, ma'am," said Fuller as he was leaving. "He's one of them Johnny Rebs we've been looking for."

"Well, I never. He says he's from Farnham, sir," said *Tatie* Dorothée.

"He's a lying, thievin' secesh, ma'am," added Beals. "He killed some people in St. Albans and we're gonna take him home and hang him."

At the road, Beals and his men tied up the lieutenant and threw him in the wagon next to Squire Teavis, who was huddled in a corner in dirty clothes and bleeding from his lip. Fuller and Beals mounted up and followed the wagon, heading south on the Vermont road.

"Where'd they catch you, Teavis?" asked Bennett.

"On the other side of town, Lieutenant," he replied.

Bennett turned to Fuller and Beals.

"You idiots can't arrest us. We're in Canada. Don't you know nothing?" he yelled.

"Can you shut him up? Stuff a rag down his throat," Fuller shouted to the wagon driver.

"We're on British soil. You have no right to arrest us," Bennett claimed.

"Maybe or maybe not," growled the driver over his shoulder, "but we're gonna hang you anyway."

Fourteen

St. Albans, Vermont

It had been a long night and Eliza was still exhausted when she heard her mother downstairs in the kitchen. She was making tea while her father had gone out to the barn. Eliza went down to check on Higbee, who was sleeping on the daybed in the parlor.

"How are you feeling this morning, Mr. Higbee?" asked Eliza.

"Awful, miss. Goddamn awful. Where's the lieutenant?"

"He left just before sunrise and took the horses."

"Damn it. He took the horses?"

"Yeah. He said he couldn't leave the horses 'cause they come from the stables in town. He wanted to say goodbye, but you were fast asleep."

"Shit, shit, shit. How am I ever gonna get to Canada?"

"You're lucky to be alive, Mr. Higbee."

"You know that vet of yours shouldn't be allowed to work on no humans. It's a cryin' shame."

"The lieutenant said you're be whinin' and complainin' soon as you woke up. He was right. Carl will be back later with some laudanum to treat the pain. Would you like a cup of tea?"

"Please, miss. I'm sorry."

Eliza went to the kitchen and returned with a cup of tea moments later.

"Are you sure Carl will keep quiet?" Higbee asked anxiously. "What makes you think he ain't gonna give me up to that damn posse?"

Eliza laughed.

"You don't have to worry about Carl, Mr. Higbee. He's a cousin of mine on my mother's side. He ain't gonna say a word about a Johnny

Reb hiding in our house. You can sleep easy."

"Well, now. That's a relief. I can give him some money for the surgery if you think—."

"Don't worry about Carl, sir. He doesn't care a whit about money or politics. All he cares about is his sick animals. Besides, Lt. Young gave me a very generous amount to cover your medical costs. How long have you known the lieutenant?"

"I met him in Chicago during the Democratic Convention. We were planning a raid on the Camp Douglas prison. We were gonna liberate a bunch of Confederate POWs from that death camp, but it was called off at the last moment. The lieutenant's a good old boy from Kentucky, miss. He was with General Morgan on his raid through Indiana and Ohio."

Frelighsburg, Quebec

Bennett was desperate to free himself. They were only a few miles from the border. He knew that once he crossed the line into the State of Vermont, he would be in real danger. The wagon moved along at a slow pace on the rough track, weaving left and right to avoid deep puddles of rainwater. They were just minutes away from crossing over the border when a local bailiff by the name of George Wells rode up.

"What you got in that wagon, sir?" Wells asked Fuller and Beals.

"We got ourselves two Johnny Rebs and we're taking 'em back to Vermont," said Fuller with pride.

Wells looked at the prisoners in the wagon.

"Who are these men?"

"I'm Lieutenant Bennett Young and this is Corporal Squire Teavis under my command," replied Bennett.

"We're gonna hang 'em soon as we get 'em back to Vermont," said Beals.

"I'm sorry, sir, but you can't take 'em with you," said Wells. "I've received orders to arrest them. They are on British soil and under British law, they can't be extradited without a full hearing."

"But sir, they stole money from the banks in St. Albans. They shot up a lot of people. They're no-good killers," added Fuller.

"I'm sorry to hear that, sir, but the law is the law. You are on

Canadian soil. You better untie them."

Bennett grinned at Teavis as the Vermont men reluctantly cut them free and they jumped down from the wagon.

Farnham, Quebec

The police detective John O'Leary climbed the stairs to the Farnham station platform, where he found several people waiting for a train. He walked along the platform until he spotted a man with mud on his clothes.

"Sorry to bother you, sir. Are you from Montreal?" asked the detective.

"Yes, sir," replied Scott nervously.

The man's dirty appearance made the detective suspicious.

"Okay, come along with me. I'm a police officer. I've got some questions for you. What's your name?"

"Scott, sir. George Scott. I've done nothing."

"We'll see about that, sir. Come along now."

O'Leary led Scott along the platform and they descended to a wagon parked out of sight at the side of the building, holding six unhappy raiders shackled to the floor. Spurr, Bruce, Collins, Lackey, Doty, and McGrorty were under guard by two soldiers of the Saint-Jean military detachment. Nearby, Colonel Ermatinger sat on a tall chestnut mare, smoking a clay pipe.

"Detective, what have you got?"

"Looks like one of them raiders, Colonel. He's been riding hard. Look at the mud on him."

"Is he armed? You better search him."

O'Leary stepped up to Scott and seized his haversack.

"Let's see them pockets, sir," ordered the detective. "Empty your pockets, man."

Scott hesitated and then acquiesced to the police detective's demand. He showed him a map of Quebec and then produced a roll of St. Alban's banknotes from his pocket.

"Well, well. You've got your proof right there, Detective," said the colonel.

O'Leary then searched the man's haversack and found great bundles of greenbacks and two Colt Navy revolvers. The total value was later determined to be around two thousand eight hundred and fifty-nine dollars.

The detective took the money and slipped it into a canvas bag before he handcuffed Scott and put him in the wagon.

Montreal

On their way into the city, Lt. Young and his men were celebrated by huge crowds of supporters lining the streets. Two wagons with shackled prisoners pulled up at the 'Pied-du-Courant' prison on De Lorimier Street near the St. Lawrence River. A joyous cry went up from the crowd as the prisoners descended one by one from the wagons. The men could hardly believe how popular they were in the old French city.

The prison had been a familiar sight in the city during the Rebellion of 1837-38, when 1,500 French Canadian *patriotes* were held there. Ninety-nine of them were condemned to death, and twelve of that number were hanged in the courtyard of the prison. Another fifty-eight were deported to a penal colony in Australia. The British government sent Lord Durham to investigate the cause of the rebellion, and his report recommended the merger of Upper and Lower Canada. Durham angered the French population by calling for their assimilation. This led to the 1841 Act of Union, which united the two regions and made English the official language.

Squire Teavis was hauled out of the wagon and told to stand next to Lt. Young as a guard removed his shackles.

"Hey, Lieutenant. I ain't heard such jubilation since Lee won at Chancellorsville," said Teavis. "You'd think we were on parade in Richmond."

"The crowds love us secesh," said Bennett. "You know why? It's because they hate the Yankee bastards just as much as we do."

The guards removed the shackles from the second wagon of prisoners as the first group headed inside the jail to shouts of encouragement from the crowd.

The prison was built around a central pavilion with three wings. The basement cells were for the condemned to death, those on the first floor were for prisoners with long sentences, and those on the second floor were for prisoners with bad debts. The raiders were incarcerated on the top floor in large, comfortable cells, including a common room.

Twelve raiders sat around the table in the dayroom, looking glum as Lt. Young and Squire Teavis entered the room. They were exhausted from their long wagon ride and several had cuts to their faces and arms from their scraps with the law.

"What happened to you, Lieutenant?" asked Lackey.

"Teavis and I were roughed up by a bunch of Vermont crackers," said Bennett. "They were takin' us back to St. Albans when a bailiff saved us less than a mile from the border."

Bennett walked around the room, shaking the hands of his friends, when he noticed how sad everyone was.

"What's goin' on, boys?" asked Bennett.

"We've lost the Shenandoah, Lieutenant. It's in all the papers," said Lackey, throwing down a copy of the New York Herald. The headline read: REBS UNDER GENERAL EARLY ROUTED AT CEDAR CREEK.

"Damn. How'd that happen?" asked Bennett.

"Jubal Early had them whipped, Lieutenant," said Lackey. "He launched an early morning attack on the Union camp and caught them with their pants down."

"Then how come we lost the battle?" questioned Bennett.

"General Sheridan arrived and mounted a counterattack," said Collins.

"It happened the same day we were in St. Albans," Scott added.

"The news is goin' from bad to worse, Lieutenant. Ain't no way we're gonna win this war," said Lackey, thinking about his family. He was an emotional young man who missed his wife and kid.

"We don't know that, Sam," said Bennett, putting a comforting hand on his shoulder. "General Lee can still whip them when he wants to."

As Bennett sat down, George Scott came over.

"Hey, Lieutenant. You hear anything about Will Teavis, Squire's brother?" asked Scott.

"Nope. He must have gotten clean away," replied Bennett.

"What's the news about Higbee and our loot?"

"I left him at a farmhouse on the Vermont side, George. He had a nasty wound. The people there are gonna patch him up and send him north in a couple of weeks."

"You ain't worried those people will turn Higbee in for a reward?" asked Lackey.

"I paid them. They are good people, they're honest."

"That son-of-a-bitch has got all our money. How do you know he won't steal it, Lieutenant?" asked Scott.

"I hid the loot when I came over the border."

The men looked indignant for a moment.

"Why? Why'd you hide our money, Lieutenant?" asked Scott.

"I had to. I didn't want to get arrested carrying it around. That loot belongs to the Confederate cause. It isn't ours."

"How'd it go with Abbott?" asked Squire Teavis.

"Abbott thinks we've got a good case. We haven't committed any crimes in Canada, so all we gotta do is fight the call for extradition."

A prison guard entered the room, looking for the lieutenant.

"There's a journalist from the Evening Telegraph," the guard told him. "He wants to talk to you."

Bennett stood up and went over to the far corner where the journalist was waiting.

Fifteen

The extradition trial was a major event in Montreal and was held with all the pomp and circumstance befitting the international nature of the case. The trial was held in the grand old courthouse on Notre Dame Street designed by John Ostell and built in 1856 with its neo-classical architecture and Doric columns. The Montreal District Court followed the British tradition with the judge and the attorneys draped in black robes and wearing white ceremonial wigs. Judge Charles-Joseph Coursol, in a full black beard, wore a long white wig as he sat behind the massive raised bench looking down at the defense lawyer, William Kerr, preparing to make a statement. Kerr was clean-shaven and a natty dresser, and wore the customary white barrister wig as did his colleagues, John Abbott, and partner, Toussaint-Antoine Laflamme. To his left sat the prosecutors, Francis Johnson, Stephen Bethune, and Edward Carter, all wearing traditional courtroom attire. Among them sat the wigless representative of the US government, Bernard Devlin, who intended to exercise a powerful influence over the proceedings. In the crowd behind the prosecution table sat two Vermont lawyers, E A. Sowles and Henry Edson, who represented the banks that had been the main victims of the raid.

There was immense public interest in the case, and the gallery was packed. It didn't seem to matter that today they were only hearing a motion for a writ of *habeas corpus* on behalf of the St. Albans raiders held in the Montreal jail.

"I have a copy of the warrant here," Kerr said, holding it up. "It is signed by Mr. Guillaume Lamothe, chief of police, sir. It says here: 'Upon the twenty-fourth day of October instant, at the said city of Montreal, between the hours of six and eight o'clock in the afternoon, I arrested a person, who has since given his name as W. H. Hutchinson, upon suspicion of his having committed a felony at St. Albans, in the State of Vermont, one of the United States of America.'"

"Yes, Mr. Kerr, I have it," confirmed Judge Coursol.

"In our application for *habeas corpus*, sir," Kerr continued. "I have filed two grounds of objection. First, the document contains no charge for any offense which the prisoner could have committed. 'Suspicion of felony' is not a charge. And secondly, the warrant contains no time limit during which the prisoner is to remain in confinement."

Kerr had hardly finished speaking before John Abbott got to his feet.

"You have something to add, Mr. Abbott?" asked Coursol.

"I would like to add, Your Honor, that the warrant omits to state the day, the place, and the time when the prisoner should be brought up for examination, sir. It is quite extraordinary, for as fast as one warrant was found defective and was on the point of being quashed by Judge Badgley, another was submitted so that the accused might be kept in jail from day to day, until the learned gentleman who drew up the first warrant learned from the prisoner's counsel how to prepare one in a legal and valid manner. I would also like to mention a further irregularity during my time at Saint-Jean as counsel for the prisoners. I found the clerk of the Crown for the District of Montreal collecting information, drawing up commitments, and acting in the capacity of the magistrate's clerk for the District of Iberville. These are not the usual duties for a clerk of the Crown, sir. I was surprised to hear that the Attorney General himself had sent him."

"Judge, I object to being described as a clerk of the magistrate," protested Carter. "I have never acted in that capacity."

Carter was then interrupted by Abbott.

"Whether the learned gentleman had acted at the instance of the Attorney-General or not," Abbott retorted, "the task he was called upon to perform was precisely that of a clerk to the magistrate. This must be the first time in the history of our constitutional government that a member of our government has been found assisting a foreign government in attempting to affect the extradition of persons found within its borders."

Judge Coursol turned to Crown Prosecutor Johnson, QC, a bespectacled man with bad skin and side whiskers.

"Mr. Johnson, what is your position regarding the warrant?"

"I believe the warrant is sufficient, sir. The information disclosed provides sufficient grounds for imprisonment and commitment for examination."

"Mr. Devlin, what is the position of the US authorities?"

"We agree with Mr. Johnson, sir. The writ of *habeas corpus* should be rejected," said Devlin, a tall thin man with a pencil mustache.

"Thank you, gentlemen," said Judge Coursol. "I must agree with the defense counsel that the original warrant was quite inadequate. It charged the prisoner with suspicion of felony and ordered his commitment for examination. As to the second objection, concerning the day, the place, and the time when the prisoner should be brought up for examination, I believe that the warrant now has been modified to my satisfaction. I am therefore rejecting the defense's application for *habeas corpus.*"

Quebec City, Quebec

John A. Macdonald rushed into the Château Louis Hotel lobby with a grey-haired older man with side whiskers and a silk top hat. They were directed to the bar on the second floor with its extraordinary view of the St. Lawrence River. They spotted Georges-Étienne Cartier having a whiskey in a booth with his male secretary.

"Thanks for seeing us on such short notice, George," said Macdonald. "We are a wee bit pressed for time. We have a train to catch for Montreal in an hour."

Cartier dismissed his secretary and invited Macdonald and his friend to sit down.

"It's a pleasure, John," said Cartier, clean-shaven with piercing eyes and receding grey hair. Cartier was a savvy, pragmatic French-Canadian politician who had worked closely with Macdonald and Brown to bring about the Canadian Union of Provinces.

"George, this is a friend of mine, Gilbert McMicken," said Macdonald. "He's doing some work for us in the Niagara area. We've had trouble with 'crimps' crossing the border and enrolling our citizens in the Union Army. But now we've got a far more serious problem."

"You mean the St. Albans affair? I've been getting daily updates from Monck."

"Good. Gilbert and I have been having a look at our borders, George. We can't afford another incident like this."

"Mr. Cartier, it's very easy for a Johnny Reb to cross into New York, Vermont, and New Hampshire from Quebec," added McMicken in a heavy Scottish accent. "They can take the train south or simply ride over the border on horseback and attack the nearest town. Of course, it's not so easy if they have to ferry men across a major river or a lake. So we think there are only a few Confederate targets worth their while along the border."

"The path of least resistance for raiders is the Quebec border, the Windsor/Sarnia border, and the Niagara peninsula," said Macdonald.

"Yes, I would have to agree with your analysis, John. What are you proposing?"

"We're thinking of raising a militia to patrol those parts of the border, George."

"We also plan to infiltrate the Confederate Service, sir, so we know what they are planning to do before they act," said McMicken.

"Those are excellent ideas," said Cartier, leaning back in his chair. "I'm not so sure how effective they will be, but what else can we do? I have put several police detectives in Montreal on the lookout for Clay and Thompson, but the news is that they have left town."

Sixteen

Montreal

In the courtroom, the prosecution was making its case for extradition. Judge Coursol looked down at the small bald man in the witness box. Cyrus Bishop had been a teller at the St. Albans Bank.

"Please tell us in your own words what happened, Mr. Bishop," said Johnson of the prosecution.

"On the nineteenth day of October last, I was fulfilling the duties of teller in the St. Albans Bank, between the hours of three and four o'clock in the afternoon when two people I didn't know entered the bank. I have since identified them and I now see them in court. Their names are Thomas Collins and Marcus Spurr," said Bishop, pointing at the two men in civilian clothes sitting in the front row of the dock.

Spurr and Collins smiled as the entire courtroom peered down at them. The raiders were a handsome bunch of young men in their early twenties and their appearance had much improved after their clothes had been washed in the prison laundry. Some of the men had shaved off their beards and others had visited the prison barber, so they wouldn't be too easy to recognize. There were fourteen men in the dock: Lackey, Teavis, Bruce, Hutchinson, Swager, Scott, Young, Wallace, Doty, McGrorty, Gregg, Moore, Collins, and Spurr.

"What about the other two men?" Johnson asked.

"They are not here, sir. I don't see them."

"So tell us what happened after they came in."

"When I saw them holding revolvers, I sprang from behind the counter to the director's room and attempted to close the door behind me, but Collins and Spurr followed me and forced the door open, and, in doing so, I was struck on the forehead. They pointed their revolvers at me and threatened to blow my brains out if I put up any further resistance."

"Can you tell us what happened to Mr. Breck?" asked Johnson.

"Mr. Breck is a customer of the bank, sir. He came in to make a payment on a loan to the amount of $393, but Marcus Spurr stole the money."

"Did you see it with your own eyes, sir?" asked Johnson.

"Yes, sir. I was in the director's room and the door was open. I saw Spurr grab him as he came into the bank."

"Thank you, Mr. Bishop."

After some ten minutes of testimony, Judge Coursol asked the witness a question.

"What was the oath about, sir?"

"Well, sir. Collins forced me to take an oath."

"What did the oath say?" asked Johnson.

Bishop furrowed his brow in concentration as he tried to recall the words.

"I do solemnly swear," he began, "that I will not fire upon Confederate soldiers and not raise the alarm, for said soldiers are here to retaliate against the barbarous atrocities of the Yankee General Sheridan in the Shenandoah Valley," said Bishop. "That's the best I can remember, sir."

"Thank you, Mr. Bishop," said Coursol.

The following day was November 8, 1864, and election day in the United States. President Abraham Lincoln of the National Union Party was up against George McClellan of the Democratic Party and it seemed highly unlikely that Lincoln would win a second term. His choice of Vice-President was Andrew Johnson, the Governor of Tennessee. In the prison dayroom, no one was certain who would carry the day. Both candidates were for pursuing the war and nothing much would change for the Confederacy regardless of who was elected. Just as the prisoners were eating their breakfast, the prison guard arrived with the American newspapers, which he sold at outrageous prices to the men. The room was soon abuzz with comments for and against the candidates.

Bennett got hold of a copy of the Boston Transcript, which mentioned that the Montreal trial of the Confederate prisoners was 'just getting underway'. As he skimmed the rest of the paper, he noticed a column about the arrest of the Chicago Conspirators: Colonel George St. Leger Grenfell, Mary Morris, Judge Morris, Colonel Vincent Marmaduke, and a third man by the name of Cantrell. There was no mention of Captain Hines, who appeared to have escaped, but the leader of the Sons of Liberty, Charles Walsh, had been arrested at his home with a cache of guns and ammunition. Camp Douglas was no longer in any danger of a Confederate attack.

As Bennett and his fellow prisoners were getting ready to leave for court, Clement Clay and George Sanders arrived to talk to the men. Sanders pulled out a chair for Clay to stand on, but Clay refused the chair and had the first word.

"Hello, I'm Commissioner Clement Clay and this is George Sanders, our agent here in Montreal. We have hired the services of the best lawyers in this town to represent you, and we are going to win this case. George will be coming in to check on you from time to time. If you need anything, talk to George. Thank you, gentlemen."

This was followed by polite applause as Sanders climbed on the chair so everyone could see him.

"Hello boys," said Sanders. "All you gotta do in court is remember that you are the proud soldiers of the Confederate States of America and the State of Vermont can do nothing against you in a time of war. The lawyers may have questions for you. Answer them honestly and they will do the best they can for you. I will be coming by every few days, but if you have an urgent problem, please talk to Lt. Young. Good luck to you all."

The prisoners stood up to applaud Sanders and then cheerfully filed out of the room on their way to court. Clay and Sanders went over to talk to the lieutenant.

"Did you see the papers, Mr. Clay?" asked Bennett. "St. Lege was arrested in Chicago."

"Yes, I saw it, Lieutenant," said Clay. "It's very unfortunate. He was an important asset. Things are not going well for us at the moment."

"I also read about the Lake Erie debacle, sir. The headline in the Toronto Globe was 'Piracy on Lake Erie,' sir."

"It was not a good plan," said Sanders.

"The plan was for Thompson's men to seize the gunboat, the USS Michigan, at Sandusky," said Clay. "They were to proceed to the prison on Johnson's Island to free the prisoners, but they failed. Beall was betrayed. It was a fiasco."

"There were too many players," said Sanders. "No wonder it failed. Thompson is pathetic."

Clay remained silent, not wanting to denigrate his partner in front of the men.

Lt. Young stood up as a guard waved him over. He nodded at Clay and Sanders and then left the room to join the others on their way to court.

A new witness was called to the box. After he was sworn in, Johnson of the prosecution asked the cashier, Marcus Beardsley, to tell his story.

"On the nineteenth day of October, I was a cashier at the Franklin County Bank. On that day, several armed men came into the bank. I recognize the prisoner, Hutchinson, as one of the armed gang that entered the bank."

Beardsley pointed to a man in the dock.

"He wore whiskers then, which he has not now, and he had no spectacles on then as he has now. When he first came into the bank, he inquired from me what we were paying for gold. I answered that we were not dealing in such an article, and referred him to Mr. Armington, a merchant of the village. There were four or five of the said armed gang that entered the bank, but I only recognize Hutchinson, who seemed to be their leader."

Beardsley's testimony dragged on for most of the morning. In the afternoon, Johnson called a new witness, Albert Sowles, who had been a cashier at the First National Bank during the raid.

"Tell us how the attack happened in your own words, Mr. Sowles," said Johnson.

"I was a bank teller on October 19 when the First National Bank was robbed. Several men entered the bank and this man, Caleb Wallace, approached me at the counter, pulling a pistol and pointing it at my head. I recognize him. He is sitting over there on the bench with the other Rebs."

"What about the others?"

"There were four of them, sir. I see James Doty, Alamanda Bruce, and Joseph McGrorty on the bench."

"So, for the record, you have identified the four men who took part in the robbery."

"Yes, sir."

Seventeen

After several days of testimony from the bank clerks and the citizens of St. Albans, Judge Coursol asked Crown Prosecutor Johnson if he had any further evidence for the charge of robbery at the St. Albans' banks. Johnson replied that he had no further evidence and argued that it was time for the depositions to be read to the prisoners to see whether they had anything to say in reply.

"Very good," replied Coursol. "It is time for voluntary statements to be taken. We'll start with Lt. Young."

Coursol handed the clerk the deposition. The clerk stood up and read a long and detailed deposition describing the actions of Lt. Bennett Young in the town of St. Albans, Vermont. When the clerk had finished the reading, Coursol addressed Lt. Young in the dock.

"Lt. Young, having heard the evidence against you, do you wish to say anything in answer to the charge? You are not obliged to say anything unless you desire to do so, but whatever you say will be taken down in writing and may be used against you at your trial."

Young nodded to his lawyers, Abbott and Kerr. He stood up and was sworn in by the court clerk before he took his place in the witness box.

"Go ahead, sir," Judge Coursol told him.

Bennett glanced at his friends in the dock as he took a folded piece of paper from his pocket and began to read, reminding himself to stay calm and to stick to the script supplied by his lawyers.

"I am a native of Kentucky, and a citizen of the Confederate States, to which I owe allegiance. I am a commissioned officer in the Army of the Confederate States, with which the United States is now at war. I owe no allegiance to the United States. I herewith produce my commission as first lieutenant in the Confederate States Army, and the instructions I received at the time that commission was conferred upon me," said Bennett, nodding to Abbott, who held up two documents that he handed to the judge.

"I reserve the right to put in evidence further instructions I have received at such time and in such manner as my counsel shall advise."

"Please explain the nature of these documents to the court, Lt. Young," asked Coursol.

"Well, sir. The first document is my commission document as First Lieutenant in the Provisional Army. It was signed on June 16, 1864."

"Yes, I can see that," Coursol said, "and the second?"

"The second document is signed by James Seddon, the Secretary of War for the Confederate States, and authorizes me to raise a company of men to carry out raids like the one in St. Albans."

"The document says that you are to organize for special service a company of no more than twenty men who will be entitled to pay, rations, clothing, and transportation."

"Yes, sir."

Judge Coursol nodded, his expression inscrutable, and passed the documents on to the clerk for circulation to the prosecution's table. A wave of consternation seemed to follow the documents as they were passed hand to hand among the prosecutors and their American colleagues.

"Do you have any questions about the documents, gentlemen?" Coursol asked.

"No, Your Honor," Johnson replied. He did not look happy, nor did any of the other lawyers at his table.

"Please continue, Lieutenant," ordered Coursol.

"Whatever was done at St. Albans was done by the authority and order of the Confederate Government. I have not violated the neutrality laws of either Canada or Great Britain. Those who were with me at St. Albans were all officers or enlisted soldiers of the Confederate Army under my command. They were before the 19th of October last and their term of enlistment has not yet expired. Several of them were prisoners of war, taken in battle by the federal forces, and retained as such until they managed to escape."

"The expedition was not planned or projected in Canada. The course I intended to pursue in Vermont, and which I was able to carry out but partially, was to retaliate in some measure for the barbarous atrocities of Grant, Butler, Sherman, Hunter, Milroy, Sheridan, Grierson, and other Yankee officers, except that I would scorn to harm women and children under any provocation, or unarmed, defenseless, and unresisting citizens, even Yankees, or to plunder for my own benefit."

The courtroom was silent as the audience hung on his words. The American Devlin frowned as he exchanged a look with Johnson of the prosecution. *It was not going to be an easy job to extradite these young men back to Vermont.*

"At this time, I am not prepared for the full defense of myself and my men without communication with my government at Richmond, and since such communication is rendered practically impossible by the Yankee government, be it by land or by sea, I do not think I can be ready for a full defense in this case under thirty days. During this time, I hope to be able to obtain important material testimony by other means from Richmond, without the consent of said Yankee government."

"Thank you, Lt. Young. You may step down."

Bennett returned to the dock accompanied by smiles and nods from his co-accused and discouraged murmurs from the prosecution table and the Americans.

On the waterfront not far from the courthouse, Charles Monck and John A. Macdonald drove along a street in a hansom cab. Monck, who liked to travel in style, had just disembarked from a paddle-wheeler that had brought him up the river to Montreal from Quebec City.

"Secretary Seward is demanding a rapid extradition of the prisoners, John," said Monck.

"It has to go through the courts, Charles. You know that, and Seward knows it. He can rail and rage against us all he likes, but nothing will change that fact."

"He talks about the 'unprovoked aggressions from Canada'," continued Monck. "He says that British neutrality policy has failed by granting asylum to active enemies of the US and allowing them to use Canada, in his own words, as a 'base for felonious depredations against the US'. Can you believe it? I have never heard such outrageous calumny against us from a foreign power."

"Our good friend Georges-Étienne talked with the US Consul, Mr.

Thurston, to assure him that we'll do all that we can to satisfy the demand for extradition," said Macdonald.

"It's incredible the papers are claiming that Cartier knew about the raid before it even happened and that we were complicit. It's ridiculous the rubbish those American papers print."

"The papers here are convinced that General Dix will invade Canada in the next week or two, and the *New York Herald* has endorsed the idea. I have requested that Dix refrain from ordering US troops into Canada to pursue the criminals, and told him we'll do everything we can to prevent future raids and to maintain British neutrality."

"The question is, will it have the effect of calming the outrage south of the border?" asked Monk.

Lieutenant Young's Commission Documents

June 16th, 1864

Confederate States of America,
War Department,
Richmond,
Virginia

Sir,

You are hereby informed that the President has appointed you First Lieutenant, under the Act 121, approved February 17th, 1864, in the Provisional Army in the service of the Confederate States, to rank as such from the sixteenth day of June, 1864. Should the Senate at their next session advise and consent thereto, you will be commissioned accordingly.

Immediately on receipt hereof, please to communicate to this Department, through the Adjutant and Inspector General's Office, your acceptance or non-acceptance of said appointment, and, with your letter of acceptance, return to the Adjutant and Inspector General the oath herewith enclosed, properly filled up, subscribed, and attested, reporting at the same time your age, residence, when appointed, and the State in which you were born. Should you accept, you will report for duty to

Signed
Jas. A. Seddon, Secretary of War.

Signed
Lieut. Bennett H. Young, &c, &c, P.A.C.S.

June 16th, 1864

Confederate States of America,
War Department.
Richmond,
Virginia

Lieut. B. H. Young is hereby authorized to organize for special service, a company not to exceed twenty in number from those who belong to the service and are at the time beyond the Confederate States. They will be entitled to their pay, rations, clothing, and transportation, but no other compensation for any service which they may be called upon to render. The organization will be under the control of this Department, and liable to be disbanded at its pleasure, and the members returned to their respective companies.

Signed
Jas. A. Seddon, Secretary of War.

Eighteen

Bennett was called to an early morning meeting with the lawyers Abbott and Kerr in a room in the courthouse. Bennett saw it as an opportunity to get an unvarnished opinion of how things stood with the trial. George Sanders was there and greeted him when he came in.

"Well, how did it go yesterday, gentlemen?" asked Bennett.

"Very well, Lieutenant," said Abbott. "You were perfect."

"I'm sorry I missed it, Lieutenant," said Sanders, genuinely disheartened.

"It's still early days, Mr. Sanders," said Kerr, turning to Abbott. "A plea for an extension will put Judge Coursol in a very difficult position."

"Well, he does owe us a favor, you know," said Abbott. "After our request for *habeas corpus* was declined and the sloppy work of the police force."

"He can hardly refuse our request for more time without appearing to favor the Crown and the Americans," said Kerr.

Back in the courtroom, Judge Coursol continued to hear voluntary statements from each of the raiders. The first was Thomas Collins from Kentucky, who read from a prepared text.

"I am a native of Kentucky and a commissioned officer of the Army of the Confederate States at war with the so-called United States. I participated in General Morgan's raid in Kentucky and became separated from my regiment at the Battle of Cynthiana. I owe no allegiance to the United States. I am a foreigner and public enemy to the Yankee Government. The Yankees dragged my father from his house and imprisoned him in Camp Chase, where his sufferings impaired his health and mind, and my grandfather has been banished from Kentucky by that brute General Burbridge. They have stolen negroes and forced them into their armies, leaving their women and children to starve and die. They have pillaged and burned private dwellings, banks, and villages and depopulated whole districts, boasting of their inhuman acts as deeds of heroism and exhibiting their plunder in northern cities as trophies of federal victories. I have violated no laws of Canada or Great Britain."

Bennett looked around him in the dock, conscious for the first time of the silence in the courtroom.

"Whatever I may have done at St. Albans," Collins continued, "I did as a Confederate officer acting under Lt. Young. If I aided in the sack of the St. Albans banks, it was because they were public institutions and because I knew the Yankee pocketbook to be the most sensitive and that they would suffer most by it being rudely touched. I cared nothing for the booty, except to injure the enemies of my country. Federal soldiers are bought up at $1000 a head, and the capture of $200,000 is equivalent to the destruction of 200 of said soldiers. I, therefore, thought the expedition 'would pay'. I guess it did, in view of the fact that they have wisely sent several thousand soldiers from the front to protect the exposed points in the rear."

"Thank you, Mr. Collins, you may step down now," ordered Judge Coursol.

Collins stood up and returned to join his friends in the dock.

In the smoke-filled prison dayroom, half a dozen young soldiers were playing poker for matchsticks at a large table observed by several attractive young ladies from town. At the other end of the room, a French barber was busy shaving a soldier and attempting to make conversation in English. There were empty beer bottles, food plates, and several baskets of apples on the table generously supplied by the lawyers from their own trees.

The raiders had been welcomed as heroes in Montreal, and the warden allowed them visits from their girlfriends during the day. The women were mainly from Toronto and Niagara, while some were local and spoke French. In the cells leading off from the dayroom, there were young soldiers writing letters and others sleeping in their bunks. From the shadowy cells in the back, you could occasionally hear erotic moaning sounds and the cries of sexual partners.

George Sanders appeared at the door, his eyes searching the room.

He saw the lieutenant sitting in the corner and made a beeline for him.

"Lieutenant, how are you doing?" asked Sanders.

"I'm fine, sir," said Bennett with a smile. "The food is terrible, but we've got other compensations."

"Yes, I can see that," said Sanders as he glanced around the sunlit room at the young soldiers and their women.

"Sure beats life in a Yankee prison, don't it?" quipped Sanders.

"It does, sir. Any news?" asked Bennett.

"Clay is on his way to St. Catharines. He says that your courier was captured a week ago as he tried to go through Union lines."

"That's bad news."

"Well, we've still got another shot at it. You know the chaplain?"

"You mean young Cameron?"

"Yeah, he left yesterday. He should have no trouble getting through Union lines."

"What about that doctor you mentioned?"

"Dr. Pallen. He'll be around in the morning to see the men."

There was a long silence as Sanders turned to a more pressing subject.

"Look, Lieutenant, we've got a problem. A large amount of the bank money is missing."

"What do you mean, missing?"

"The banks estimate you took over $210,000 in St. Albans, but the chief of police says they only got around $80,000 off our men. So, where's the rest of the money?"

Bennett said nothing but was disturbed by the question.

"Clay is concerned. He gave you strict orders to destroy the town, not to stop and rob the banks."

"It was a retribution raid, Mr. Sanders. We went there to destroy the town, steal from the banks, and damage whatever else we could with the time we had. We tried to burn it down."

"Well, you're going to have to account for the money, Lieutenant."

"I have no idea who has what. We didn't have time to count the banknotes before we left. We grabbed what we could."

"What about Daniel Butterworth, Louis Price, Will Teavis, John Moss, Charlie Higbee, and the others? Where the hell are they?"

"They were supposed to go to your headquarters on the docks after the raid. They didn't show up?"

"We haven't seen hide nor hair of any of them. Your buddy, Squire Teavis, was captured in Frelighsburg, but not before he hid $17,500 in a house there. Was he hiding the money for his brother, who got away? Was that the plan?"

"I don't know, sir. You're saying that we stole the money for ourselves?"

"That's about it, Lieutenant. Clay is mighty pissed. You were supposed to burn down the goddamned town, but all your men did was rob the banks and line their own pockets."

"That's a damned lie, Sanders!" said Bennett, standing up.

"Well, you'd better find that money fast," Sanders said in a more conciliatory tone. "This war ain't over yet and we've got plans that cost money, including your defense in court."

Bennett said nothing. Sanders tried to stare him down, but in the end, he got up and left. Bennett watched him go, then sighed as he sat down again.

Bennett had hidden the loot so that Higbee couldn't abscond with it, and now he was under suspicion of stealing the money for himself. Even his friends were suspicious of his motives after he told them what he had done with the money.

There was one point he couldn't argue. He was guilty of being naive. He was a true believer in the Confederate cause, and he had made the mistake of thinking that his men felt the same way, but they were tired of the war and simply wanted to move on with their lives. And large amounts of free money would be very helpful in facilitating a return to civilian life.

Nineteen

After the voluntary statements were taken, Judge Coursol was ready to hear the defense arguments. He listened as William Kerr questioned the Vermont attorney, Edward A. Sowles, a small man with a smug, arrogant air. The Crown Prosecutor Johnson listened attentively while Devlin looked visibly annoyed by the questions. He was convinced that the defense was tying up the case with nonsensical quibbles and that Judge Coursol was being manipulated. He also found British colonial law to be extremely opaque.

"From the facts deposed to in your presence and after hearing the witnesses, what criminal offense was committed in the State of Vermont on the nineteenth day of October last?" asked Kerr.

"Robbery, sir, as testified to by the witnesses," said Sowles with a patronizing air. "Samuel Breck called them robbers after they took $393 from him."

"According to the laws of the State of Vermont, would the facts disclosed in evidence bring home the robbery charge against all the prisoners?"

"Yes, sir. All of them would be charged."

"I am sure you know that Congress passed a law on the 17th of July, 1862, Chapter 195, entitled an 'Act to suppress Insurrection, and to punish Treason and Rebellion, to seize and confiscate the property of Rebels.'"

Sowles nodded as Kerr continued.

"The act says that any person engaged in war or committing the crime of treason against the United States is liable to imprisonment and fine, and the property of that individual is liable to confiscation. In your opinion, Mr. Sowles, should a detachment of United States soldiers, under the command of an officer in your army, do like acts to those charged against the prisoners in this courtroom, your soldiers and officers being in Georgia, would they be guilty of robbery?"

Devlin stood up to object, but Judge Coursol overruled him. He sat down, red in the face and steaming.

"I think not. Georgia is in a state of active rebellion against the authorities of the United States," said Sowles. "War is going on there. It is a battleground. The State of Vermont is not in rebellion against the authorities of the United States but is a loyal state. Its citizens are not committing acts of treason, but those in Georgia are doing so. The two cases are not analogous. I consider the actions of the prisoners as robbery. I do not consider it an act of treason against the State of Vermont."

"What is your definition of treason, sir?" asked Kerr.

Devlin tried again to object, but Judge Coursol waved him down.

"The Constitution of the United States defines it, sir," said Kerr, reading from the document before him. "Treason against the United States shall consist only in levying war against them, or in adhering to their enemies, giving them aid and comfort."

"Were not these Confederate soldiers who attacked the town of St. Albans committing a treasonable offense?"

"That is a matter of opinion. In my opinion, they were not."

"So treason against the United States depends on which state you live in? Is that what you are saying, Mr. Sowles? It is robbery in Vermont and treason in Georgia?"

The courtroom erupted in laughter. Sowles, thoroughly deflated, was only too happy to vacate the witness box when he was dismissed and stepped down.

"Your Honor," Abbott stood up, carefully masking a smile. "Lt. Young asked this court a few days ago in his testimony for an extension of thirty days to obtain evidence necessary for the defense. The extension is to allow the accused to collect further evidence from Richmond. Let me read to you the affidavit signed by prisoners Young, Collins, and Wallace under oath:"

"That deponents and the other prisoners charged with the offense now under investigation require certain testimony which is necessary and material to their defense, and which they are unable to procure in Montreal, or even in Canada. That they desire to prove and can prove if time be allowed them to procure the requisite evidence, that every one of the prisoners now in custody is an officer or soldier of the

army of the Confederate States of America, duly enlisted, enrolled, or commissioned respectively, and their term of service has not expired."

Johnson got to his feet, furious.

"What would be the effect on the Court of granting this application?" he demanded. "Why, it would be to oust the courts of the United States of their jurisdiction. If thirty days were granted, then these gentlemen might, at the end of that time, ask for a hundred days. One request would be just as reasonable as the other. To grant such a demand would be to deprive the United States courts of their jurisdiction."

"I'm happy to see," Kerr said, rising to defend his colleague, "that the counsel for the Crown has at last shown his true colors. The conduct of the Crown in the management of this prosecution had been marked from beginning to end by an exhibition of the most disgraceful despotism on the part of its ministers and of those who attend to its interests in this province. The prosecution has shown an ignorance of constitutional law which will draw upon it the reprobation of the law officers of Great Britain."

There was a murmur of sympathy in the courtroom for Kerr's argument. Johnson was openly siding with the US representatives.

"It should be noted," Kerr continued, "that Great Britain has been an asylum of political refugees from time immemorial and has received and protected refugees from France since the time of the First Revolution, including its present Emperor from the hands of his enemies. It is hard to believe that Great Britain would authorize her officers to appear in any case of extradition in order to deliver up men whose only offense was their condition of being political refugees, to use their own words 'thrown by the fortunes of war on her soil.' The Crown has forgotten its duty in employing its officers to prosecute this case, for it has been evident from the start that they have appeared against the prisoners conjointly with the counsel of the United States."

Frelighsburg, Quebec

Eliza left St. Albans in a hay wagon at dawn, hoping to make Stanbridge East by the end of the day. The road was little more than a winding rutted track through the wilderness. *At this pace,* she thought, *it would take me a week to get to Montreal.*

"We just crossed the border, Charlie," said Eliza. "You are out of danger. Are you happy?"

"Can't you go any faster, Eliza?" said a muffled voice behind her. She could feel the wagon rock as Higbee shifted his weight under the hay. "My shoulder is killing me."

Higbee was lying on a blanket under the bales of hay and struggling to find a comfortable position with his wounded shoulder.

"Not with this old mare, Charlie. A little patience. We'll be there soon. You want to sit up here?"

"Let's wait until we are on the other side of town."

The watcher stood at the hotel window, fighting boredom and the urge to doze off. There wasn't much to see, just an unprepossessing main street lined with wooden walkways and little shops. Still, it was what McMicken had hired him for and it was easy money.

He perked up a bit when he saw the girl driving the hay wagon. She was young and pretty. He knew he would have remembered her if he'd ever seen her before. She was just passing his window when he felt a tug at his sleeve.

"So guv, what are you militia chaps looking for?" asked a small boy.

"We're keeping an eye on the border, Jimmy. We're gonna stop the damn Yankees from invading the town," said the agent.

"Ain't seen no Yankees in town for weeks, guv. Not since that posse was running around."

"Well, they can come at any time, Jimmy. That's why we're here."

"You think they'll come at night, guv?"

"Sure, they will, Jimmy. They'll come when everyone is sleeping."

Jimmy jumped up and ran off to tell all his friends to get ready for a Yankee invasion. The watcher looked back at the street, hoping to see the young lady on the hay wagon again, but she had disappeared.

Twenty

Montreal

After the lunch recess, Judge Coursol returned to the courtroom with his decision. He waited patiently for the crowd to quiet down and then read from his notes.

"An application on the part of the prisoners to obtain a delay of one month for the production of evidence for the defense has been very urgently and ably argued before me this day. This application has been opposed by Mr. Johnson, representing the Crown, and Mr. Devlin, representing the American authorities, upon the ground that although in cases of local offenses, I possess the power of granting such an application, under the treaty I do not possess that power, as I would be thereby virtually assuming the jurisdiction of the American Courts to try the accused. I do not agree with this view and for this reason, I am granting the defense an extension until the 13th of December next to produce the evidence they need to defend themselves."

Abbott and Kerr stood up as Judge Coursol left the room. They were jubilant, as were the prisoners in the dock, who burst into unseemly cheers, as Johnson and Devlin, enraged by the decision, stormed out of the courtroom.

Frelighsburg, Quebec

Eliza waited until she was well past the town before she stopped the wagon.

"You can come out now," she told him.

He didn't have to be told twice. Eliza stifled a laugh as Higbee hauled himself out of the hay with great difficulty and brushed the straw off his hair and coat. He shook out his black fedora and tried to poke it back into shape after it had been squashed underneath him. Then he started looking for something on the bed of the wagon.

"Hurry up," she urged him.

Higbee glared at her. The last thing Eliza needed was a curious passerby seeing a skinny scarecrow stumbling around on her wagon.

"Lost my damn feather," he whined, showing a faded spot on his hatband.

"We'll get you another one."

Higbee sighed loudly and clambered up onto the seat beside her.

"How's your shoulder?"

"It hurts, but it's not as bad sitting up."

"There was a man back there at the hotel watching us, Charlie."

"Probably just a busybody, Eliza."

"He didn't look like a local to me. You better be ready to jump under them bales again when we get to the next town."

Montreal

"They searched everywhere?" asked Bennett in the prison dayroom.

"Yeah, 'course they did," said Squire Teavis. "That was more money than I ever saw in my life. With money like that, I'd be in high cotton, old chum."

He glanced uncomfortably around him. They were in a quiet corner and neither of them wanted to be overheard.

"I did my best to hide it, but they found my stash only minutes after they went into the barn."

"So you were gonna go back and collect it later? Was that the plan?"

"Yeah, that was the plan, but that ain't gonna happen now."

"Sanders has been asking after the money," Bennett said grimly. "He came around with that new guy who calls himself Benton Wood. He said we're gonna need the money to pay for our defense."

"Yeah, I heard that."

"What happened to your brother?"

"I don't know," Teavis shrugged. "He went west with a bunch of the fellas. He's probably back home in Kentucky by now."

Stanbridge East, Quebec

It was late in the day when Eliza and Higbee pulled up at the Stanbridge Hotel on Main Street and climbed down from the wagon. The town was bigger than Frelighsburg and had a few shops, restaurants, and taverns. The streets were empty, as most people were at home having their supper.

"I'm going to get a room, Charlie."

"You go on, Eliza. I'll look after the wagon and horse. I want to get a feel for the place."

Eliza collected her old red carpet bag from the wagon and walked over to the hotel. Higbee took the reins and drove the wagon down the street to the livery stable.

Stanbridge was a farming community, and it got dark early in November. Benton Wood stepped out of Elder's tavern and looked up and down the shadowy street. He was a strong, wiry man in his forties, prematurely bald on top, with a broken nose. He put on his wide-brimmed hat and lit a cheroot, revealing the silver rings he wore on his fingers. He noticed a wagon loaded with bales of hay outside the livery stable and walked over to have a look. He spotted a man with a familiar face sitting on a chair in the stable. He grabbed his Colt 44-caliber Army revolver and went inside.

The man was drinking whiskey straight out of the bottle and was so intent on his drinking that he didn't notice Wood until he stepped into the dim light from an oil lamp.

"Hey, Charlie," Wood said, grinning and pointing the Colt at his head. "Ain't seen you in a long time."

"Shit. If it ain't fuckin' Benton Wood," blurted Higbee. "What do you want?"

"What the hell do you think I want, you son-of-a-bitch? You stole my share of the Quantrill money back in Wisconsin. You don't remember nothin'?"

Higbee looked disconsolate.

"You bailed on me that night. You took off in the boat for Canada. Well, it's payback time now, Charlie."

"I only took my share of the money, Benton. You know that. You can't have my share. I invested every last penny of that money when I got to Toronto."

"We took $75,000 from the bank in Lawrence. Without my help, you would never have gotten into the damn safe."

"Well, you can't have what I ain't got, can you now, Benton?"

Wood grabbed Higbee and wrestled him to the ground. He pummeled him with blows and then kicked him in the head. Higbee cried out in pain.

"Please, Benton!" Higbee gasped. "I got shot in the Vermont raid. You're gonna open up the wound and I'll be bleedin' all over the damn place again."

"I want my share, Charlie," Wood growled, "and you're gonna get it for me. I've been followin' you for weeks, all the way from St. Catharines."

"What share, Benton? I ain't got nothing but the clothes on my back."

"You're gonna go to Lieutenant Young and get it for me, Charlie."

Wood effortlessly whacked Higbee over the head with the butt of his gun, knocking him unconscious. He led his horse out of its stall and was throwing a saddle across its back when a young boy appeared in the doorway.

"You leavin' us now, Monsieur Wood?" inquired the stable hand, holding a harness in one hand and a brush in the other.

"Yeah, it looks like it," Wood grunted as he casually hooked a thumb over his shoulder to where Higbee lay motionless on the floor. "I'm gonna need a horse for my friend, Pierre."

Pierre looked down at Higbee lying unconscious on the floor, bleeding through his shirt.

"*Pas de problème, Monsieur* Wood. Is your friend gonna be OK?"

"Yeah, he was drunk and hurt himself. He'll wake up soon enough."

The following morning, shortly after sunrise, Eliza stood in the doorway of the livery stable looking for her horse and wagon. She found the wagon parked behind the stable, but there was no horse and her charge had vanished.

"Mr. Higbee," called Eliza. "Charlie! Are you in here?"

"Can I help you, ma'am?" asked Pierre, appearing from behind a bale of hay.

"I'm gonna need my wagon and horse, young man. Can you get it ready for me?"

"Sure, ma'am. That'll be tuppence for the water and hay."

"Tuppence?" asked Eliza.

"Ten cents in dollars, ma'am."

Eliza searched her purse for a dime.

"You seen my traveling companion, Mr. Higbee?"

Pierre shook his head and went off to get Eliza's horse.

Twenty-one

Montreal

It was snowing as Eliza arrived in a horsecar and descended at the corner of Notre Dame and De Lorimier Streets. She crossed the road to the Pied-du-Courant Prison and was admitted by a guard. She climbed the stairs leading to the top floor.

She had expected to find Bennett languishing in a dingy cell in the basement. She was surprised when she entered a spacious dayroom with a dozen men and women sitting around a large table playing poker for matchsticks. Eliza was shocked to see the women carousing with the prisoners, sitting on their laps, and drinking beer with them. The women were well-dressed and pretty, and Eliza felt unattractive and frumpy. She scanned the room and felt a sudden *frisson* of excitement when she spotted Lieutenant Young in a quiet corner of the room writing a letter. She hurried over to see him.

"How are you, Bennett?" asked Eliza.

Bennett's face lit up when he saw her. He stood up, nearly knocking over the bottle of ink.

"This is a surprise, Eliza. I wasn't expecting you so soon."

"Well, Lieutenant, I have some good news and some bad news."

"Start with good news, please."

"Your friend Higbee is in Canada."

"That's wonderful," said Bennett, "and the bad news?"

"I tried to bring him to you, but he ran off when we got to Stanbridge East."

"What do you mean, he ran off?"

"He skedaddled, Bennett, without a thank-you and nary a farewell. That ungrateful man just disappeared in the night, so I went home to St. Albans. Then I saw your letter to Mr. Skinner of the Tremont Hotel in the *St. Albans Messenger,* so I decided to take the train to Montreal to see you."

"Ha, ha. It was just a joke. I sent Skinner a five-dollar St. Albans' banknote to pay for my hotel bill."

"Yes, and you told the bank teller, Cyrus Bishop, to remember that he had sworn allegiance to the Confederacy. I thought that was pretty funny, but I can tell you that no one in St. Albans enjoyed it."

"I'm sorry, Eliza. I was being facetious and having a bit of fun."

"Everybody wants you dead in St. Albans, Bennett. There is still talk of hanging all you secesh when they extradite you. How are you holding up?"

"I'm fine. We have very little to do here, but sit around, write letters, and play cards."

"And all these women?" Eliza glanced around the room. "Are they prisoners too?"

"No, of course not," said Bennett, surprised by her comment. "They've, uh, taken a shine to some of the fellas."

"I see."

Bennett decided it was time to change the subject.

"Where are you staying?"

"A fancy hotel on Saint-Jacques Street, the St. Lawrence Hall. You know it?"

"Yeah, that's the place the Confederate Commissioners stay at."

"This is my first time in Montreal, Bennett. Guess who I saw in the lobby?"

"I wouldn't know, Eliza."

"Go on. Make a guess. A famous person?"

"I give up."

"John Wilkes Booth, the actor. He's staying there. The papers call him the most promising young actor in American theater."

"I've read about him. He has that famous father, Junius Brutus Booth, and I believe a brother."

"Yes, that's him. He's very handsome. He started his stage career in Baltimore playing *Richard III.* He's played in theaters across the country."

"He's also played in Richmond and towns across the south. He's secesh!"

"No!" Her striking green eyes went wide with surprise and her full lips formed a perfect 'O'.

"Yes, he is," said Bennett, smiling.

"Well, no matter what he is," Eliza gushed. "He's performing Shakespeare's *Merchant of Venice* tonight at Corby Hall. I think I might go and see it."

"That's a wonderful idea. You should go."

Young reached into his pocket and discreetly slipped her a five-pound note.

"Here, take this. See the play and go shopping while you're in town. You could use a new coat. I wish I could go with you."

Eliza looked down at her threadbare beige coat as she slipped the banknote into her pocket.

"It's an old hand-me-down, Bennett."

"You look lovely just as you are."

Eliza turned to look at the barber, who had just arrived and was setting up to cut hair. He was making a joke with a French woman across the room and laughing. While Eliza was watching the woman flirt with the barber, Bennett admired the nape of her neck and the curls of her chestnut-brown hair.

"I've brought you a present," Eliza said shyly, taking a thin volume from her bag and handing it to him.

It was a book of poems. He looked through it and stopped on a page of poems by Emily Dickinson. He read several lines.

> *"Hope is the thing with feathers*
> *That perches in the soul*
> *And sings the tune without the words*
> *And never stops at all."*

"What a wonderful gift," said Bennett, moved by her generosity.

"You must not lose hope, Bennett," she said softly as Bennett looked away, trying to hide his emotions.

He was hugely in her debt. She had done the impossible for him while her dear brother was fighting for the other side in the war. She had nursed Higbee back to health and smuggled him across the border at great risk to herself and her family. She had opened his eyes to the richness of life beyond the war and its cruel exactions, and he felt an irresistible attraction for her.

"You can win this case," she added. "Maybe they'll set you free. I hope they do."

Higbee was locked up in an old house on the Montreal docks which belonged to the Confederate Secret Service. There was an armed man posted outside his door on the second floor at all hours. Not long after the guard had brought up a breakfast tray, there was a knock on the door and Dr. Pallen entered the room in the company of Benton Wood.

"Here he is, Doctor," said Wood. "I'll leave you to treat his wound. Call the guard when you're finished."

"What happened to you, Mr. Higbee?" asked Pallen.

"A gunshot wound, sir. I think it has reinfected. It hurts."

"Take off your shirt."

Higbee did as he was told, revealing blue welts on his back and arms.

"You've been in a fight, Mr. Higbee," Pallen said nonchalantly. "Your wound has reinfected. I am going to have to wash out the pus and disinfect it. We'll need to change the bandage."

"You've met the lieutenant at the prison, have you not, Doctor?"

"Ah, yes. I've been over there twice already."

Higbee pulled a two-dollar St. Albans' banknote from his pocket and handed it to the doctor.

"Do me a favor, would you, Dr. Pallen? Give this banknote to the lieutenant when you go over there again. Tell him you've seen me."

Pallen nodded as he slipped the banknote into his pocket.

"Guard," shouted Pallen.

For a moment, Higbee thought Pallen was going to tell the guard about the banknote. He held his breath as the guard opened the door and stepped inside.

"I'm going to need a basin of hot water," said Pallen.

The guard stood rooted to the spot, then opened his mouth to object.

"Go on now," Pallen said. "I don't have all morning."

In the kitchen downstairs, Wood poured Sanders a cup of tea as they waited for Dr. Pallen to finish with the prisoner.

"So you think Higbee can get to Young?" asked Sanders.

"He's our best chance, sir," Wood told him. "I was lucky to catch the bastard in Stanbridge East, otherwise he would have been long gone."

"The men told me that Higbee had a pack horse loaded with greenbacks, banknotes, and silver loot until the lieutenant took off with it."

"Yeah, that's the story I heard. The lieutenant hid the money before he was captured in Frelighsburg. He had nothing on him when they arrested him."

"Higbee doesn't know where he hid the money?"

"No, sir. I beat the son-of-a-bitch black and blue. He ain't got a clue."

"He would have told you if he'd known?"

"Yep, Higbee ain't no martyr. The lieutenant's got the money stashed somewhere in the area. We just have to find it."

Twenty-two

December 13, 1864

"I wish to bring to Your Honor's attention a question of jurisdiction in this case," said the defense lawyer, William Kerr, standing before Judge Coursol in the courtroom.

There was a resounding groan from Bernard Devlin and the Americans before Crown Prosecutor Johnson stood up to object. The trial of the Confederate raiders had resumed in the District Court after a one-month delay. The courtroom was full of journalists from every major newspaper in New England and Canada. The fourteen Confederate soldiers sat nervously in the dock, waiting to see what was to become of them.

"Your Honor," Johnson said, feigning exasperation, "this inquiry has been adjourned until today to enable the accused to provide evidence in their defense, and the Court is now in session to hear this testimony. It is not in session to hear an argument about the law of the case. I call on the defense to proceed with their witnesses."

"Your Honor, my objection goes to the jurisdiction of the Court. If it has no jurisdiction, it has no right to hear witnesses. I allege that all the proceedings are wrong."

"The objection is to my jurisdiction in this matter?" asked Judge Coursol.

"Yes, Your Honor. I deny your right to sit at all."

"You deny my right to sit?" asked Coursol, astonished.

"Well, well, Mr. Kerr. I'm interested to hear this," said Coursol with a wry smile. "The objection cannot be disregarded. I am bound to hear any exceptions to my jurisdiction."

"I have no objection, Your Honor," said Johnson, showing great patience, "but we must move on."

"Please proceed, Mr. Kerr," said Judge Coursol.

Kerr exchanged a look with his associate, John Abbott.

"The state of the law is that in lieu of our provincial statutes, or any of them, being in force, the Imperial Act regulates all proceedings for extradition," said Kerr. "It is absolutely essential that in order to give you jurisdiction in this matter before anyone is arrested and charged with the commission of a crime, a warrant be issued by the Governor General according to the provisions of the Imperial Act. No such warrant, however, has been issued and you therefore have not, nor have you had at any time, jurisdiction in these cases to arrest the prisoners."

"Your argument," said Coursol, "is that, according to the Imperial Act, it would be necessary for the arrest of the accused that a warrant of apprehension be signed by the Governor General. Is that what you are saying, Mr. Kerr?"

"Precisely. Since no warrant has been issued by the Governor General, you have no jurisdiction."

Mr. Devlin stood up, shocked by Kerr's legal argument.

"I would like to remind Your Honor that you have acted at present under the law of the land," he argued. "Is the Webster-Ashburton Treaty for the extradition of the prisoners still in force, yes or no? One might assume from the argument just heard that we have been living in blissful ignorance of our rights and of the law of the land in this matter till the present moment."

"I firmly believe," added Johnson," that it is within Your Honor's power to issue a warrant for the apprehension of a fugitive before waiting for other authority, or a warrant from the Governor. The opposite pretension would cause a frustration of justice and render it impossible to carry out the provisions of the Treaty."

Judge Coursol looked thoughtfully at Kerr and then turned his attention to several legal documents he had before him on the bench. The public in the gallery watched as Coursol took his time to read the documents. Even the court officers were growing restive by the time Coursol abruptly stood up and motioned for silence.

"We are adjourned, gentlemen," he said, his face an inscrutable mask, "until two o'clock."

Coursol slipped out of the courtroom, leaving the lawyers

ambivalent as to the meaning of the adjournment.

In the prison dayroom, Young and his colleagues were having lunch and waiting for the call to return to the courtroom. Dr. Pallen was busy treating Wallace's sore shoulder. After finishing with the prisoner, the doctor came over to shake Bennett's hand.

"Hello, Lieutenant," said Dr. Pallen.

Bennett looked up at the doctor and then got to his feet.

"Hello, sir."

Pallen quietly slipped the St. Albans' banknote into the lieutenant's hand.

"Doctor Pallen, I haven't thanked you enough for taking such good care of my men," said Bennett, as he put the note in his pocket.

"You're welcome, Lieutenant. The patient said you would know what it means."

"Is he all right?"

"He was in a very sorry state when I first saw him. His wound was infected and someone had beaten him up."

"I'm sorry to hear that. Where is he?"

"He's under arrest and being held at the house in the old port."

"What's he done?"

"I don't know, sir. Good day to you."

Dr. Pallen smiled, collected his medical bag, and left the room. Bennett sat down and furtively took the note from his pocket. *Sanders is holding Higbee against his will*, thought Bennett. *He knows I hid the money, so he's putting pressure on Higbee.*

The tension in the courtroom was palpable as Judge Coursol returned to the bench. Only moments before, the courtroom had been buzzing with speculation about his abrupt adjournment a few hours earlier, but as soon as he took his seat and swept an imperious glare across the courtroom, the noisy crowd was cowed into silence. The Confederate raiders who had been whispering among themselves stopped talking and turned their attention to the judge, as did the defense and prosecution lawyers.

On the bench, Coursol took out his spectacles and wiped them clean with a handkerchief before putting them on. He opened the file before him and began to read.

"The point I am now called upon to decide," he said, "is one of very great importance, inasmuch as my jurisdiction and my authority to act in this case has been put in question and is now for the first time directly denied."

"It is contended on behalf of the prisoners that the Treaty being a national act, the Imperial Act must be regarded as the Supreme Law and our colonial legislatures being subordinate to it. The arrest of the parties charged can only have been made upon a warrant signed by the Governor General himself or by a person administering the government of Canada according to the terms of the Imperial Act."

"I have therefore decided that having not received any such warrant from the Governor General to authorize the arrest of the accused, as is required by the Imperial Act, I have no jurisdiction in this case. Consequently, I am bound in law, justice, and fairness to order the immediate release of the prisoners from custody upon all the charges brought before me. Let the prisoners be discharged."

It was a bombshell. There was a brief instant of complete silence as the import of Coursol's words sank in. Then the courtroom exploded with cheers and applause. The raiders jumped up and down in the dock, hugging each other and exchanging jubilant handshakes as they savored their victory, while the prosecution team and the Americans looked on, disconsolate. The reporters raced out of the room to write their stories as cheers were heard from the gallery.

The American lawyers swarmed the bench while Kerr, Abbott, and Laflamme were still recovering from Coursol's astonishing decision.

"Your Honor!" Devlin protested, failing to hide his disgust. "The prisoners have been charged on seven counts, but you only heard one of them."

"Yes, that is exact," Coursol replied, fixing Devlin with an implacable stare. "I hereby discharge them in every case before me."

Devlin, sputtering with rage, was about to say something else when Johnson intervened before the American made things worse.

"Get him out of here," Johnson barked at a clerk, who ushered Devlin toward the door.

"Your Honor, there has been no application for the discharge of the prisoners on the other accusations?" blurted Johnson.

"Having no jurisdiction in the one case," Coursol added, "I would certainly have none in the others."

"With all due respect, sir," Johnson said, reminding himself to keep a civil tone. "I dissent from the soundness of the judgment in this case."

"Not a word more on this matter, gentlemen," ordered the judge. "I know the weight of the responsibility of such a course, but I am bound as a magistrate to do what my conscience and duty direct, without regard to influences, feelings, or consequences."

Twenty-three

The Governor-General Lord Charles Monck walked briskly into a Montreal office building and was met by MacDonald, who led him to a conference room on the first floor.

"I just got the news, Charles," said Macdonald. "That wretched pig of a police magistrate set the raiders free. The Americans are already saying that Coursol was bought by the Confederate commissioners. This is not what I had hoped for."

"Nor I, John," Monck shook his head in disbelief. "This is going to infuriate them. Secretary Seward will be on a war footing, with General Dix right behind him. We need to act quickly."

"I don't know about President Lincoln's taste for a second front. There are going to be a lot of loud voices demanding war with Britain."

"I just got a telegram from Washington. Our ambassador, Richard Lyon, has been talking to President Lincoln. You know he'll be leaving his post there shortly, for health reasons. He says the President and Seward are furious. We are this close to a war with the Americans."

"I'm working on a new warrant for the prisoners, but it will take some time. I couldn't get the chief of police to re-arrest the men before they got away."

"Talk to Judge Smith and see what he can do. We don't have a leg to stand on. We've got to put this right."

In the prison dayroom, there was a great cheer for the raiders as they came in. Bennett smiled at his friends and there was a lot of hugging and back-slapping going on as Sanders and Wood appeared at the door.

"Wonderful news, Lieutenant. We just heard that you are all to be released," said Sanders.

"Yes, sir. It's amazing," said Bennett, who felt ill at ease in Sanders' presence.

"We are putting on a little celebration for the men tonight," said Sanders. "Word is out that Lamothe is going to release the bank money this afternoon. We're going to send several cabs here to collect you around five o'clock."

"That would be fine, sir," said Bennett. "I'm sure the men appreciate it. Thank you."

Sanders clapped Bennett on the back and left. He seemed unaware of Bennett's reserve.

Not that long ago, thought Bennett, *this man was accusing me of theft and now he's holding Higbee against his will. A reckoning is coming.*

The Lieutenant held up his hand for silence. The party was already in full swing and he needed his men to concentrate on the situation at hand.

"We just won our case, boys. Soon, we're going to be free," said the Lieutenant. "We need to collect our things and get ready to move out of here."

Abbott and Kerr arrived at the prison an hour later. Half the men were already drunk after smuggling several bottles of whiskey into the dayroom, so the lawyers commandeered a tiny interrogation room on the same floor.

"The police chief will soon be coming by to process your men out of here, Lieutenant," said Abbott.

Bennett nodded and looked at the wistful faces of his legal team.

"We've come to warn you," said Kerr. "The prosecution team and the Americans are not at all happy with this result."

"You think they might change their minds?" asked Bennett.

"Anything is possible," confirmed Abbott. "The Crown may try to arrest you again."

Bennett's spirits sagged. *He'd had the uneasy feeling all afternoon that Coursol's decision was almost too good to be true. What would happen now?*

"It might be a good idea," Abbott continued, "for you and your men to lie low over the next few days. We understand that this verdict is cause for celebration, but public drunkenness and disturbing the peace will just give the authorities cause to go after you."

Kerr was less circumspect.

"Lamothe will be returning your money soon, so we suggest that all of you leave town as soon as possible."

Bennett thanked the lawyers and saw them out just as Eliza Miller appeared in the vestibule, coming up the stairs. Eliza waited for the lawyers to descend to the floor below before rushing forward to embrace Bennett. She looked very elegant in a dark blue coat over her print skirt and bodice.

"Eliza, they're letting us go. We'll be out of here by five o'clock."

"Wonderful news. I heard it at the hotel and rushed over to see it with my own eyes."

"If you have time, let's go have a drink together to celebrate. I need to be back here by five o'clock."

A horsecar rumbled past the fashionable St. Lawrence Hall on Saint Jacques Street, where Bennett and Eliza occupied a booth in Dooley's bar.

"What do you want to drink, Eliza?"

"A whiskey, a very small one, please."

The waiter arrived, and the lieutenant ordered their drinks.

"A whiskey for the lady and a mint julep for me, sir."

The waiter left to get the order as a man lurked in the shadows across the street. He looked very much like one of Sanders' men and seemed to be keeping an eye on the lieutenant and his girlfriend.

"This is the only place in town where you can get a mint julep, Eliza," said Bennett. "A lot of secesh stay at this hotel."

"I have tickets to the play tonight. Why don't you come with me? It starts at seven."

"I'd love to, my dear, but I've got some business to attend to this evening."

"John Wilkes Booth is playing Shylock, Bennett. You don't want to miss it."

Bennett smiled at Eliza as they were interrupted by the waiter bringing their drinks. The mint julep was served in a frosty glass just the way Bennett liked it, with mint leaf, bourbon, syrup, and crushed ice.

"Do you want to taste it?" asked Bennett.

Eliza nodded and took a sip. She shivered when the bourbon hit her.

It was already dark at five o'clock as the hansom cabs arrived at the prison on De Lorimier Street and parked in a line out front. The prisoners left in small groups and climbed into the cabs with their girlfriends. They wore heavy winter coats and tuques and carried their leather haversacks full of banknotes with them. The cabs made the short run down to the old port area. The men were drunk and laughing with their women friends as they made their way across town. Local citizens cheered the men as they passed by on the snowy street. It was going to be a long night of celebration.

There was no sign of the lieutenant, who decided to ignore Sanders' invitation for a night out with the boys and went to the theater instead. Bennett and Eliza went to see Booth playing Shylock in *The Merchant of Venice* at Corby Hall. They were fascinated by the play. On stage, Antonio went to see Shylock to borrow money for his friend Bassanio.

"Signor Antonio, you've often insulted my money and my business practices in the Rialto," said Shylock. "I have always just shrugged and put up with it because Jews are good at suffering. You called me a heathen, a dirty dog, and you spat on my Jewish clothes. And all because I use my money to make a profit. And now it looks like you need my help."

Bennett looked around the theater at the people enjoying a night of entertainment. He was astonished at how good it felt to be a normal person in peacetime. He squeezed Eliza's hand and smiled at her. *Eliza was right*, Bennett thought. *Booth had an amazing stage presence with his curly black hair and drooping mustache.*

"You come to me saying 'Shylock, we need money.' You say that even though you spat on my beard and kicked me like you'd kick a stray mutt out your front door. And now you're asking for money. What can I tell you? Shouldn't I say 'Does a dog have money?' Is it possible for a mutt to lend three thousand ducats? Or should I bend down low, and in a humble and submissive voice say: Sir, last Wednesday you spat on me. You insulted me on this day and another time you called me a dog. And out of gratitude for these favors, I'll be happy to lend you the money?"

Antonio stepped forward to confront Shylock.

"I'll probably call you those names again, and spit on you, and reject you again. If you're going to lend us this money, don't lend it to us as if we were your friends. When do friends charge interest? Instead, lend it to me as your enemy. If your enemy goes bankrupt, it's easier for you to take your penalty from him."

At the house on the docks, there were half a dozen raiders gathered around a table in the downstairs kitchen near the wood stove. The women had left earlier at the request of George Sanders because they had important things to discuss at their meeting. They were drinking whiskey at an open bar, laughing and making jokes. They were quite drunk as Sanders stepped out of the shadows in the company of Benton Wood.

"Where are the other men?" asked Sanders.

"These are the only ones who showed up, sir," said Wood. "I heard some of the men took a coach out to Dorval and are heading west. The others must be celebrating somewhere else in town."

Sanders frowned. He had hoped to gather everyone in the same place. Still, it was a start. He put a foot on an empty chair and raised his hand for silence.

"Okay, boys," he shouted, then waited until they had settled down and were paying attention. "I know you're having a good time and I'm glad of it, but it's time to divvy up the cash and separate your personal assets from company assets."

The raiders were upset by Sanders' words and looked uneasy. They knew they were sitting on a small fortune with their stolen funds. They could never earn as much on a shop floor or working on a farm.

"But sir," one man objected. "We've earned our share of the bank money. We risked our lives getting it while you boys were sittin' on your asses, pickin' your noses."

"He's right, George, and you know it," said an older man. "We did all the work and got little or nothing in pay. It ain't fair."

Sanders, who had always fancied himself a Southern aristocrat, couldn't believe the aggressive tone of the men and their lack of respect. He had always been so supportive of the men, and he felt they owed him their loyalty.

"Look boys, most of them bank bills ain't worth nothing," said

Sanders, trying to reason with the men. "The banks are gonna refuse to honor them pretty soon."

"Yeah, but we still got greenbacks with Lincoln's picture on them," said another. "They should be good."

"You can keep the bank bills," said Sanders, "but we're gonna need the rest of the loot. The greenbacks, the treasury notes, and the silver."

"All of it?" roared somebody from the back of the room. "What about us?"

"I ain't givin' up one cent of my money to the Rebel cause. I earned it," said a drunk raider, falling off his chair.

Sanders knew better than to try to explain his position further or get into a shouting match. He was expressionless as he got up to leave. There were ragged cheers and catcalls from the raiders. They assumed they had won their point, and did not notice that as Sanders left the room in apparent defeat, he had directed a nod at Benton Wood.

Wood stepped out of the shadows with two pistols in his hands and a menacing look. He picked a raider at random and shot him in the chest. The man pitched backward out of his chair onto the floor.

"Now that I have your attention," said Wood calmly. "It ain't your money or my money. Jefferson Davis needs it to pay for your defense and the cost of the war."

"You killed him, you son-of-a-bitch," said another.

"I'll only say it once. Lay down your money or lay down your life."

Wood had either overestimated his own reputation or had underestimated the raiders, who were all hardened ex-soldiers. Suddenly, all hell broke loose.

It was after ten o'clock and it had started to snow as Bennett and Eliza took a hansom cab through the old town. They arrived at the house on the docks and descended from the cab. They paid the driver and looked around, unsure of the address. They walked arm-in-arm along the dock and eventually found the house.

The house was eerily quiet as they slipped into the darkened hall. *Where is everybody?* wondered Bennett. *They must have missed the celebration.* A moment later, Eliza stumbled over the body of a dead man on the floor as they made their way along the corridor in the dark.

"What the hell happened here?" exclaimed Bennett, pulling Eliza away. "Stay near the door, Eliza."

"Be careful, Bennett."

"I'll take a look. I'll only be a moment."

"Why don't we just leave?" asked Eliza.

The lieutenant removed his pistol from his satchel and cocked it as he advanced silently along the corridor. He took his time, allowing his eyes to adjust to the darkness. The hall led to a large meeting room lit by a couple of sputtering oil lamps. Overturned tables and chairs littered the floor, and Bennett could make out two dead men still sitting in their chairs.

"Hey, Lieutenant."

Bennett whirled around at the sound of the voice, his revolver coming up and his finger tightening on the trigger. Then he saw who it was.

"Higbee!" said Bennett as he lowered his revolver. "What the hell happened here?"

Higbee was standing in the open doorway of a small room at the back, a strange expression on his face. He was about to say something when he was shoved into the room from behind and a man Bennett didn't immediately recognize appeared close behind him. He had the muzzle of one revolver against the back of Higbee's head. The gun in his other hand was pointed at Bennett.

"You're late, Lieutenant," Wood smiled menacingly. "Too late to save these fellas. They didn't want to give up their loot, so I had to shoot the lot of them."

"Higbee, what's goin' on?"

Higbee looked around sheepishly as Wood stepped into the room.

"Where's Sanders?"

"He's gone. He got tired of waiting for you. So you're still holding on to most of the loot."

"Who is this guy, Higbee?"

"His name is Benton Wood, Lieutenant."

Wood paused, apparently expecting that his name would trigger some kind of reaction from Bennett.

"Charlie's my old partner from our days with Quantrill's raiders. You remember that town in Kansas, Charlie?"

"Yeah, I do. I remember Lawrence, Benton."

"We robbed the banks, Charlie and me, and killed a lot of people. They were great times, weren't they, Charlie?"

This had gone on too long, Bennett thought. He still had his gun, but he'd made the mistake of lowering it to his side the moment he'd seen Higbee.

"OK, Wood," he said, looking at Higbee, who seemed to be trying to distance himself from Wood. "You want me to fetch the money? Is that what you want?"

"Yeah, that would be a good first step, Lieutenant."

Higbee slammed his elbow into Wood's stomach, doubling him over, and jumped to one side. Bennett brought up the Colt and fired, then ran for the door. Higbee was right behind him. Bennett had no idea if he'd hit Wood or not, but he stopped at the door only long enough for Higbee to get past him.

"Go Eliza!" he shouted, firing a second shot into the room with no real hope of achieving anything but keeping Wood's head down long enough for them to get away. Then he bolted down the hall and followed Higbee and Eliza out into the street.

Twenty-four

It was still snowing as Bennett, Higbee, and Eliza raced off into the night, followed at a distance by Benton Wood. They ran down Rue de la Commune and found a hansom cab on Saint-Gabriel, which took them back to the St. Lawrence Hall on Saint-Jacques at the corner of Saint-Laurent. On the way, Bennett noticed they were being pursued by a second hansom cab with no lights. Bennett stuck his head out and told the driver to go north at the next turn. The cab swung north on Bleury and sped up the hill, followed by the mysterious carriage. Bennett then ordered the driver to go east on Saint-Antoine.

As they headed east again, Bennett noticed that the dark carriage never made the turn. They returned to Saint-Jacques and continued east until they arrived safely at St. Lawrence Hall. They entered the lobby and Bennett booked three rooms for the night. Bennett and Higbee went directly to the hotel bar while Eliza, visibly shaken, left them to go to her room.

"What were you thinking, Charlie?" asked Bennett as he drank a glass of ale.

"Wood has been after me for some time, Lieutenant. He's a crazy son-of-a-bitch. He grabbed me in Stanbridge East. He wanted me to give him the Quantrill money."

"You stole Quantrill's bank loot? Are you mad, Charlie?"

"It's not as crazy as it sounds, Lieutenant."

"The attack on Lawrence was a massacre, Charlie. How could you participate in all that killing? Men, women, and children."

"I was in charge of attacking the banks, Lieutenant. I had nothing to do with the killing of civilians."

Bennett wasn't sure he believed him.

"What about this Wood fella?" he asked. "He's gonna be coming after us now."

"I think we can buy him off, Lieutenant, if we have to. He's only interested in the money."

Bennett wasn't convinced. He'd seen men like Benton Wood before, back when he rode with Morgan. In wartime, men killed because they had to. Men like Wood killed because they enjoyed it.

Bennett stopped talking as Eliza entered the bar. He gave Charlie a pointed look. This wasn't a conversation he wanted to have in front of her.

"Are you all right, Eliza?"

"I just came down to say good night, Bennett," said Eliza with a brittle smile. "I had a lovely time at the play. I'll see you both in the morning."

They wished her good night, watching her as she turned and left the bar.

"She's a real lady, isn't she, Lieutenant?" Higbee said admiringly.

"Yes, Charlie, she is," said Bennett.

Sanders returned to his headquarters on the docks, which was covered with several inches of snow. He found Wood pulling one last body out of the building and throwing it in a boat tied to the wharf.

"How'd it go, Wood?"

"The money's on the table, sir. Two of the men got away. Higbee escaped with the lieutenant and the girl just as we planned it."

"Good. All you gotta do now is follow the breadcrumbs, right?"

"Yep. I'm gonna dump the bodies first and then go by their hotel."

"I don't want to see any more dead raiders, Wood. If the authorities find their bodies, they'll kick us out of the country."

"Ain't nobody gonna find these bodies, sir. I got lots of chains in the boat to hold 'em under."

"The same goes for the lieutenant and Higbee. Let them live, but get back our money."

"Yes, sir."

Sanders nodded and left.

On a cloudy day, the lieutenant in a beige overcoat and a tuque accompanied by Higbee in his army-issue greatcoat and a black fedora rode east on a snowy track to the town of Saint-Jean. Eliza followed the men on a grey mare bundled up in her blue coat and fur hat with her red carpet bag tied to the saddle horn.

They had gotten up early and left at dawn, taking a ferry across the river to La Prairie on the South shore where they had acquired three horses in a livery stable. It would be slow going, but Bennett wanted to avoid the train to Saint-Jean, which would have made them easy targets for Wood and Sanders.

"How much money do you think we got, Higbee?" asked Bennett.

"I don't know, Lieutenant. We never counted the bank bills, the greenbacks, the silver and what have you, but I would think it must be over $50,000."

"Sanders thinks we have a lot more than that, maybe around $100,000. What is Wood's role in this?"

"Wood is a bagman, Lieutenant. He took the money from the raiders and gave it to Sanders to prove his loyalty. If he hadn't, Sanders would have sent men after him. He doesn't put up with insubordination."

"Wood is coming after us, isn't he, Higbee?"

"'Course he is, sir. That son-of-a-bitch never gives up. He's a dangerous man. I wouldn't put anything past him."

"Well, I've had it with both of them," Bennett declared suddenly. "How about this? We dig up the loot, divide it between us, and split up before they can find us."

Higbee gaped at him, incredulous.

"You ain't gonna return the money to Sanders?"

"Why would I do that?" Bennett snapped. "After he had all those guys killed for their money. I don't trust Sanders anymore. I think those two are just going to line their own pockets and not a penny will go to the Confederate cause."

Higbee remained silent.

"I thought about it last night and again this morning. I think we should just take the money for ourselves. We fought for it. Whaddya say, Charlie?"

Higbee didn't answer. He just exploded in laughter.

"What's so funny?" demanded Bennett.

"You, Lieutenant," Higbee chuckled, shaking his head. "I didn't think you had it in you."

Saint-Jean, Quebec

Bennett and Eliza had reserved adjoining rooms in a small hotel on Main Street, with Higbee down the hall. The lieutenant stopped by Eliza's room and knocked on the door. Eliza appeared on the threshold, all cleaned up and wearing a nice new dress.

"That dress is new?" said Bennett with admiration.

"Do you like it?" she asked shyly. "I bought it in Montreal."

"You look beautiful, Eliza. Are you ready to go down for supper?"

"Yes, I was waiting for you."

Heads turned as the couple descended the stairs and entered the hotel dining room. Bennett thought Eliza looked gorgeous as they sat at a corner table. Higbee was nowhere to be seen.

"I've been thinking, Bennett," she leaned forward and gently brushed his hand with her own. "I'm not going with you tomorrow. I'm going to return to St. Albans."

Bennett felt like he had been punched in the gut. It took him a moment before he trusted himself to speak.

"Are you sure?" he asked.

"Yes, I am," she said firmly. "I don't want anything to do with stolen bank money."

"I understand, Eliza."

"You and Higbee can keep the money."

There was a long silence between them as a young boy arrived with two bowls of soup and a bread basket from the kitchen. Bennett said grace.

"For what we are about to receive may the Lord make us truly grateful, Amen."

There was little to say after that. The meal seemed to take forever. Their conversation was awkward, each lost in their own thoughts. Finally, Bennett spoke.

"I'm thinking of leaving for England, Eliza."

Eliza stared at him, stunned.

"There is nothing here in Canada for me and the war is lost."

"You're serious, aren't you, Bennett?"

"Yes, I am. You met Teavis and Swager. They'll be in Quebec City tonight along with Hutchinson and Spurr. We've talked about catching the next boat for England."

Eliza looked at Bennett in a new light.

"Come with me, Eliza," he implored her. "With the money, we can catch the next boat for England and spend a year doing whatever we like. Just imagine that!"

Eliza was astonished by Bennett's bold plans. *He wasn't going after the money to get rich. He was going to use it to get away from the war. She liked him more than she cared to admit. Her parents liked him. Her mother had even warned her to be careful around the handsome young Southerner. But could she simply drop everything for a Johnny Reb and leave for England, the dream of every American girl?*

After Eliza had gone to bed, Bennett crossed the road from the hotel to a tavern where he spotted Higbee sitting quietly at the bar drinking bourbon. He stepped inside and went over to his friend.

"How's your wound holding up, Charlie?"

"Much better, sir, since Dr. Pallen fixed me up."

"You think Wood will find us?"

"I don't see how. I think we got away clean. Taking the ferry was a great idea."

They sat in silence for a moment.

"You seem to be taking quite an interest in Eliza, Lieutenant."

"Yeah, I suppose I am," said Bennett, deciding to change the subject. "The way the war is going, it will all be over in a few months. I'm looking forward to the peace. What are your plans when the war is over, Charlie?"

"Head back to Texas. Maybe start a business if they let me."

"Well, that sounds like a good plan. You could take the boat from Halifax to Havana, and then on to New Orleans. It would be easier than going through Union lines. They catch you, they might hang you."

"Yeah, I was thinking the same thing."

The lieutenant stood up and looked around at the men nursing drinks at the bar.

"We're gonna be up early, Charlie. See you in the morning, old chum."

"Night, Lieutenant."

Bennett stepped out of the tavern and looked across the street at the hotel. There was a lot to think about, and every time he tried to figure things out, he always ended up coming back to Eliza. Now he was doing it again as he remembered the look that had come over her face when he'd told her about England. He had no idea what she thought of his plan. He had first to get his hands on the money. There was the threat from Wood and Sanders. They wouldn't stand idly by if he and Higbee were to take off with the loot. *We've just got to get there first*, he thought as he crossed the road and entered the hotel.

Twenty-five

It was a cold, wintry day as Bennett, Eliza, and Higbee rode along the winding trail to the southeast. It had snowed again overnight, but the day was getting warmer. The trail took them through the hill country of Eastern Quebec with its mix of English and French farming communities. Occasionally, Bennett would turn in the saddle to check whether they were being followed, but he could only see a short distance behind them because of the tree cover. *Anybody could be back there*, thought Bennett.

Somebody certainly was.

A mile or two behind them, a horseman followed at a slow pace. He wore a hood over his head and kept his eyes on their tracks in the snow. He was in no hurry. He had all the time in the world.

Higbee rode ahead, followed by Bennett and Eliza.

"I find the winters here are very cold, Eliza," said Bennett. "I'm from Kentucky, so I'm used to snow, but Charlie's from Texas. He's probably never seen snow before. Have you, Charlie?"

"We get snow down south too, Lieutenant."

"Not like we do, Charlie," said Eliza. "I doubt you have sleigh rides in the winter and fish from holes in the ice."

"No, ma'am, we don't, but we do get northers back home and the temperature drops real sudden like. I ain't never seen a river froze over back in Texas."

Bennett's thoughts returned to Eliza, who had been her usual cheerful self at breakfast. They had made small talk together, neither of them mentioning Bennett's plan to sail to England.

Stanbridge East, Quebec

Wood stood in the shadows behind Elder's Hotel on Main Street. He watched the lieutenant's party enter the hotel after their evening meal in a café down the street. Bennett was laughing at something that Eliza had said, and Higbee was smiling. *They don't suspect a thing,* Wood thought. *Tomorrow, he'd catch up to them. He had full control of the situation now. Things were going well.*

Wood left the dark alley and mounted his horse. He rode out of town on the road to Frelighsburg. A couple of miles out of town, he stopped near a farmhouse overlooking the road. He paid the owner a small amount to feed and look after his horse while he slept in the barn.

In the early morning, the lieutenant and his party left for Frelighsburg. Bennett and Eliza rode ahead, followed at a distance by Higbee, who was having trouble keeping up. He'd stopped once already, complaining about some kind of stomach ailment, and Bennett was starting to lose patience.

"You all right back there, Charlie?" asked Bennett.

"I'm fine, Lieutenant," said Higbee. "The horse is a bit slow today."

Bennett turned to look. He could see Higbee's horse favoring one hoof and trailing them badly.

"Get off your horse, Charlie, and check the left back leg. If that horse goes lame, we're in big trouble."

"I can keep going for a while," said Higbee before Bennett cut him off.

"You heard me," growled Bennett.

Higbee shrugged and slid out of the saddle. He took out a folding knife and dug around the horse's hoof, prying out a stone and tossing it aside.

"Got it," he said to Bennett as he remounted the horse.

Bennett gave him a curt nod and then followed Eliza onward to Frelighsburg.

From a distance, Wood observed them from the barn. He stood in the doorway and drank a cup of tea provided by the farmer's wife. Then he climbed on his horse and left. It was going to be a very long day.

Saint-Jean, Quebec

Gilbert McMicken in a heavy winter coat and bowler hat rode into the old fort built in 1666 by the French. He was met by armed soldiers in greatcoats and shako hats. He waited in the freezing guardhouse for an aide-de-camp to come and fetch him, and was taken to Colonel Ermatinger's office.

"Good morning, sir," said the colonel, standing up to greet him. "Macdonald sent word you were coming. It seems you are having trouble rounding up your Johnny Rebs."

"Thank you, Colonel. Yes, we are and the Governor-General is losing faith."

McMicken hurried over to the fireplace to warm himself up and was joined by the colonel.

"Sounds like a right cock-up to me, sir. It would have been a good idea not to release them in the first place."

"I agree wholeheartedly, but now we have to clean up the mess we've made. I have put men on the roads leading to Montreal and along the border, but I think they're long gone."

"I would suspect they'd go west to Toronto or east to Halifax to avoid arrest. They can't return to the States without great risk to themselves."

"True. The warrant is only good in Quebec, so we need to catch them before they get to Ontario or New Brunswick."

"So where should my men be looking for them, Mr. McMicken?"

"That's a very good question, sir. I wish I knew."

"Would you like a cup of tea, Mr. McMicken?"

"Gladly, sir."

"I think we need to put on our thinking caps. I have an officer who knows the country well. It might help to talk to him."

"Of course, sir. That would be wonderful."

Frelighsburg, Quebec

Benton Wood followed the Pike River, which ran near the mill on the outskirts of the town. He had let the lieutenant's party get way ahead of him so he wouldn't spook them when they went searching for the loot. Their tracks were easy to follow in the snow. As the mill was just coming into view, a man jumped out from behind some rocks and fired a pistol at him. Wood slid off his horse as the bullet went wide. He was drawing his own gun and diving for cover when another man appeared out of nowhere, firing a rifle. The rifleman missed and Wood got off a lucky shot. He fired once, purely on instinct, and the man toppled to the ground, killed instantly.

Wood didn't spend time reflecting on his good fortune. The other shooter was still out there, so he crawled through the snow into a copse of trees. He lay very still, looking around for other assailants. He could hear the first shooter breathing hard and coming for him. Wood drew his knife and started crawling toward the muffled sounds of footsteps in the snow. He finally came upon the man, who was only a few feet away with his back turned. Wood launched himself on his assailant, pulling his head back with his free hand and slitting his throat with the other. He stepped clear of the geyser of blood as the man fell forward. When he looked down at the man, he realized he knew him. He was one of the minions who did odd jobs for Sanders.

Wood knew better than to stay where he was. He'd seen two men shoot at him, but there might be a third assailant out there somewhere. He crawled away to the cover of some trees and waited, keeping his eyes and ears open while he thought about what he'd do to Sanders.

The Confederate agent no longer trusted him. He had sent men to bushwhack him. That was clear. As soon as he had the money, he'd go after that stuffed shirt of a politico. He won't die as easy as these two, thought Wood. *I'll track him down and gut him like a deer.*

Iris was playing in the woods near the farm when she saw the lieutenant arrive at the farmhouse, accompanied by a young woman and a man in a black fedora. She instantly recognized the young American and was not at all surprised to see him return to the farm. She was going to run out to meet them, but thought it would be more fun to wait and then surprise them. She hid behind a tree and watched as they got off their horses and knocked on the front door. Nobody came to open the door and after a few moments, the lieutenant turned to the others and shook his head. He said something Iris couldn't make out, and then he and Higbee went around the house and headed to the barn while the woman stayed with the horses.

Bennett continued past the barn and searched the long rows of corded firewood.

"I unloaded the bags right here," said Bennett. "I hid them in the gap between the rows."

The trouble was that he couldn't remember exactly where he had put the bags between the rows of firewood.

"Let's start over there," he suggested to Charlie.

It didn't take long to check the rows.

"Well, they ain't here no more," said Charlie. "Somebody took 'em."

"I'm tellin' you, Charlie," insisted Bennett. "I hid the bags right here. No one could have found them."

"What the hell did you do with them, Lieutenant?"

"I just told you where I put them, but they're no longer here," protested Bennett as a scream came from the front of the house.

"You got my money, Higbee?" Wood bellowed as he came around the house, one arm around Eliza's neck. He held a revolver in his other hand and it was pointed directly at Bennett.

Bennett cursed himself. Like a fool, he'd left his own gun belt draped across the saddle.

"Higbee left a nice trail for me," said Wood, grinning at Bennett. "It wasn't hard to follow. Where's the loot?"

Bennett glared at Charlie, who had betrayed him.

"Son-of-a-bitch!" Bennett could hardly believe it. "You helped him after he killed all our friends?"

"I didn't have a choice, Lieutenant." Higbee turned to Wood. "It looks like someone got here before us."

"Sure they did," said Wood sarcastically. "I don't believe either of you."

Bennett's heart nearly stopped as Wood kicked the legs out from under Eliza and pointed his pistol at her.

"Someone took the money," said Bennett. "It was right here."

"I think you're lying to me, and I'm a lot smarter than Higbee. You go find the money, lieutenant, wherever the hell you left it. If you don't find it, I'm gonna blow her head off."

"All right," Bennett held up a hand. "I'll get it."

He had no choice but to play for time.

"I'm gonna take a look in the barn," said Bennett.

"Stay where you are, Lieutenant. Higbee will go."

Higbee went to the barn and rummaged around inside. As Wood watched Higbee, Bennett caught a brief glimpse of movement in the trees off to his left. At first, he thought he was seeing things, but out of the corner of his eye, he saw the closely cropped blonde head above a brown hand-me-down coat sneaking around in the woods.

Iris was standing behind a tree, using it to block Wood's view of her. She waved at Bennett and pointed to something in the woods that he couldn't see. He walked toward the point in the woods Iris had indicated.

"Hey, where you goin', Lieutenant? Don't move."

"I'm gonna have a look over there by the creek."

Wood watched Bennett walking along the dry creek bed covered in snow. He stopped after a moment and looked down.

"What you got, Lieutenant?"

As Wood started after Bennett, Eliza stood up and pulled Bennett's revolver from her coat pocket. She tried to shoot Wood, but the revolver wouldn't fire with the safety on. Wood turned around and laughed at her as she fumbled with the gun.

"You wouldn't try to shoot me, would you, miss?"

Eliza struggled with the gun.

"Drop the damn gun, bitch, or I'll shoot you."

The lieutenant hurried back just as Wood grabbed the revolver from Eliza and smacked her across the mouth with the back of his hand. She fell to the ground.

"Leave her alone, Wood."

"The damn bitch tried to shoot me."

Higbee emerged from the barn.

"Ain't nothin' in the barn, Benton," said Higbee.

"It's over there by the creek," said Bennett.

Wood and Higbee hurried over excitedly and watched as Bennett got down on his hands and knees in the snow and started to dig. He found the first sack of silver in the sandy soil and pulled it out. Higbee emitted a jubilant shout as he retrieved a sack of greenbacks and another of bearer bonds.

Bennett let them continue the search and stepped back away from the creek. He joined Eliza near the barn. He wiped the blood from her nose and tried to comfort her. He looked for the child in the woods, but she had disappeared.

Twenty-six

It was getting dark as Bennett and Eliza sat near the stove in the kitchen while they waited for Higbee and Wood to return. Thin and tomboyish in breeches and a torn vest, Iris brought them steaming bowls of vegetable soup and chunks of her aunt's bread.

"Iris, how have you been?" asked Bennett.

"Fine, sir," said Iris, fidgeting in her chair. She couldn't remain still for a moment, so much so that Bennett was worried about her. He said grace and then both he and Eliza started on the soup.

"Thank you, Iris. It's very good," said Bennett.

"Bennett tells me you live with your aunt and uncle," said Eliza.

"Yeah. They went to Farnham for provisions. They'll be back tomorrow. This is yours, Lieutenant."

Iris put Bennett's miraculous medal on the table near the soup bowls.

Bennett was surprised to see Reuben's medal again. He thought he had lost it somewhere on his way to Montreal.

"You found it after the fight in the kitchen?" he asked.

"Yes, I thought you would need it."

"You are an angel, my dear," Bennett said, smiling. "And you hid the money?"

"My uncle would've found it hidden in the woodpile, sir. I knew you'd come back, so I put it where he couldn't find it."

"Well, thank you, Iris. You probably saved our lives out there."

Iris held up an elegantly dressed male doll in a tailcoat and top hat.

"You know who he is?" she asked Bennett.

"I'm not sure."

"You get three guesses, Lieutenant."

"My dear, could he be Prince Albert?"

"Good guess, Lieutenant. He's Prince Albert of Saxe-Coburg and

Gotha. That's someplace in Germany."

"Well, I never," said Eliza as Iris presented Bennett with a ragged doll representing Queen Victoria in a black mourning dress and white cap.

"This is Queen Victoria, Lieutenant. Do you recognize her?"

"Yes, I believe I do."

"*Tatie* Dorothée says that the Queen was very sad when Prince Albert died. That's why she's wearing the mourning dress. You know how many children they have?"

"I don't know, Iris," said Bennett. "Maybe five or six."

"The number is eight or nine, I think," said Eliza.

"Eliza's right. The Queen has nine children: four boys and five girls."

"You are a fount of information about the Royal Family, Iris," said Eliza.

"The queen wears her black mourning clothes every day. She's so sad."

"They say he died of typhus," said Eliza.

"Wednesday was the third anniversary of his death, Lieutenant. He died on December 14. I wore black on Wednesday, just like the Queen."

Iris showed them a black smock that she pulled from a box of clothes behind them just as Wood and Higbee came in.

"Who's the girl?" asked Wood.

"She lives here. It's her home," replied Bennett.

"Well girl, you just got two more mouths to feed," said Wood with a laugh.

Iris nodded at Wood and took two bowls from the cupboard. She filled the bowls for the men, who sat on the daybed and chairs near the door examining the loot.

"Where's your ma, Iris?" asked Eliza.

"She lives with my grandpa at Lac-Brome, miss."

"Why aren't you with her?"

"She wants to keep me, but my grandpa won't have it. See, my *maman* was unmarried when I was born."

"I'm sorry to hear that, my dear."

"Grandpa sent me here to live with my aunt and uncle. They are good to me, but I miss my *maman* a lot. She comes to visit, but not often."

"But Iris, you're such a sweet child. I'm sure your mother would love to keep you," said Eliza.

Iris smiled and carried the soup bowls to the men.

"Well, ain't that nice. Just like home. Thank you, girl," said Wood, who tucked into the soup as Iris handed a bowl to Higbee. Iris returned to the kitchen for the bread basket.

"Maybe I won't have to kill you all before I leave," said Wood. "Whatcha think about that, Higbee?"

"Fuck off, Benton. Don't you have any manners?"

"Yeah, you got a lot of manners. You do. These people ain't seen you murderin' women and children in Kansas like I have."

"Don't listen to them, Iris," said Bennett. "I guess you and Eliza will sleep in the bedroom while we sleep out here near the stove."

Eliza nodded at the lieutenant and went to the bedroom to get things ready. Iris silently observed Wood and Higbee gulping down the soup and eating thick chunks of bread, before following Eliza out of the room.

"I'm gonna keep a close eye on you, Lieutenant," said Wood. "If you even twitch an eyelid, I'll shoot you down like a dog."

"You and your friend have got all the St. Albans' money. I can't wait to see the last of you," said Bennett.

Iris appeared, carrying in extra blankets for her guests. She set them down on a chair before returning to the bedroom.

It was an hour or two before dawn as Iris stepped gently around the men camped out in the parlor. She spotted the haversacks containing the money in the corner and tried to wake up the lieutenant, but gave up when he wouldn't stir. She tiptoed back to the bedroom, where Eliza was asleep in the large bed.

"Eliza, wake up," whispered Iris in her ear.

"What is it, Iris? Can't you sleep?" asked Eliza, rolling over.

"We gotta get up. We can't stay here."

Eliza nodded and quickly rose, putting on her coat and boots. Iris silently slid the window up and a cold draft entered the room. She put on her coat and boots, and slipped silently out through the window, jumping down into the wet snow. She was followed a moment later by Eliza. They disappeared around the side of the house in the dark, heading for the trees. When they got to the creek, Eliza called to Iris.

"Hold on, Iris. We can't leave the lieutenant alone in the house with those men. They'll kill him for sure."

"You're right. We've gotta help the lieutenant."

"What can we do?"

"Stay here, Eliza. I've got an idea."

Iris ran off before Eliza could call her back.

Inside the house, Higbee was asleep on the floor near Bennett when he was awakened by the sound of scratching on the windowsill. He turned to look at the shadow of a person standing in the moonlight outside the window. He sat up and prepared to go have a look when Wood woke up. The men jumped as a large rock smashed the window and they heard footsteps running off into the night. Wood seized his revolver and took a shot out the window. He pulled on his coat and boots and rushed out the door.

Bennett got up and went to the bedroom to see whether the girls were all right when he noticed the open window.

"The girls are gone, Charlie. Wood is after them."

"You better get the hell out of here, Lieutenant. I'm sure Benton is gonna kill you and the girls before we leave in the morning."

Higbee pulled on his boots, grabbed his coat and fedora, and dashed out the front door after Wood. Bennett got dressed in a hurry and emerged from the house by climbing out the back window. He headed as silently as he could towards the copse of trees beyond the creek. He figured that Eliza and Iris would go east, away from the road. As he approached the creek, he saw Wood stumbling about in the trees, looking for a target followed by Higbee. He hid in the snowy underbrush until they gave up and headed back to the house. He pushed on, banging into branches and tree trunks, slipping and sliding in the wet snow until he found Eliza and Iris hiding behind a snowbank.

As the dawn light was coming up, three horsemen rode through the snow-covered countryside near the mill on their way into town. Sanders' men had left Stanbridge East in the middle of the night and were supposed to hook up with their advance party when they accidentally found their bodies lying in the bushes on the side of the road. They suspected the lieutenant and his party were responsible for killing their friends and hurried into town, hoping to catch up with them. They followed the tracks south of Frelighsburg and spotted a farmhouse in the trees by the side of the road.

Higbee was in the barn saddling a horse. After he finished, he led the horse out of the barn and left it tied to the railing near the front porch for loading. He went inside the house to collect the bags of loot and carried them outside. He tied the bags one by one to the saddle horn while Wood appeared on the stoop, watching him with a cup of tea in his hand.

"Things are looking up, Charlie. It's gonna be a nice sunny day. We're gonna make good time without the lieutenant and that damn woman."

Twenty-seven

Higbee went to the barn to fetch the horses, one for Wood and one for himself. He left Eliza's grey mare behind for the lieutenant and Eliza if they returned to the house. As Higbee came out of the barn, leading the horses, he called to Wood.

"What did you do with the bag of greenbacks, Benton?"

Wood looked at him with an interrogative air, when suddenly all hell broke loose as gunfire erupted around them. Sanders' men were firing at the house with muskets and pistols from the trees. Wood crawled off the porch and hid in the bushes.

Unarmed, Higbee dropped to the ground and found refuge behind the house. He climbed in through the bedroom window as Wood fired at Sanders' men with his pistol. Higbee searched for the lieutenant's revolver in Wood's bag in the parlor. He carefully loaded the weapon and crawled out the front door. Sanders' men were getting closer and maintaining a terrible barrage of gunfire on the porch. Higbee sneaked up behind Wood, hiding in the underbrush, and shot him in the back of the head. He then raised his arms to show he was giving up as Wood lay immobile in the snow.

"Charlie? Charlie Higbee?" said one of Sanders' men behind a snowbank.

"Looks like I beat you to it, boys!" said Higbee, grinning.

"Was it you or the lieutenant who shot up our friends?" asked the older man named Tattersall.

"We didn't shoot nobody," replied Higbee. "You can come and get your money now. Wood's dead."

There was a long silence before the three soldiers appeared near the house with their guns drawn. They looked down at Wood, unconscious and bleeding from a head wound in the snow.

"You shot that son-of-a-bitch, Benton Wood. Good for you,

Charlie," said Tattersall.

"He's gonna die," said Higbee. "Ain't no way someone can survive a wound like that."

As the other men searched the house, Tattersall stayed with Higbee on the porch.

"We were watchin' for you and the lieutenant, Charlie. My guys set a trap for Wood, but it looks like he got to them."

"Wood's a hard man to kill."

"Where's the lieutenant and the girl?"

"They ran off at dawn. They must be some miles back there in the woods."

Bennett wasn't sure how much time had passed since he had heard the gunshots coming from the house. It must have been close to an hour before Bennett, Eliza, and Iris quietly returned to the house, listening for any movement inside. As Bennett came around the front, he spotted Wood lying in a pool of blood near the porch and quickly led Iris and Eliza into the house. They sat in the kitchen, getting warm and drying their clothes near the stove. Iris put the kettle on to make tea for her guests.

"So what are your plans now, Bennett?" asked Eliza.

"I expect I'll return to Montreal. We can't go to England without any money, Eliza."

"I think I'll go home for a spell. I don't need all this excitement."

"I'm sorry about the window, Iris. I'll cover it up with a piece of wood for you."

"Don't worry, Lieutenant. *Tatie* Dorothée will look after it."

"Are you sure?" asked Bennett.

"She's always complaining about me breaking things and hiding stuff."

"What kind of things do you like to hide?" asked Eliza.

"Lots of things, miss. Clothes, food, a walking stick, sometimes..."

Iris stood up suddenly and went over to the daybed in the corner. She searched behind a hidden panel in the wall and returned, carrying a leather satchel. She unfastened the straps and flipped it open. A pile of greenbacks fell onto the table.

"Iris, this is a small fortune!" Bennett exclaimed, hugging her.

"Where did you find it?"

"I tried to wake you up last night, Lieutenant," said Iris, "but you wouldn't wake up. Then I saw the bag with the Lincolns on the floor near that bad man, so I hid it for you."

Bennett and Eliza looked down at a real treasure chest of greenbacks, close to ten thousand dollars' worth. There was a mix of ten-dollar bills with the picture of Lincoln and twenties with the liberty statue, showing the sword and shield on the front.

"You're quite amazing, Iris," said Eliza, looking at Bennett. "I think we're going to London after all."

Bennett couldn't believe their luck and smiled at Eliza, who would be coming with him to England after all.

"You must go to Buckingham Palace to see the Queen, Lieutenant."

"Well, yes. Of course, we'll go, won't we, Eliza?" said Bennett, as Iris beamed with delight. She danced away from them, holding up her dolls as if they were participating in some courtly palace event. The girl's fantasy life was complete. Eliza and the lieutenant were going to see the Queen at Buckingham Palace and she was the one who had made it all possible.

Bennett exited the house and went to the barn to look for a spade. In a forested area behind the barn, he started to dig a grave in the sandy soil. Eliza left the house and approached.

"I told Iris to stay indoors. A dead body is not a pretty sight for a young girl," said Eliza.

"Thanks, Eliza. We better be on our way before her aunt and uncle get home. I don't want to cause any more trouble for the family."

Eliza kissed him on the cheek, and he put his arm around her.

"What was that for, Eliza?" asked Bennett, looking into her lovely green eyes.

"For saving us, Bennett."

"It seems to me that Iris played a big part."

"She did, didn't she? She has asked to come with us as far as Lac-Brome. It's on the way. She wants to see her *maman*."

"Do you think her aunt will mind?"

"She said she'd leave a note for her aunt."

"Well, that's wonderful, Eliza. It will be a pleasure to take her with us. She's a delightful child."

Eliza returned to the house, leaving the lieutenant to dig the grave. A moment later, there was a scream coming from the front of the house.

Montreal

In the backroom of a tavern, Macdonald and Cartier were having drinks together in a private room as they awaited a third man. Both men were in good spirits.

"I just got a letter from Brown in London, George," said Macdonald. "He met with the Colonial Secretary Cardwell and submitted his brief. Cardwell is for it. He supports our plan for Confederation, anything that will help him reduce the cost of defending the colonies."

"Did Brown meet with the prime minister, Lord Viscount Palmerston?" asked Cartier.

"Yes, he did. Palmerston invited him out to his country estate for the weekend, so I imagine it went well. He also met with the members of the cabinet and got on well with William Gladstone, the chancellor. It looks like it's going to be a waiting game until January when we should have a decision on the defense proposal."

The cost of defending the British colonies in North America was expensive and involved building forts and maintaining a military force along the 5,000-mile border with the US. A new Canadian Confederation meant that Canada would have to pay for its own defense by raising taxes, so it was a popular idea in government circles in London.

There was a discreet knock on the door and Gilbert McMicken appeared on the threshold looking cold and exhausted with snowy eyebrows and side whiskers. He shook the snow from his scarf and hat, before shaking hands with Macdonald and Cartier. He had just come from Fort Saint-Jean.

"It was a long ride, gentlemen," said McMicken, after exchanging pleasantries.

"I imagine it was," Macdonald said, glancing at Cartier. "Thanks for coming, Gilbert. How did it go with the colonel?"

McMicken was about to reply when a waiter entered to refresh their drinks. He ordered a whiskey, shrugged off his coat, and sat down.

The waiter departed with their orders.

"It went very well," McMicken said finally. "The colonel's a good man. He's got men at Fort Henry, near Kingston, and a small contingent at Fort Ingall on Lake Temiscouata, near the border with New Brunswick. They're going to keep an eye out for our Johnny Rebs."

"The Montreal police are looking for them, John," said Cartier, "but the new police chief is not optimistic."

"Clay and Sanders have disappeared, sir," added McMicken. "We believe Clay is on his way to Halifax and then home. As you know, James Holcombe left in August, but we've still got Jacob Thompson under surveillance at the Queen's Hotel in Toronto."

"Keep up the good work, Gilbert," said Macdonald. "We'll catch them soon enough."

"If those Rebs try to return to the States, sir, they're going to need a passport. It's a complete muddle at the border. We're getting lots of complaints from people in Toronto who have tried to cross, but have been turned back."

"It's all Seward's doing," said Macdonald bitterly. "He's punishing us for the Coursol affair. He wants us to pass a neutrality act to stop the Confederates from mounting cross-border attacks."

"It would be worth it, John, if it will keep the Americans from waging war against us," said Cartier.

"I agree, George," Macdonald sighed. "A small inconvenience for the greater good."

Frelighsburg, Quebec

Bennett ran to the front of the house where Eliza was standing on the porch, looking down. She was shaking uncontrollably with fear. Iris came out on the porch and took her hand.

"He's gone," said Eliza.

Bennett looked around for the body, but it had disappeared.

"I don't believe it. He was dead. Where'd he go?" asked Bennett.

"I don't know," said Eliza. "He's alive, and he's out there somewhere."

The lieutenant followed Wood's tracks in the snow. They crossed the road and disappeared among the trees on the other side. He returned to the house to comfort Eliza and Iris on the porch.

"He may be watching us, Eliza. Let's get out of here."

Eliza returned to the kitchen while the lieutenant went out looking for Wood's horse that had run off. He returned with the horse and then went to the barn to saddle Eliza's grey mare. As he worked, he remembered friends of his in Kentucky who had been shot in the head in battle. *Sometimes, the bullet would bounce off the skull when it struck at a certain angle. He had never heard of a soldier with a bullet in the head managing to walk away like Wood had done.*

Sanders' men rode west on the road to Stanbridge East, accompanied by Higbee. Tattersall was in the lead with the pack horse loaded down with the bags of loot. Anderson was just behind him, and Higbee followed the pair. The other man named Wells trailed them a hundred yards back.

Higbee knew Tattersall from his time in Montreal. He had never had any trouble with the man, which was borne out when Tattersall made no effort to disarm him. Higbee wasn't so sure about the other men. He'd caught a suspicious glance between Anderson and Wells as they left the farmhouse after Tattersall had ordered Wells to take up the rear position. The men didn't trust him, and he knew he was on borrowed time.

After an hour on the road, Higbee suddenly pulled up and dismounted. He squatted to look at some tracks in the snow. He called out to the men.

"Hey, boys. It looks like we got company."

Higbee stood up and looked around at the vast emptiness of the country.

Twenty-eight

Anderson and Tattersall turned their mounts around and came back to have a look at the tracks in the snow. Anderson was the first to arrive and stared down at Higbee.

"OK, Higbee. What you got?" asked the young man with an arrogant air.

Higbee slipped the revolver from his pocket, cocking it in almost the same motion, and shot an aghast Anderson in the head. He then fired a shot at Tattersall, which went wild and climbed back in the saddle. He fired a shot at Wells some fifty yards away to the rear and chased after Tattersall, who was trying to get away, but was slowed down by the pack horse. Higbee came at Tattersall at a full gallop, firing his revolver as the man tried to get clear. The first bullet struck him in the back, and then Higbee shot him in the face as he came around. Tattersall fell off his horse as Higbee turned to confront Wells.

The third man charged Higbee but at the last moment skirted him when he saw Tattersall on the ground. He didn't even try to pursue him and simply rode off toward Frelighsburg. Higbee grabbed the reins of the pack horse and scattered the soldiers' mounts, before riding off, leaving two dying men in the snowy field.

Higbee smiled as he thought how easy it had gone down. He had planned the attack soon after he had killed Benton Wood at the house. He knew the soldiers would be easy to kill after they allowed him to keep the lieutenant's Colt revolver. All he had to do was wait for the right moment. *He had learned a lot from his days riding with Quantrill's men: ruthlessness pays a dividend every time. He had no empathy for these men nor for the women and children he had killed during the Lawrence massacre. He wasn't worried about Wells finding him. He would be long gone by the time Sanders' men regrouped and tried to track his movements.*

A hunter in a fur hat dragged a white spruce through the snow, followed by his young son. The plan was to install it in their home and bring all the joy of Christmas to the family. As they approached their modest shack in the woods, they noticed a man lying on his belly in a ditch with a bloody head wound.

"Sir, are you all right?" asked the hunter, alarmed. He released his grip on the tree and hurried to the man's side, kneeling to examine the wound more closely. The man made no response, although his head was still warm to the touch and the hunter thought he could detect his breathing.

"Let's get him inside," the hunter said to his son. "He's got a nasty wound."

The hunter reached down to turn the man over so he could help him onto his feet when Benton Wood rolled over onto his back and plunged his knife deep into the man's throat.

The hunter dropped like a stone, bleeding out as Wood staggered to his feet and made a move towards the young son, who stood nearby frozen in fear.

Lac-Brome, Quebec

It was a miserable day. It had been raining all morning, only letting up after they stopped to eat at noon near Sutton. Bennett rode Wood's chestnut stallion, letting Eliza take the lead on her grey mare. Most of the time, Iris sat behind Eliza, but after a while, Eliza installed Iris in front so she could nap in her arms if she fell asleep. They headed north, following the western contour of the lake as the sun came out of the clouds. After a while, they turned down a deeply furrowed track towards the Yamaska River.

Bennett had spent most of the day thinking about Benton Wood. There was something preternatural about a man who could survive a horrific wound to the head and then somehow marshal the physical strength and mental awareness to run off into the wild. *I should have known better,* he chastised himself. *I thought he was dead because I wanted him to be dead.*

Bennett looked ahead and saw a stone cottage with a steep, gabled roof, and small gabled dormers in the French style overlooking the river. Two women were outside hanging clothes on a long clothesline. They turned when they saw the horses approaching from the road. Eliza pulled up on the grey mare and Iris jumped down. While Bennett and Eliza waited, Iris started walking toward the women at the clothesline. Agnes, the younger of the two, was jabbering away at the older woman.

"It's Iris!" she shouted, hardly able to contain herself. "I tell you, it's Iris."

Iris ran forward and then stopped.

"It's me, *Maman*," she exclaimed timidly.

"Iris, I can't believe it," said her mother. "Did you run away?"

"No, *Maman*. I came with my friends."

"*Viens ici, Iris. Serre-moi fort*. Give me a hug."

Iris ran to her mother, who swept her up in her arms.

Bennett, Eliza, and Iris sat at the kitchen table surrounded by a flock of children, with the youngest barely two and the oldest around sixteen. Agnes and several young women were busy serving them their supper. The children were curious about Iris' friends and attempted to communicate with them in halting English. A six-year-old girl piped up.

"Iris say you are American?"

"Yes, dear. I'm from Vermont," said Eliza.

"Where's this Vermont?" asked another child.

"It's a good day's ride south of here, my dear."

"Is Iris gonna stay with us, *Tatie* Agnes?" asked the youngest.

"We'll talk about it later when Papa comes home," said Agnes.

Eliza and Bennett smiled at the kids as they ate their supper.

Grandpa Gagnon sat silently in his rocking chair, stuffing his pipe with tobacco. A cup of tea was on the table near his chair. He had arrived home about an hour ago and was annoyed to learn that Iris had run off again and had come to Lac-Brome with two strangers.

"I'm sorry for the inconvenience, sir," said Bennett, sitting across from him.

The old man said nothing until he had finished lighting his pipe. Eliza and the children had already gone to bed.

"You ain't one of them Johnny Rebs I seen in the paper, are you, Lieutenant?" asked Gagnon.

"Yes, sir. I'm a Confederate soldier and proud to serve. The judge let us go."

"I heard that. Where do you come from, young man?"

"Kentucky, sir."

"Ain't you Southern boys tired of makin' war?" asked Gagnon with a cynical air.

"We are, sir, very much so."

"You've seen our house full of children, Lieutenant. That's a lot of mouths to feed. So there ain't no way we can keep Iris, sweet girl that she is."

"I understand, sir."

"Agnes has lived a sinful life, Lieutenant. She ain't married, you know."

"I understand that, sir."

"This isn't the first time Iris has run away, Lieutenant. Each time I gotta send for Dorothée to come and get her."

"Eliza and I want to do something for Iris and her mother, sir. We want to help if we can."

Grandpa Gagnon got up to fetch a bottle of homemade wine and two glasses from the nearby cabinet.

"Can I offer you a drink, Lieutenant?"

Bennett nodded, and the old man poured him a glass of wine.

"I think you call it elderberry wine, Lieutenant? It grows along the river. The berries are called *'baies de sureau'* in French."

Bennett tasted the wine and was pleasantly surprised.

"It's good, sir. I have a proposition to make."

"A proposition!" Gagnon exclaimed with a laugh and a twinkle in his eyes. "You want to buy my land or marry my Agnes? You can have her if you want, Lieutenant."

"Not that kind of proposition, sir," said Bennett with a smile. "I was thinking that we could contribute to Iris' upkeep if she stayed with her mother."

"You want to give me money to keep Iris and her *maman* together? I cannot accept your money, sir."

"It would go to Agnes. It would pay for the girl's education."

"You don't understand, Lieutenant," Gagnon sighed. "The *curé* in this parish is an ornery old whoreson. If he hears that the love child is back, he'll raise all kinds of hell in the village. The church doesn't approve of women having children out of wedlock. He'll say we are encouraging a sinful act."

The lieutenant nodded as he thought about Agnes' predicament. He understood the pressure the old man was under from the Catholic Church but figured he had to find a way to help Agnes and Iris. It was getting late and Grandpa Gagnon got up to go to bed.

"*Bonne nuit*, Lieutenant."

"*Bonne nuit*," replied Bennett.

As the oil lamp dimmed in the Gagnon house on the river, a lone horseman came from the south, following the tracks in the wet snow. He dismounted and walked ahead, leading his horse. He examined the tracks that went off toward the cottage on the river. He got back on his horse and headed for the trees, away from the river.

After sunup, Bennett and Eliza prepared to leave as Agnes, Iris and the children watched them from the front porch. The lieutenant arrived from the barn with their horses saddled up. He turned to Agnes, who handed him a sandwich lunch for the journey.

"*Merci*, Agnes. *Nous voulons vous aider.* We want to help you," said Bennett.

He pulled an envelope from his saddlebag and thrust it into her hands.

"*C'est un secret entre nous*, Agnes. This is for you and Iris."

Agnes's eyes widened in surprise when she peeked at the US greenbacks in the envelope.

"The money will help you cover the costs of maintaining the child and pay for her education. She's a bright, intelligent girl. She needs to go to school."

"Thank you, Lieutenant!" said Agnes, throwing her arms around him.

Agnes turned to Iris: "*Donne-lui un baiser*, Iris."

Iris timidly planted a kiss on Bennett's cheek as he hugged her.

"*Merci, Iris.* Good luck, my dear."

Eliza hugged Iris and then went over to say goodbye to the little ones on the porch.

Bennett then helped Eliza into the saddle and mounted his own horse.

"Follow the river to the south, Lieutenant, then take the bridge," said Agnes.

"Lieutenant," said Iris, looking up at him. "Don't forget to go see the Queen."

"I will Iris, I promise."

"Will you write me a letter, Lieutenant?" blurted Iris, and then almost regretted it after her mother gave her a disapproving look.

"Of course I will, my dear," said Bennett, feeling homesick already. It was hard to leave such a warm and loving family. He felt an unexpected catch in his throat.

They followed the trail next to the Yamaska River and waved again to the children. Iris had tears in her eyes as she stood next to Agnes, watching her friends leave. She had been alone for much of her young life, despite the efforts of her aunt and uncle to provide for her basic needs. It seemed like everyone she cared about was always leaving her behind. She felt abandoned and lonely. No one had ever come back for her.

Twenty-nine

Frelighsburg, Quebec

After an hour's ride, they came upon the bodies in a field, partially covered in snow. The doctor in black funeral garb and a top hat climbed down from his wagon and was already kneeling by the bodies when Colonel Ermatinger and his men in winter greatcoats and shako hats arrived on horseback. A farmer had discovered two bodies some distance from town and had gotten word to the constable, who had then notified the doctor.

"Voici, deux autres victimes, Colonel. Ils ne sont pas d'ici," said Dr Boivin, looking relieved.

"You say these men aren't locals, Dr. Boivin?" asked the colonel.

"No, sir. I never saw them before. See this one with the bullet in his head. He's got an old wound on his neck, probably from a gunshot. I think they are soldiers, sir."

"Let's have a look at the other one."

The colonel and doctor walked over to have a look at the second man, who had been shot in the back and the face. Sergeant Wilson joined them.

"They look like those other men we found dead near the mill, sir," said the sergeant.

"Oui, monsieur. Ils sont pareils," murmured Boivin.

Colonel Ermatinger had to agree. He'd been in the military all his adult life and knew soldiers when he saw them. The ones at the mill had looked like rough customers, and these two had a similar look. He had served in the Crimea and seen similar wounds on the battlefield. These fellows weren't ordinary farm laborers.

"So we have four dead soldiers, Sergeant. Let's load up these two and return to town."

Ermatinger observed the tracks of two horses leading off in a westerly direction as Sergeant Wilson ordered his men to load the bodies in the wagon.

"Dr Boivin, where does this road lead to?"

"Bedford, sir."

The colonel nodded his thanks and considered going after the killers, but quickly realized they had no chance of catching them.

Waterloo, Quebec

Bennett and Eliza rode through town and stopped at the railway station. The town of Waterloo was located a short distance north of Lac-Brome in the Eastern Townships. The rail link would take them through Farnham and Saint-Jean, and east to Quebec City. They dismounted and tied their horses to the railing before entering the station.

Inside the station, there were numerous posters advertising rail travel on the Grand Trunk and Central Vermont Railways. Eliza went to the ticket counter, where a clerk in a green visor was busy with a customer. As Eliza and Bennett waited in line, Eliza noticed a picture on the wall behind the clerk. She quickly stepped in front of Bennett.

"Can I help you, ma'am?" asked the clerk, as the elderly man collected his ticket and left.

"No thanks, we've changed our minds," said Eliza to the clerk. She stepped away, pulling on Bennett's sleeve.

"What's going on, Eliza?" asked Bennett as she turned him around and marched him toward the exit.

"Dammit, Bennett," Eliza hissed. "They've got a wanted poster of you on the wall. You didn't see it?"

"No, I—."

"Shush," Eliza cut him off as they went out the door and into the busy street. She had his arm firmly locked in hers as she headed to their horses.

"Are you sure?" asked Bennett, looking perplexed.

"Of course, I'm sure. Keep your voice down," Eliza snapped. "It's your picture on the wall, Bennett. They're looking for you and your friends. We can't take the train."

"But that can't be right," Bennett protested, not wanting to believe it. "We won our case. We were released. We're free."

"No, Bennett, you're not. Not anymore."

Stanbridge East, Quebec

It had been a long day in Frelighsburg for Colonel Ermatinger and his men before they rode north and west. Several hours later, they entered the lobby of Elder's Hotel on Main Street and booked rooms for the night. They planned to leave in the morning in search of the fugitive raiders. Colonel Ermatinger took a moment to make an inquiry of the clerk, a small man with rheumy eyes.

"We're looking for several men who may have stayed here in the last few days," said the colonel. "May I see your reservation book?"

"December is a slow month, sir," said the clerk, "but you can have a look if you like."

He turned the large book around on the counter and pushed it across so the colonel could read the names. It had indeed been a slow month, the entries for the month barely filling a single page. The colonel ran his finger down the page and then peered at the clerk.

"I see some names here, sir. B. Young, E. Miller, and a C. Higbee, I think it reads," said the colonel, squinting as he tried to decipher the handwriting. "Do you remember seeing these people two days ago?"

"No, sir," said the clerk, "but my daughter might remember them. She's in the dining room."

Colonel Ermatinger turned and entered the dining room, leaving the sergeant and two other men in the lobby. A young woman was setting out cutlery on the tables as the colonel approached. They talked for a few moments and then the colonel returned.

"The lieutenant has been here, Sergeant. There was a woman with him and another man."

"Maybe a girlfriend, sir?" ventured Wilson.

"Perhaps. The other fellow's name is Higbee."

"I don't recognize the name, sir."

"Neither do I. He may be just a traveling companion."

Sorel, Quebec

Bennett and Eliza rode on staying the night in a hotel in Roxton Falls. The next day they headed north again, riding all day and all night through the snowy flat land. They arrived at dawn in the town of Sorel, a river port on the St. Lawrence with several *goelettes* moored along the dock. They dismounted at a café opposite the dock, stiff and cold from their overnight ride. They stepped into the warm interior of the café, looking exhausted just as several young men headed out for work on the boats. The place was crowded with workmen, drinking tea and downing shots of gin to fend off the cold.

A sweaty beef of a man in an apron welcomed them and assumed from their dress and demeanor that they were a cut above his usual clientele and hence might have more money to spend. He was disappointed when Bennett ordered a breakfast of eggs, ham, and cheese with a pot of tea and two shots of gin.

"Let's get some food into you, Eliza, and warm up a bit before we go out looking for a boat," said Bennett.

"Bennett," Eliza said, interrupting his thoughts. "Aren't you worried someone might recognize you?"

"I've learned not to worry about things I can't control, Eliza. It's unlikely anyone here has the time to follow the trial in Montreal. We're safe for the time being."

The tea and gin arrived, and their demeanor improved. They were going on a boat ride and a bit of an adventure.

"I don't drink gin this early in the morning," said Eliza, laughing.

"Come on, Eliza. Drink it. It'll warm you up," chided Bennett, as he took a slug of gin and shivered as it went down.

Two hours later, they were comfortably installed on the deck of a two-masted *goelette* sailing east around *Île de Grace* before entering the Saint-Pierre Lake, a huge inland body of water on the St. Lawrence River. They were soon surrounded by water as far as the eye could see. With the help of the ebb current running at a knot and a half, the *goelette* was making good time down the river. After a time, Bennett and Eliza sought refuge in the cabin huddled around a wood stove with the other passengers.

"We should be in Quebec City tomorrow morning, Eliza. We'll get a room there and get cleaned up."

"I'm looking forward to seeing the town, Bennett. While we're there, I want to get a Christmas present for my parents."

"We can mail it before we leave on the boat."

They had come a long way in a very short time and it was not long before Eliza was fast asleep, nestled against Bennett's chest while he struggled to stay awake.

Magog, Quebec

Colonel Ermatinger and his men rode hard throughout the day and late into the evening before they arrived in the little town on Lake Memphremagog. They sat in the hotel bar and drank drafts of pale ale before the evening meal was served. They were conscious of the stares of the locals, who were not used to seeing the red serge uniforms of British soldiers in their town.

"What do you think are our chances of catching the lieutenant and his girlfriend, sergeant?" asked the colonel.

"I think the men at Fort Ingall will catch them for us, sir," replied Wilson.

"I sent their names along by telegraph this afternoon, but it might not be easy to recognize the fugitives without a physical description. I think we need to get ahead of them."

"Ahead of them, sir?" asked a corporal. "They've got a good start on us. If they're heading east to New Brunswick, we'll never catch 'em in time."

"There's been a change of plan," Ermatinger told the young man. "I've decided that Sergeant Wilson and I can travel faster on our own. I'm sending you men back to Fort Saint-Jean while I travel east with the sergeant."

The men were surprised by this turn of events but not unhappy. It would mean avoiding a long and futile race against time to catch up with the fugitives.

"In two days, the sergeant and I will be meeting a man in St. Georges on the Chaudière River. He's a tracker who will take us through Northern Maine into New Brunswick."

Thirty

Quebec City, Quebec

Bennett and Eliza stepped into a small hotel near the docks in the Port of Quebec. They were exhausted from their boat trip. Bennett's beard had grown, and he was starting to look like a different person. There were no wanted posters on the walls at the front desk when Bennett asked for a room for himself and his wife. He looked at Eliza, who smiled back at him. She had told him to get one room for them both. The police would be looking for single men, not for a married couple. The clerk handed Bennett the key.

"Here you go, Mr. Miller. Room 21 on the second floor. The dining room opens at five."

"Thank you, sir."

They headed upstairs, with Bennett carrying their bags. Once inside the small plain room with its double bed, the lieutenant went to look out the window at the harbor. There were boats of every size imaginable and, further out in the *Bassin Louise*, he could see two huge transatlantic liners.

"Look at those ships out there, Eliza."

Eliza approached the window, and Bennett put his arm around her and kissed her.

"We're almost newlyweds," said Bennett with a laugh.

"No, we aren't, Bennett. We're fugitives."

"Yes, I suppose we are."

"I'm going to have a nap. You have things to do."

"I need to find Swager and Teavis. After that, we can go shopping and book our passage for the next departure."

Eliza rummaged through her bag as Bennett left the room to search for his friends.

Bennett was running out of places to look when he entered a music hall in a side street, a block away from the docks. The place was crowded with sailors and workmen listening to a buxom young woman in a long dress singing *Bonnie Mary of Argyle*. She was accompanied onstage by a guitarist and an accordion player. She had the rapt attention of the nostalgic and predominately male customers.

> *I have heard the mavis singing*
> *His love song to the moon*
> *I have seen the dewdrop clinging*
> *To the rose just nearly born*
> *But a sweeter song has cheer'd me*
> *At the evening's gentle close*
> *And I've seen an eye still brighter*
> *Than the dewdrop on the rose*
> *'Twas thy voice, my gentle Mary,*
> *And thine artless winning smile*
> *That made this world an Eden,*
> *Bonnie Mary of Argyle*

The lieutenant listened to the loud applause and made his way around the smoky room past the sailors and painted ladies until he spotted Charles Swager and Squire Teavis seated at a table drinking large glasses of ale. Despite the joyous mood of the music hall, both men looked rather glum.

"Boys, what's up?" asked Bennett.

It took them a moment to recognize him.

"Lieutenant!" Swager exclaimed. "We'd almost given up on you."

"What happened to you?" demanded Teavis.

"It's a long story, fellas," said Bennett, pulling up a chair. "How are you doing?"

"Well, it would be a whole lot better," Swager allowed, putting his hand on Teavis' shoulder, "if I didn't have to put up with this asshole all the time."

"Ah, fuck off, Swager. Lieutenant, we've got a problem. The police are looking for us. Your picture is in all the newspapers."

"I know. There's also a wanted poster with my name on it," replied Bennett.

"Are you still courting that pretty Miller girl, Lieutenant?" asked Swager.

"Yeah, she's here with me."

"You look a lot different with the beard, Lieutenant. You could wear spectacles and I swear nobody would recognize you," said Teavis.

"Let me get you a drink. Ale?" asked Swager.

"Yes, please."

Swager waved down a waiter who left to get the lieutenant's drink.

"Where are you staying?" asked Bennett.

"We've got rooms across the street," said Teavis.

"Have you heard from Hutchinson and Spurr?"

"Nope. They never showed up," said Swager. "We don't know where they got to."

When Bennett returned to the hotel, he saw Eliza having tea in the dining room off the lobby. He hurried over to her.

"Eliza, I found them," he said triumphantly, his eye going to the brown paper package on the table. "You've been out shopping?"

"Yes, I had a nap and then went out," said Eliza. "I bought a dress for my ma and a shirt for my pa. They wrapped them up for me real nice in the shop. So what's our plan?"

"We're thinking of getting on a ship using false names. You and I would go as a couple."

"Nobody will recognize you if you wear spectacles, Bennett. That beard already changes your looks."

"That's what Teavis said. If you're not too tired, we could go over to the shipping office and buy the tickets."

Eliza looked like a young and sophisticated woman about town as she entered the shipping office on the docks. There were large posters announcing transatlantic voyages to Liverpool, Southampton, Rotterdam, Bremen, and other destinations.

"Good day, ma'am. Can I help you?" asked the clerk, hastily putting away the rag he'd been using to wipe down the counter.

"I want to inquire about ships leaving for Europe."

"When do you want to leave, ma'am?" asked the clerk.

"As soon as possible, sir. My husband and I are traveling for business reasons."

"Well, there's the SS Hibernia, an Allan liner, leaving tomorrow for Liverpool and the S.S. Belgian on Wednesday next for Londonderry and Liverpool."

"I've never been on a transatlantic voyage, sir. How much does it cost?"

"Cabin class on the Hibernia goes from 12 to 20 guineas, madam. It's a steamer and takes about twelve days to make the crossing."

Eliza looked puzzled for a moment.

"How much is that in dollars, sir?"

"The US dollar is trading ten to the pound, madam. That would be 126 dollars for the least expensive cabin."

"That's very expensive, sir."

"Well, there's a war on, ma'am," the clerk reminded her.

"Thank you, sir. I'll be back."

Eliza looked over the clerk's shoulder at the wanted poster on the wall before leaving the office. The poster showed a photograph of Bennett and the Royal Coat of Arms above the words:

WANTED:
LT. BENNETT FLEET
REWARD OF £100 FOR INFORMATION
LEADING TO THE ARREST OF
THE ST. ALBANS' RAIDERS
LAST SEEN IN MONTREAL
ON DECEMBER 13, 1864

Eliza crossed the street and entered a café where Bennett and his friends were waiting. Bennett was wearing his newly acquired spectacles and looked like a different man.

"How'd it go, Miss Miller?" asked Swager, smiling at her.

"It went well, Charles. The S.S. Hibernia is leaving for Liverpool tomorrow. It's very expensive, Bennett."

"We need to get on that ship. I don't care what it costs," said Bennett.

"How much is it, miss?" asked Teavis.

"Cabin class is 126 dollars," said Eliza.

Swager raised an eyebrow.

"Your picture is on the wanted poster, Lieutenant, but no one is looking for Swager and me," said Teavis.

"It looks that way. You boys should have no trouble buying tickets," Bennett said as he took two hundred and fifty-two dollars of greenbacks from his pocket and counted them out in two piles on the table.

"Here's my contribution to your passage, boys. Don't try to pay anything with those bank bills of yours."

"Thanks, Lieutenant," said Swager as he put his share of the money in his pocket.

"So Higbee and Sanders got all the loot and Wood got a bullet in the back of his head," mused Teavis with a suspicious air. "So, what did you get, Lieutenant?"

"We got our lives," Bennett told him, annoyed by the question. "Mine and Eliza's."

"Wood has a reputation, Lieutenant, from his time with Quantrill's raiders," said Teavis. "They say he is unkillable. He has nine lives."

"It only takes one bullet, Teavis," Bennett told him, his eyes flat. "You know that. Even the toughest among us are gonna die sometime."

Eliza stifled her surprise at Bennett's lie. She lowered her head and busied herself looking for something in her purse as Teavis collected his share of the greenbacks on the table.

"I'm gonna go have a look," said Swager, getting up to leave.

"Be careful, Charles," Bennett warned him. "Say as little as possible."

Swager nodded and winked at the lieutenant as he left.

"I don't know, Lieutenant," teased Teavis, "whether I should trust you."

"Why?" asked Bennett. "I just paid for your ticket on the steamer."

"Cause you're a no-good liar," Teavis burst into laughter, clapping Bennett on the back. "You shoulda seen the look on your face! I'm just pulling your chain, Lieutenant. You've always been straight with us."

Bennett glanced at Eliza, but she was watching the crowd in the street with its sailors, merchants, hawkers, and street urchins. She spotted Swager as he entered the shipping office.

Bennett turned back to Teavis.

"So what are your plans, Squire?"

"I'd like to find my brother."

"He might have gone to see Thompson in Toronto. You could write him a letter care of the commissioner at the Queen's Hotel."

"I don't know, Lieutenant," Teavis shook his head. "He might not show up there after hearing about the shooting in Montreal."

"Bennett!" Eliza squeezed his arm, her voice an urgent whisper.

Bennett looked up just in time to see Swager hurrying across the street and coming toward the café. *Not here*, Bennett thought desperately. *Don't come in here!*

It was as if Swager had heard his voice. At the last moment, he broke into a run, veering away, and disappeared from their view in the window. Bennett glanced back toward the shipping office and saw the clerk standing in the doorway, shouting and gesticulating at a nearby constable.

Bennett turned away from the window as the police whistles shrilled in the street.

"Swager must have blown it with his big mouth," said Bennett. "You better get after him, Squire."

Teavis stood up and put on his coat.

"We'll be at our hotel," Bennett murmured. "One hour, Squire, no longer."

Teavis left as Bennett put some coins on the table and helped Eliza into her coat. They took their time leaving the café and walked slowly arm-in-arm back to their hotel, conscious of the number of constables converging on the docks. Three more men, in plainclothes but unmistakably police, dashed past them toward the shipping office.

Thirty-one

Quebec City, Quebec

Macdonald arrived at Government House in the Spencer Wood Estate in a snowstorm. The butler brushed the snow from his shoulders and led him into Lord Monck's study, with its view overlooking the St. Lawrence River. The river would freeze up starting in January and an ice bridge would form, allowing the townspeople to drive their buggies across the huge waterway.

"Would you like some tea or coffee, John?" asked Monck, "or maybe something stronger?"

"Coffee would be fine, Charles."

"What brings you back to town?" asked Monck, nodding at the butler as he gestured to Macdonald to take a chair.

Macdonald sat down and didn't reply until he heard the discreet *click* of the door behind them.

"I've just come from a meeting with Cartier."

"We tried to rearrest the rebels," Monck sighed, his frustration evident, "but Lamothe dithered. He wouldn't sign the arrest warrant. I had to go to Judge Smith."

"I think you did very well, sir, under the circumstances. We're still looking for them."

"I've ordered an investigation into the conduct of Coursol and Lamothe."

"Very good, but we've still got to find those men. Nothing less will appease Secretary Seward and General Dix. A resumption of the extradition trial will go a long way to calm the threats in the newspapers, sir."

"Ambassador Lyons believes Washington will wait before taking any further action, John. We do have some time to put things right."

"Have you heard about Lyons' dinner parties in Washington, Charles?"

"I've heard they are extravagant, *bien arrosé*," said Monck. "The ambassador is amazing and has Seward and Lincoln eating out of his hand most of the time. It's just very unfortunate he's leaving his post."

"I can only agree with you."

Richard Lyons had been British ambassador to the United States since 1858 and was hugely influential in the American capital. All of Washington wanted to be invited to his luxurious dinner parties. Lyons' most famous diplomatic success had been the resolution of the Trent Affair during the autumn of 1861 when two Southern politicians who were on their way to Europe had been abducted from the *Trent*, a British mail steamer, by a Union ship. The resentment in Britain was so acrimonious that a war between Britain and the United States seemed imminent. Lyons had convinced the authorities in Washington to release the two envoys to avoid a declaration of war by Britain.

Time was almost up, thought Bennett, sitting in a quiet corner of the hotel lobby. They had gathered their things and already checked out as they waited for their friends to arrive. Eliza was at the front desk looking at the railway schedules, when Teavis stepped into the lobby.

"No sign of him," said Teavis. "He didn't return to the boarding house."

"What was he thinking?" asked Bennett. "I did warn him."

"I know you did, Lieutenant, but we're talking about Swager here. He does dumb things sometimes. Maybe he tried to make a joke or gave an address in Kentucky. Who knows?"

"They're onto him now. They'll be checking every passenger on every ship from now on. We better get out of town."

"Well," Eliza said, holding up a railway schedule, "there's a train from Levis that goes east as far as Rivière-du-Loup. We could try to catch it. It leaves at eight o'clock."

"I think we should go," said Bennett. "What do you think, Squire?"

Teavis nodded his agreement.

It was cold and snowing heavily as the lieutenant, Eliza, and Teavis made their way to the embarkation area for ferries crossing the river.

There was a lot of traffic on the river. Schooners, *goélettes*, and small runabouts were coming and going while large coastal steamers belching black smoke from their smokestacks made their way up the river. At the ferry landing, there was a queue of passengers waiting to get on the next boat for Levis. Teavis looked around for Swager, but he was nowhere to be seen.

"We can't wait for him, Squire," said Bennett. "He'll have to find his way out all by himself."

A sailor beckoned to the passengers to come forward. They bought their tickets and descended the gangway to the ferry boat deck. The boat was about twenty feet long, with oak planking, an interior cabin, and an exterior sitting area. Moments later, the little boat whisked them across the river, first heading upstream against the current and then downstream along the shore to Levis.

Daaquam, Quebec

Ermatinger and Wilson followed their guide past a rustic trading post in the small border town. Their first meeting with him the day before in Saint-Georges had not been encouraging. The wizened old man did not look the part of the tough-as-nails frontiersman, and he rode an old swaybacked nag that looked ready to drop. Now, into their second day of following him through the frigid Quebec outback, they had wordlessly conceded that appearances could be deceiving. The old man followed landmarks and turnings that were virtually invisible to the military men, and his elderly mount made such steady, implacable progress over the difficult terrain that the soldiers' proud Canadian Pacers could hardly keep up. The trail was covered in snow and followed the St. John River south into the State of Maine, but was still passable on horseback in the wet month of December. It ran all the way east to the town of St. Francis, at the junction of the St. Francis and St. John Rivers near the US-Canada border.

Levis, Quebec

The lieutenant's party stood on the platform among a crowd of country folk carrying boxes of supplies and live animals in cages. A locomotive belching black coal dust and pulling two passenger cars came to a stop. They stepped into a car and sat down on the wooden seats. A minute later, the train horn sounded, and the stationmaster called to close the doors.

"Damn it," said Squire sadly. "Swager didn't make it."

"You did the best you could, Squire," Bennett assured him. "You left him a message at our hotel."

"I know, Lieutenant," Squire nodded as the train departed.

Bennett had never seen him so discouraged. He was trying to think of something he could say to cheer him up when the door to the second car opened and Swager came in and plopped himself down in the seat next to his friend.

"Can I join you fine people?" Swager asked, a grin on his face.

Squire jumped up and gave his friend a bear hug as he danced around him. Bennett and Eliza laughed to see the two men happily together again.

MAP OF ST. JOHN RIVER

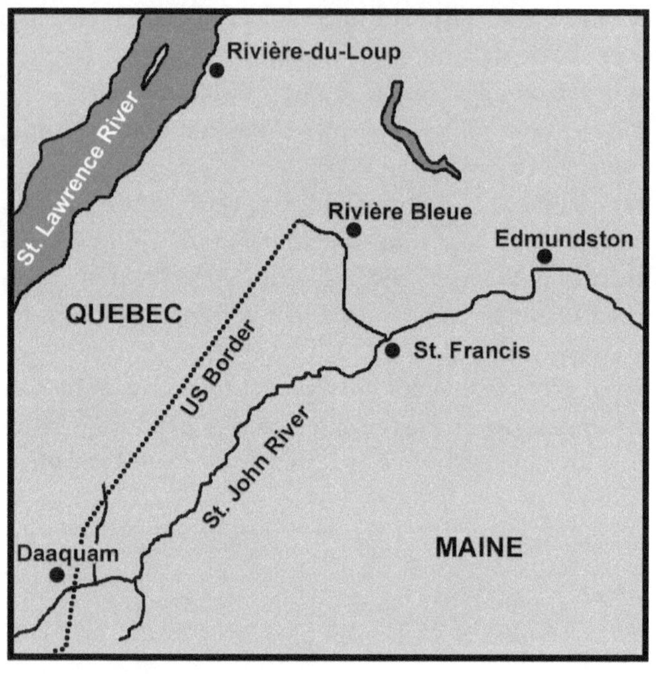

Thirty-two

St. John River, Maine

It was snowing heavily, and a blizzard was on its way. The snow had obliterated their tracks through the woods. Colonel Ermatinger and Sergeant Wilson followed their guide to a log cabin on the edge of a lake. The old man dismounted at the cabin.

"Colonel, we better stay here until the storm has passed," said the guide. "The horses go in the shed in back. I'll get the stove going."

Ermatinger looked up at the dark, overcast sky. He was frustrated by the delay but said nothing. He got off his horse and handed the reins to Sergeant Wilson, who led the horses over to the shed. He knew from experience that there was nothing you could do when a winter snowstorm threatened to shut you down in Canada. He had learned this lesson the hard way during his first year in the country. Sometimes you just had to wait and see and hope for the best.

We're running out the clock, the colonel thought bitterly. *We have to catch those damn fugitives before they leave the province. The warrant is only good for Quebec, and won't apply in New Brunswick or Nova Scotia. None of this would have happened if that judge had not released the men.*

Rivière-du-Loup, Quebec

It had been a long day of traveling, and it wasn't over yet. The lieutenant and his friends had debarked at the train station in the small town on the St. Lawrence River without any idea of how they would get farther south until their chance meeting with a gregarious, red-haired Scottish transplant. David Barrie had offered them a ride in his wagon as far as Rivière-Bleue, close to the border with New Brunswick. He had insisted that Eliza sit up front with him while Bennett, Teavis, and Swager made do with the sacks of grain in the back.

"So, Miss Eliza, when you expectin' to marry the young lieutenant here?" teased Barrie, his eyes twinkling.

Eliza smiled awkwardly. Undeterred, Barrie decided to torment her young man instead.

"When you gonna pop the question, Lieutenant?" he asked. "Time's a-wasting, my man."

Barrie laughed at the embarrassment he had created and burst into a song by Robbie Burns.

> "O my luve's like a red, red rose,
> That's newly sprung in June.
> O my luve's like the melodie
> That's sweetly play'd in tune.
> As fair art thou, my bonny lass,
> So deep in luve am I,
> And I will luve thee still, my dear,
> Till a' the seas gang dry..."

Barrie wasn't ready to let the young couple off the hook.

"You like Robbie Burns, Miss Eliza?" he asked innocently.

Eliza nodded shyly.

"I don't know," Bennett ventured, "whether Eliza has any plans for marriage yet, Mr. Barrie."

"You don't know?" Barrie asked, feigning surprise. "I think she may be hidin' something from you, Lieutenant. She may have another pretendant that you don't know about. A bonny lass like Miss Eliza can pick and choose. You better marry her quick 'fore she gets away."

Eliza laughed at this, as did the men in the back.

St. John River, Maine

After several hours and a nap in the warmth of the log cabin, the snow clouds had moved on. Sergeant Wilson brought out the horses and, as before, their guide wordlessly took the lead on his old brown nag. Heavy snow sat on the branches of the pine trees as they rode through the thick snow drifts. The trail was barely visible. After a couple of miles, they crested a rise and started to descend on the other side. The footing was treacherous, and yet the guide's old mount negotiated the incline more comfortably than those of his clients. They reached the bottom unscathed and their guide, noting landmarks known only to him, led them through a turn, following the bend in the river.

Colonel Ermatinger fished out a compass from his pocket and noted their new direction.

"Northeast by east, Sergeant," he said with authority.

"Very good, sir," Wilson replied. "We're going east again."

They followed a rough track parallel to the turbulent water and had to ford several creeks and avoid low-lying areas before they could get back on the footpath that ran along the river.

Rivière-Bleue, Quebec

In the tiny settlement on the Maine border, Barrie put up his new friends in the barn behind his rustic log cabin. His family was having an early Christmas party and his wife Beatrice was drawing off jars of homemade whiskey from a barrel near the still in the barn. She was helped by a grey-haired neighbor named Ti-Guy Laroche.

"Let us drink to Ti-Guy and our new friends," said Barrie, lifting his glass. "*Santé* and cheers to our southern guests."

For Bennett Young and his friends, it was much more than just a Christmas celebration; it was a celebration of their newfound liberty. There was laughter and gaiety in the room as Ti-Guy served up the jars of moonshine. Eliza chatted with Barrie's two teenage children, Ian and Marie, who were bringing in food from the house.

"If you don't mind, Mr. Barrie," said Teavis, already quite drunk, "I'd like to raise a glass to the Confederacy and its valiant struggle for freedom. I raise my glass to those that have died and to the living who have to carry on."

"Cheers to your struggle for freedom," said Barrie.

"Now after so many years of war, I'd like to see... I'd like to breathe the peace," Teavis struggled as he got to his feet, his voice choking with emotion and his eyes welling up with tears. "I'd like to see an end to the killin' and murderin' goin' on south of the border."

Bennett and Eliza applauded Squire's heartfelt words as Swager strummed on an old guitar and launched into a favorite song, *Poor Wayfaring Stranger.*

"I am a poor wayfaring stranger.
I'm travellin' through this world of woe.
Yet there's no sickness, toil nor danger,
In that bright land to which I go."

"I'm going there to see my father.
I'm going there no more to roam.
I'm only going over Jordan.
I'm only going over home..."

Teavis hadn't finished with his toasts.

"Lieutenant, sir, I wanna raise my glass to you for commandin' us Kentucky boys and leading us into battle."

Bennett struggled to hold back the tears when he heard the words. It had been a long time since he had cried in public, but now the long struggle seemed to be coming to an end. Eliza put her arm around him. Everyone applauded the lieutenant and then laughter erupted in the room as Teavis stumbled and nearly knocked over several jars of whiskey. The song played on as Barrie picked up his accordion and joined Swager.

"I know dark clouds will gather 'round me.
I know my way is rough and steep.
But golden fields lie just before me,
Where God's redeemed shall ever sleep."

"I'm going home to see my mother.
And all my loved ones who've gone on.
I'm only going over Jordan.
I'm only going over home."

Eliza sat close to Bennett and whispered in his ear.

"I can't believe we're going to Europe, Bennett. I'll need to write to my folks to tell them."

"We'll be in Halifax in a few days, Eliza. We'll catch a steamer from there."

Ti-Guy picked up his fiddle and added sweet, emotional notes to the song.

"I'll soon be free from every trial.
My body sleep in the church yard.
I'll drop the cross of self-denial.
And enter on my great reward."

"I'm going there to see my Savior.
And sing His praise forever more.
I'm only going over Jordan.
I'm only going over home."

Shortly after sunup, Barrie's son Ian arrived at the barn with a pot of tea and stopped when he noticed a St. Albans bank bill nailed to the door. He collected the ten-dollar bill and looked at the footprints leading off into the woods. Inside the barn, Teavis was snoring loudly in the hayloft as Ian came in with the tea. The Barrie family had invited Eliza to sleep in a real bed in their house while the men made do with the barn. He put the tray down on a bale of hay near the lieutenant.

"Lieutenant, here's your tea," said Ian.

Bennett was a light sleeper. He opened an eye and looked at the boy.

"What is it, Ian?"

"Look what I found stuck on the barn door, Lieutenant."

Bennett rubbed his face as he watched Ian pull the bank bill from his pocket.

"It's a tenner, sir."

Young got up quickly.

"Where'd you find it, Ian?"

"It was stuck on the door, sir."

"Show me," said Bennett, putting on his boots.

Ian led Bennett outside, where the boy pointed to the rusty nail on the outer face of the door.

"It was right here, sir."

The lieutenant glanced at the rusty nail. Ian saw him tense up as looked at the footprints in the snow leading off into the dense woods.

It happened very fast. The lieutenant grabbed Ian and shoved him back into the barn, throwing his body over the boy as the blast of a fowling piece tore a hole in the wall above their heads.

Thirty-three

"Stay down, Ian," Bennett ordered. "Don't move."

Teavis and Swager were instantly awake and stumbling down from the hayloft.

"What the hell is going on, Lieutenant?" asked Teavis.

"We got company."

Bennett went over to the still and pulled an old caplock musket off the wall. He checked the barrel and found percussion caps and balls nearby. He quickly loaded the musket as a scream was heard coming from the log cabin, followed by Barrie's Scottish brogue booming across the courtyard.

"Ian. Where are you, boy?"

The lieutenant opened the barn door a crack.

"He's with us, sir," yelled Bennett. "He's safe."

"Thank God, Lieutenant. What's going on?" asked Barrie.

Teavis and Swager jumped down next to Bennett.

"Who is it, Lieutenant?" Teavis asked. "Is it that son-of-a-bitch, Higbee?"

"I don't think so. You got your pepperbox derringer with you?"

"Yep, but it ain't no good against a rifle."

"Swager, you still got your pistol, right?" asked Bennett.

"Yes, sir. Let's go get the bastard."

"No, we're gonna take the wagon," Bennett said. "Can you get a harness on that horse?"

"Sure, Lieutenant. We gonna ride outta here?" asked Swager.

"Yeah, that's the plan," Bennett told him. He turned to Ian. "I want you to climb into the hayloft, son. Stay there until it is safe enough for your daddy to come and get you."

Ian nodded and did what he was told. Bennett collected a pitchfork and an axe from the wall and threw them into the back of the wagon, along with a few heavy planks of wood.

Across from the barn, Barrie and his wife were looking out their windows to see whether they could spot the shooter when Eliza suddenly appeared, dressed and ready to go.

"Tell the lieutenant to take the wagon," Barrie told her. "He can leave it in St. Francis."

"I'm so sorry, Mr. Barrie."

"Not your fault, miss. Don't worry about us."

Eliza went to the door and was about to step outside when another shot from the fowling piece blew another hole in the barn. The lieutenant's voice could be heard from across the courtyard.

"Eliza!" Bennett yelled. "Stay where you are. He's up that hill and can't see you. We'll swing by and pick you up at the house."

The door of the barn opened, and Teavis waved a piece of cloth on a stick. The stick disintegrated as it was struck by buckshot. Moments later, Bennett drove out of the barn as Swager opened the doors as wide as possible. As the wagon burst out of the barn, Teavis and Swager ran after it, climbing on board as it made a turn toward the cabin.

Bennett had no idea if there was more than one gunman, so he bent low as he reined the horse hard to the right. He had to get to Eliza, and that path would take them closer to the man with the shotgun. He urged the horse left toward the shelter of the cabin and gasped as Eliza calmly stepped out, her carpet bag in one hand as if she was waiting for a horsecar on a street in Montreal. He pulled the wagon up next to her.

"Get in the back!" Bennett yelled. "Keep your heads down. We're gonna make a run for it."

Teavis took Eliza's bag and then pulled her into the wagon, hiding her behind the wooden planks. Bennett whipped the horse, and they took off at a frantic pace. As they came out from the cover of the cabin and the trees, the lieutenant laid low on the front bench with one hand holding the reins. They soon arrived at the open road.

St. Francis, Maine

Colonel Ermatinger and Sergeant Wilson followed their guide into the tiny settlement on the St. John River. They were exhausted from the ride and stopped at the trading post. Across from the road, there was a cable barge floating in a deep pool of slow-moving water. The locals used it to pull themselves across the St. John River into Canadian territory.

"Let's have a drink," said the colonel. "We've come a long way."

"A capital idea, sir," said the sergeant, smiling.

The colonel tied his mount to the railing and turned to their guide.

"*Est-ce je peux vous offrir à boire et à manger, monsieur?*"

"*S'il vous plaît,*" said the guide, following them into the bar next to the trading post.

The taciturn old man had not said a word for over two days, but he had gotten them safely to their destination. The colonel was determined to show his appreciation for a job well done. He had already paid the man, but he would stand him dinner, drinks, and a healthy tip before sending him off on his return trip.

The colonel led the men into the bar.

"You think you catch your man, Colonel?" asked the guide.

"We remain hopeful," said Ermatinger. "We always get our man, don't we, Sergeant?"

"Damn right, we do," said the sergeant with a laugh.

Riviere-Bleue, Quebec

Bennett drove the horse at a fast trot for over ten minutes until the poor animal was all lathered up and begging for a rest. They stopped and Eliza climbed up on the front seat next to the lieutenant.

"Who can it be, Bennett?" asked Eliza.

"Yeah, who is this guy?" asked Swager. "We ain't done nothin'."

"It can't be Higbee, Lieutenant," said Teavis. "He can't shoot worth a damn."

"It's got to be Benton Wood," said Bennett. "Who else can it be? He's come after us."

"But you said Wood was dead," said Teavis.

"Higbee shot him in the back of the head," said Bennett. "Maybe he survived somehow."

"What's the bastard want with us? We ain't got nothing," said

Swager.

Bennett shrugged uncomfortably and kept a watchful eye on the woods. He tapped the horse with the reins, and they headed south again at a slow pace across the snowy fields. After an hour or two, they followed a winding creek bed, which led them into a densely forested area. The lieutenant stopped the wagon and jumped down off the wagon to have a word with his men.

"What is it, Lieutenant?" asked Teavis.

"It's a trap. I want you two to go around. Our man is gonna be on the other side waiting for us when we cross the creek."

"Got it. Come on Teavis, we can do this," said Swager, pulling his six-gun from his bag.

"Take the musket, Teavis, leave me the derringer."

Bennett watched his men descend to the creek bed and cross to the other side by jumping from one boulder to another. This was familiar terrain for Bennett. He had been a soldier behind enemy lines during his time with Morgan's raiders, sniffing out enemy positions and watching for ambushes. He knew exactly what to do to put pressure on the enemy. He gave Eliza a reassuring kiss on the cheek while they waited for his men to get into position.

"You think he's lying in wait for us, Bennett?" she asked.

"Yeah, that's what I would do. He'll do the same."

"Can't we go back, Bennett?"

"No, Eliza. He'll just catch up again and bushwhack us when we least expect it."

Eliza put her arm around Bennett as he tapped the horse with the reins. They advanced slowly along the trail to the turning that would carry them across the creek. Bennett stopped the wagon. Eliza stared at him for a long moment, her eyes wide. Then she kissed him and stepped down from the wagon.

"Take your bag with you, Eliza, and stay put until I come back," said Bennett.

"Be careful, Bennett."

Eliza disappeared behind a line of trees as the wagon moved slowly into the turn.

Thirty-four

The wagon advanced slowly, closing in on the creek. The horse stepped into the icy water and then, with enormous effort, pulled the wagon up the slope to join the trail. The lieutenant held Teavis' Nock four-barrel derringer in one hand and ducked down, holding the reins. Wood appeared behind a tree, holding his fowling piece at the ready. He had planned on the lieutenant's party leaving the farm in the slow-moving wagon so he could get ahead of them on horseback and set the trap.

"So, Lieutenant, you got my message?" yelled Wood.

"I figured it was you," admitted Bennett.

"I bet you thought I was dead. Well, I'm back. No one can kill me, Lieutenant."

Bennett remained silent.

"So you know why I'm here. I want them greenbacks that you stole from Higbee and me."

"You're mistaken, Wood. It was Higbee who shot you and took all the loot."

"They say you're a patriot. Are you a patriot, Lieutenant?"

"What do you want, Wood? Why don't you ride away and get lost?"

"You hid the money so you could return it to the Confederate cause, didn't you? That was pretty stupid."

"The purpose of the raid was to provide funds for Confederate operations in Canada. That's why we did it."

"What about that little bag of greenbacks, Lieutenant? You were saving it for the Confederate cause."

Bennett remained silent. He still had Iris' bag of greenbacks, and he had no intention of giving it to Woods or anyone else. He had contributed an amount to help his friends, Teavis and Swager, pay for their passage to England, but he would need the rest to cover his own expenses in England with Eliza.

"You self-righteous little whoreson. You're stealing money belonging to the Confederacy. You think I believe any of your shit about defending Jefferson Davis?"

"I don't care a whit about what you believe, Wood. You should've died back there at the farm. I was going to dig a grave for you and put a nice little cross on it."

"Gimme the greenbacks, Lieutenant, and I won't kill you."

"Sure thing, Wood. Come and get 'em."

Just as he dropped into the bed of the wagon behind a wooden plank, a volley of buckshot struck the wagon, driving the horse crazy with fear. It bolted headlong into a ditch, dragging the wagon with it.

"You think I'm stupid, Lieutenant. You hoped Swager and Teavis would get the drop on me."

As Wood finished speaking, Teavis took a shot at him with Barrie's musket. Wood ducked down and reloaded, quickly advancing towards the wagon.

"I'll give you one last chance, Lieutenant. Throw out that bag of greenbacks and I won't bother you no more."

There was a long silence.

Bennett threw out a nondescript canvas bag that he found lying on the floor of the wagon. For all he knew, it contained Teavis' or Swager's clothes. The bag fell into the ditch near the wagon. Wood crawled closer through the dry leaves and forest debris just as Teavis took a second shot at him and missed. Wood scrambled into the ditch to collect the canvas bag and found it full of dirty laundry.

"You secesh whoreson. I want my money," yelled a furious Wood.

"Come and get it. I'm waiting for you."

Bennett put his head over the edge of the wagon and took a shot at Wood in the ditch with the derringer. The shot went wild. Bennett looked around for Swager and Teavis, but he couldn't see either of them. There was complete silence on the hillside. *Why weren't they picking off Wood with the musket and pistol?*

Bennett examined the four-barrel pepperbox and knew he had just one bullet remaining. Then he would have to face the music from Wood's fowling piece. A volley of buckshot fired at close range could easily tear a body apart. He was outgunned, and his only chance with the derringer was to bring Wood in even closer. Another blast of the shotgun hit the side of the wagon. Wood reloaded and came in closer. He raised the musket to fire down into the bed of the wagon when the Bennett popped his head over the side and fired the derringer clipping Wood's shoulder.

"Damn you, Lieutenant," screamed Wood. "I'm gonna enjoy killin' you."

Bennett was out of luck. He was at the end of the road. He had nothing to defend himself against the coup de grâce. Wood stood up and took aim over the side railing, but he couldn't see Bennett, who was hidden behind the wooden planks. As he circled the wagon with his musket to get a clean shot, Bennett looked down at the rusty axe and the pitchfork with its five metal tines. The axe was far too heavy to throw, so, in desperation, he seized the pitchfork and launched it with all his force over the side at his assailant's last position. The pitchfork's tines caught Wood in the neck and his shotgun went off as he fell to the ground.

Bennett sneaked a peek over the edge of the wagon, and could hardly believe his eyes when he saw Wood pinned to the ground with his neck pierced by the pitchfork tines. Bennett was so shaken he could hardly stand up. It was not a novel experience for him. He'd had the same reaction before, perhaps once or twice, after an especially close call on the battlefield. This one may have been the closest of all.

He thought he could hear Eliza's voice calling from afar. The blast of the shotgun at close range had made him deaf. He looked up and saw her running along the trail to join him. She stopped suddenly, her eyes widening in horror at the sight of Wood's body with the pitchfork grotesquely upright in his throat. Bennett climbed down from the wagon and managed to take her in his arms. They clung to each other for a few moments, neither wanting to let the other go until she suddenly pulled away.

"Bennett!" she said urgently, pointing up the hill behind him.

Bennett turned to see Swager and Teavis being shepherded down the hill at gunpoint by two armed men in red serge uniforms and shakos. Bennett turned back to Eliza.

"You still have the bag?" he whispered.

"Yes," she told him. "It's with my things back where you left me."

He turned to watch the four men coming down the hillside. They were a study in contrasts. Swager and Teavis looked sheepish, ashamed of themselves, having failed to protect the lieutenant and now under arrest. Bennett recognized Colonel Ermatinger and thought he recognized the other man, a sergeant. Both men wore a smug look on their faces.

"Ah, the notorious Lieutenant Bennett Young," said the colonel, grinning. "What's going on here, Lieutenant?"

"A local bandit, sir," Bennett shrugged. "We were defending ourselves."

"I suspect," said Ermatinger, "the man on the ground over there might feel differently about that."

The colonel went over to examine the body of Wood, bleeding out on the ground.

"You were making so much noise. We thought you might be celebrating the Christmas season, but I see otherwise. You are all under arrest."

Eliza stepped closer to Bennett and put her arm around him.

"But Colonel, we ain't done nothin', we're free men," protested Teavis. "You can't arrest us."

"We're in New Brunswick now," said Swager with a confident air. "You don't have any authority here."

"We crossed over into New Brunswick back at the lake head," added Eliza.

"I agree wholeheartedly with you, young lady," said Ermatinger, unperturbed. "The warrant for your arrest is only good in Quebec. We're just going to borrow that wagon of yours, gentlemen, and haul your arses back to Quebec, where you'll be legally arrested."

"Who is the dead man, Lieutenant?" asked Ermatinger.

"I have no idea, Colonel," said Bennett, careful to keep a respectful tone in his voice.

"You're lucky he died in New Brunswick, otherwise I might have had to arrest all of you for murder," said Ermatinger. "Sergeant Wilson, did you see a dead man here just now?"

"No, sir. I did not," Wilson replied.

"Thank you, Sergeant, neither did I," said the colonel, winking at Bennett. "There appears to be no evidence of a crime."

Bennett turned to look at Eliza, who was heartbroken. Her dreams had just been shattered. Teavis and Swagar were in a state of shock. They could hardly believe their bad luck. Bennett just looked relieved to be alive.

"Well, Colonel," said Bennett. "It looks like we're your prisoners again."

Thirty-five

November 1865
Dublin, Ireland

A raucous, unruly crowd of foppish undergraduates from Trinity College, Queen's University in top hats and frock coats gathered around the ring, shouting and haranguing the bare-knuckle fighters as bets were taken. They were the pampered sons of some of the wealthiest families in America. They wore extravagant facial hair in mutton chop sideburns, handlebar mustaches, goatees, chinstraps, full Shenandoahs, and door-knockers. They were studying law at Queen's University, known to be one of the best law schools in the world. Americans were obliged to go abroad to complete their studies since many American universities had gone bankrupt or been destroyed by invading armies during the Civil War.

It was late afternoon in a green park behind a pub. The ring was a roped-in area between four vertical posts where fights were scheduled once a week. Boxing was the national sport for young men in Ireland and an amateur boxer could win a handsome prize against a professional fighter. But today, it would be a friendly fight between the American undergraduates studying law at Trinity College: the Johnny Rebs against the Yanks.

Among the Northerners was a young Irish-American fighter named Jake Doyle from New York who could beat most of the local talent in bare-knuckle boxing. He was in his mid-twenties but bore little resemblance to the callow young men cheering for and against him. He looked older, the epitome of the square-jawed, working-class Irishman with massive shoulders and a hard stare. He had been a Union Army sergeant and had fought at Gettysburg in 1863.

For a mountain of muscle, Jake was a fast learner and got better marks at Trinity than most of his compatriots born to wealth. He was a serious student, but he enjoyed making extra money in the ring during his free time. He had challenged his Southern colleagues to a friendly fight, which had been received with great enthusiasm by his friends and the Irish punters, who loved any opportunity to lay a bet. His reputation had preceded him and, for some time, no one seemed willing to go up against him.

By the day of the fight, only one student had thrown his hat in the ring. Bennett Young had boxed at Center College in Danville, Kentucky, for two years before he had enlisted as a private in the Confederate 8th Kentucky Cavalry. Bennett did not look like a boxer. He was of medium height with wiry limbs and looked like a picket fence next to a fireplug like Jake. Bennett knew Jake, and they got on well together in the classroom and outside. There was no animosity between them, which was surprising because a lot of expatriate Americans couldn't stand their old enemy and were often ridiculed in Ireland for their unnecessary war.

Jake warmed up by jumping up and down in the ring while the bets were still coming in. He was already a six-to-one favorite among the Irish punters so he felt very confident. He reckoned it would take him less than two minutes to knock Bennett down. The young Southerner removed his top hat and stripped off his frock coat and shirt as he climbed into the ring. In his undershirt, he looked older and wiser than he had during the endless extradition trial in Canada. He rolled his shoulders and started his warm-up routine. The fight promoter in a green leprechaun hat and velvet tailcoat arrived and climbed into the ring.

"Gentlemen, let's agree on some rules," declared the small man. "It's going to be London Prize Ring and Irish stand down. If a fighter goes down, the round ends. Each fighter has eight seconds to get up and toe the line before he is declared the loser. No kicking, head butting, or biting. Are we clear, gentlemen? Let the fight begin."

The promoter allowed the punters a minute or two to add to their bets before he rang the bell and the fight began. The student crowd cheered wildly, as did the Irish punters. The two fighters toed the line and started exchanging blows, bobbing and weaving around their opponent's fists. While Jake was looking for a knock-out blow that would bring the fight to an end quickly, Bennett was busy targeting

Jake with body blows and avoiding his massive fists. This went on for a while, with no one scoring a winning blow until Bennett slipped on the wet grass and briefly went down. He jumped back up and toed the line again, but the promoter had already called for a new round.

Round Two began with Bennett bobbing and weaving again, always just out of range, while he worked on Jake's body. This was not to the liking of Jake who looked tired and uncomfortable as the Southerner nonchalantly slammed his fists into his chest, stomach, ribs, and even his back when he turned. In Jake's world, you went for the face and tried for the knock-out, but Bennett was not doing any of that. Instead, his punches came in flurries, landing anywhere and everywhere he saw an opening. Jake was frustrated and tiring fast. He lunged at his opponent with his massive fists, but Bennett ducked and Jake slipped, falling on the wet grass.

Round Three began with Bennett coming out of his corner and attacking Jake with fast and furious jabs to the face. This new tactic encouraged Jake, who could hear the crowd cheering for a knockout. He retaliated with a huge roundhouse that would have nearly decapitated Bennett if it had connected. It didn't. Jake found himself lying on his back and wondering how he had gotten there. He could hear the promoter calling out the seconds and knew he had to get up. He also knew it was taking him far too long. Still groggy, he got to his feet but couldn't toe the line before the eight seconds were up.

Bennett's friends were mad with joy. They had beaten the tough Yankee in a fair fight and some of them had won some serious money. They raised his arm and pranced around the ring, yelling the Rebel war cry—a yowling holler, halfway between a hog call and an Indian war whoop. It was an unnerving sound for any Union man, and the Irish punters didn't know what to make of it. The writer Ambrose Bierce declared the Rebel yell was the "ugliest sound that any mortal ever heard."

Bennett ignored the cheers and went over to shake Jake's hand. At first, Jake refused, but seeing his opponent's friendly demeanor, he relented and took it.

"The war is over, Mr. Doyle," said Bennett. "We're all Americans and we're enjoying a lovely evening in Ireland."

They repaired to the pub for a huge celebration paid for by several wealthy Southerners. With his prize money, Bennett bought rounds of

Irish whiskey for all his friends, and, after a long evening, they stumbled back to their college rooms quite drunk.

The Criminal Law class on a Friday morning was full up with not a seat unclaimed. There were sixty-odd male students crammed together on long benches with wooden desks and inkwells. The aging professor was a famous jurist at the Court of King's Bench. In a dark suit and gown, the flamboyant old man was going on about criminal intent in the commission of a crime and how it referred to the mental state of the offender. This could include intent to cause harm, knowledge that an act was illegal, or recklessness in disregarding the potential consequences of an act. The students were taking notes, knowing that these basic notions of the law would soon appear on a test that could determine their suitability for a career in law.

"Mr. Doyle, can you give me an example of a defense strategy for an accused person?" asked the professor.

"Well, sir. One of them might be insanity," said Jake.

"Thank you, Mr. Doyle. Any others?"

Bennett raised a hand.

"Self-defense, sir."

"Of course. Does anybody else want to make a guess?"

"Innocence," said another young man in the front row.

"Of course," said the professor. "A man can simply be innocent of a crime."

"Somebody else committed the crime," said Jake.

"Very good," said the professor. "Anything else?"

"An innocent person can provide an alibi, sir," said Bennett.

"Duress," said Jake, smiling at Bennett.

"The criminal act was committed under duress. That's a good one, but there's another very common defense," said the professor. "Can you think of it?"

No one raised a hand.

"Involuntary intoxication," said the professor. "As in, I was too drunk to commit the crime."

There was laughter in the room.

"You can see," said the professor, "that a barrister has numerous tools to work with when defending an accused person. Thank you, gentlemen. I'll see you again next Friday."

Jake and Bennett left the class together. They had become fast friends since the boxing match. They crossed the quadrangle to their rooms in the college and Bennett stopped by the mail room before following Jake up the stairs to his room.

"Any mail for Young, sir?" asked Bennett.

The mail clerk looked in the post boxes along the wall.

"I think there is something," said the mail clerk, handing a letter to Bennett.

Bennett looked at the childish handwriting on the envelope. He put it in his pocket and left. Once inside his room, Bennett sat down and opened the short letter from Iris.

Dear Lieutenant,

Thank you for your news. I am well. Maman is well. We are staying in Lac-Brome. I am going to school here with the other kids. Sorry, you did not see the Queen.
Your friend,
Iris

He put down the letter and smiled at the memory of the little French-Canadian girl who had saved his life. He had written to her a few weeks ago, sending the letter c/o the Gagnon family, Lac-Brome, Province of Canada. He wasn't sure she would get it, but he had promised to keep in touch.

After he was arrested the second time with Teavis and Swager, he had spent several months in the Pied du Courant jail along with Hutchinson and Spurr, who had been arrested around the same time on the north shore of the St. Lawrence River. The new judge in the case was Judge Smith. He had been appointed by the Governor-General to retry the five raiders on the same charges as his predecessor had done back in November. Meanwhile, Eliza had returned to Vermont to be with her family while they awaited the arrival of her younger brother Byron, who had been wounded at Cedar Creek with the 8th Vermont Infantry Regiment.

In March 1865, Judge Smith issued a decision almost identical to that of Judge Coursol, claiming that the men could not be extradited under the Webster-Ashburton Treaty because they were acting on military orders from the Confederate states. They were not simply robbing banks, but were soldiers engaged in an authorized military operation against the forces of the US government. The prisoners Teavis, Spurr, Swagar, and Hutchinson were released on April 6, 1865, while the Crown pondered trying Bennett again on new charges.

Six days later, the war was over. On April 12, General Robert E. Lee surrendered his Army of Northern Virginia to Union General Ulysses S. Grant at the Appomattox Court House. Three days after that, John Wilkes Booth assassinated President Lincoln at Ford's Theater in Washington. The Union had won the war but lost its president. Nothing would ever be the same again.

The Canadian judiciary didn't give up easily and Bennett was sent to Toronto while a new judge determined what charges could be laid against him. In the summer of 1865, Bennett was finally released. He had spent almost a year fighting extradition charges and could no longer return home to Kentucky for fear of being arrested. He took the train to Montreal and decided to try to see Eliza one last time before going to Europe.

Thirty-six

Three months earlier
Stanbridge East, Quebec

Elder's Hotel looked rundown after barely one year and a change of ownership. The grey, weathered walls were almost black and looked foreboding in the light rain as Bennett Young waited in the dimly lit tavern across the street. With the end of the Civil War, farmers in Lower Canada were suffering from increased competition from producers of wheat, barley, and oats in the western states and from Upper Canada. US grain prices had dropped so much that all that remained for farmers was the local domestic market. Times were tough and small towns depended on local farm production for their well-being. Bennett sat on the porch and watched a few people saddling horses at the livery stable and loading provisions on their wagons at the store on Main Street. After a year in and out of prison, he felt great joy in observing the simple gestures of country life.

Bennett had made a practice of not arguing with fate after his experiences in the war. He was still in love with Eliza, but the chances that she still held him in esteem were low or non-existent. The rule was that people got on with their lives after disruptive events like the Civil War. An attractive young woman like Eliza would have numerous suitors in a farming community like St. Albans. He had written to her every week from jail during the first few months of his incarceration, but after he had been remanded to prison in Toronto, her letters arrived less frequently. *With his Christian upbringing, he knew that life had no value if it didn't include love. Was there a worse fate than not loving and not being loved in return?*

He had written to Eliza a week ago from Montreal and hoped to see her briefly before he left on a ship for England. He told her that he would arrive in Stanbridge East and stay at the hotel. He would wait for her for three days before he had to leave. He figured that if she was over him, she might not come at all or, if she did, he would know it immediately. He would then get on with his life wherever it might lead him.

On the second day, Eliza arrived in town in a buggy from the Stanbridge rail station. She had taken the train from St. Albans and descended at the station a few miles east of the town. In her letters, Eliza had talked about her brother's growing frustration with the medical staff at the hospital in Burlington. He blamed the amputation of his leg on the doctors at the field hospital, calling them incompetent 'sawbones'. He would soon be released, and he spent his time being pushed around the hospital's long corridors in an invalid chair.

Bennett was in his hotel room when he spotted Eliza on the street and ran out to meet her. She was wearing a paisley print skirt and bodice, with a blue bonnet.

"Eliza," he called. "You came! How are you?"

"I'm fine, Bennett."

"I was worried I'd miss you."

"I got your letter only yesterday and had to make an excuse to come north."

They fell silent for a moment, standing in the street looking at each other nervously before Bennett took her arm and her bag and they crossed the road to the hotel lobby.

"I almost didn't come, Bennett."

"Yes, but now you are here."

They sat in the hotel dining room having afternoon tea. Bennett watched Eliza play nervously with a simple pearl necklace that belonged to her mother.

"My mother says you are a hopeless case, Bennett. A Johnny Reb who can't ever come home. And now you're running away again, going overseas."

"Well, your dear mother is right, Eliza. I am a hopeless case."

"Why do you have to go to Europe, Bennett? You could study law here in Canada. They've stopped trying to arrest you."

"I want to see the world, Eliza."

"You'll probably stay there forever and won't ever come back."

Bennett put a lump of sugar in his tea and changed the subject. *There was no point in lying to her. He had no idea what his life would look like in five years.*

"How are things in St. Albans, Eliza?"

"Ma and pa are fine. We see Carl from time to time. My uncle fixed the leaky roof with the money you gave me."

"When is your brother coming home?"

"In a few weeks. I'll fetch him with the wagon. It won't be easy getting around with an artificial leg."

"He'll receive a disabled pension from the army, no doubt."

"Yes, that would help, but it won't amount to much."

"I was thinking of going to see Iris and her ma before I depart, Eliza. Perhaps we could go together."

"I need to get back, Bennett."

"We could go tomorrow and be back in two days."

"You really are attached to that child, aren't you?"

"Yes, I am. I want to know how she's doing. She saved our lives."

"Yes, she did."

Lac-Brome, Quebec

It was a warm sunny day as scores of local men wearing wide-brimmed hats, colorful bandanas, and traditional red 'ceintures fléchées' (arrowhead belts) swung their scythes in the field of golden wheat, severing five-foot arcs and collecting the stems against the snath. The scythe took the hand sickle—a tool that has been used since time immemorial—and made it larger and more efficient. At the end of the arc, a simple tip of the scythe dropped the wheat into a neat pile, heads on one end and cut stems on the other.

It was a hallucinating ballet of scythes moving slowly across the field along the banks of the Yamaska River and climbing the hill to the west. It was brutally hard work and only men who had grown up on a farm could do a long day of scything. Behind the men came the women in long dresses and bonnets, accompanied by children, who collected the sheaves in bundles and arranged them in stooks to keep the grain-heads off the ground before they were hauled away for threshing. The stooking was necessary to dry the grain while protecting it from vermin. Already half the field along the river was occupied by stooks as midday approached.

On the hill overlooking the river, near the French-style farmhouse, a long table had been set for the midday meal that the Gagnon family would provide their neighbors and friends. With the bad economy, most farmers were producing just enough to provide the basics to support their families. They grew cucumbers, melons, broccoli, cabbages, and root vegetables that could be kept for long periods. The wheat, barley, and oats were cash crops, but they were often too costly to ship to market.

As they rode up the hill to the farmhouse, Bennett and Eliza heard French voices in the fields reacting to their arrival. They rode past the main house and descended toward the river, watched closely by the workers in the field. Young Iris was now eleven years old and wearing her blonde hair in a braid down her back. She still had her tomboyish air as she carried a bundle of sheaves and placed them in a stook. She looked up and spotted the lieutenant and Eliza riding down toward her.

"*Maman,*" shouted Iris, running toward them. "*C'est le lieutenant et Eliza!*"

Bennett climbed down from his horse and Iris jumped into his arms.

"Iris, how are you?" asked Bennett.

"I'm fine, Lieutenant."

Eliza dismounted and embraced Iris. All eyes were on Iris and her English-speaking friends.

"You've grown, Iris," said Eliza. "*Vous êtes si jolie.* You are so pretty."

"Pretty?" asked Iris, who had never imagined the word could apply to her. "I'm pretty."

"Yes, you are," said Eliza. "Isn't she lovely, Bennett?"

"She certainly is," said Bennett. "We're so happy to see you again, Iris."

Iris stood apart in the tightly knit French-Canadian community where girls were supposed to be feminine and show an interest in clothes and womanly pursuits. Iris had no interest in clothes and in being fashionable. She was blunt and opinionated and would often say the most outrageous things. Agnes often recounted how *Tatie* Dorothée had raised her as a wild child in the woods of Frelighsburg. Iris could be a clumsy and unladylike child, but Bennett and Eliza loved her just as she was.

Agnes emerged from the house with a large basket of bread for the midday meal and spotted Iris talking to the lieutenant and Eliza. She came down the hill to greet them.

"I'm sorry to arrive in the middle of the harvest, Agnes," said Bennett. "We wanted to see how you were doing."

"You must be hungry," said Agnes. "Please join us for the meal, Lieutenant."

"The war is over, Agnes. I'm just plain old Bennett Young now, no longer a lieutenant. And yes, thank you. We would enjoy that."

They followed Iris and her mother up the hill to the house, leading their horses. A dozen curious children followed them.

The midday meal was a joyous family affair with a lot of laughter and jokes. There were some forty perspiring men, covered in dust from the fieldwork, sitting at the long table served by their wives and children. Bennett and Eliza sat next to Iris at one end of the table opposite Agnes and Grandpa Gagnon. Pitchers of elderberry and dandelion wine circulated among the men who talked loudly in French, laughing among themselves.

"Lieutenant, I heard from Agnes that they finally let you go," said the grandpa. "What are you going to do now that you are a free man?"

"I'm going to Ireland, sir. I hope to study the law."

"Ireland? Why not stay here and marry Eliza?"

Bennett smiled at Agnes's dad while Eliza looked away.

"He don't need no marriage advice from you, *Père*," said Agnes, raising an eyebrow.

"My Agnes just got married this summer to a man from Lac-Brome. Life is that simple, Lieutenant."

"See that quiet fella at the end of the table?" asked Agnes. "That's Antoine. He's shy and doesn't speak much English."

"Well, good for you, Agnes," said Bennett.

"How is Iris doing at school?" asked Eliza.

"Iris is a clever girl," said Agnes. "She's at the top of her class."

"Is she now?" exclaimed Eliza.

Iris smiled timidly, happy to be the center of attention.

"What do you think she'll do when she grows up?" asked Eliza.

"She won't tell me," Agnes said. "She has her secrets, don't you, Iris?"

Iris smiled, embarrassed by all the attention.

The men moved to a neighboring field in the afternoon and Bennett joined them with a scythe belonging to the Gagnon family. It had been a long time since Bennett wielded a scythe at his father's farm back in Kentucky, but it was a technique that you never completely forgot. Although scything was not as hard as a lot of traditional farm work, it put a lot of strain on one's back. In the afternoon heat, Bennett found the work to be exhausting and had to rest frequently, drinking water from a bucket carried around by the children.

The women and children followed the men, collecting and arranging the sheaves in bundles. The men and women sang a song as they worked their way across the field. It was about a man visiting his girlfriend on a Sunday. The girl refused to see him and hid in the field disguised as a doe. The man then threatened to become a hunter to hunt down the doe, and so on.

The men sang:

> *"Je me suis fait une blonde y a pas longtemps,*
> *J'irai la voir dimanche, dimanche j'irai,*
> *Je ferai la demande à ma bien-aimée."*

The women sang:

> *"Ah ! si tu viens dimanche, j'n'y serai pas,*
> *Car je me ferai biche dans un beau champ:*
> *De moi tu n'auras pas de contentement."*

The men sang:

> *"Ah! si tu te mets biche dans un beau champ,*
> *Je me ferai chasseur pour te chasser :*
> *Je chasserai la biche, ma bien-aimée."*

Thirty-seven

At the house, a dozen women in long dresses and bonnets sat in the shade spinning flax, some using spinning wheels and others using drop spindles and distaffs. As they worked, the women talked endlessly, telling funny stories in French. Iris sat beside Eliza using a drop spindle to spin the flax. They laughed as they worked together. From time to time, Eliza got up to break the flax on a wooden contraption that separated the woody core or boon, which fell away, leaving the long, flexible flax fibers intact. After the harvest, the women soaked the flax in pond water for a week to free the fiber from the flax stalks. Then came the drying and breaking until the flax was ready for spinning.

During a break in the spinning, Iris showed Eliza around the house. Iris slept in a room at the top of the house with half a dozen young girls and boys, the children of various aunts and uncles living near the Gagnon family home. There was a cry of alarm from the kitchen. A woman suddenly appeared on the landing, calling for Iris. The child followed her down to the kitchen, where a small boy was crying and bleeding from a cut on his arm.

"*Peux-tu arrêter le sang, Iris? Robert a été blessé par ma faucille,*" said the mother. "Can you stop the bleeding? Robert was playing with my sickle."

Eliza saw Iris sit down quietly near young Robert and concentrated all her attention on the boy, who looked despondently at the wound on his arm. A few minutes later, the ordeal was over. Robert had stopped bleeding and his mother had returned from the pump with fresh water to clean the wound.

They left at dawn the following day just as the sun rose over the fields. It was going to be another lovely summer day. Bennett saddled up the horses and brought them around to the house. Eliza and Iris emerged from the house dressed for the journey. After Agnes had suggested that Iris needed to improve her English, Eliza had invited her to visit her family in Vermont. Iris was overjoyed. Agnes had insisted that Iris help with the household chores and make herself useful during her stay. She was to return in two weeks after the harvest was complete and school resumed. Bennett had topped up Iris's educational endowment from the stolen greenbacks and had given Eliza a generous sum to cover Iris's travel expenses.

They set off for Stanbridge East, with Iris sitting behind Bennett and Eliza following in his tracks. Iris loved to talk and, after a time, Bennett found her seemingly endless stream of chatter quite tiring, and tactfully suggested to Eliza that she might like to ride with her for a while. Iris transferred to Eliza's horse, and the girls chatted the hours away before lunch.

It was late afternoon by the time Bennett and Eliza arrived at Stanbridge Station to catch the Central Vermont train, which ran north to Saint-Jean and Montreal, and south to Burlington. They crossed the tracks to the western platform and waited for the train to pull in. It was a tearful separation for Eliza and Bennett. Eliza doubted she would ever see him again. Bennett embraced her, reminding himself not to make any promises he couldn't keep. He released Eliza and gave Iris a big hug. His fear of losing Eliza and his doubts about leaving were written on his face.

"Are you lonely, weary, and sad, Lieutenant?" asked Iris with a playful air.

Bennett recognized the phrase from a popular Civil War poem by Lt. Seth Wallace Cobb.

"Yes, my dear," he said with a sorrowful look. "I'm lonely, weary, and sad."

Eliza fought back tears as Bennett and Iris gleefully recited the poem together.

> *"I'm thinking of thee in this twilight hour,*
> *And I'm lonely, weary, and sad,*
> *For the day is done and the night has come.*
> *And there's nothing to make me glad."*

They stood there in silence as the train pulled in and it was time to get on board. Then Eliza nudged Iris toward the steps.

"Write to me, Bennett," she said, kissing him, "and send me some lovely poems."

"I'll write to you both," said Bennett, smiling. He watched as Eliza scrambled on board after Iris.

They found a seat just as the train started to move. Eliza opened a window so they could lean out and wave goodbye to Bennett. They waved until he disappeared from view.

As the train wound its way south to the Vermont border, Eliza turned to Iris with a serious air.

"You mustn't tell my brother about Bennett," Eliza cautioned Iris. "He wouldn't approve."

Iris looked perplexed. She loved Bennett as much as Eliza did.

"Byron was a soldier in the Union Army and fought against the Rebels," Eliza explained. "My ma and pa have both met Bennett, but they will never talk about him. You must not say a word about Bennett to anyone in Vermont. It will be our secret."

"Are you in love with him, Eliza?"

Eliza remained silent. She hardly knew how to reply to such a question from an eleven-year-old. *There was that fear again, the fear of rejection and unrequited love, the fear of unfamiliar feelings welling up in her heart. She had never met a man like Bennett before.*

"When I see you look at him," said Iris. "I think you are in love."

"Stop it, please," said Eliza. "Of course I like him. He is a good man."

"I like him too, Eliza," said Iris. "He's the best papa in the world."

Eliza looked at Iris, astonished by her comment. The child had already adopted Bennett and was not going to give him up.

"But Iris, sometimes men don't come home."

"Don't worry, Eliza. He'll come home. You'll see him again."

St. Albans, Vermont

Within the hour, they arrived at the train station in St. Albans, and Eliza hired a buggy to drive them home. The town looked a lot like it had a year earlier, except for one thing. There were homeless veterans everywhere, standing outside the bars and hotels in town with caps in their hands, looking for handouts. Some had amputated limbs and others had horrific head wounds. There was not much work in St. Albans for able-bodied men, let alone disabled veterans. The general feeling in town was one of sympathy for the veterans, but time would soon work against them. It wouldn't be long before the population would turn against the 'lazy' amputees haunting the public space, cap in hand.

It was just getting dark as Eliza's pa showed Iris around the farm. The sky was pink and the foliage on the trees was ablaze with the fall colors. They walked through the fields down to the Missisquoi River, where a herd of Merino sheep was grazing in the long grass. The sheep had been washed and sheared in the summer and were marked with a painted brand. The rocky landscape of the hills around St. Albans was perfect for the Merinos. Their characteristic cleft lips allowed them to graze on just about anything.

Vermont was home to more than a million sheep in the mid-nineteenth century and they were raised for their wool, which was much softer on the skin than other types of wool. Merino wool soon became the standard for expensive woolen goods, but by the Civil War, the industry was in decline after the loss of protective tariffs and competition in the West. The war brought some relief with the need for uniforms and blankets. Wool was going at a dollar a pound as it replaced articles formerly made of cotton that were no longer available in the North.

The harvest was over in Vermont, but there would always be work around the farm as the Miller family prepared for the long winter. Behind the barn, Carl was busy chopping wood and waved to Eliza as she went to talk to her mother on the porch.

"She's that little French-Canadian girl you talked about," said Eliza's mother, spinning flax with one hand on her distaff and the other on the spinning wheel.

"Her name is Iris, Ma. You remember I told you I met her in Frelighsburg with the lieutenant?"

"What's she doing here?"

"She wants to improve her English. She won't be staying long. Her mother will come and fetch her in two weeks."

"You should take her with you when you visit Byron at the hospital."

"Yes, I was thinking of doing that."

"How's that old boyfriend of yours doing?"

"He's gone, Ma. Gone to Europe."

"Gone for good, maybe?"

"I don't know, Ma."

Burlington, Vermont

The old Marine Hospital was located in a large, Italianate-style brick building with a spacious verandah off the Shelburne Road. The two-story hospital commanded a fine view of the town of Burlington and beautiful Lake Champlain, which ran south into Lake George and north into Canada. The rooms were high and airy, with closets and bathrooms on each floor.

Byron had been wounded at Cedar Creek in the Shenandoah Valley. After the amputation of his leg, he was transported by train north to the Sloan Hospital in Montpelier for further treatment. As his health improved, they moved him to the Marine Hospital so he would be closer to his family. There were few deaths among the war wounded in Vermont's hospitals because the patients had been chosen for their ability to survive the journey north. Soldiers with important head or chest wounds were rarely sent north.

Iris sat in the waiting room near the front desk while she waited for Eliza to return from the administration office upstairs. Her brother was being sent home, and Eliza needed to sign the papers for his release. The doctors' offices and the surgery were in the back of the building on the first floor. From her seat in the waiting room, Iris could hear the voice of a man screaming in pain, followed by the angry voices of the medical staff. The receptionist got up and left her desk, passing through the swinging doors to investigate.

Iris was curious and had nothing else to do, so she followed the woman through the door, where she could better hear the screams. The man was in great pain, and the doctor was trying to calm him down, but it was not working. She peered down the long corridor leading to the doctor's office and tip-toed down the hall.

"You are hurting me!" the patient screamed.

"*Parbleu!*" said Dr. Dubois. "*SVP, Monsieur, arrêtez vous un instant.*"

"Doctor, he's going to open up the wound, pulling at the stump like that," said the nurse.

"Don't touch me," yelled the man. "Just don't touch me."

Iris sneaked a peek inside the office, where a young man was sitting on the examination table as a doctor probed the stump of his amputated leg. With every exploratory tap, the young man's body contorted in pain.

"I see nothing wrong, sir," said the doctor, clearly mystified. "There's no infection."

"The muscles are clenched so tight," said the man. "It feels like it's on fire."

"The surgeon did a good job. I see no evidence…"

"*Vous ne voyez pas qu'il se tord de douleur, Docteur,*" blurted little Iris from the doorway.

"*Qu'est-ce que vous faîtes là?*" asked the doctor. "What is that girl doing in here?"

The nurse looked confused by the presence of Iris in the doorway and the exchange in French.

"He is in pain, Doctor," said Iris. "You must do something."

"Get that kid out of here," ordered Dr. Dubois, who stood up to fetch a bottle of laudanum.

"Come along, miss. You have no business in here," said the nurse as she tried to drag the little scamp away, but Iris twisted out of her grasp and darted back to the stricken young man.

She gently put her hand on the soldier's stump and left it there for a long moment. The soldier felt the warmth of the child's hand and the burning sensation began to subside.

After a minute or two, Dr. Dubois reappeared with a syringe of laudanum and saw Iris with her hand on the young man's leg.

"I told you. Get her out of here!" he roared at the nurse.

The flustered nurse grabbed Iris and hustled her out of the room. Dubois prepared the syringe and turned back to the patient, who was breathing normally and had closed his eyes, looking calm and composed.

"This should help reduce the pain," said Dubois.

"Thank you, Doctor," said Byron, shaking his head, "but I feel better already."

The doctor was astonished by the transformation in the young man's demeanor. He looked relaxed as if an immense weight had been removed from his shoulders.

"Don't you dare go in there again, miss!" the nurse scolded Iris as she marched her back to the waiting room.

"He was in pain, miss," Iris protested.

"No, he wasn't," the nurse snapped. "He was faking it! They're all faking it to get the laudanum. Don't trouble your pretty head, young lady."

"What's going on here?" Eliza demanded from the doorway.

"Your daughter's been causing trouble in the doctor's office, ma'am. You should keep her on a tight leash."

The nurse glared at Eliza and returned to the doctor's office.

"I was not," protested Iris. "I wasn't causing trouble."

"Iris, what's going on?" asked Eliza.

Eliza was about to reply when the same young man appeared near the front desk, walking unsteadily on his artificial limb.

"Byron, how'd it go?" asked Eliza.

"There you are," Byron said, smiling at Iris. "You are my guardian angel."

Eliza looked at her brother in total incomprehension.

"I had an attack in Dr. Dubois' office, Eliza. Then, this kid came in and helped me get over it."

"Are you feeling better?" asked Iris.

"Yes, I am now. Thanks to this young lady."

"Byron, this is Iris. I told you about her. She's French-Canadian."

"Hello, Iris. Nice to meet you."

Iris nodded timidly.

"Iris, what were you doing in the doctor's office?" demanded Eliza.

"I heard your brother cry out in pain, Eliza. I thought I could help by laying my hands on his leg. My uncle lost an arm in an accident on his farm. He often complained of a burning pain, just like your brother."

"So, how long will you be staying with us?" asked Byron.

"Two weeks. My *maman* is coming to get me."

"Let's go home," said Eliza as the angry nurse reappeared in the reception area with a husky young orderly.

Outside the hospital, Byron struggled to climb into the buggy. He had to swing his artificial leg over the side of the carriage before he could sit down next to Iris. Eliza took the reins, and they drove off, heading toward Burlington and the lake.

"How are you adjusting to the artificial leg?" asked Eliza.

"It's a Palmer, made in New Hampshire," Byron said. "It cost seventy-five dollars, paid for by the government. The man came to the hospital for the fitting. He says Palmer's legs are the best. I don't know, it sure took me a lot of time to get used to wearing it."

"So have you thought about getting your disability pay, Byron?"

"I ain't gonna depend on no handouts, Eliza. I can move around slowly. I can get work just like before the war."

"It's not so easy now that the war is over."

"I talked to some fellas at the hospital. They said the foundry will be taking us back, so I won't be needin' no disability."

"I don't know. You should go in and talk to the foreman."

"It's gonna be fine, Sis. You'll see."

Iris smiled at her brother. She loved him dearly, but sometimes he had his head in the clouds and couldn't adjust to the practicalities of life.

"Why does she smile all the time?" asked Byron.

"She's a sweetie, Byron," Eliza laughed. "You'll have to smile more to keep up with her."

Thirty-eight

St. Albans, Vermont

In the night, Iris heard a whimpering animal sound coming from downstairs. At first, she thought it must be the dog that had been let into the kitchen and wanted to go out. The sound started and stopped, and then went on for a while before there was the occasional muffled cry, that sounded almost human. She sat up in bed next to Eliza.

"Go back to sleep, Iris," said Eliza. "I'll go have a look."

Eliza put on her robe and headed downstairs, closing the door behind her. Iris fell asleep again but was soon awakened by Eliza's mother, who tiptoed into the room and stopped near the bed.

"Are you awake, my dear?" she asked Iris. "Please come. Byron thinks you can help him."

Iris got up quickly and followed Eliza's mother down to the kitchen in her bedclothes. Byron was lying on a daybed in the small room off the kitchen. His artificial leg lay on the floor near the bed. He was in terrible pain again and looked ashamed to have to ask Iris for help.

"I'm sorry, Iris, to get you up," said Byron. "You were sleeping?"

"No, I'm fine," said Iris, standing near the bed. "Can you sit up, please?"

Byron sat up and Iris squatted, taking his stump in both her hands. She remained immobile for several minutes as Mrs. Miller prayed for relief for her son. After a few minutes, Byron started to relax.

"She's done it again," he smiled gratefully. "Thank you, Iris."

"How long have you had the gift?" asked Mrs. Miller.

"About a year or two," said Iris. "It started with my uncle."

"She can stop the bleeding too," added Eliza. "It's quite remarkable. I saw her do it when we were at Lac-Brome."

"Well, we love her, don't we, Eliza?" said Mrs. Miller, taking Iris in her arms. "Thank you so much, my dear."

Byron was so exhausted that he fell asleep almost immediately. The family moved to the kitchen to let him sleep. Mr. Miller put the kettle on the hob for tea and asked Iris about her folks in Canada.

"So what does your dad do, Iris?"

"She doesn't know him. Iris was born out of wedlock, Pa," said Eliza.

"I'm sorry, miss. I didn't know."

"I have another papa now, Mr. Miller," said Iris with great pride. "He's my real papa. His name is Bennett."

The Millers shared a glance, knowing full well who Bennett was. Eliza smiled but remained silent as her mother went to make the tea and find something sweet for Iris.

"What do we know about the pain?" asked Mr. Miller.

"A doctor at the hospital explained it to me. Amputees get this sensation of pain in a missing limb," said Eliza. "They call it 'phantom limb pain' and it's quite common. At the hospital, they treat it with laudanum and alcohol."

"Does it help?" asked Mr. Miller.

"They say it helps," said Eliza.

"How is that even possible?" Mrs. Miller asked as she placed the tea tray on the table. "The pain, I mean. How can it exist if the limb isn't there?"

Two days later, Eliza drove Byron and Iris into town. The plan was for Byron to go to the foundry to look for work while Eliza and Iris went shopping. After that, they planned to meet in town for lunch at the café near the foundry, so Byron would not have to walk too far on his artificial leg.

After visiting Miss Beattie's Millinery shop where they looked at the new fall dress fabrics, Eliza and Iris left through the alley and arrived at the café well in time to catch up with Byron.

"St. Albans is a pretty place, *Tatie* Eliza," said Iris. "I have never been in a town this big."

"It is quite big for Vermont," said Eliza.

"I've never seen so many shops and cafés. Back home, we don't have many shops and the towns are so small."

The waitress arrived with the menu and Eliza decided to spoil Iris and ordered two Wiener Schnitzels, the house specialty. The food was delicious and young Iris was sorely tempted by the apple strudel, another specialty of the Viennese owners.

"Go on, Iris," said Eliza, smiling indulgently. "Try it."

"Are you sure, *Tatie*?" asked Iris.

"Of course, I'm sure, Iris. The lieutenant is paying and wants you to eat well. He said you were too thin when we met him in Lac-Brome."

Eliza waved to the waitress, who brought over the strudel. While Iris tucked in, Eliza looked out the window to see whether Byron was coming their way, but there was no sign of him.

They waited for another hour and then left the café to go looking for Byron in the streets. They went by the foundry, but the guard at the gate told them that Byron had left an hour ago. They walked around town, but Byron was nowhere to be seen. They reluctantly returned home to announce that Byron had gone missing.

"We looked everywhere, Pa," said Eliza.

"He can't have gotten far, Eliza, with that leg of his," commented her father. "He's probably in some bar somewhere."

"What are we going to do?" asked her mother.

"I'll go in later and bring him home."

"So you had a nice time, then?"

"We had a lovely time, Ma," said Eliza. "We went to that Viennese place."

It was after seven when Miller had finished his chores around the farm and took off in the buggy. It was a Friday night, and the bars were buzzing with lots of young men and painted ladies, looking to turn a trick. The men were farmers or war veterans drinking away their disability pay, or losing it laying bets. Five-card stud poker and dice games like Chuck-a-luck or Hazard were popular among the crowd, and the women liked to hang close to the high rollers, hoping to snare a customer.

The older men talked with reverence about their time on the battlefields in the South while the younger men complained about how miserable life had been in the army. They were an unhappy lot because they had no way of supporting a family in the rotten post-war economy.

As Miller came into the bar, he spotted Ezra dealing a game of Chuck-a-luck with five men, including several veterans of the 8th Vermont Regiment. Chuck-a-luck was a game of chance and favored the dealer rather than the players. One man had only one hand while his amputated limb was pinned inside an empty sleeve. The game fascinated the men. There was a cloth marked with six spaces numbered one to six on the table. Players put money on their chosen numbers and hoped their number would come up with each throw of the dice.

"You seen my Byron?" asked Miller.

"Yeah, I saw him earlier, sir," said Ezra. "Place your bets, fellas."

"Where'd he go, Ezra?"

"He had a brick in his hat, sir," said Ezra. "Gone out back in the alley to get some air."

"Go on, Ezra. Throw the dice, dammit," said Newton Landry, a brash young farmer who loved the game and the chance to make a winning bet.

Ezra rolled three dice. Two players won some money, while the other three lost their bets. Miller went out the backdoor into the cold night air but couldn't see his son anywhere. He walked north and discovered Byron sprawled on a wooden bench near a young black woman in the shadow of an overhanging roof. The woman was smoking a clay pipe while Byron was clutching his artificial leg in his arms.

"Byron, let's go, Son," said Miller. "You've had enough to drink."

"This is Ginny, Pa," said Byron, slurring his words. "She works at the hotel."

"Evening," said Miller to the young woman.

"Good evening, sir," said Ginny in a Jamaican accent.

"Time to come home, Son. Meet me in the street out front."

Miller said nothing more and headed back to the bar. As he entered, he heard angry words exchanged at Ezra's table. A man was complaining about losing his disability money at the game.

"Son of a bitch," the man roared. "Them dice are loaded. You stole my money!"

"Ain't no way," Ezra told him, unmoved by the accusation, "to load the dice in Chuck-a-luck. Your number comes up, and you win. It's that simple."

"He's right, Billie," a gambler retorted. "It can't be done."

For a moment, it looked like Billie was going to take a swing at Ezra. None of the players were on his side, so he just stood up and told them all to go to hell as he staggered away.

Miller watched him go, then looked around the room. *The war had changed everything,* he thought, *and not for the better. The drinking and the gambling in this town had gotten a lot worse after the veterans came home.*

He headed outside to wait for his son in the street.

Thirty-nine

It was almost noon the next day when Eliza went looking for her brother. He had returned late the previous night, but his father had refused him entry into the house because of his drunkenness. Eliza found him asleep in the barn when she went looking for him with Iris.

"Dad told me about last night," said Eliza. "How are you feeling?"

"I'm fine, Sis. How's my little Iris doing?" asked Byron, smiling at the girl.

"Iris was asking after you."

"Well, little sister, I'm doin' just fine," said Byron, who strapped on his artificial leg, and pulled down his pant leg to cover it.

"So what happened at the foundry?"

"They ain't hiring, Sis. They don't need nobody, no casters or mould makers. They've laid off lots of people."

"Times are bad, Byron. You could learn a new trade."

"Who's gonna hire a one-legged veteran like me, Sis?"

"I don't know, Byron, but there are sit-down jobs you could do. You've got two hands and you're smart. You could work as a clerk in a shop or as a bookkeeper. There are lots of jobs that you could do."

"Yeah, well, I ain't gonna be no clerk, that's for sure," said Byron, as he stood up and left the barn in a huff.

Eliza looked at Iris and put her arm around her.

"He'll come around, Iris. You'll see. He'll find something."

When Eliza and Iris returned to the house, Byron was arguing with his dad in the kitchen. They sat on the porch but didn't dare enter the house.

"You have no choice, Byron," said his father.

"I ain't gonna collect no disability pay," Byron replied. "No way."

"There's no shame in it," said his mother. "You fought for the Union.

They owe you."

"It's $15 for a leg or a foot," said his father, "and it's paid every month. You earned it."

"I seen the amputees in the bars in town, Pa. Nobody respects them. They just take their money and laugh at them."

"Nobody is laughing at you, Byron," said Mrs. Miller. "We're proud of you, aren't we, Pa?"

"We're real proud of you, Son. You survived the war, now you gotta find a way to live through the peace."

Byron shrugged and retired to the small bedroom, shutting the door.

Two days later, Byron took the buggy and went into town to sign up for his Union pension at the post office. As he exited the building, he saw a gathering of angry men in the street near the tavern. He had to fight his way through the hubbub to get inside. The regulars at the bar were incensed and yelling at one another, many teary-eyed and others drunk.

Byron soon learned that his friend Ezra had been murdered in the alley. His body had been discovered in the early morning hours. The veterans of the 8th Vermont Regiment were furious that one of their own had been murdered and his money stolen after all he had suffered in the war. Byron left them and went into the alley to have a look at the body. Ezra was under a muslin sheet. A deputy guarded his body after the town doctor had examined it.

"What happened to Ezra?" asked Byron.

"Someone knifed him and took his money," said the deputy.

"You find the knife?"

"Nope."

"Mind if I have a look?"

"Go ahead."

Byron pulled back the sheet to reveal a wicked chest wound. Ezra had been stabbed through the heart and probably died instantly. Byron knelt to get a better look. He had seen lots of dead soldiers during the war and there was something familiar about the puncture wound. It had a triangular shape, which was unusual for a civilian weapon.

"You're looking for a bayonet," said Byron to the deputy.

"What you sayin', Son?"

"I'm sayin' it looks like a bayonet wound. I've seen enough of 'em during the war."

"You think so?"

"Yeah, it will have a socket at the end. It fits over the end of a musket."

"Well, if that don't beat the Dutch. Killed by a veteran?"

"Looks like it."

Byron returned to the bar and was soon accepting drinks from his friends. He knew a lot of the men. Some had served in his unit and others he had seen on the battlefield. The killer could be any one of these men; they had all lost money playing dice with Ezra. He looked around at the familiar faces, but couldn't imagine any of them being the killer.

"Ezra was nothin' but a bottom-line sharpie," said one man. "He was a dealer. He was winnin' all the time."

"Goddamit, Allan! Ezra was no sharpie. He was a good man," said another.

"You ain't gonna make no spondulicks playin' Chuck-a-luck in this town," said a bearded newcomer.

"He was killed with a bayonet," said Byron. "Stabbed to death by a soldier."

"What you saying, Byron?" asked a drunk.

"Cause I seen it. The triangular shape of the entry wound."

"None of us would kill Ezra, Byron. No way. We fought with him. He was one of us."

"I know that, but the bayonet doesn't lie."

"He was a good man, had a wife and child," said another.

A chill fell over the group. Every man in the room was wondering who might be next on the killer's list.

A memory came back to Byron from the war. The day before the battle at Cedar Creek, a soldier on guard duty in his company had been murdered with a bayonet, just as Ezra had been. His sergeant thought a Johnny Reb sneaking around the perimeter of the camp had committed the murder. Byron had forgotten the incident, because the day after, he was having his leg amputated at a field hospital.

When Byron arrived home several hours later, he was suffering such terrible pain in his leg that he couldn't get down from the buggy. Eliza and Iris were spinning flax on the porch, but pride prevented him from calling for help. He removed his artificial leg, thinking that somehow it might relieve the pain, but it had no effect at all.

"Byron!" Eliza called.

He could hear his sister and Iris getting up and coming around to have a look. Eliza quickly took charge of the situation.

"Iris, see what you can do," Eliza said with calm reassurance at the sight of her brother grimacing as he lay on the front seat.

"Ask him to sit up, please," said Iris.

"Of course, Iris."

"Sit up, Byron," Eliza ordered her brother as she climbed up on the buggy and reached for his hand.

"Iris says you gotta sit up."

Between Eliza pulling with one hand and Byron pushing with the other, he sat upright. He refused to cry out, even though the pain was excruciating. Iris put her hands on his stump and a smile passed over Byron's face as he felt the pain going away. They sat there in silence for a good five minutes before Iris removed her hands and the pain was gone.

Eliza helped her brother down from the buggy, and he hopped over to a chair on the porch. He sat down heavily as his mother appeared.

"What happened to you?" asked his mother.

"I'm okay, Ma, thanks to Iris."

"He was having an attack and couldn't get down off the buggy," said Eliza. "Iris made it go away."

"Well, isn't she the splendid child?" exclaimed his mother.

"Is Pa around?" asked Byron. "I have some news."

"He's in the barn, Byron."

"I'll get him," said Eliza, leaving the porch to find her father.

Ten minutes later, Miller arrived in a dirty pair of overalls and sat down next to Byron on the porch. Iris and Eliza had gone into the kitchen with Mrs. Miller for a cup of tea and a treat for the child.

"I signed up for the disability pay," Byron told his father.

"Good to hear, Son."

"I've got some bad news, Pa. Ezra is dead. He was murdered. Somebody stabbed him to death in the alley during the night."

"What? That's just terrible! Ezra's a good boy. We know his folks."

"It's true."

"Why would anyone want to kill him? It doesn't make sense."

"Well, someone did. The sheriff is looking for a man with a bayonet. That can only be a veteran, maybe someone with the 8th Vermont."

"You think so?"

"I ain't never seen no bayonet outside of the army, Pa. It has to be a veteran."

In the afternoon, Agnes arrived in St. Albans by train to fetch her daughter. The driver dropped her off at the Miller farmhouse and Iris ran out to greet her mother. She was looking forward to seeing her friends and returning to school in Lac-Brome. The Miller family would miss Iris, whom they had adopted as their own.

Mrs. Miller prepared a special meal to celebrate Agnes' arrival. She worked for hours in the kitchen, cooking a rack of lamb dipped in a blend of mustard, garlic, and herbs along with tomatoes and potatoes from the farm. It was a special occasion, and her husband proudly brought out a couple of bottles of his best elderberry wine to go along with it. The evening meal was a joyful moment for the Miller family and their guests.

In the morning, as Agnes and Iris ate their breakfast and the conversation turned to work around the farm, Iris got up and went to see Byron in his room.

"How you doin', little sister?" said Byron, who stopped talking when he saw the girl's serious air.

"I can help you, Byron," said Iris, "with the pain."

"I know you can."

"If you feel the pain coming on, you just have to think about me and I will know it is you."

"You can stop the pain from afar?"

"Yes, it works with my uncle, so it should work with you. Do you understand what I'm saying?"

Byron wasn't sure he did, but then he didn't understand how Iris could make the pain go away just by touching him. Even if what she was saying sounded impossible, it wouldn't hurt to humor her after all she had done for him.

"I think so," he said, smiling at the girl's grim expression.

"If you feel the pain coming on, stop what you are doing and sit down in a quiet place. Then think about me sitting next to you. I will know it is you and stop the pain."

An hour later, Eliza and Byron drove Agnes and Iris in the buggy to catch the train. They escorted them to the platform and waited until the train arrived. They embraced the mother and daughter and helped them climb aboard. Eliza knew she was going to miss Iris. The presence of the child had been a godsend for her brother and a welcome distraction for her when her mind wandered and she thought about Bennett.

Half an hour later, Eliza and Byron were on their way home when they were stopped by two men on horseback. One man was the deputy who Byron had seen guarding Ezra's body in the alley.

"Pull over, ma'am," said the deputy.

Eliza stopped the buggy, and the deputy climbed down off his horse and came over.

"Mr. Miller, you are under arrest."

"You must be mistaken, sir," said Eliza. "This is my brother. He can't be under arrest."

"I'm sorry, ma'am," said the deputy. "He has to come with us."

"Why am I under arrest, sir?" asked Byron.

"Murder."

"Murder, but that is not possible," exclaimed Byron. "I haven't killed anyone since the war."

"Doesn't matter one bit, sir. The constable has some questions for you. Now turn the buggy around."

Eliza did as she was told. Then the deputy tied his horse to the buggy and climbed in next to Byron. Eliza whipped the horse, and they headed back to town while the second deputy brought up the rear.

Forty

Dublin, Ireland

Dear Bennett,

Byron was arrested yesterday, just after Agnes and Iris took the train to return to Lac-Brome. They suspect him of killing a friend of his, Ezra Williams, who fought with him in the 8th Vermont Regiment. Ezra was stabbed to death behind a bar with what appears to be a bayonet. But my brother would never kill anyone. He is not capable of such violence.

We had a lovely week with Iris, but the death of Ezra has turned our lives into a nightmare. I'll write again when I have more to tell you.
Your affectionate friend,
Eliza

In a darkened pub, Bennett sat reading Eliza's worrisome letter while his American friends were drinking beer and having a good time.

"You know what was the greatest advantage of the Confederacy?" asked Jake Doyle with a grin. "I've always been a fervent believer in Confederate superiority."

"The army?" ventured Bennett.

"Nope," said Jake.

"The generals? Robert E. Lee, Stonewall Jackson, J.E.B. Stuart," said another Southern boy.

"The great people of the South," said another man.

"That may be true, but no. The railroads," replied Jake. "And why is that, gentlemen?"

"I suppose it was the fastest way to move men and supplies," suggested Bennett.

"Yep, give the man a prize. Richmond was connected by rail to every part of the Confederacy. Remember the Richmond and Danville line in Virginia. That was 140 miles of track."

"I read that there's a boom in railway construction going on in the States."

"You're referring to the Great Transcontinental Railroad, Bennett," said Jake. "We'll soon be able to cross the country from Chicago to California. President Johnson's government is pushing hard to complete the rail link."

"Doesn't your brother work for the New York Central, Jake?" asked another Southerner.

"Yeah, he does. The New York Central runs from Albany to Buffalo and there is talk of merging it with the Hudson River Railroad. Imagine that, going from NYC to Buffalo by train."

The young law students were intrigued. They came from wealthy Eastern families and had lived privileged lives, never having to do a day of work in their short lives, but there was Doyle, an Irishman, telling them about career opportunities beyond their wildest dreams. For many of them, their sole ambition had been to work as a clerk in their father's firm. Working for the railroads sounded much more exciting.

"You're lucky, Jake. You can go home whenever you want," said one Southern boy.

"Not to worry, gentlemen," said Jake. "Johnson will soon have a pardon in the works for all of you."

"I don't know," said Bennett. "It could take time to forget about the past."

"Johnson can't afford to wait, Bennett. He needs people to rebuild the South. It's gonna take lots of people to do that. Lots of lawyers like you fellas to do all the contracting work."

A hearty cheer went up from the dozen young men in the pub and a new round of drinks was ordered at the bar.

St. Albans, Vermont

"Miller, you told my deputy that it was a bayonet that killed Ezra Williams," said Paul Harris, the old town constable with grey mutton chops and a handlebar mustache. "How could you know that?"

They were sitting in Harris' office at the back of the dry goods store. The walls were dark pine with deer antlers and moose heads, while behind Harris there was a dusty, old bookcase full of ancient law journals. Byron sat in a chair opposite the constable while a deputy stood inside the door, keeping a watch on him.

"It was obvious, sir," replied Byron. "The triangular shape of the wound."

"Are you some kind of expert on war wounds, young man?" asked Harris.

"No, sir, but I've seen a lot of them after three years of war," said Byron.

Harris was a wily old bastard, thought Byron. *Maybe he is trying to fit me up for the crime.*

"As the town constable, Governor Smith has urged me to find this killer before he kills again."

"All I can tell you, sir, is that I saw a similar stabbing one night in the Shenandoah before the Cedar Creek battle. The man was on guard duty when he was stabbed to death with what looked like a bayonet. My sergeant said it was probably a Johnny Reb, prowling around the perimeter of our camp."

"So you think the deaths might be linked?"

Byron stared at him, dumbfounded. The two incidents were separated by a thousand miles. A year had passed, and the war was over. There could be no connection between the incidents.

"Of course not, sir," said Byron. "It was just that I remembered the incident and the triangular wound. That's all."

"We checked with your regiment. There were twenty men in your platoon at Cedar Creek, including Williams and Baker."

"Yes, sir. I knew them both."

"Baker died a few weeks ago. He was run over by a wagon loaded with corn. And now we have Sergeant Williams stabbed to death with a bayonet. So if you didn't kill Sergeant Williams yourself, then you must know who did."

"I have no idea, sir."

"Come on, Miller. You must know something. Tell me about the 8th Vermont?"

"Well, sir, we were mustered in February '62 and sent to Louisiana.

We served in the Red River campaign, Port Hudson, and later in Virginia."

"So you were with Sheridan's forces when he laid waste to the Shenandoah Valley?"

"Yes, sir. I was at the Smithfield Crossing, Berryville, and the Third Winchester battles in August and September."

"I heard you fellas burned crops and farms on your way south. You were making a thorough nuisance of yourselves?"

"Yes, sir. We burned barns and crops, and we slaughtered thousands of sheep, hogs, and cattle. Those were our orders."

"Was everyone in your platoon happy with the orders?"

"No, sir. We hated destroying the property of those farmers. They were good people, just like here in Vermont. What were their families going to eat over the winter months and where would they stay? It was inhuman. Sheridan was an ass. We hated the bastard."

"But you were winning the war?"

"Yes, we were, but we were doing terrible things. A man in our company was tried for the rape of a white woman at Winchester. I remember her name. Mary Dryden. She had a fourteen-year-old boy named John who would come around the camp with milk and eggs to sell. He was a nice kid. His ma did the sewing and laundry for our regiment and we used her house and stable as a temporary hospital for our wounded."

"What happened to the rapist?"

"I would think he was locked up and condemned to hard labor or the firing squad. Desertion or murder got you the firing squad."

"Do you remember his name?"

"No, sir. All I know is that it happened a week before the big battle."

"Was Sergeant Williams involved in the arrest?"

"Come to think of it, yes, he was. It was Ezra who found the woman. The man had tied her up with her apron strings and bound her mouth with a leather strap. Ezra freed her and took her to see Lt. Baker."

"So you don't have any further knowledge about the trial?"

"I know the man was found guilty. That's all I know. You think he's the killer?"

"I don't know. It could be a revenge killing."

Byron nodded.

"You can go, Miller."

Byron got up to leave as a young man stuck his head in the doorway.

"Hey, Miller. How are you doing with your new leg?" asked Newton Landry, whose family owned a sawmill south of St. Albans.

"I get around now, which is the important thing," replied Byron.

"Keep in touch, Miller," said the constable.

Byron waved to the men and left.

Forty-one

Dublin, Ireland

Bennett sat in his room at Trinity College, Queen's University reading Eliza's letter. She told him that Byron had been released and the constable suspected someone else of killing Ezra. She mentioned that she had gotten a letter from Iris who had enjoyed her stay and how her parents just loved the kid. She told him that her brother had come home and had a burning pain in his missing leg. and Iris had stopped it. She had no idea how she did it, but the girl was amazing. Bennett had fond memories of their lovely time together on the Gagnon farm in rural Quebec. Eliza and Iris spinning flax and laughing together. He was homesick for his parents' farm in Jessamine County in Kentucky. He worried about his parents, brothers, and sister. He wrote to his mother as often as he could, but the news was not good.

The Civil War in Kentucky had been one of quick military incursions against specific targets and sudden withdrawals with a few major battles. The war had left the state hopelessly divided against itself. Many Kentuckians balked at the freedom of their black slaves, and hatred often prevailed. After the surrender, the government in Washington imposed martial law in the state.

Bennett came out of his daydream to heavy knocking on the door to his room. He went to the door to find two burly constables in dark blue uniforms from the Dublin Metropolitan Police.

"Mr. Bennett Young?"

"Yes, sir."

"You are under arrest."

"Arrest? What have I done?" asked Bennett, astonished.

"We have orders to round up all the Americans in the college, sir. You must come with us."

They cuffed Bennett like a common criminal and pushed him down the stairs and out of the building. Bennett had read in the newspaper about the four Fenian leaders—Charles Joseph Kickham, John O'Leary, Thomas Clarke Luby, and Jeremiah O'Donovan Rossa—who had been arrested in September. They had been sentenced to long prison terms for publishing treasonable articles in *The Irish People's* newspaper. Ireland was in a state of extreme tension and a nationwide uprising against the British was coming. Most of the funds to finance it were coming from sympathizers in the United States.

The Fenians were a secret organization known as the Irish Republican Brotherhood. The term Fenian came from the Irish Gaelic term *Fianna Eirionn*—a band of mythological warriors. In the United States, the Fenians operated freely and aimed to secure Ireland's independence from Britain. It was believed the Fenians in Ireland numbered over fifty thousand men, including some eight thousand who were soldiers serving in the British Army. In response to the perceived threat, the authorities were moving against the brotherhood and arresting as many senior leaders as they could.

Bennett Young was thrown into a room with a dozen other American men of all ages, some of whom were students at the university and others who were businessmen with American connections. Shortly after he arrived, he saw a policeman lead Jake Doyle down a corridor into a tiny conference room.

"Jake," called Bennett to his friend. "What's going on?"

"It looks like we Americans are all suspect, Bennett. They're looking everywhere for Fenians."

"How long will they be keeping us here?"

"I have no idea. I heard the American Consul is on his way. We should be out of here in a couple of hours."

The Irish had suffered numerous famines under British rule, starting with the potato crop in 1845. The famine had killed over a million men, women, and children over a period of seven years. The "Great Hunger", as it was called, forced Queen Victoria and Parliament to act by repealing the Corn Laws, which made food such as corn and wheat prohibitively expensive. One of the most glaring causes of the famine was the fact that vast tracts of land belonged to absentee English landlords who rented small plots to the local population in return for labor and cash crops. The Irish often had no rights to the land they farmed nor to any improvements they might make, except in parts of the country dominated by the Protestants. They were landless serfs exploited by foreign owners. The situation had festered for over a century and now a reckoning was coming.

Burlington, Vermont

It was a bright sunny morning as Eliza drove her brother south to Burlington to make inquiries at the regimental office of the 8th Vermont. The sun shone off the lake as they rounded a turn on their way south.

"So what do you think we'll find?" asked Eliza.

Byron admired the scenery, holding his artificial leg in his hands as the buggy bounced along the rough track.

"I don't know. Harris thinks it could be anyone, but I'm not so sure. Why go after Ezra?"

"You need to be careful, Byron. Ma is worried about you."

"No need to worry, Sis," said Byron, removing a six-shot Colt Army revolver from his kit bag.

"Where'd you get that?"

"I borrowed it from a friend."

"Does it work?"

"Sure it does."

"Are you afraid of an attack?" asked Eliza.

"No, but it is always better to be prepared."

It was getting late as they arrived in town and drove along Main Street, looking for the regimental office. They found it in a dusty street behind a bank. They arrived just as a young woman in pigtails was closing up the office for the day.

"Hello, miss," said Byron. "We're looking for some information."

"Are you a veteran, sir?" asked the young woman.

"Yes, I'm with the 8th Vermont."

"Come in, sir. I'm Fabienne."

"I'm Byron Miller and this is my sister, Eliza."

"Where you folks comin' from?"

"St. Albans."

They followed Fabienne into a poorly furnished office with large wooden filing cabinets and chairs.

"What can I help you with? I see you've got your artificial leg. There's a waiting list, you know. Congress has yet to increase the funding, that's why it's so slow."

"Sorry to hear that," said Byron. "We're here for information. See, just before I was wounded at Cedar Creek, a man in our company was found guilty of raping a white woman in Winchester, Virginia. We figured you might have some information on that."

"When did it happen?"

"September '64."

Fabienne shook her head.

"I'm sorry, sir."

"You have nothing about the trial?"

"During the war, we had reports from the front coming in every month. But somebody broke into the office a few weeks ago and took the reports from September through October. I can't help you."

"Damn! You have nothing?"

"I'm so sorry, sir," said Fabienne, looking distressed. "They broke a window to get in."

"Isn't that a bit strange, miss?"

"First, we thought they had stolen something of value, but no. Nothing was missing except those reports."

"Do you have a list of the veterans in the area?" asked Eliza, exchanging a look with her brother.

"Sure, I've got a list of veterans in Burlington and St. Albans, but it's not complete."

"Doesn't matter, we'd like to take a look," said Byron.

Fabienne went to a file cabinet and pulled a register with the names of local veterans.

After ten minutes of running his finger down the names on the list, Byron stopped at the name of Joel Johnson.

"I remember Sergeant Johnson," said Byron. "He worked with Lt. Baker."

"Yeah, he's from Burlington," said Fabienne. "He's at the old Marine Hospital. I hear he's not doing so well."

At the hospital, the male nurse was happy to take the visitors up to see Sergeant Johnson in the ward on the second floor.

"Joel will be happy to have visitors," said the nurse. "He doesn't get many. His family never comes."

"I was a patient here not so long ago," said Byron.

"I see you got your new leg," said the nurse. "How are you doing?"

"Better," said Byron. "It takes some time to get used to."

"Sure does. Look, Sergeant Johnson is in bad shape, so don't get him excited."

When Eliza and Byron arrived on the second floor, they soon realized they were in for a shock. The men in the ward were the worst kind of casualties. Missing limbs was one thing, but missing faces, ears, and noses was something else. Here were the worst of the worst. Johnson was a quadriplegic, with four missing limbs and a terrible scar across his face. His family had abandoned him. The nurse led them to his bed. The poor man would require constant nursing and surveillance for the rest of his life. He couldn't eat by himself nor move about without the help of the nurses.

"Hello, Sergeant Johnson. You remember me, Byron Miller?" asked Byron. "I remember you down in the Shenandoah."

It was clear Johnson was making an effort to remember, but finally, he just shook his head in frustration.

"It don't matter none," Byron reassured him, recalling the nurse's admonition not to get him excited. "This is my sister Eliza. I was in the ward downstairs a couple of weeks ago, then I got my new leg."

"Nice to see you, Miller. Yes, I remember you. You got hit at Cedar Creek, same as I did."

"Yeah, we were in a right firefight. I remember seeing your men in the fog when the Rebels were coming for our flags."

"Yes, sir."

"They were comin' at us from every direction. It was a slaughter. It was hand-to-hand fighting with clubbed muskets and bayonets."

"It's nice to see you again, Miller. I never thought I would see your face again."

Byron wasn't sure if Johnson truly remembered him or not, but the man appreciated the company. Byron got chairs for himself and his sister, and they sat down.

"You were the best of the best," Byron told him and meant it. He found himself tearing up as he laid a hand on Johnson's shoulder and recalled the desperate fight for the flags. Johnson had been in the thick of it.

He was conscious of the nurse hovering protectively nearby. They wouldn't have much time to talk.

"Sergeant," Byron said softly. "I have to ask you something. We are looking into the trial of a company man. He raped that white woman, Mary Dryden, in Winchester."

"Yeah, I remember that. I gave Lt. Baker a hand preparing the brief."

"You do? Do you remember the name of the rapist?"

"Of course I do. Still got my memory up here," said Johnson, tapping his head with the stump of his arm. "That was Lionel Howard, the son of Silas Howard, the richest man in Vermont. He runs the foundry in St. Albans."

"Lionel Howard. I never met him, maybe saw him once or twice. A small guy with a mustache."

"Yeah, that's him. He got six months of jail time, as I remember."

"Well, thank you, Sergeant. You're a good man."

A nurse arrived with the evening meal. Byron and Eliza stood up to give the man room as he set the tray on the bed near the sergeant.

"Thank you, Sergeant Johnson," said Byron as the nurse sat down on the bed and began to spoon-feed the sergeant.

"Come back to see me anytime, Miller. I like talking to you and your sister."

Byron didn't trust himself to speak. He could only manage a warm smile in response. It wouldn't have done to break down and cry in front of a war hero. He could feel Eliza's firm but gentle grasp on his arm as she guided him out of the room.

Byron sat in silence in the buggy as Eliza drove them back to the town in the failing light. They could see the sun reflected off the lake in the distance as they went looking for a café in town.

"I'd forgotten the fight for the flags at Cedar Creek until I recognized the sergeant, Eliza," said Byron quietly. "That was the worst firefight I ever saw."

"Try to forget the war, Byron. It won't do you any good. Put the past aside."

"It was a crazy fight, Eliza. The Johnny Rebs were comin' at us from every direction out of this thick fog. Colonel Thomas had us fire a volley and then we fell back to avoid being surrounded. They were demons coming at us for those damn flags. We lost over a hundred men on that hill."

"Poor Sergeant Johnson, abandoned by his family."

"Without men like Johnson, we would all have been slaughtered. We held the line. The 8th Vermont held the line and it allowed General Emory to reorganize the battle lines."

Forty-two

Dublin, Ireland

"Mr. Young, what are you doing in Ireland?" asked a massive Irish constable with striking blue eyes and a black beard. The Dublin Metropolitan Police officer was looking down a list of names with an intense expression. Bennett Young was the last name on the list.

"I'm here to study law, sir," said Bennett.

"So, you are a student at the university?"

"Yes, sir."

"How much money did you bring with you from America, sir?"

"Not enough. I have to pay tuition, and then there is my room and board."

"You Americans always seem to have money on you. Do you have any wealthy friends at your college?"

"I don't think so, sir. Most of us are students trying to complete our studies and then return home."

"Queen's is an expensive university, Mr. Young. A lot of Irish boys would like to study there, but can't raise the tuition."

"I'm sure that's the case."

The constable smiled as a thought came to him.

"You seen the boys playing rugby football at Trinity?"

"Yes, I have. It's a strange game for us Americans with all that pushing and shoving in the mud."

"We call it a scrum, sir. It's just a way of restarting the game. You have to hook the ball back to your side."

"You seem to know a lot about it."

"Well, that's because I sometimes play at Trinity with the boys."

"You do? Well, I'll try to come out and see you play, sir."

"Thank you for coming in, Mr. Young. Good luck to you."

St. Albans, Vermont

Eliza and her brother had spent the night at a rooming house in Burlington before heading back to St. Albans in the morning. They had no idea whether the information they had collected would be useful to the constable. When they arrived in St. Albans late in the afternoon, they were tired and hungry and stopped to eat in town. As they were finishing their meal, Byron left Eliza and went out to make his report to the constable.

The constable was in a meeting when he arrived at his office, so Byron waited outside until he saw several town council members leaving. Silas Howard, owner of the Howard Foundry, passed within feet of Byron. He was a stooped old man in his sixties with a bald crown and flushed cheeks. The foundry was located near the Central Vermont passenger terminal and produced railroad and machine castings, boiler stoves, and just about anything made of metal. Byron watched the other town councilors file out and then went inside.

"Ah, Mr. Miller." Harris gestured him to a chair. "How are you?"

"I'm fine, sir. I found the name of the rapist. His name is Lionel Howard, sir. He's the son of Silas Howard, who was just in here."

"How did you find that out?"

"Easy, sir. I talked to a sergeant at the hospital down in Burlington. Howard got six months' jail time for the rape."

"So what's your theory, Miller?"

"I don't know, sir. But I can investigate some more if you like."

"No, I think we're good. I find it hard to believe that the Howard boy had anything to do with the murders. He got his punishment and did his time."

"Yes, I can see that, sir."

"I think it's more likely that someone had a grudge against Ezra Williams winning at dice."

"There is something strange going on, sir. The woman at the regimental office told me they had a break-in, and the thief took all the regimental paper for September and October."

"Regimental paper?" asked Harris, looking perplexed.

"Yes, sir. The regiment keeps a copy of the reports from the front. It can be anything, sir. Casualties, arrests, absentees, purchases of beef cattle, ammunition, and what have you. It all goes in the report."

"Good work, Miller."

"The woman told us the report on the trial would have been in the September report. That's when young Howard was tried."

"Maybe someone just borrowed the files." Harris shrugged.

"They broke a window to get in, sir," Byron said as he watched Harris take out a clay pipe and start stuffing tobacco into it.

It was clear that their little chat was over, thought Byron. *The constable was not very interested in solving the murder.*

"Well, I'll leave it with you, sir," Byron said.

"Yes, do that, Miller," said Harris, busying himself with his pipe. "I'll let you know if we arrest anyone."

Byron felt he'd done the constable's work for him and he'd just been dismissed like a schoolboy.

Eliza drove her brother home. It had been a long day, and they were both tired. As they came over the bridge that took them home, a bullet whizzed over their heads from the trees. Byron instantly ducked at the sound of gunfire, pulling Eliza off the seat onto the buggy floor as he seized the reins and whipped the horse to go faster. The horse took off along a rough track along the river. Two horsemen with bandannas covering their faces took up the chase. Byron pulled a pistol from his bag and gave the reins to Eliza, who whipped the horse into a mad dash.

"Slow down a bit," yelled Byron, turning to face their pursuers. Eliza looked at him like he was crazy, but pulled back on the reins.

After a moment, the wagon's motion steadied enough for Byron to take a shot. The horsemen were gaining on them. As they came around a turn, the lead horseman fired wildly at Byron but missed. Byron ignored the impulse to duck and returned fire, toppling the man from his horse. He thumbed back the hammer and waited for the second man to make his approach. As the assailant raised his weapon, Byron shot him in the shoulder. The impact knocked the man sideways in the saddle, but he didn't fall off his horse. He galloped away, abandoning his partner, and the attack was over.

Eliza brought the buggy to a stop and Byron stepped down, wincing as he stood on his artificial leg. He walked back to the man lying in the ditch.

"Is he alive?" asked Eliza.

"No, he's dead," said Byron. "I know him. He's a mould maker at the foundry."

"Why were they coming after us, Byron?"

"I have no idea, Sis."

Byron found the man's pistol lying in the road and picked it up. He went after the man's horse and attached the reins to the back of the buggy. He climbed up onto the seat next to Eliza and they drove off.

"What did you say to the constable, Byron?"

"Nothing much. I gave him the name of Lionel Howard, that's all."

"Somebody doesn't want us looking into the death of Sergeant Williams."

"I'm thinking the same thing."

When they got home with the news of the attack, their father wasted no time going to the barn. Moments later, he returned with two old muskets he used for hunting game. He removed the oily rags covering them and put them on the kitchen table to clean them.

"The Howards are rich as Croesus and are always bullying people in town, Byron. I won't have them comin' round here."

"What's going on, Byron?" asked Mrs. Miller.

"It's got something to do with Ezra's murder, Ma. We just haven't figured it out yet."

"I'm gonna fetch Carl and have him stay with us tonight," said Mr. Miller.

He set the powder and ball on the table and started to clean the muskets.

"We can set up a hide in the barn and another on the second floor," said Mr. Miller. "If those bastards come tonight, we'll drop 'em in their tracks."

"We should be all right, Pa," said Byron. "I've got two pistols here, and whatever Carl brings with him. If they come for us, we'll be ready."

Forty-three

Dublin, Ireland

It was a rainy Saturday afternoon and a game of rugby football was being played on the Trinity College pitch between the University and the Dublin Metropolitan Police Union players. The DMP players were big, tough-looking young men compared to the more diminutive university players. The Police Union was winning the match at half-time when one of the University players pulled a hamstring and stumbled off the pitch. The team was one player down with no replacements and little hope of winning against the stronger Police Union team.

On the sidelines watching the game, there was a crowd of American expats, including Jake Doyle and Bennett Young. A University team member came over to ask whether any of the Americans knew the game and might replace the player who was out for injury.

"Here's the man you need," said one expat, jokingly pointing to Jake. "He knows how to play. Don't you, Jake?"

Jake laughed when he heard his name had come up as a replacement for the injured player.

"Go on, Jake," shouted Bennett and his friends. "Go on, show them how we Americans play the game."

The University man called to Jake.

"You'll be playin' outside center, Mr. Doyle. You think you can do it?"

"I'm not sure," said Jake.

"If you can run fast, you can do it. Remember, never pass the ball forward, always back. That's all you need to know."

"Got it. Let me get changed," said Jake, happy to accept the challenge.

"Ten minutes," warned the player.

Jake ran off to get kitted out for the team while the University man pulled a number 13 from the injured player's shirt. When Jake returned, he was given the number to pin on his jersey and told where to play.

Jake Doyle was a strong, natural athlete and could run very fast over short distances. He even looked like a rugby player with his massive shoulders and chest, but the game could be very confusing for a first-timer. On the first play, he ran the wrong way but soon learned to follow his teammates when they had the ball and were moving up the pitch. His job was simple enough—wait for the pass from the inside center and pass it along to the wing. After failing to make the pass the first time, the disgruntled wingman set him right, and he made each subsequent pass even when he had two massive Police Union players wrapped around his legs.

"Go on, Jake," yelled Bennett. "You can do it, go for it."

The Police Union scored a try, one of their forwards plunging over the goal line. Rugby was still evolving as a sport at the time and carrying the ball over the line and touching it down did not result in a point or points being given. Instead, the act of doing so allowed the team to score a 'goal' by kicking the ball over the crossbar between the uprights. The Police Union did just that, 'converting' the try and giving them a point.

They were going for another try when Jake collected a dropped ball and hightailed up the pitch and over the goal line, getting a first try for the Trinity boys. This was followed by a well-placed kick with the ball soaring over the goalposts for the conversion. The score was 1-1, but it was not enough.

The Police Union team wore down the university players, scoring two more goals and winning the match 3-1. Still, it was a good showing for the younger and less experienced Trinity players, who congratulated Jake on his remarkable run. His American colleagues were ecstatic.

A Police Union player wearing a red scrum cap came over to say hello to Jake.

"So you're playing for the effin' uni team now, Mr. Doyle?"

Bennett recognized the man as the police interrogator who had questioned him after he was arrested. He didn't look so formidable without his uniform.

"My first time," said Jake.

"Well, you did good. Maybe those Trinner wankers will keep you on."

"I don't think so," replied Jake.

"I'm only codding ya, mate."

Jake and Bennett laughed and shook hands with the man before heading off to the pub.

St. Albans, Vermont

The Miller family had spent a sleepless night waiting for an attack that never came. In the morning, Carl drove Byron to town in the buggy to report the attack. Byron's mother had insisted that Carl go with her son for protection. With his large mustache, beard, and bowler hat, Carl looked formidable enough to scare off any potential assailants all by himself. Byron wore a wide-brimmed hat and scarf to hide his identity and carried two pistols, while Carl had brought a musket with him. They kept their heads down as they raced along the rough track, watching the trees for hidden bushwhackers. On the way, they stopped to collect the dead man. They loaded his body into the buggy and turned onto the bridge that took them into town.

Byron and Carl entered Constable Harris's office as the old man was pouring himself a cup of tea. Byron walked right up to his desk while Carl remained by the door.

"Mr. Miller. What brings you to town?" asked Harris, taken aback by Byron's angry intrusion.

"My sister and I were shot at yesterday, Mr. Harris," Byron told him. "It happened after we came here to make our report to you. What do you know about that?"

"I have no idea. I hope your sister wasn't hurt?"

"No, she wasn't. Thank God. We were lucky."

"Where did it happen?"

"After the turnoff to our place. We were attacked by two men on horseback. One man worked at the foundry. He's dead. The other man escaped, but I think I wounded him."

"You aren't making this up, Miller, are you?"

"Why the hell would I do that?" Byron exploded. "I've got the dead man in the buggy parked outside. If you don't believe me, go out and take a look at him."

"No need to get worked up, young man," said Harris. "We'll look into it. We can't have innocent people being shot at."

"The dead man worked for Silas Howard, sir. The Howards have something to do with the murder of Williams and the attack yesterday."

"Look here, Miller. You can't come in here and accuse the good citizens of this town without a shred of evidence."

"Goddammit, Harris! Go out the door and take a look at the dead man. He worked for the Howards. What more proof do you want?"

"Calm down, Miller," Harris ordered. "There's a rumor going around that your family may be mixed up with those Rebel soldiers who attacked our town last year."

"My family? What are you talking about?"

"Your sister was seen in Montreal with that southern boy. What's his name? The young raider, Bennett Young, that they talked about in the paper."

"My sister Eliza ain't never been to Montreal. Get your facts straight, man."

"He's that fella who sent a stolen five-dollar St. Albans banknote to pay for his room. You weren't here, Miller, but those rebels murdered Elinus Morrison right here in town during the attack."

"You're mistaken, Harris," Byron shook his head, mystified. "My family had nothing to do with the Rebs."

"Well, your sister did. She was seen talking to the same man just before the attack. She could be arrested at any time for aiding and abetting the enemy."

"Aiding and abetting my ass," Byron snarled. "The war is over, sir, or hadn't you noticed?"

Byron turned and stormed out of the office, followed by Carl.

Byron and Carl dumped the body of the dead man on the wooden sidewalk in front of several disapproving local citizens before heading across the street to the tavern. The usual barflies were there, spending their disability money on gambling and alcohol.

"Any of you boys still capable of shooting a musket?" asked Byron with a grin. "We're looking for able-bodied men who can walk and shoot?"

Almost immediately, he was deluged with a chorus of voices.

"Sure can," said a man at the bar. "I was in the war just like you, Byron."

"I can shoot, but I cain't walk none," said another.

"Count me in," said a burly man who was almost as big as Carl.

"There's Hank and Wilbur come in regular," said the bartender. "They were in many a scrap with the Rebs."

They don't even know why I'm asking, Byron thought, *and they don't care. They just miss a good fight.*

"Tell them we'll be back tonight," he told the men clustered around him. "We're gonna need a dozen men. Tell 'em to bring their guns."

Forty-four

The men returned home. Byron was eager to learn if his sister had ever met with the Rebel lieutenant Harris had mentioned. *How could he not have heard about something like that? Of course, he had been in the hospital for a long time and only saw Eliza from time to time when she came to visit. He wondered whether Carl had heard anything about this, but Carl was his usual self, silent as the grave.* Carl was busy driving the wagon and keeping the wheels out of the ruts on the road. They arrived at the farm and went into the kitchen, where his mother was preparing the evening meal.

"Well, how did it go?" she asked.

"There was no one waiting on the road, Ma. Maybe they've given up."

"Good. I'm glad Carl went with you."

"We spoke with the constable and got nothing from him, so we dumped the body of the dead man outside the dry goods store."

Byron and Carl sat down. Byron looked at his mother, who smiled at him in the usual way, but he knew she was hiding something. She disapproved of his offhand description of how they had dealt with the body. *Better if I hadn't said anything*, Byron thought. He watched his mother as she busied herself chopping up meat and transferring it to the frying pan.

"What did he say about the attack?" she asked.

"Nothing. The son-of-a-bitch is not going to do anything against the Howards. He told me that Eliza was seen in Montreal with that Rebel lieutenant. Is there any truth to that?"

The mother lifted the frying pan with the chopped meat and put it on the counter while she tried to formulate a reply to her son's question.

"Yes," she said finally, but wouldn't meet his eyes. "Eliza went to Montreal. She met with Lt. Young."

"So it's true," Byron said, disgusted. "The constable says that Eliza could be arrested for aiding and abetting the enemy."

"That's ridiculous, Byron," said his mother, shaking her head. "The day of the attack, Eliza and I ran into the lieutenant on Main Street. He told us to get out of town for our own safety. After the attack, he came here with a wounded man. He begged us to help his friend."

"I can't believe you helped those secesh raiders, Ma?"

"Yes, we did." She faced him, defiant. "That was the only Christian thing we could do. Carl extracted the bullet, didn't you, Carl?"

"Yep, sure did. That man was in bad shape; the infection would have killed him."

"Ma, do you know what you've done? You could be arrested and sent to prison."

His mother put the frying pan on the hob, and the meat started to sizzle.

"We are good Christian people, Byron. We help others in need as we help ourselves. And then there was the money."

"The money?"

"The lieutenant gave Eliza one thousand dollars to look after his friend and to take him across the border to safety in Canada. We were desperate, Byron."

Byron's anger deflated as he shook his head, astonished by the news.

"The lieutenant is not a bad man, Byron. Eliza says he's in Ireland now."

"So Eliza was involved with this secesh. I can hardly believe it."

"Where do you think little Iris comes from?"

"Isn't she one of our cousin's children?"

"No, dear. Lt. Young was arrested by the Canadian authorities at her aunt's house in Frelighsburg. That's where he met Iris and later, she saved his life."

"Iris saved his life?"

"The lieutenant is a good man, a religious man. He loves that kid and gave money to Iris' mother to pay for her education."

"Yeah, the same money he stole from the St. Albans' banks."

Eliza looked at her brother as she came into the kitchen to help her mother prepare the meal. She realized the cat was out of the bag.

"You never told me, Sis," said Byron.

"I couldn't tell anyone, Byron. We've kept it secret. Haven't we, Ma?"

"Well, it ain't a secret no more. Constable Harris says someone saw you in Montreal with that man."

"So what? I'm not a criminal because I met with someone."

"They think you were a spy working for the secesh just like that Mary Surratt who was hanged this summer."

"That's ridiculous," said Eliza. "They can think what they want. Nobody knows what we did."

"You never told anyone about that night, did you, Carl?" asked Mrs. Miller.

"No, ma'am," said Carl.

There was a long silence before Mrs. Miller looked up at her son.

"What are you going to do, Byron?"

"Carl and I are going to town later tonight to talk to some veterans."

"Don't go," said his mother. "Stay here. You'll be safer at home."

"She's right," said Eliza. "These killings are out of your hands, Byron. Let the constable handle it."

While Byron and Carl were having their midday meal, Eliza saddled up a horse and left to visit Ezra Williams' wife and children. They lived on a farm south of the Millers and had a large spread on some of the best land in the region. They raised sheep like the Millers, but unlike their neighbors, the Williams farm was perfect for cash crops like wheat and barley. Eliza caught Beatrice Williams on her knees in the vegetable plot, digging up potatoes with her twins, a boy and a girl around six years old. She was in her thirties with a brown, weathered face from working long hours in the fields. She had raised her two children without a husband for most of their lives.

"I'm so sorry for your loss," said Eliza, getting off her horse. "My brother said Ezra was a fine, courageous man."

"Well, thank you, Eliza. I'm not going to miss him. He was gone from my life for three long years of war, so it was not easy when he returned. He was angry all the time and drank too much. He wasn't easy to live with, and the war only made him worse."

"I'm sorry to hear that."

"How is your brother holding up with the amputated leg?"

"He's going to be all right."

"Let's go inside and have a cup of tea."

"Yes, I would like that."

Eliza followed Beatrice and the twins, leading her horse.

Ten minutes later, they were sitting in the kitchen around the stove.

"It's been very hard for me without a husband, Eliza. Last year was especially bad. It's been a struggle for me to keep the farm going."

"I know. It was bad for us, too."

"I'm thinking of selling the house and the land and going south to stay with my sister in Burlington. Her husband is an accountant and they live in a very nice house. The twins would be better off there."

"My dad always said that you Williams were sitting pretty compared to us while we struggled to get any kind of crop out of our rocky soil."

"Well, there's a lot of truth to that. This is fine farmland, Eliza, but I'm not up to it anymore. I want out."

Through the kitchen window, they could see a man on horseback riding along the southern edge of the property.

"Who is that man?" asked Eliza.

"That's Newton Landry. He's ever so rich. He's gonna make an offer for the house and land. He just bought Baker's farm south of us."

"You mean Lt. Baker? His farm?"

"Yeah, Lt. Baker was Ezra's commanding officer in the war, but he had an accident a few weeks ago and died. He lost a brother in the war, so there was no one left to run the farm."

"You don't say," said Eliza, whose interest had perked up. "That's quite a coincidence, Lt. Baker, and then Ezra."

"Landry told me about it. He was there at the time. Baker was bringing in a load of corn when he slipped off the wagon and fell behind the horses. The loaded wagon ran over him and he died a few hours later."

Forty-five

By the time Eliza got home, Byron and Carl were already gone. She stopped by the barn where her father was repairing the sleigh for winter travel. Snow was on its way, and there would be days when their horse-drawn sleigh would be the only way to get to town.

"The night you saw Ezra Williams playing Chuck-a-luck at the bar, Pa. Do you remember who was at the table?"

"Well, Herman Greenwood, Fred Plumtree, Newton Landry, and Amos Bosley were there. That's it. Why?"

"I think Newton Landry is trying to steal the Williams' farm."

"I've seen him over there at the house. He seems to have some business with Ezra's wife."

"He's going to make an offer for the property, according to Beatrice."

"Landry's dad owns the sawmill and a good deal of land. They have money."

"Landry was never called up?"

"Nope. I heard a rumor that Newton was called up in '63 and his old man paid a Polish immigrant \$300 to serve as a private in his place in the 4th Vermont. I don't know if it's true."

"Beatrice told me he bought the Baker property after Lt. Baker died in an accident."

"Well, Landry knows a good deal when he sees one. The family will soon own most of the good farmland in the region."

Eliza climbed back on her horse.

"Where are you going, my dear?"

"Dad, Byron doesn't know about Newton Landry. I have to warn him before he does something stupid."

"Don't go, Eliza! I'll go—."

Eliza pretended not to hear. She kicked her horse's flanks and took off at a gallop.

The Main Street of St. Albans was unusually quiet as Eliza dismounted at the dry goods store. She ran into the constable's office, hoping to find Byron and Carl, but the front room was empty. She was about to leave when the constable appeared from the cells in the back. He didn't look happy to see her.

"What are you doing here, Miss Miller?"

"I'm looking for my brother. Have you seen him?"

"Seen him," Harris roared. "The damn fool's got a bunch of veterans all worked up and they're going after Lionel Howard—they say he killed Ezra Williams."

"Well, they've got the wrong man," Eliza said. "It was Newton Landry who killed Ezra, not Lionel Howard."

"Do you have anything to prove that?"

"Not much," she conceded. "I've got to stop my brother. Are you going to help me or not?"

He isn't going to help, thought Eliza. *I'm just another hysterical woman. Who is going to believe me?*

They stared at each other for a moment, and then Eliza wheeled around and headed back out to the street. Harris swore under his breath. He took his coat and followed her out.

Eliza and the constable could see a group of men assembled in the street near the railway depot, but her brother was not among them. The town folk smelled blood, and they were out in the street waiting for something to happen. The atmosphere was tense. There were angry voices, and it was not long before a shot was fired from a foundry window. A dozen veterans in the buildings along the street returned fire.

Eliza looked on in horror. The shouting match had exploded into a deadly gun battle. There would soon be bodies in the streets, and her brother might be one of them. She turned to Constable Harris.

"Tell them to stop!" she cried.

"It's too late for that, miss," he said, shaking his head. "There's nothing we can do."

"The hell there isn't!" she snapped.

Byron was busy reloading his musket when he looked up to see Eliza calmly walking into the middle of a gunfight.

"Stop shooting!" she yelled, raising her arms and waving at the men in the foundry.

The constable followed her, advancing reluctantly on the belligerents. He repeated the call for calm. The shooting diminished a bit and then started up again.

"Damn you all to hell," shouted Eliza. "I'm Eliza Miller and I'm telling you idiots to put your guns down."

Byron ran toward his fearless sister, standing in the street waving her arms. The gunfire from the foundry had stopped and there was only silence in the street.

"You are bringing shame on your families. You just came home from the war and now you are starting a new one. We know who killed Ezra Williams and it wasn't the Howards."

Byron looked back to see his men mesmerized by his beautiful, imperious sister standing alone in the street. Eliza looked at the crowd watching her from a distance and imagined herself taking flight and rising slowly over the heads of the veterans and the foundry workers. *I can fly*, thought Eliza. *I can rise above the foundry walls and fly down Main Street like I do so often in my dreams. I can be Joan of Arc on the ramparts of Orléans raising the morale of the French defenders against the English attack. I am a force to be reckoned with in this town.*

Then suddenly, the illusion was crushed and she was knocked off her feet by her brother Byron. He hadn't meant to hit his sister so hard. He'd caught a flicker of movement in one of the foundry windows and barreled into her just before a musket ball passed within inches of where she'd been standing. He'd been in enough firefights to know when a shot was close or when it wasn't. This one had been close.

Eliza was quite unaware she'd been the target. She screamed at Byron and pounded him with her fists.

"Get off me. Are you out of your mind?"

"Quiet now, Sis," Byron said, shielding her body from the shooters in the foundry.

"That was Landry!" One man yelled. "I saw him take the shot. He nearly killed Miss Eliza."

"That's what I was trying to tell you," Eliza said, shoving her brother. "Now, get off me."

The shocking attempt on Eliza's life had taken the fight out of everybody. Constable Harris took advantage of the lull to assert his authority.

"You in the foundry," he bellowed. "This has gone far enough. We have witnesses down here who saw Newton Landry take a shot at Miss Eliza."

"Witnesses?" scoffed a voice from the foundry window. "How do we know they are telling the truth?"

"I saw it myself," shouted Harris. "That good enough for you? Now come out so we can settle this thing."

Byron smiled at the constable's quick recovery. He was now the man of the situation after riding on Eliza's coattails from the start of the confrontation. There were raised voices coming from the foundry windows and a brief scuffle was heard before Newton Landry came out, surrounded by several foundry employees who were not there to protect him.

Nobody wanted anything to do with a man who would shoot an unarmed woman in the street. They walked Landry right up to Constable Harris, and one of them dropped a haversack on the ground.

"What's that?" Harris asked.

"It belongs to Landry," said the man. "And this is his musket."

"I ain't done nothin' wrong, Constable," said Landry, managing a smug smile that defied anyone to blame him for anything.

Landry was used to talking his way out of trouble and the smile was too much for Byron, who launched at him with his fists.

"You son-of-a-bitch!" Byron yelled at him. "You took a shot at my sister."

"Stop it, Byron," Eliza said, pointing at Landry's haversack. "Take a look in his bag."

Byron started to object, but then he picked up the haversack and rummaged through it.

"Landry bought up the Baker farm," said Eliza, turning to the constable. "Now he's going after Beatrice Williams' farm. He's the only one to benefit from the deaths of the two men."

"That don't prove nothin', Constable," shrugged Landry.

"Miss Miller, is that all you have?" asked Harris. "That's mighty slim."

"Maybe not," said Byron, grinning as he pulled a bayonet out of

Landry's haversack and held it up.

"Take a look at this."

"Goddamnit, Landry's got a bayonet," said one veteran.

"Whatcha doin' with a bayonet, Newton?" asked another. "You ain't never been in no war."

Byron handed the bayonet to Harris.

"I bet you a dollar," he told the constable. "If you let these boys take off his shirt, you'll have all the proof you need."

Harris looked at him thoughtfully for a moment, then nodded. Two burly veterans yanked Landry's coat off and tore his shirt away to reveal a crude, bloodstained bandage on his shoulder.

"He's wounded," said one man.

"That's 'cause I shot him," said Byron. "He's the same fella who attacked us on the road, Sis."

Byron walked up to the cowering Landry and ripped the bandage away to expose a bullet wound, made uglier by clumsy attempts to extract the bullet.

Eliza approached her brother and hugged him.

"Lucky, I got here in time, Byron."

"Thank God you did, Eliza."

"Constable, arrest this man," said Byron, quietly. "I'll be pressing charges."

The veterans seized Landry, and Harris took him away.

An hour later, Byron and Eliza were sitting in the constable's office, drawing up an official complaint against Newton Landry, who was being held in the town jail and his wound treated by the town doctor. The constable was writing up the complaint on a piece of foolscap while Eliza helped him with the wording. After they had finished, Silas Howard and his son Lionel appeared in the doorway.

"You shot up my business, Miller," said Silas. "We were lucky you didn't kill anyone. You gonna have to pay for damages."

"Mr. Howard, we know a few things that might change your mind," said Eliza. "We know you or your son broke into the regimental office down in Burlington."

"Don't say a word, Lionel," Silas ordered his son. "Go home, I'll handle it."

Silas waited until Lionel had left, then turned and glared at Eliza.

"How do we know that Eliza?" asked Byron, who now seemed very reticent to jump to conclusions.

"Who else would do such a thing, Byron? Only a Howard would try to hide the details of the rape."

"Young lady, you don't have no proof," said Silas.

"Miss Eliza and Byron here have done a pretty good job of proving things so far, Silas," said Constable Harris.

"I ain't admitting nothing, Harris. My boy didn't do nothing."

"Silas, the only damage I can see to the foundry is a couple of broken windows. If I were you, I'd just shake hands with Byron and his sister here, and say you're done."

Silas Howard suddenly looked ten years older, but he knew a good deal when he saw one. He had done everything he could to protect his son from the scandal of rape, but the theft of the regiment reports would only worsen his situation. He reluctantly stood up and exchanged a brief handshake with Byron before leaving the room without a word.

Forty-six

September 1868
Stanbridge East, Quebec

Bennett Young and Eliza Miller were married in the Stanbridge Ridge Stone Chapel, a typical meeting-house-style Baptist church built in 1842, without a bell tower and any exterior religious symbolism. After the American Revolution and the arrival of the Loyalists in the Eastern Townships, preachers would travel from town to town on foot or horseback, and worship services were held in homes, barns, or anywhere people could assemble. Meeting-house places of worship were built at the crossroads between villages and were often used to hold public meetings.

The bride was given away by her father. The best man was Jake Doyle. Iris, now fifteen, was a bridesmaid, along with a cousin from Lac-Brome. Agnes and her husband, Antoine, sat in a box pew near Mrs. Miller and her son, Byron. Nobody from Bennett's Kentucky family made the trip east. The bride wore a colorful print dress made by her mother with her face hidden by a veil, while the groom looked handsome in his new frock coat, vest, and ascot. The minister stood before them as Bennett slipped a plain gold ring on Eliza's finger. An exchange of marriage vows, communion, and prayers followed this.

Marriages were solemn ceremonies in the 19th century and there was no such thing as a kiss-the-bride moment. The couple was not even permitted to acknowledge friends and family during the ceremony. White was not worn by brides, because it was impractical without modern bleaching techniques. As they emerged from the chapel, Iris and her cousin threw grain—the symbol of fertility—after them as they crossed the street to a hotel where the wedding breakfast would be served. The couple received their guests in a private room accompanied by their bridesmaids. The Millers were the first to arrive and congratulate the couple. They were followed by Byron, Jake, and Agnes. The breakfast treat was a dark fruitcake with white frosting.

"I heard about your injuries at Cedar Creek," said Bennett to Eliza's brother.

"The worst fight I've ever been in," said Byron. "The Union lost over 5,000 men against Jubal Early."

"Early was one of Lee's best generals," said Bennett. "You know that he published a memoir about the last year of the war."

"It doesn't matter what Early says," Jake scoffed. "Philip Sheridan whipped his ass in the Shenandoah. The Rebs didn't stand a chance."

"Early was a force to be reckoned with, Jake," Bennett argued. "He almost beat Sheridan at Cedar Creek."

"I agree with Bennett," said Byron. "Early surprised us with that dawn attack."

"Want some cake, Lieutenant?" asked Iris as she came around with her cousin distributing portions of cake to the guests.

Iris still called Bennett 'Lieutenant', even if the Confederate Army no longer existed.

"Thank you, Iris, my dear."

"What about you, Byron?"

"Yes, please."

It had taken a long time before Eliza's father finally accepted Bennett's marriage proposal for his daughter's hand. It looked like an impossible marriage. The groom was a hated Confederate raider and was barred from ever returning to the United States. Even if he were pardoned one day by the government in Washington, it was not clear whether he could ever set foot in the State of Vermont again because of the crimes he had committed there. And worse still, the man didn't seem to have any means of support, although he had been very generous with the family, paying for numerous expenses over the years with stolen greenbacks.

Eliza's father was not blind to the fact that his daughter was desperately in love with her lieutenant. It became difficult to ignore the voices of his wife and son, who both supported the marriage. Byron felt that his sister had earned the right to marry whoever she wanted after her courageous attempt to stop the violence against the Howard family. And they were all in agreement when Bennett had suggested the marriage be held in Stanbridge East close to the border and a short distance from St. Albans.

Bennett had returned to Quebec by ship from Liverpool in the summer of 1868 and had met Eliza in Montreal as he waited for his pardon to come through. Although President Andrew Johnson had issued a proclamation in May 1865, extending amnesty to most former Confederate officials and soldiers, there remained a group of officers and soldiers who had played an important and visible role in the Confederacy and needed to be punished in his eyes. The amnesty proclamation included fourteen exception clauses to the general pardon. These applied to soldiers who had attended the United States military and naval academies, former Confederate governors and officials, high-ranking officers, and participants in the rebellion who had property valued at more than $20,000.

Bennett Young was prevented from returning under the eleventh exception: 'All parties who have been engaged in the destruction of the commerce of the United States upon the high seas, and all persons who have made raids into the United States from Canada, or have been engaged in the destruction of commerce on the lakes and rivers that separate the British Provinces from the United States.' The Johnson government was not willing to tolerate the return of the St. Albans' raiders.

The couple started their married life together, penniless and stuck in limbo, waiting for a pardon. Bennett had spent the last of the St. Albans' money studying law in Ireland, followed by a year in Scotland at the University of Edinburgh. Jake Doyle had returned to New York during the summer and was working for the Erie Railroad Company, which ran trains between New York City, Buffalo, and Chicago. He was a junior assistant to the director, Daniel Drew, in Piermont on the western bank of the Hudson River. The company was looking for up-and-coming young lawyers and had offered Bennett a job when he returned to the States.

After the marriage, the couple had been invited to stay at the Gagnon farm in Lac-Brome while they waited for news of the pardon. Jake had advanced some money to Bennett to help with his expenses, but it wouldn't last long. Bennett went to work on the farm, swinging a scythe in the fields of wheat while Eliza taught English grammar to Iris and the children.

Forty-seven

December 1868
New York City

In New York, there was a major battle looming between the robber barons for control of the Erie Railroad. The main characters in this extraordinary drama were Cornelius Vanderbilt, the transportation magnate known as 'The Commodore', and two Wall Street traders, Jay Gould and Jim Fisk, who were famous for their shady, unethical business practices. The war was playing out on Wall Street and also captivating the public in newspaper reports. Vanderbilt was the richest man in America and he planned to add the Erie Railway to his vast holdings. He believed that by adding the Erie to his network of railroads, including the New York Central, he would control much of the nation's rail networks.

This put him in direct opposition to Daniel Drew, a former cattle drover who had made his fortune driving herds of beef cattle from upstate New York to Manhattan. Vanderbilt had known Drew for decades. They had been opponents in various Wall Street battles and, at other times, allies. They started collaborating again in 1867 to allow Vanderbilt to buy up the majority of shares in the Erie Railroad. But later, Drew formed an alliance with Gould and Fisk, who were plotting against the Vanderbilt takeover. Using a loophole in the law, they began issuing additional shares of the Erie stock, forcing Vanderbilt to buy the diluted stock. He was outraged but could do nothing against the board composed of Gould, Fisk, and Drew.

A New York judge eventually ordered the board members to appear in court. To avoid prosecution, the board fled across the Hudson River to New Jersey and barricaded themselves in a hotel, protected by hired thugs. The newspapers covered every twist and turn in this bizarre story, and the Erie Railroad earned itself a nickname: the 'Scarlet Woman of Wall Street'.

To avoid litigation, the trio brought in the Tammany Hall political party, which ran New York. They made Boss Tweed a company director and drew up a bill for the state legislators that would legalize their fraudulent stock issue. The drama moved to the state capital in Albany, where Vanderbilt sent his lobbyists to kill the bill. To counter the Commodore's efforts, Gould took Jake Doyle and a satchel full of cash valued at some $500,000 to Albany to bribe the lawmakers. One senator pocketed $75,000 from Vanderbilt and then took another $100,000 from Gould for his vote. The bill passed and the stock was deemed legal. Gould, Fisk, and Drew were saved by the legislation, but Vanderbilt eventually got his revenge by forcing the Erie Railroad to buy back all his diluted stock.

While all these backroom deals were playing out, a new and glamorous investor from Scotland arrived in New York. His name was Lord Gordon-Gordon, also known as Lord Glencairn. He told Gould that he would help him gain control of the Erie Railroad with the help of some European investors who had bought stock in the company. The Scot had one condition. Gould must give him a million dollars in negotiable stock in what he described as a 'pooling of interests', but as soon as Gould had delivered the stock, Gordon-Gordon went out and sold it on the open market. Gould was out a million dollars and sued Gordon-Gordon, but before the trial could start, the Scottish swindler was given bail and escaped to Canada.

Lac-Brome, Quebec

The package arrived in the week before Christmas. The Gagnon house was decorated with homemade candies, cakes, and pine cones painted by the children. Colorful paper garlands were fixed to the walls, and there was a small tree near the door to the kitchen. Bennett and Eliza were playing card games with the children when the package was delivered. It was a heavy brown parcel with a New York postmark. Bennett opened it and found an envelope full of banknotes, along with a revolver wrapped in newsprint. He slid out the letter written on cream vellum with the Erie Railroad Company logo at the top and read:

Dear Bennett,

Jay Gould has asked me to contact you to help us find Lord Gordon-Gordon, a Scot who stole a million dollars from the company. The fugitive is headed for Montreal, but he could be anywhere in Canada. Here is an advance of $1,000 for your expenses and something for your protection. You need to leave right away and try to find the bastard. As soon as you track him down, send me a telegram. Jay wants us to find out what he is doing with our money and to persuade him to come back for trial.

Warmest regards,

J. Doyle

Bennett read the letter twice before looking at Eliza.

"It's a letter from Jake," said Bennett. "I'm to go to Montreal."

"For how long?" asked Eliza.

"It's hard to say."

"I want to go home for a while to see my folks, Bennett. Christmas is almost upon us."

"That's a good idea, Eliza. I may be gone for a couple of weeks."

"What about Iris?"

"She can go with you if Agnes approves."

They set off in the sleigh. There was already a foot of snow and ice on the roads as Agnes drove north toward the town of Waterloo, Quebec. Bennett sat up front with Agnes while Eliza and Iris sat in the back, covered by a canvas tarp and blankets.

"Why do you want to be a nurse, Iris?" asked Bennett.

"I like to help people, Lieutenant," replied Iris, putting on her mittens. "I don't like to see people in pain or suffering."

"But nursing is a hard job. It means working long hours and putting up with a lot of guff from sick people."

"I don't care. I like working with people."

"Don't try to dissuade her, Bennett," said Eliza. "She's been fixated on nursing for quite some time. You never saw her stop the pain my brother was in."

"Well, we are all very proud of her," said Bennett, "but it may not be easy to get into that nursing school you mentioned."

"We'll work something out," said Eliza. "If she starts school in St. Albans in January, then she'll be ready for whatever training she wants to do in the fall."

Two hours later, they arrived at the railway station in Waterloo. Trains on the Stanstead, Shefford, and Chambly line joined up with the Grand Trunk Railway going north to Montreal. Eliza and Iris would have to change again at Saint-Jean for St. Albans, while Bennett continued to Montreal.

Forty-eight

Montreal

Bennett entered the St. Lawrence Hall on snowy St. Jacques Street in the early evening. There were Christmas decorations over the entrance and a tree in the lobby, with colorful glass ornaments and garlands hanging on the walls. A dozen carolers sang the usual Christmas hymns, including *Hark! The Herald Angels Sing, Good King Wenceslas,* and *O Tannenbaum* to the hotel guests as they entered the richly decorated dining room. Just as Bennett was admiring the Christmas cheer in the lobby, he did a double take when he spotted a grey and haggard Jefferson Davis, ex-president of the Confederate States of America, entering the dining room accompanied by his wife Varina and several distinguished-looking businessmen. Davis was barely recognizable, walking with a cane and looking like a man broken in health and fortune. Bennett had read about Davis' turn of fortune in the Montreal newspapers.

The former politician had been thrown in prison at the end of the war and spent two years at Fort Monroe, near Norfolk, Virginia. Many Americans wanted to punish him, while others favored a more conciliatory approach. After the government had failed to link Davis to the assassination of Lincoln, they decided to charge him with treason for organizing the invasion of Maryland and the District of Columbia in 1864. The trial was to start in the spring of 1868 and then the defense suddenly decided to go to the Supreme Court to contest the litigation. To bury the case, President Johnson decided to pardon Davis and everyone else who had participated in the rebellion. But no date had been set for the pardon.

When Davis was finally released on bail in May 1867, he quickly left the country to join his family in Canada. As his train passed through towns in the Northern States, it was pelted with rotten fruit and crowds jeered the passage of their archenemy. Things changed for the better when he arrived in Toronto by ferry boat on May 30, 1867. Thousands of well-wishing Canadians cheered the famous man as his steamer docked at the foot of Yonge Street. While Davis had been in prison, his family—Varina, Davis's mother, and their three children—had found refuge in Montreal. The family was penniless after their Brierfield and Hurricane plantations in Mississippi had been destroyed by Union troops at the end of the war. John Lovell, a wealthy publisher in the city, stepped in and offered to lodge the family in a three-story house on Mountain Street near McGill University. For Canadians, Davis remained a tragic, even noble hero.

Bennett returned to the reception desk.

"Do you have my reservation, sir? The name is Young," said Bennett. "I work for the Erie Railroad."

"Yes, sir," said the clerk, pushing the register toward him. "Please sign here."

"Do you have any Scottish gentlemen at the hotel?"

"Scottish? Why yes, I believe we do."

"That wouldn't be the famous Lord Gordon-Gordon, would it?"

"Yes, sir. That's the name. Hold on a second."

The clerk's face clouded as he consulted a note in the register, then looked up at Bennett.

"Do you know the gentleman, sir?"

"No, sir," Bennett said. "I've never met the man."

"He left earlier, but he didn't pay his note."

"That does sound like him, sir," Bennett grinned. "Did he say where he was going?"

"No, sir. Mr. Gordon's party was here for a full week." He looked hopefully at Bennett. "I wonder who is going to pay the note?"

"I can't help you there," Bennett replied. "How many were in his party?"

"Three, sir. Gordon and two other men."

"I see. Anything else you can tell me about them?"

"They were loud, sir. They made a lot of noise in the dining room, as I remember. Mr Gordon was a big spender."

"So nothing was paid?"

"No, sir."

"Do you have an address for Mr. Gordon in Montreal?"

"No, I don't," said the clerk, handing him the keys to his room.

Bennett went up to his room. He was tired from his journey. Tomorrow, he'd check on the other hotels in town.

After Davis joined his family in Montreal, he remained in seclusion, staying away from public view and declining invitations. It wasn't until July that he finally acquiesced to his friends' insistence that he attend a performance of Richard Sheridan's comedy *The Rivals* at the Montreal *Theatre Royale*—the same theater where John Wilkes Booth had performed in the autumn of 1864. The proceeds from the play were to go to the Southern Relief Association, a charity that provided aid to Southerners.

The crowd cheered when they saw him appear in his loge, an august and dignified presence in a dark suit and broad-rimmed white hat. To honor the famous visitor to the city, the orchestra struck up 'Dixie', the rallying cry of the Confederacy. The crowd sang along.

> *"Oh, I wish I was in the land of cotton*
> *Old times there are not forgotten*
> *Look away! Look away!*
> *Look away! Dixie Land"*

As the music faded away, Davis stood up and acknowledged the cheering crowd. After the play, as he waited with his family in the street for a carriage, a man pushed forward and thrust a piece of paper into his hands. There was only one word in block letters on the slip of paper: ANDERSONVILLE

It was the name of the dreaded, hellish prison in Georgia, a name and place that had burned its way into the minds of every Union soldier. Some thirteen thousand prisoners had died there from starvation, exposure, and disease. This was Davis' last public appearance in Montreal before he returned to the States with his family in 1870.

Bennett returned to the lobby an hour later and requested directions to the nearest Western Union telegraph office. He left the hotel and crossed the street. The telegraph office was full of customers standing at a long counter composing messages in block letters on special pads. Bennett composed a message for his friend Jake:

G.G. LEFT ST. LAWRENCE HOTEL.
B. YOUNG.

It was a long wait to have his message transcoded, but the line finally advanced until just one man remained between Bennett and the clerk at the counter. The clerk looked up from the message the man had just handed him.

"Is this Glasgow in Scotland, sir?" asked the clerk.

"Is there another?" asked the red-bearded man facetiously.

"Right. That will be two dollars, sir."

As soon as the man left, Bennett quickly stepped up to the counter and gave his message to the clerk. He paid, not waiting for the change, and hurried out of the shop. The street was thronged with hansom cabs and pedestrians, and for a moment he thought he had lost the Scot.

Bennett's luck held. He spotted him waving down a cab in front of the hotel. Bennett hailed a cab of his own and told the bemused driver to follow the first cab. They raced down Saint-Jacques and eventually turned into the GTR's Bonaventure Station. Bennett stepped down, paid the driver, and followed the man into the station, where he met up with Lord Gordon and another man in the waiting room. Bennett watched from a distance. The confidence trickster was flamboyantly dressed in a Glengarry hat with a white cockade. He was easy to pick out in the crowd. He had a relaxed, cheerful arrogance about him as he talked to his two companions who were lackeys of some kind, judging by their dress and apparent deference to Gordon. The heavily built man with a reddish beard that Bennett had followed looked like a general factotum or even a bodyguard. The smaller man looked like a valet, or possibly a secretary. They had lots of baggage as they waited to board a train.

Their destination was easy to determine. Bennett looked up at the announcement board and saw that the only departure to a place of any size was the night train to Toronto. That allowed Bennett time to go back to the hotel to collect his bag and, unlike Gordon, pay his bill before returning to the train station. He had been looking forward to a decent meal and a good night's sleep, but now that he had located the man himself, he felt obliged to trail the Gordon party all the way to Toronto.

Jake had trusted him to find Lord Gordon, and he had done so. He was not paying him to find where he had just been, but where he was going. He returned to his hotel room and freshened up, changing his clothes and having a wash. He hurried back downstairs, paid the bill, and took a cab to the station, where he bought a ticket to Toronto.

Forty-nine

Gananoque, Ontario

The train left the Bonaventure Station at nine o'clock sharp. Bennett sat in the Pullman sleeper car, a new invention in rail travel with pull-down sleeping berths along a long corridor of comfortable seats. He watched as the train entered the metal tubular structure of the Victoria Jubilee Bridge. Built in 1859, it was the longest bridge in the world at 1.7 miles. The passengers were relieved when the six-minute crossing to the South Shore ended because of the eye-irritating coal smoke from the locomotive's smokestack that entered the car.

Bennett expected to be in Toronto by eleven o'clock the following morning and he hoped that would spell the end of his new career as a Pinkerton detective trailing Lord Gordon. He would send Jake a telegram in New York at noon and then go on to Niagara Falls to wait for his pardon before crossing into Buffalo, where a job awaited him. The Erie Railroad needed young lawyers to handle the expansion of the rail network. The plan was for Eliza to join him as soon as he was set up in Buffalo.

The night was uneventful. The train arrived at Prescott on the St. Lawrence River at dawn. When they got to Brockville, the porter came around and rolled up the top and bottom beds so the passengers could sit up and enjoy the view. This was followed by tea and sandwiches just as a blizzard blew in from the west. It raged with terrific fury, reducing visibility to next to nothing. The snow brought the train to an abrupt stop near Gananoque, a small town near the Thousand Islands that led into Lake Ontario.

A second locomotive arrived from the east and tried to push the train forward, but the wheels were locked in the ice and snow. Bennett joined the passengers in the open door, watching the crew try to disengage the wheels with shovels while snow gusts blew into the carriage. Gordon's red-bearded secretary stood behind him looking out the door.

"We could be here for days," said one man, turning away in disgust and returning to his seat.

"We ain't gonna leave here 'til this damn storm dies down," Red Beard complained. "Look, they're giving up already."

Bennett nodded as the rail crew gathered up their picks and shovels and filed past, looking for shelter from the storm.

"They're gonna try to get us some help in the village," said one onlooker.

Red Beard pulled a flask of whiskey from his coat pocket and took a swig. He turned to Bennett and offered him a shot. Bennett drank from the flask and handed it back.

"You play cards or dice, sir? We're going to get a game going later."

Bennett hesitated, unsure he wanted to be drawn into any interaction with the confidence trickster's party.

"Sure," he said finally. "Why not?"

Red Beard called to another man who was well-dressed and looked like a businessman. There were other men nearby, but Red Beard declined to invite them. It occurred to Bennett that the Scot was looking for people with money. *He's done this before*, Bennett thought. *He's looking for a couple of pigeons.*

"What you playin'?" asked the first pigeon.

"Hazard's a favorite," said Red Beard. "You in?"

"Well, sure," said the man, nodding.

"Good," said Red Beard with a smile. "Later tonight, I'll come looking for you fellas."

During the long afternoon, the rail car sat immobile on the tracks, buffeted by the wind and snow. Some passengers disembarked and headed toward a house in the distance. As they moved off, they sank up to their waist and vanished like ghosts into the swirling curtain of snow. After an hour, they returned with food and a jug of hot tea. One man offered sweet cakes and apples to two boys alone with their father. The storm continued with unabated fury as Bennett found copies of the Toronto Globe and several Montreal papers. He looked for news about the Johnson pardon in the papers, but there was nothing.

After nine o'clock, the porter came by and turned down the beds. Red Beard appeared in the corridor and nodded to Bennett and several men nearby. They stood up and went to the end of the car where Lord Gordon had set out the dice and a leather table set.

"This is my boss, Mr. Gordon, gentlemen," said Red Beard. "I'm Callum, we're from Glasgow."

They shook hands with Gordon, whose eyes gleamed in the poor light with predatory enthusiasm. This was his favorite game, and now he had his three pigeons as entertainment for the evening.

"I'm Fred," said the first pigeon to Red Beard. "Where are you heading?"

"Out west, first to Toronto and then onwards," said Gordon, turning to Bennett. "We're exploring your beautiful country. Who are you?"

"I'm Bennett. I'm on my way to Toronto."

"I'm Jim," said a small man. "I live in Toronto."

"Well, gentlemen. Take a seat and let's begin," said Callum. "Each caster throws for his main. Gordon here is the bank. Bets are at 10 dollars, gentlemen."

Callum put two bone dice on the game table.

"Let's throw the dice to see who starts. The high number goes first," announced Gordon.

Jim, Fred, and Bennett threw the dice, with Fred coming up with the high number.

"Fred, you're the caster," said Callum.

Fred threw the dice and got a six.

"Six is the main," said Callum. "All bets on the table."

Fred put down a ten-dollar bill followed by Gordon.

Fred threw a 1 and 2 called a 'crab' and lost. Gordon collected the money on the table.

"Come on Fred," said Jim. "You can do better than that."

Fred threw the dice again and got a 4. He threw again and got a 9.

"Nine is the main," said Callum. "Place your bets."

Fred put a ten on the table, followed by Gordon and Bennett. Fred threw again and got a 5.

"Five is the chance," said Callum.

Fred threw again and got a 4. Next, he threw a 5 and won. He collected his 10-dollar bet and took 20 dollars from Gordon and Bennett. He continued to play. The rules allowed the caster to keep playing until he lost three times in a row or when he tired. The next caster was the man on his left.

After the second hour, Fred and Jim were out about 100 dollars each while Bennett had hardly played at all, but had lost each time he placed a bet.

"Go for it, Bennett," said Jim.

Bennett threw the dice and came up with a 7.

"Seven is the main," announced Callum. "Place your bets."

Bennett put a ten on the table and was followed by Gordon, Jim, and Fred.

Bennett threw again and came up with a 5.

"Five is the chance," said Callum.

Bennett threw another 5 and won 45 dollars based on odds of 3/2 (30 dollars x 3/2).

What the hell, Bennett thought. *He might as well go for it again.*

He threw the dice and got an 8.

"Eight is the main," said Callum. "Place your bets."

Bennett increased his bet to 50 dollars, followed by Gordon and Fred. There was growing excitement around the table as Callum offered the men whiskey from his flask.

Bennett threw again and came up with a 6.

"Six is the chance," said Callum.

Bennett threw the dice, winning with two sixes for a total of 12.

"Damn," Fred exclaimed. "You're on a lucky streak!"

Bennett collected 100 dollars from the table on odds of 1/1. He threw the dice again and got a ten. He threw again and got a four. He continued until he got a main of 5.

"Five is the main," said Callum. "Place your bets."

Bennett bet his entire win of 100 dollars on the next throw. He didn't care as long as he was winning. He was followed by Gordon while Fred and Jim decided to stay out.

Bennett threw the dice again and got a 10.

"Ten is the chance," said Callum with a grin, anticipating a win for his boss.

Bennett hesitated before he threw the dice. He examined them carefully, trying to influence the way they fell. He threw the dice, and a six came up followed by a three, which fell on its side and became a four. Bennett grinned at Gordon, who looked rather glum.

"You play quite a game, Bennett," Gordon growled.

Bennett said nothing as he collected 133 dollars from Gordon based on odds of 4/3. This was a big win for Bennett.

"Want to double your money?" goaded Gordon. "Go on, you're on a winning streak."

"You aren't tired of losing, Mr. Gordon?"

"He's never tired of losing, are you, sir?" asked Callum. "Let's have another round."

Bennett threw the dice again and got a 3. It took him three more throws to get a 7, a very favorable number in the game of hazard.

"Seven is the main," said Callum.

Bennett put 200 dollars on the table and Gordon smiled at him as he followed.

"You fellas want in?" Callum asked Fred and Jim.

"No, thanks," they said.

"How about I spot you 100 dollars?" suggested Gordon to Jim. "You double your money if he loses."

"Sure," said Jim, but Fred refused.

There was now a pot of 600 dollars on the table.

"You fellas ready?" Bennett asked before he threw the dice again and got a 4.

"Four is the chance, gentlemen," said Callum, glancing at his boss. The tension in the air was palpable. Bennett blew on the dice and rubbed them between his hands. He threw a ten and collected the dice for a second throw. He threw an 8. Still, there was no winner or loser as the tension around the table mounted. Time passed as he got a 9, then a 6, and finally a 4, winning the jackpot.

"Damn lucky," Gordon observed, apparently unperturbed by the size of his loss. Bennett knew better than to crow about his big win in a room full of strangers. He stifled a smile and quietly collected the pot, including his 200-dollar bet plus 800 dollars from Gordon and Jim based on odds of 2/1.

Jim looked disconsolate. He had lost 200 dollars of his own money and now owed Gordon another 200. Fred saw the expression on Jim's face and stood up.

"Let's get some air," he said.

Bennett followed Jim out the door to have a look at the storm. The blustery gusts of wind were gone, but the snow was still coming down heavily. They climbed down on the tracks. Once outside, Bennett slipped Jim 400 dollars to cover his losses.

"Gordon can afford to gamble, you can't," said Bennett.

"Thank you, Bennett," replied Jim, nearly in tears. "I don't know how I would explain it to my wife."

"You're a good man, Bennett," Fred said, giving him a pat on the back.

The men walked along the tracks with other passengers and lit up their pipes and cigars as they chatted among themselves.

Callum followed Bennett along the tracks away from the others.

"So Bennett, you're a lucky man, or you've played the game before?" asked Callum.

"I played in Ireland, and your home country."

Bennett remembered the long evenings in camp playing Chuck-a-Luck for match sticks during the war. Hazard was different, but dice were dice. It all depended on a man's luck.

"Well, that explains it then. I saw you in the Western Union," said Callum as he seized Bennett by the neck and stuck a brass double-barreled derringer in his face.

"*Ya broon nose basterd.* You're working for Jay!"

"Jay?" replied Bennett, struggling to breathe. "Who's Jay?"

"Jay Gould sent you. You've been trailing us since we left New York."

"Why would I want to do that? I'm from Kentucky."

Callum hesitated, then released Bennett, pointing his gun at him.

"New York?" muttered Bennett, thinking fast, as he blew warm air into his cold hands. "Jim's from New York."

Callum stood there for a minute, his mind working overtime, and swore under his breath. He brushed past Bennett and went looking for Jim.

Now I've done it, thought Bennett. He climbed through a snowdrift to get back to the car. He went to his seat and removed the gun from his bag. He slid the gun into his pocket and retraced his steps, pushing past the returning passengers until he saw Fred, half unconscious, lying in a snowbank after he had been knocked flat by the Scot. Callum had Jim pushed up against the side of the car with one hand wrapped around his throat and the other holding the derringer.

"Callum!" said Bennett, raising his gun and walking toward the big Scot. "I lied about New York. Let him go."

"*A mhic-na-galla*," swore Callum. "So Jay is payin' you, after all?"

"Nope," replied Bennett. "Drop the gun!"

Red Beard released Jim, who followed Fred back to the Pullman car. He realized he had been played. His attention had been on Jim and Bennett had got the drop on him. He tried to brazen it out.

"You ain't got it in you, Bennett," he said. "You won't shoot me."

Bennett cocked his revolver and stepped closer to the Scot. By this time, all the passengers had returned to the car, and they were quite alone with the snow swirling around them.

"I was a Confederate soldier," said Bennett and then whacked Callum across the ear with his six-gun. "I've lost track of how many Union boys I've killed. I'll shoot you dead and, by tomorrow, I won't even remember your name. Drop the gun."

Callum held his sore head and dropped his gun in the snow.

"Now step back," Bennett ordered him as he reached into the snow to pick up the derringer. "See that house over there? I want you to walk over to that house."

Callum glanced over his shoulder.

"*Dagone*, Bennett," said Callum. "It's damn cold out here."

"Start walking," commanded Bennett.

Fifty

Shortly after sunrise, the tinkling of sleigh bells was heard coming from the south. The conductor and engineer arrived with provisions from the village. The porter turned down the beds and soon the passengers were eating sandwiches and drinking tea. The conductor made his way through the car, talking to passengers and relating his adventures. He had struggled through the storm to get to Gananoque and telegraphed the office in Kingston for food and assistance. A train had set out from Kingston but got stuck in the snow a few miles west of them. The good news was that they were sending a snowplow along with three locomotives to set them free and take them on to Toronto.

Bennett watched Lord Gordon and his valet looking out at the snow, apparently trying to figure out what had happened to Callum. Bennett had returned late the night before to find all the passengers had retired to their berths, including the Gordon party. It was only in the morning that anyone had noticed that Callum was gone.

"You seen Callum?" asked Lord Gordon.

"No, sir," said Jim.

"He went to that house across the way," said Bennett. "Didn't he come back?"

"No, he's disappeared," said Lord Gordon, looking puzzled.

Bennett shrugged and ate a sandwich. A series of whistles were heard, and the train started to move again as the locomotives and snowplow went to work. The train arrived in Kingston, twenty miles to the west, around six o'clock, and the Grand Trunk Railway offered a hot meal to all one hundred and fifty passengers. They left the station again at nine and chugged along at a slow pace until they arrived at the small town of Grafton, halfway to Toronto. The passengers were then obliged to leave the train and trudge westwards with their suitcases to board another train that would take them on to Toronto. It was slow going, encumbered as they were with their luggage, and the monotony was relieved only when they passed an equally disgruntled group of eastbound passengers walking in the other direction, on their way to board the train that Bennett and the others had just left.

Bennett found a seat in the Pullman car and immediately fell asleep. The train started its slow journey west and finally arrived in Toronto the following morning at eleven o'clock. It had taken a full sixty-two hours to complete the trip. Bennett was looking forward to finding a hotel and sending a telegram to Jake. His mind was made up. He was not going to trail the Scots across the country. He was going to strike out on his own. It had been six years since he had been home. He had sufficient funds in his pocket, along with his hazard winnings. He longed to see his parents and family back in Kentucky. He was going home even if he risked being arrested.

Tomorrow was Christmas Eve, and the streets were decorated for the occasion. Bennett followed Lord Gordon and his valet out of Union Station to the Queen's Hotel on Front Street, where he first met Colonel Thompson in 1864. They passed carolers in the street near the hotel, but Bennett felt little Christmas cheer. He was exhausted as he stepped into the lobby and watched the Gordon party get a suite of rooms at the front desk. After they left, he got a room for himself and went upstairs for a wash and a nap.

When he awoke, it was after five in the evening. He dressed quickly and went down to the lobby. He crossed the floor to the Western Union office, where he composed a message to Jake in New York.

G.G. IN TORONTO AT QUEEN'S HOTEL.
GOING HOME TO KY. B. YOUNG.

As he left the office, he noticed Lord Gordon and his valet heading for the hotel bar. There was no sign of the delinquent secretary. He walked down Front Street and descended Yonge Street to the wharf. There he bought a ticket on a steamer leaving for Niagara-on-the-Lake the next day.

In the morning, as he was checking out of the hotel, Bennett ran into a bedraggled Red Beard, coming into the hotel. His hair and clothes were a mess. He looked like he had spent the night in a barn and walked all the way to Toronto.

"*Dagone*, Bennett," said Callum. "You haven't seen the last of me."

"Your boss was asking after you, Callum. He looked concerned about your welfare."

"You're gonna pay for what you did."

Bennett smiled as he watched the Scot go looking for his master. He stepped out of the hotel into the sunshine and hurried to catch the ferry. He felt good. He was on his way home and Lord Gordon and Red Beard could go to hell.

St. Albans, Vermont

The Christmas decorations were everywhere in town. Byron, Eliza, and Iris took the train south to Burlington through the snow-covered countryside. From the train station, they hired a driver to take them to the old Marine Hospital. It was a cold windy day, and they made good time arriving in the early afternoon.

Byron had an appointment for a checkup with Dr. Dubois. Eliza had decided to accompany him, taking Iris with her. Byron knew his sister had an ulterior motive for bringing Iris along. She had read in the local paper about how the good doctor had worked at the Royal Charité Hospital in Berlin before moving to Boston. She was sure that he was a former colleague of the Polish-American physician who had founded the New England Hospital for Women and Children in Boston and was now opening the first training school for nurses in America.

Both Eliza and Byron thought that Iris, gifted and determined as she was, would be a perfect candidate. The problem was that after their last encounter with the doctor, he might not feel the same way.

Dr. Dubois welcomed the three of them to his office. Eliza was pleasantly surprised. The doctor was perfectly cordial and, if he remembered their last meeting, he gave no sign of it.

"So, Mr. Miller, let's have a look at that leg of yours," said Dubois after Byron climbed onto the examination table.

The doctor began his examination, looking closely at the stump and artificial leg.

"A nice fit," said Dubois. "Any irritation or skin issues?"

"No, sir."

"What about balance and walking problems?"

"Sometimes I get a pain in the knee. I try to rest up as much as possible when it starts."

"Any back pain?"

"Sometimes," Byron admitted.

"The only advice I can give you, Mr. Miller, is to take your time with the artificial limb. It takes a while to adjust to a new way of walking."

"Thank you, sir," said Byron as he got off the examination table and stood up. "Do you remember Iris, Doctor?"

Eliza held her breath.

"Yes, she does look familiar," Dubois said.

Eliza was about to stammer an apology, but Iris beat her to it.

"*Docteur Dubois, c'est moi qui a enlevé la douleur à Byron,*" said Iris.

"*Ah, c'est vous, la gamine. La petite Canadienne-française.* Yes, of course I remember you," Dubois said with a laugh. "I had to kick you out of my office."

"I'm so sorry about that, sir," said Iris, all sweetness and light.

Eliza had not expected Iris to be so forthcoming. She had just admitted to being the same loathsome kid who had criticized the great doctor for his lack of understanding of phantom limb pain.

"No need to excuse yourself, Miss Iris. You were one of the first people to open my eyes to the phenomenon. I've had numerous cases since then. Byron here was one of my first."

Eliza decided to jump in and profit from the doctor's goodwill.

"Iris wants to train as a nurse, sir. We were hoping you could write a letter of recommendation for her to Doctor Zakrzewska, who runs the New England Women and Children's Hospital in Boston."

"*Ah, oui.* I know Dr. Zakrzewska," said the doctor. "She's a medical doctor like me trained in Berlin. There's talk she is opening a training school for nurses."

Dubois turned to Iris, curious about the girl's interest in nursing.

"Why would you want to become a nurse, young lady?"

"I like to help people in need, sir," said Iris. "I am not squeamish at the sight of blood. I can change dressings and clean up messes."

"There are a lot of very sad moments in the medical profession,

Miss Iris."

"Yes, sir," said Iris.

"*Des moments extrêment pénibles, vous savez, quand un patient meurt malgré tous nos efforts pour le sauver.* Very difficult moments when a patient dies despite all our efforts to save them."

Iris nodded.

"There are infectious diseases and awful injuries."

"Yes, sir."

"You have to be tough to be a nurse."

"I'm tough, sir."

"You can be a kind, caring, compassionate person, but sometimes the work can be too much for one person to cope with."

"Yes, sir."

"During the last year of the war, we had some terrible cases here at the Marine Hospital. Some of them were beyond hope. Terrible wounds."

Dubois shook his head at the memory.

"So you need to ask yourself if you have it in you to become a nurse?"

"I have it, sir."

The doctor smiled at her, sensing the girl's determination and strong character.

"She has it, Doctor," Eliza assured him. "I've never seen anyone who was more a born nurse than Iris."

Fifty-one

Niagara on the Lake, Ontario

In his mind, he was running toward Frelighsburg, just beyond the Canadian border. His breathing was fast and shallow. He could feel the sweat pouring off his body as he raced toward the trees. He inhaled the fresh air of freedom: the fragrance of flowering plants and pine trees after the omnipresent stink of the camp latrines. The sounds were soft and reassuring and spoke to him. He'd forgotten how good it felt to escape. He could move and breathe without feeling constricted by the prison walls.

Bennett started awake, eyes wide and mouth stretched in a silent scream. He calmed down when he realized that he had fallen asleep near the stove in the overheated cabin of a fishing boat. They headed out into the Niagara River and he could make out the stone gunpowder magazine and bastions of Fort George, virtually all that remained after its destruction by American forces from Fort Niagara during the War of 1812. The overgrown stretch of land was being used as farmland and for grazing cattle. They crossed the river and the boat dropped him at the wharf in Youngstown in the State of New York before it headed north into Lake Ontario for a day of fishing.

He collected his bag and started walking south. He caught a coach in town for Lewiston and Buffalo. No one asked him his name or where he was from. People were getting on with their lives, and no one cared anymore about a dangerous Confederate spy walking in their midst. From Buffalo, he took the train to Cleveland and on to Cincinnati. The next leg of the journey took him south into Kentucky. It was the first time he had seen his home state since 1863. From the train, he could just make out what appeared to be the Cynthiana battlefield under the snow cover. It was where John Hunt Morgan had defeated the Union forces at Licking Creek in July 1862.

The second battle of Cynthiana in June 1864, however, had been a total disaster. Union forces had driven Morgan's newly formed battalion back into the town of Cynthiana itself, killing or capturing many of his men. It had been a decisive victory for the Union, as well as a sign that the strength of Union arms was starting to take its toll on the Confederacy. Morgan and some of his officers escaped, but it marked the end of his war effort. A few months later, he was killed in Greeneville, Tennessee, by a bullet in the back.

Lexington, Kentucky

Arriving in Lexington, Bennett was astonished at how small and dirty the place looked. The soul seemed to have gone out of the town and its people. There were sullen, hollowed-out war veterans everywhere, struggling to put food on the table while they watched 'carpetbaggers' with money buying up land and businesses. Bennett hired a dogcart to take him south to Nicholasville. As they drove out of town, he recognized the Hunt-Morgan House located on the corner of North Mill Street and Old South, named after the 'Thunderbolt of the Confederacy'.

When they got to the small town of Nicholasville, Bennett asked the driver to pull over so he could have a look at his father's old hat factory, which had burned to the ground along with a row of houses. There were a few shops open, but not many people about. They continued their journey south again and passed by what remained of a huge military camp that Bennett had never seen before. It looked a lot like Camp Douglas without the security fence. There were numerous barracks for soldiers.

"What is this place?" asked Bennett of his black driver. "It wasn't here before the war."

"It's Camp Nelson, sir."

"Camp Nelson?"

"Yep, I came here in '64 with my family. I was given my freedom when I signed up."

"You got your freedom when you signed up?"

"Yes, sir. All of us slaves who enlisted in the Union Army became freedmen."

"Well, I congratulate you, sir. President Lincoln did the right thing."

"Thank you. We were 25,000 colored soldiers here at the time."

"Where'd they send you to fight?"

"We fought in Tennessee and Virginia, sir. I fought at Saltville in '64."

Two miles south of Camp Nelson, they drove past a huge cemetery.

"This is the cemetery for the folks who died in the battles at Perryville, Richmond, and Covington, sir," said the driver.

"It's amazing how things have changed."

They drove on until they came to the Young farm. Nothing seemed to have changed since he left for the war. He paid the driver and stepped down. The dogcart took off as he approached the main house. An elderly woman opened the door to the kitchen. It took him a minute to realize the woman was his own mother. She struggled with a bucket of slops, which she carried to the pigs' trough in the yard. She poured it out and looked up, but from the puzzled look on her face, she didn't recognize him.

"Ma," he cried. "It's me, Bennett."

"Bennett!" called his mother joyfully.

Bennett ran to her and hugged her. They stood like that for a long minute with tears in their eyes until she pulled away and looked closely at him.

"Bennett, my boy. I was just saying to your pa that you might be coming home with the pardon and all."

"The pardon, Ma?"

"Yeah, it's in all the papers, Son. President Johnson pardoned all our soldiers the day after Christmas."

Bennett sagged with relief and embraced his mother all over again. He had hoped for a pardon but had never been sure it would come through.

"How are you, Ma?" he asked her.

"I'm fine," she said dismissively. "Just a bit older, Son."

"Where's Pa?"

She hesitated a moment, looking sad.

"He's not been well, Bennett."

A moment later, Bennett's father appeared at the kitchen door. He looked emaciated and weak. Bennett managed to mask his surprise at his appearance. It was not a time to ask more questions. He let his mother take his arm and guide him to the door so his father would welcome him home.

"So what happened to the factory, Pa?" asked Bennett, sitting at the kitchen table after finishing a meal of salt pork, pinto beans, and cornbread.

"It was in '64 when the Union troops came to town," said his father. "They burned it down to punish us."

"We don't know whether that's true, my dear," added his mother. "It could have been an accident."

"I can't believe I'm home," said Bennett. "I've so longed to see you all."

Bennett put his arm around his younger brother, Melancthon, and kissed him on the top of his head. His brother had just turned twenty and greatly admired Bennett for all his adventures and the sights he had seen.

"Have you heard anything about Elizabeth's husband?"

"Not a thing," said his father. "It's been three years and not a word."

"We know Bert was discharged in Virginia from the 3rd Tennessee under Colonel John Vaughn, but he never returned," said his mother.

"My poor sister. How is she getting by without a husband and two boys to feed?" asked Bennett.

"She's in Lexington, Bennett. Pa gives her money when he can," said his mother. "And she gets help from Bert's brother, but it ain't easy."

"Well, I'm going to leave you some money, so that should help."

"You're married now," said his mother. "How is your Eliza?"

"She's fine, Ma. She's staying with her family in Vermont for Christmas."

"So, what are your plans?"

"Well, I was thinking of having a look around. I have a job working for Jake and the Erie Railroad. We'll see."

"Daniel is still in Chicago, Bennett."

"He should stay there. He never liked Kentucky."

"Don't be so hard on him, Son."

"Robert is in Louisville, Bennett," said his father. "He never went to the war."

"Good for him," said Bennett. "Is he still working in the feed yards?"

"Yeah, you should look him up."

"Hey, Pa. Guess who I saw in a hotel in Montreal a week ago?"

Mr. Young looked blankly at his son.

"Jefferson Davis, Pa. Jefferson Davis, and his family. He's a famous man in Canada and the people love him."

"Well, I never," said his mother. "Here, they want to string him up."

"The Canadians love us Confederates, Ma," Bennett smiled, "even if we did lose the war."

It was late January when two horsemen appeared on a small hill overlooking the town of Lexington. A freak snowstorm had blown in and the men shivered in the cold wind. They stopped to look down at the town before descending the slippery slope to the outskirts. Bennett led the way on a tall, bay horse, followed by Melancthon on a dark mare. They wore wide-brimmed hats and were wrapped in blankets against the chill. They rode through the wintry streets before they came to a rundown tenement building off Main Street. They dismounted and climbed the stairs.

"Which floor?" asked Bennett.

"Top," replied Melancthon.

They looked up to see a woman carrying a washing basket downstairs. They moved to one side to let her pass, but she stopped them.

"You lookin' for the woman on the top floor?" She asked. "She's gone. Left with her two boys after the landlord kicked her out."

"Kicked her out?" Bennett gaped at her in shock. "Where'd she go?"

"She's staying with that old bag who lives in the shack down the alley."

"Thanks," said Bennett.

They hurried back down the stairs and were walking down the alley when they saw two boys throwing snowballs. Melancthon laughed as a snowball whizzed over his head.

"Stop it, you two," he grinned. "Harry and Jimmy, you remember your Uncle Bennett?"

"Hello, boys," said Bennett smiling. "We are here to see your mother. Is she around?"

"She's workin' in the kitchen," said Harry.

"How long since you moved?"

"About a week. Ma's lookin' for something else," said Jimmy.

They knocked on the door of a weather-beaten shack on the edge of the creek. Elizabeth appeared in the doorway in an apron with a scarf covering her hair.

"Bennett! You've come home," she exclaimed, hugging her brother.

"I've missed you, Sis," said Bennett. "I've missed you all."

"Come in, it's cold out there."

The two brothers entered a tiny kitchen with a large stone fireplace. Elizabeth was cooking a meat stew over an open fire.

"Sit down," she ordered her brothers.

"I'll just have a word with Ma Coutts. She's not been well."

Elizabeth left for a moment and the men could smell the stale odor of the sick room off the kitchen. There was a lot of whispering going on in the other room before Elizabeth returned.

"I got kicked out of the flat last week," said Elizabeth. "So I moved in here with Ma Coutts for a time."

"I'm sorry to hear that," said Bennett.

"You do know, Bennett, that my Bert never came home."

"Pa told me."

"He wrote me a letter after the surrender. He said he was thinking of going to Mexico with Jubal Early."

Bennett and Melancthon were astonished to hear the news.

"Elizabeth," Bennett said softly, "General Early's been in Canada. I hear he's writing his memoirs."

It was Elizabeth's turn to be shocked. She just stared at him, dumbfounded. It took her a moment before she found her voice.

"So that was just another lie," she said finally. "Bert abandoned us. He left us with nothing."

"A lot of Confederate officers escaped to Mexico, Sis," said Bennett. "A judge in Norfolk charged General Lee and Early with treason, along with thirty-nine Confederate officers. They faced death by hanging if found guilty."

"Don't make no excuses for the bastard," said Elizabeth.

"But didn't General Grant promise them that they could go home after the surrender and wouldn't face prosecution?" asked Melancthon.

"Yeah, Grant was against any further punishment of the South, but not Johnson. President Johnson wanted retribution along with a lot of Northerners."

"But you were pardoned, weren't you, Bennett?" asked Elizabeth.

"Yes, I was and now I'm back home. Maybe your husband—."

"Don't say it, Bennett. He ain't never comin' home."

Louisville, Kentucky

The smell from the Bourbon House stockyards on Main and Johnson Streets was atrocious. It was a mix of garbage, meat, and animal shit. It permeated the area with a putrid smell that nothing could erase. Kentucky was a major supplier of livestock to the south and the east. It was not unusual to see immense droves of hogs, sometimes counting more than 800 animals, making their way east through the famous Cumberland Gap—a passageway through the otherwise impenetrable Appalachian Mountains—to Virginia and the cities of Baltimore and Philadelphia. The Union Army needed beef and pork to feed the large number of men fighting in the war. The slaughterhouses were located in Louisville's Butchertown district, and even though the war was over, many were still in operation. Bennett's brother Robert had been a drover at the stockyard throughout the war and still worked there. He had been exempt from military service but had been suspected from time to time of being a Southern sympathizer by his mates.

It was late in the day when Bennett entered the Bourbon House building on Main Street and asked to talk to his brother. He wasn't sure what kind of reception he'd get as he took a seat in the waiting room.

"You're Bob's brother, right?"

Bennett looked up, surprised to see the man looking at him from the doorway. He was well dressed, somewhere in his fifties, and wore a white Stetson. There was a casual authority about him. He had to be Robert's boss.

"Yes, sir," said Bennett, standing up. "Is he here today?"

"Bob's here every day. He works down the road. I'll send someone down there to get him. Why don't you come into my office for a chinwag, Bennett?"

"Thank you, sir," said Bennett, shaking hands.

"I'm Mike Pope, the superintendent."

Pope took off his Stetson and told his assistant to fetch Robert from the rail yard. Then he ushered Bennett into his office and motioned him to a chair while he went to the credenza along the wall and poured two glasses of whiskey. He handed one to Bennett and sat down at his desk.

"You're the famous Bennett Young we've been hearing about in the papers. The man who took on the town of St. Albans single-handed and pissed off President Lincoln to no end."

"It wasn't single-handed, sir," Bennett said, "but no, I can't deny it."

"Where have you been since the end of the war?"

"I just returned from Canada, sir. I was pardoned a week ago."

"Canada? Your brother mentioned that you were in Ireland for a time."

"Yes, sir. I studied law at Queen's University in Dublin."

"So what are you plannin' on doing now that you're back home?"

"I don't know, sir. I just got married. I'm gonna look for work."

As Pope finished his whiskey, Bob appeared in the doorway in a torn workman's vest and overalls, wearing a dusty old bowler hat.

"Bennett," he called to his younger brother.

The two brothers embraced.

"How are you, Bennett?" asked Bob. "I didn't know you were back."

"I'm doing just fine, Bob. I just came from Lexington after seeing Elizabeth."

"Sit down, boys," Pope gestured expansively. "Let's have a drink together."

"Thank you, sir," Robert said as he settled into a chair. "You know I ain't seen Bennett now for over five years. He fought with John Hunt Morgan."

"You picked the wrong side," said Pope, "but you're still a hero in my book. Not many men dared to fight alongside Morgan's raiders."

"I don't expect any sympathy, sir, but I do appreciate your honesty."

"How would you like to continue your battle with the Union Army, Bennett?"

"Sorry, sir. I'm not sure I understand. The war is over."

"It ain't never over with those scheming bastards in Washington," growled Pope. "We're still waiting to get paid for a large shipment of beef we made last year. Since you're now a fancy lawyer, Bennett, I was thinkin' that you might help us get our money."

"Bennett's a smart guy, sir," said Robert. "He can do anything."

"Well?" Pope was staring at him, a half smile playing across his face. *He's serious*, Bennett thought. *He's looking for a lawyer.*

"I would need to register with the local bar association, Mr. Pope," said Bennett, trying to buy himself some time, "so I could practice law in the State."

"Think you can teach those stuffed shirts in the Army a lesson, Bennett?"

"Well, yes, sir. We could sue them in state court."

"Good," Pope said as he raised his glass and waited for the brothers to raise theirs.

Fifty-two

September 1872
Boston

It was three a.m. when they heard the cry in the women's ward on the third floor. It was a strangled scream that came and went. The person was obviously in pain but was slipping into unconsciousness between her calls for help. Iris and Betty provided care for twelve patients in the third-floor ward. Betty was a short, bespectacled ward maid in her early twenties and a hard worker, but she had no pretensions of becoming a nurse. It was dark as they approached the patient. There was barely enough light to see her face. The gas lamps were turned down at the end of the day shift to save money and turned off completely in the early morning hours. A similar procedure was followed for the heating in the ward. The steam was turned off at precisely midnight and only came back on with a loud crackling sound in the morning. During the night, the patients moved about in the dark, cold ward, often getting into all kinds of trouble that kept the nurses busy during the long hours.

The woman appeared to suffer from severe stomach cramps and had vomited all over her bedclothes. She looked feverish and shivered under a grey blanket. Betty and Iris went to work cleaning her up as best they could by the light of a single candle. Betty held the candle while Iris washed away the vomit on her face, chest, and hands. They put her in a clean nightdress and removed her soiled bedclothes, replacing them with clean ones.

It was only Iris' third day on the ward. Her first day had started bright and early on a Monday morning. They had put her right to work, although none of her tasks had anything to do with nursing. Instead, she found herself at a washtub in the dingy basement, washing assorted poultice cloths, bandages, and rags. After that, they had her working long hours in the dining room, serving meals and washing dishes. On the second day, she was ordered by the matron to go into the wards to wash the faces of patients, to make beds, to sweep floors, and to clean until the end of her shift. The third day had been a repeat of the second day, and Iris felt thoroughly fed up by the experience. *I didn't come to Boston to learn how to be a scullery maid. I came here to train as a nurse.*

Everything had been a disappointment. The New England Hospital for Women and Children did not provide uniforms for the nurses in training. Iris had admired the pictures of the British nurses under Florence Nightingale at the St. Thomas Hospital in London in their striped gingham dresses, crisp white bib aprons, and white muslin caps. They looked like real nurses, while in Boston the matron had ordered them to wear washable clothes and not to worry about fancy uniforms. The hospital was located in two buildings, one on Warrenton Street and the other on Pleasant Street. The hospital was a warren of small, badly ventilated rooms with narrow passages leading from one to another. The wards were always overcrowded and there were not enough baths and toilets for the number of patients. The tiny mortuary in the basement was insufficient for storing the dead before burial or transportation.

Iris was up every morning at five a.m. and never left the ward before nine p.m., when she would go to her bed in a small room between the wards which she shared with Betty. They were responsible for their patients during the day and were on call at night. They were obliged to get up several times most nights to look in on their patients. Matron had told them that it was a great honor to work at the hospital and that they should not expect to be coddled in any way since all the ward maids were subjected to the same harsh routine during their first weeks on the job.

An hour later, after they had cleaned themselves up and returned to bed, they were again awakened when a confused woman strayed onto their ward. She was making a lot of noise, trying to find her way back to her own bed. It took a lot of soothing talk and infinite kindness to lead her back upstairs to the nurses on the upper floors. After the second interruption, Betty and Iris gave up trying to sleep and made some tea. They drank it as they watched the dawn light coming through the windows. Betty looked exhausted, while Iris seemed wide awake and ready to go for another day. Iris was a good five years younger than Betty and had remarkable energy. She never seemed to tire.

At the end of the second week, Iris and the other training nurses were given their first lecture by Dr. Susan Dimock in a room off the ward. The training nurses were from all over the Northeast and had been selected from a list of young women recommended for the training. There were three nurses from the Boston region, one from New York, one from Rhode Island, and Iris from Quebec. Dr. Dimock thanked them for enlisting in the training program and told them that the hospital's goal was to train women physicians in the practical study of medicine and to train women nurses for the care of the sick.

"You have heard of our founder, Dr. Zakrzewska, who was trained in Berlin and has always shown an interest in providing learning opportunities for women in medicine. Some of you may have met our woman surgeon," Dr. Dimock said, as a wave of incomprehension swept through the room.

"You don't believe me. Yes, we have a woman surgeon right here at the hospital," she repeated as the astonished murmurs grew louder and more animated.

"Her name is Dr. Anita Tyng," said Dimock with pride. "She graduated from the Woman's Medical College of Pennsylvania. She was the first woman in the US to become a surgeon. We are very proud of her."

Few women were allowed to enter a medical faculty in the US. The medical profession was almost totally dominated by men. Dr. Dimock herself had studied in Europe at the University of Zurich after the Harvard Medical School had rejected her candidature. Although modest in appearance and soft-spoken, the nurses found Dr. Dimock's enthusiasm for her profession contagious.

"You will be given twelve lectures by visiting staff during your year of training," she said. "You will need to be attentive to our women interns, who are learning to become medical doctors. They need your support. They will teach you the duties of the nurse: how to take the temperature of a patient, how to count the pulse rate and respirations, how to prepare dressings, and other nursing duties."

"Ask them questions. Don't be shy. We need all of you to succeed in your new careers."

It was going into the third week that it happened. Iris and Betty were back in the basement along with at least twenty other women, all of them relegated to the drudgery of washing poultice cloths, bandages, and rags using soft soap and a scrub board. Water had to be carried by hand from a pump outside and heated in a large kettle on a coal-burning stove. The larger items, including dirty clothing, towels, and bed linens, were washed by a dozen laundresses and run through hand wringers before being laid out on drying racks. Sheets and clothing often had to be boiled to kill lice and insects or soaked in chamber lye (urine) to rid them of stubborn stains and dirt. The heat in the room was quite unbearable and there was a strong smell of coal dust and perspiration.

Iris had just finished washing a whole tub of dirty poultice cloths when a short, angry redhead with a pox-scarred face approached her.

"So you're the new nurse?" the redhead demanded, her lip curled in an insolent tone. "You talk with a funny accent. You're one of them 'Frenchies' taking away good jobs from us South Boston Irish."

The redhead was emboldened by a phalanx of tittering friends, most of them distinguished only by their bad complexions and rotting teeth. They crowded in on Iris and Betty, trying to intimidate them.

Iris ignored the redhead and turned away from her.

"Hey, I'm talkin' to you, Frenchie," said the redhead. "Don't you turn your back on me!"

Iris was a farm girl and had grown up hauling water and doing manual labor. She wasn't impressed by the redhead and turned to face her. It wouldn't be the first time she'd thrown a punch. The maids were watching them closely, hoping for a catfight.

"What's your name?"

"Iris."

"Iris, that's the name of a flower," laughed the redhead. "Where you comin' from, milkmaid?"

"Quebec."

"Ah, so that explains it, does it? A feckin' French milkmaid from Canada. You think you're better than us 'Southies'?"

Iris found the remark ridiculous and grinned at the redhead.

"I've milked better cows than you," said Iris, chuckling to herself. She turned her back on the troublemaker and picked up the washtub.

"Hear that, girls," the redhead said, looking around to drum up support. "The bitch called me a cow. She thinks she's better than us."

Betty looked frightened and moved away, convinced that Iris was about to get her comeuppance. As Iris turned with the heavy washtub, the redhead shoved her and Iris lost her balance and her grip on the slippery edges of the washtub. It dropped directly onto the redhead's foot.

"Ow!" screamed the woman, doubled over in pain.

Iris figured that was as good a distraction as she was going to get. She picked up the washtub and headed off while the redhead stood on one leg and screamed.

"You did that on purpose, bitch. I'm gonna get you."

Betty followed Iris out the door while some twenty ward maids and washerwomen watched the redhead blow her top. She was a bully and had just found herself a new target among the newly arrived nurses.

"Her name's Polly," Betty told her.

Iris just nodded. It was the end of their shift and she was having a cup of tea with Betty before going to bed for a few hours.

"She ain't gonna give you a free pass, Iris," said Betty. "She's the worst of the lot."

"What should I do?" asked Iris.

"She's gonna come after you. She cut a girl last year she didn't like. She had to have stitches, and then up and left the job."

"I don't want to lose my job," said Iris. "She's not going to run me out of here."

"She's gonna try for sure."

"I don't care who she is. I've always dreamed of being a nurse."

"You have?"

"Yes, I have, ever since I was a little kid."

"All I'm sayin' is watch yourself after what you did to her."

Iris assumed an expression of wide-eyed innocence.

"But I didn't do anything."

"Iris," Betty snorted. "You dropped that washtub on purpose."

"Maybe," Iris admitted with a laugh.

"I knew it," Betty shook her head. "She's comin' for you."

"Good," Iris said. "Let her come. I've dealt with bullies before."

Iris fell asleep thinking about how she might go after Polly herself.

Fifty-three

It was going to be another long night in the ward. Iris had spent part of the day working with a hospital intern named Elsie, applying poultices to the chest of Mrs. White who was suffering from a grave case of pneumonia. Dr. Dimock had come by in the afternoon to see how her patient was doing, but it was going to be touch and go. The doctor feared she might not pass the night. Elsie and Iris were instructed to take her temperature every hour, apply dry cupping, and change the poultice every eight hours. They were to give her water or soup if she was hungry.

At precisely nine o'clock, Elsie went home just as Iris and Betty applied the cupping to the patient's back. This was an age-old treatment dating back to ancient Egyptian medicine. A pinch of lint was ignited and placed in a glass cup, which was then applied to the patient's skin. A vacuum was produced by the burning of oxygen and as the air cooled inside the cup, a partial vacuum was created, drawing out toxins and pathogens from a round area of inflammation. Mrs. White soon had half a dozen glass cups fixed to her back.

Since the next poultice application was scheduled for 2 a.m., Iris and Betty went to bed for an hour or two. At eleven, Iris got up to have a look at the stump of a diabetic woman whose foot had been amputated by Dr. Jones. Betty held the candle while Iris swabbed the wound with a diluted carbolic acid solution and put on a new dressing. Mrs. Bigelow had nerve damage and poor blood circulation, which led to the amputation of her foot. She complained of the burning sensation, and then promptly fell asleep.

The use of carbolic acid as an antiseptic had been discovered by Joseph Lister, a surgeon at the Glasgow Royal Infirmary. He rejected the then-prevalent 'miasma' theory of disease—that diseases were caused by inhaling 'bad air'—and embraced Pasteur's germ theory. He promoted the use of carbolic acid as an antiseptic in surgery and managed to reduce the incidence of wound sepsis and gangrene in his patients. The only downside to carbolic acid was the burning sensation on the skin, so it had to be used sparingly.

As Iris was finishing up, the confused woman from upstairs returned to the ward and started waking up patients as she went from bed to bed. Iris told Betty to take her back upstairs while she prepared Mrs. White for the poultice. The poor woman was feverish and half unconscious. Iris sat her up and washed her face and chest with cloth dipped in a warm soapy solution.

"Mary's got her," said Betty, returning. "I don't know what's going on up there with that damned woman."

"OK, Betty. We're ready for the poultice."

Betty went to fetch the poultice from the kitchen. She returned and held the candle close to the patient while Iris applied a thin layer of olive oil to her chest. Iris then removed the kitchen plates that were keeping the poultice warm and quickly applied the flannel poultice, tying it off with straps around her shoulders. Mrs. White gasped as the heat hit her. Iris covered her with a blanket and stood back. She wiped the sweat from the woman's brow and Mrs. White fell asleep before Iris could give her water.

"She's still running a fever," said Iris to Betty. "What was her temperature an hour ago?"

"Over 103 degrees."

"Let's check again in an hour."

It was after three a.m. when Betty called Iris to Mrs. Adams' bed. As Betty held a candle near the woman's face, Iris took her pulse but couldn't find one. She checked to see whether the woman was still breathing by holding a mirror close to her mouth. Mrs. Adams had passed away. The poor woman was in her sixties and suffered from an undiagnosed malady. She had been bedridden with red, painful sores for over a month which had turned purple and the doctors couldn't find any remedy to heal them.

"Go find the captain, Betty," said Iris. "Tell him that Mrs. Adams has passed away. I'll wait here for you."

Betty nodded and left. Iris sat in the dark ward and reflected on the hopeless situation of so many of their patients. There were a lot of infectious diseases in the city: smallpox, whooping cough, typhoid, rheumatic fever, typhus, scarlet fever, diphtheria, and tuberculosis. It was reported in 1865 that, in the sixteenth ward of New York City alone, there were more than 1,200 cases of smallpox and more than 2,000 cases of typhus. Things were not much better in Boston, with deaths from tuberculosis standing at 300 per 100,000 population, and infant mortality at around 200 per 1,000 live births. No one went to a hospital in the city if they could avoid it because one's chances of surviving the experience were not good at all.

Betty arrived with the captain and two male stretcher-bearers. They loaded up Mrs. Adams' wasted body and left while Iris and Betty collected the bed linens and the woman's few personal things, then remade the bed in the dark. After the exertion, they headed off to their quarters for an hour's sleep. Betty threw herself on her bed and was soon fast asleep. Iris took her time and went out on the ward again to check on Mrs. White. She returned to bed and as she lay down, she jumped up in shock. Her bed was wet with something that smelled suspiciously like urine.

"Betty!" Iris hissed. "My bed stinks of pee."

"What?" Betty asked, groggy with sleep.

"Someone emptied a chamber pot on it. The mattress is soaked."

Betty sighed loudly and got out of bed.

"That's Polly's work," she said, wrinkling her nose at the smell.

"She wouldn't dare do that."

"It may be one of her friends, but that's the kind of thing she likes to do."

"God, it stinks. Help me get rid of the bedding."

Together the women hauled the sheets and blankets out of the room and deposited them in the dirty sheets hamper. They returned and removed the mattress straw, which they set out to dry. Betty went to fetch a replacement mattress while Iris changed her clothes. They remade the bed and ten minutes later, both women were fast asleep.

At five a.m. Iris and Betty woke up and dressed for the day. It was the time in the morning when chamber pots were emptied, windows opened to air out the wards, bed linens changed and floors scrubbed. The chamber pot brigade, composed of nurses and ward maids from every floor, collected the pots, the bedpans, and the dirty linen on each floor and headed downstairs with them.

Matron went from ward to ward to see that the work was progressing before giving the order to serve breakfast to the patients. She was a kindly older lady who, nevertheless, could bark orders like a drill sergeant if the work wasn't done to her satisfaction. Nothing escaped her and the ward maids feared losing their jobs if they weren't up to snuff. Iris was surprised when the matron stopped to talk to her while Betty was scrubbing the floor.

"I seen you had a right busy night, Iris, with Mrs. Adams passing away."

"Yes, ma'am. Betty found her," said Iris, looking depressed. "She was fine earlier in the evening."

"It happens, my dear. Mrs. Adams was with us for a long time. She will be missed, but we do the best we can."

"Thank you, Matron."

"What happened to that mattress?"

The mattress was leaning against the wall in the maids' quarters.

"We had a bit of an accident last night, ma'am."

"Oh?" questioned the matron.

"It's mine, ma'am. Someone emptied a chamber pot in my bed last night."

"Sounds like someone is playing dirty tricks on you nurses. We've had a rash of those. A nurse on the sixth floor and now you."

"I'm sorry, ma'am. I'll replace the straw and we'll be fine."

Fifty-four

At 8:30 a.m. Dr. Dimock arrived on the ward accompanied by Elsie to check on her patients.

"We lost one last night," said the doctor.

"Yes, we did," confirmed Iris.

"How is Mrs. White doing this morning?"

"Her temperature is down a bit," said Iris. "Betty took it an hour ago."

"Good, so she had a good night?"

"Yes, Dr. Dimock," said Elsie.

Iris nodded but said nothing as Elsie took all the credit for the successful treatment of the patient.

"What's the matter, Iris?" asked Dimock, detecting the worry on her face.

"Doctor, I think we may have a problem with the new patient."

The doctor, Elsie, and Iris went down the row to have a look at the young woman at the end.

"Miss Peters complained last night of having a terrible headache and now she's got a rash," said Iris. "I was thinking she might have… the way you described it."

Dimock nodded and examined the woman.

"How are you feeling, Miss Peters? You look feverish."

"I'm hot, Doctor," said Peters, turning around. "I feel terrible."

"How's your head?"

"It hurts," said Peters.

Dimock noticed the dull red rash on her neck, chest, and stomach.

"She's got the rash alright," Elsie said, confirming the glaringly obvious.

"Yes, she does," said the doctor. "Try to get some sleep, Miss Peters."

Dimock let her go back to sleep while she finished her round of patients. Then she joined the others in the nurses' quarters.

"Iris, I think you're right. It looks like typhus. We need to move her upstairs right away and get her bedsheets and clothes washed."

"Yes, Doctor," said Elsie.

Iris nodded at Dimock and realized she would have to tell the laundry service to boil the bed linen to kill any suspect lice.

After Miss Peters had been moved upstairs, Elsie appeared with Dr. Jones, a kindly older physician, to check up on Mrs. Bigelow.

"How are you this morning, Mrs. Bigelow?" Jones asked with a cheerful air.

"Not so good, Doctor," said Mrs. Bigelow.

"Let's have a look at your foot."

Dr. Jones removed the dressing and examined the stump carefully. The wound was closed and seemed to be healing well.

"It's looking better, ma'am. There doesn't appear to be any purulent drainage. No pus and fluids."

"The skin burns, Doctor."

"That's from the carbolic acid solution, ma'am. We need to keep the wound clean from infection."

"So, Elsie, you were the one who removed the dressing during the night?"

"Yes, sir."

"You are tying the dressing too tight. You need to keep it loose so air can get to the wound."

"Yes, sir. That was the nurse. It was Iris who tied it too tight."

"I see, well keep that in mind when you are changing her dressing."

"Of course, sir," said Elsie as Iris arrived.

"The dressing is too tight, nurse," said Dr. Jones. "See that it is looser the next time."

"Yes, sir."

As Dr. Jones left the ward, Iris looked at Elsie, who came from a privileged old family in Boston. Iris had realized from day one that the intern was a shirker. She was lazy and always blaming others for the mistakes she made. Iris said nothing and smiled at her colleague. She had no intention of making an enemy of Elsie. She loved her job too much for that.

"I won't be here this afternoon, Elsie. Dr. Dimock is sending me to nurse an outside patient."

"Does she want me to go along?"

"No, I think she needs you here. It's another case of pneumonia. I'm going to be applying poultices throughout the night."

"Well, good luck then."

Iris traveled north in a hansom cab along Charles Street, through the Boston Common, where there were a lot of well-dressed women pushing baby prams and kids playing in the park. Iris promptly fell asleep as they drove through Beacon Hill and took the Craigie bridge across the Charles River into Cambridge. They arrived at a brick row house and the driver had to touch Iris' shoulder to awaken her. She climbed down with her bag and collected a large sack from the driver that the matron had given her. It held a supply of clean flannel poultices, a container of linseed meal and mustard, a bottle of olive oil, a thermometer, glass cups, and other indispensable items. Dr. Dimock said the Codmans would provide anything else she needed.

Iris was quickly ushered into the servants' quarters, where she was shown a room. Mrs. Codman arrived moments later and led her upstairs to meet her daughter, a pretty 18-year-old named Emily. The girl was highly congested and hot to the touch.

"So you are one of Dr. Dimock's new nurses?" asked Mrs. Codman.

"Yes, ma'am. I started this year."

"What's your name?" asked Emily.

"Iris, miss."

"You seem to be very young to be training as a nurse?"

"I'm 16 years old, miss."

"That is quite young," replied Mrs. Codman with a smile.

"Mother, Iris is younger than I am."

"Well, Dr. Dimock thinks she's very talented," said the mother, giving her daughter a reassuring pat on the arm. "She says you are French."

"French Canadian, ma'am."

Iris put her hand on Emily's shoulder. Her skin was very hot.

"Where does it hurt?"

"Mostly my chest."

"Not in the back?"

"Not so much."

"Did Dr. Dimock explain the treatment, miss?"

"No, she didn't."

"The treatment involves dry cupping and the application of poultices. We are going to start with the poultice. My instructions are to change it three times a day. I'll need access to the kitchen," said Iris, turning to Mrs. Codman.

"Of course. Anything you need," said the mother.

"Can you sit up, please?" asked Iris.

Iris gently helped Emily sit up in bed while she took her temperature. It was 102 degrees.

"She's got quite a fever," Iris said, careful to hide her concern. "I better get to work. Be back in a jiffy."

In the kitchen, the bemused cook and servant watched with interest as Iris prepared a poultice, which so many mothers and grandmothers prepared time and again. Poultices were believed to 'draw out' the infection. They were considered essential for treating colds, congestion, and any sickness of the lungs, but were also used for other kinds of complaints. Iris' poultice was made with three parts linseed meal and one part mustard. She mixed the meal and mustard into a paste with water, heating it on the stove, and then spread the hot paste out on two layers of flannel. She placed two warm kitchen plates over the poultice and carried it upstairs.

Emily sat up as Iris entered the bedroom.

"It's going to be a bit of a shock, miss," Iris warned her. "It's quite hot and we need to apply it quickly."

Iris spread a thin layer of olive oil on Emily's chest and then applied the poultice. The girl gasped as the heat hit her. Iris wrapped the flannel straps around her shoulders and tied them in the back. She covered her up with a blanket and stood back.

"Is it uncomfortable?"

"It's hot, but it feels good."

"Good, Emily," said Iris, smiling. "Try to get some sleep. I'll be back again in a few hours for the cupping."

Pneumonia was called 'the most fatal of all acute diseases' by Sir William Osler, the father of modern medicine. During the Civil War, the mortality rate for pneumonia was twenty-four percent among soldiers, making it the third most common cause of death from disease during the conflict.

It was a grueling schedule, but at least Iris could sleep every few hours without being disturbed by other patients demanding her services. She ate her meals at the dining room table with the Codman family, who were very generous and helpful. She even spoke French with Emily's father, who had lived in France for several years.

Emily's condition quickly improved under Iris' care. Two days later, Emily was on her stomach and covered by a sheet as Iris removed the last glass cups from her back, leaving purplish circles on her skin.

"How is she?" asked her mother.

"She's better, ma'am. The fever is gone, and she says her appetite is back."

"Well, that's wonderful!"

"I feel fine, mother," said Emily.

Iris was sufficiently encouraged by Emily's progress to stop the treatment. The family was overjoyed at the news. They had all been terribly worried by Emily's illness. Mrs. Codman invited Iris to stay on for the rest of the week, and sent a note to Dr. Dimock, informing her of Emily's recovery. Iris had enjoyed her time with the Codmans and had become fast friends with young Emily.

The following afternoon, Dimock arrived to check on her patient. She auscultated Emily and confirmed that her lungs were clear and she was out of danger. There were tears in Mrs. Codman's eyes as she heard the news. The Codmans thanked the doctor and embraced young Iris as they boarded a hansom cab and drove away.

"You did very well, Iris," Dr. Dimock told her. "Thank you. The Codmans are friends with Dr. Zakrzewska and our benefactors."

"They were very kind to me, Doctor."

"I'm sure they were. By the way, you are looking much better yourself after your stay. I will need to send you out more often for home care," said Dimock with a laugh.

"Thank you," said Iris, grateful for the praise.

"By the way, my dear, I'm giving you the night off so you can see your parents. They sent a message to the hospital today."

"I'm sorry, Doctor. I wasn't expecting them until next week."

"They're staying at the Parker House, my dear. You have a dinner invitation, so you must get ready and look your best."

Fifty-five

November 9, 1872

"Parker House is an immense hotel, with all manner
of white marble public passages and public rooms.
I live in a corner, high up, and have a hot and cold bath
in the bedroom connecting with the sitting room
and comforts not in existence when I was here before.
The cost of living is enormous, but happily we can afford it."
Charles Dickens in a letter to his daughter.

Parker House on School Street was one of the oldest hotels in Boston, a richly furnished old building with heavy drapes and chandeliers near the Boston Common and just down the road from the Massachusetts Statehouse. When it opened in 1855, the visitors were surprised and delighted by the gorgeous furniture, the beauty of the dining room, and the style of the rooms.

Bennett and Eliza had come east to New York to meet with a group of investors in the railway business who were interested in buying a rail line in Kentucky. They continued their journey to Boston to see how young Iris was getting on at the nursing school. They invited her to have dinner with them in the elegant hotel dining room, with its white tablecloths, silver cutlery, and crystal wine glasses. Iris wore a tightly laced corset over a bodice paired with a red embroidered skirt and wore her blond hair in a chignon with small curls in a silk snood. Eliza wore a similar outfit in blue alongside her handsome husband in a black tailcoat, vest, and stiffly starched white shirt and ascot. They had never seen Iris looking so lovely and so well dressed. Eliza soon learned that Iris had borrowed the dress and accessories from Dr. Dimock after the doctor had insisted that she dress appropriately for the event.

During dinner, Iris entertained them with stories about her patients at the hospital, never alluding to the threats she was receiving from one pesky ward maid. They had just finished a wonderful duck confit cooked with thyme and garlic and polished off a bottle of French wine. Iris had never eaten anything as delicious before, and it was a welcome relief after the tasteless, overcooked meals at the hospital.

"Thank you for the wonderful meal, Papa Bennett," she said with a smile.

"Stop it, Iris," said Eliza, grinning. "Stop teasing your papa. I think she's had too much to drink, Bennett."

"Eliza," Iris giggled, her eyes wide with feigned surprise. "I wouldn't dare!"

Bennett laughed. He was used to Iris' sense of humor. She took a wicked pleasure in teasing him and making him ill at ease in front of guests who knew her family name was Gagnon. She adored old-fashioned, stick-in-the-mud Bennett and loved to pull his leg.

"It's my pleasure, Iris," said Bennett, returning the smile. "We've missed you so much, my dear."

"Bennett asks after you," said Eliza. "You must write to us more often."

"I don't have the time, Eliza. The days are so long."

"We think about how hard it must be working in that hospital of yours. You're so thin and pale."

"The first month was the very worst, Eliza. Now things are better and I have more moments to myself. I love the job. I like working with Dr. Dimock. She's an excellent physician."

"How's your mum?" asked Eliza.

"She's fine. She writes to me about the crops, the weather, the neighbors, and of course the children. I do miss Lac-Brome, Eliza, but my life is here now. This is where I feel useful."

"Good for you, Iris," said Bennett.

"How is your brother faring, Eliza?" asked Iris.

"He works in a shop selling and repairing clocks and pocket watches," said Eliza. "Hard to believe that Byron, who is never on time, is now repairing clocks."

There was a sudden noisy disturbance in the kitchen, followed by the wait staff bursting into the dining hall. The maître d' stood in the center of the group and clapped his hands to get the attention of the dinner guests.

"Ladies and gentlemen, we have an emergency on our hands. There's a fire in the city. We want you to collect your things and go to the lobby."

Bennett motioned for Eliza and Iris to keep their seats as he went to the window to have a look. He could see smoke in the air and panicked people congregating on the street corner. He could hear the faint sound of fire alarms going off outside. He went back to the table, his face expressionless. Panic was contagious, so he had no intention of scaring the women as he returned to the table.

"We'd better go," he said quietly.

They followed the dinner crowd out of the restaurant and into the lobby. The doors to the street were wide open and there was the acrid smell of smoke coming in from the street.

"Stay here," said Bennett. "Let me have a look."

Eliza and Iris stood near the front door and listened to the voices of the panicked guests. The Great Fire of Chicago was on everyone's mind. It had happened the previous year and killed some 300 people, destroying over 17,000 buildings. There was a real fear among the hotel guests that the same thing was happening in Boston.

Bennett followed the crowd, heading south toward the fire. As he turned right on Washington, he saw the first fire engine struggling to make its way toward the fire on Summer Street, near the corner of Kingston. A stiff breeze was blowing in a southeasterly direction, sending sparks and burning debris onto the roofs of nearby buildings. The crowd was full of people intent on lending a hand to the families trying to escape the burning buildings. A fire engine arrived on Summer to help fight the fire, but Bennett could see it was already too late to extinguish the blaze. The wind blew sparks and burning debris over the heads of the crowd toward the buildings behind them. It wasn't long before fires were breaking out in the adjoining streets and the crowd was boxed in.

In his dark coat and dinner attire, the CEO of Louisville Southern stood out in the crowd, but he wasn't alone in helping the women and old people collect their possessions and rush north out of danger. Americans from all walks of life, from street sweepers to university professors, assisted in the mass exodus. Old couples stumbled down the front steps of tenement buildings loaded down with boxes of precious possessions; shabbily dressed children hauled cardboard suitcases into the street and then ran back to collect more; frightened horses were released from stables and ran wild down the streets while others were harnessed to heavily loaded wagons and trotted away to get clear of the fire and smoke. A young mother with two frightened children in tow was having trouble dragging a heavy bag along behind her when Bennett picked it up and followed her down a narrow alley. As they emerged from the alley, the building behind them collapsed in flames. They reached safety on Washington Street and the woman took back her bag. She thanked Bennett, who returned to the hotel.

Eliza gasped in shock when she saw Bennett pass through the lobby doors. His hat and coat were covered in ash.

"Bennett," Eliza exclaimed, brushing the ash from his shoulders. "We were worried about you."

"I'm all right," Bennett assured her, taking off his hat and shaking it out, "but the fire is out of control. It's on Summer Street, just a few blocks south of here."

"You think we might have to evacuate the hospital?" Iris asked, alarmed. "I must get back."

"I wouldn't worry, Iris. The wind is blowing to the southeast. I think your hospital will be safe."

"I should go, Papa. They might need me."

Bennett nodded. He would have expected nothing less of Iris. They left the hotel, walking away from the fire up School Street to Tremont.

From the Boston Common, they observed the blaze on Summer and Franklin, with the flames jumping from one tenement building to another. Fire alarms sounded across the city, and fire engines arrived from the surrounding towns. They caught a hansom cab which took them west away from the fire. They arrived at the hospital and noticed a small crowd standing in the lobby. Iris ran inside and saw the matron working in triage and issuing curt orders to the ward maids.

"What are you doing here?" the matron asked. "I gave you the night off, remember?"

"I just thought—."

"We're fine, Iris. We've got it under control."

Iris looked around the hall and saw the matron was right. Women and children were coming in with burns, but the numbers were nothing like she'd feared.

"It's early days yet," the matron said. She looked Iris up and down. "You're not dressed for it. Now go away, I'm busy."

Bennett and Eliza joined Iris in the lobby just as Betty and a ward maid Iris had never seen before helped an elderly woman into a chair. The burns looked relatively minor, but because of her age, they were very gentle with her. Betty spotted Iris in her fancy evening clothes, observing the triage from the doorway. She waved to her and gave her a tired smile. She looked dead on her feet. She admired Iris and felt only shame when she looked down at her shabby work clothes.

Iris hurried over to see her friend, followed by Bennett and Eliza.

"This is my friend, Betty," said Iris. She then looked at Betty's colleague. "I'm sorry, I think you must be new here. What's your name?"

"I'm Ida, miss. I'll be replacing Betty on the third floor."

"Betty and Ida," Iris said proudly. "This is my papa Bennett and his wife Eliza."

They shook hands, and Iris was surprised to find herself staring at the new girl. Ida was petite, almost waif-like, with dark hair and milky blue eyes. Iris came back to herself in time to notice that Eliza was looking at the scene with genuine concern.

"How bad is it?" Eliza asked Betty.

"It's just starting, ma'am," said Betty. "Just a few burn victims have come in."

Betty smiled at Iris.

"You look so beautiful, Iris, in your new clothes," blurted Betty.

"These are Dr. Dimock's clothes, Betty," said Iris, smiling. "She lent them to me."

"Well, you look wonderful in them," added Ida.

"Thank you, Ida," replied Iris.

"We better go. Matron says I have the evening off. I'll see you tomorrow."

"Bye, Iris," said Betty as they left the lobby and returned to the hotel.

Back at the hotel, they watched as firefighters and hotel personnel hosed down the exterior walls and roof in case the fire suddenly turned north. The hotel lounge was packed with people, but Bennett managed to find three seats near the bar. He ordered a brandy for himself and tea for Eliza and Iris while they watched the progression of the fire through the hotel window. A city employee sitting nearby turned away from the window and looked at Bennett.

"Our fire chief warned the mayor about the risk," he said, shaking his head, "but no one would listen to him."

"I would think the Chicago fire would have sounded the alarm across the country," said Bennett.

"Well, it should have. Captain John Damrell suggested improving the city's water mains to fight fires, but nobody listened to him."

"Do you think they can stop it?"

"It's blowing toward the docks, sir, so it won't be long before it runs out of fuel."

Bennett was about to reply when he felt a nudge on his arm. He turned and had to smile. Iris had fallen asleep on Eliza's shoulder.

"I'm going to take her upstairs, Bennett," Eliza told him as she gently helped get Iris to her feet. "The poor girl needs a good night's rest."

Iris swayed slightly, her eyelids fluttering, and was about to lose her balance when Bennett stood up to steady her. Together, Eliza and Iris stumbled out of the lounge while Bennett remained behind, chatting with the local people.

In the morning, Boston woke up and there was a great sigh of relief across the city. The fire had spread rapidly overnight. Although many buildings were made of brick or stone, their window frames and other fixtures were made of dry wood and these exploded in flames, allowing the fire to jump across streets. The firefighters made a last-ditch effort to create firebreaks by blowing up buildings in the fire's path.

Bennett and Eliza slept fitfully, aware that an evacuation order could come at any time. Iris was dead to the world until she was awakened by Eliza around six o'clock in the morning. They quickly got up and went downstairs to see what had happened during the night.

The desperate tactic of firebreaks had worked, but not before two

Boston firefighters and eleven civilians had lost their lives. The fire destroyed 776 buildings over an area of 65 acres.

The atmosphere in the lobby was one of subdued relief, tempered by regret at the destruction and loss of life elsewhere in the city. The hotel itself had never been in danger, and the staff were making a determined effort to care for their guests.

Bennett and Eliza insisted that Iris join them for breakfast before they took her back to the hospital.

Fifty-six

When Iris arrived back on the third floor several hours later, there was a new case of diphtheria, a disease so dangerous it had a nickname —the 'strangling angel'. The patient was in her forties. She had a sore throat and swollen glands in her neck. Dr. Lucy Sewall wasted no time, placing her at the far end of a row of beds to isolate her from the other patients. She issued strict instructions to the ward maids and nurses to wear face masks when they were in her vicinity. Diphtheria was a major killer of young children and older adults. It was caused by a bacterial toxin that destroyed the cells lining the throat and windpipe, making it difficult to breathe. The woman had a maddeningly persistent cough, which kept the other women awake. There was no known cure for the disease and not much could be done to help her except to keep her hydrated.

When Elsie came in later that morning, she told Iris to give the woman water every few hours to calm her coughing. She then left to go home, complaining about fire damage to her parents' home. It was a busy day for Iris and the new ward maid, Ida, with new burn victims coming in every few hours. Day soon turned into night, and Elsie didn't return. It ended up being a relatively quiet night on the ward.

In the morning, after the chamber pot brigade and cleaning crew had completed their tasks and the patients had been fed, Iris and the other training nurses were summoned to a lecture given by Dr. Sewall who wasn't much older than most of her students. She had graduated from the New England Female Medical College in 1862 and had spent a year studying in London and Paris before coming to work at the hospital. Tired as they were, the nurses were all looking forward to it. Lectures were a welcome break from the interminable drudgery of their everyday routines. They were eager to learn something about the art and science of medicine.

As the nurses arrived one by one in the lecture hall, Dr. Sewall was struck by how exhausted and unhealthy they looked. *No wonder,* she thought. *We've been working them day and night, without a break, for weeks on end. They'll need a rest soon or they will drop out of the program from sheer exhaustion.*

Dr. Sewall shook off the thought and did her best to offer a bright, welcoming smile.

"Have you ever heard of the Kaiserswerth Deaconesses of Germany?" she asked.

No one replied.

"The Kaiserswerth Deaconesses are Protestant nuns trained in caring for the sick, the poor, orphans, and homeless children. The motherhouse was founded in 1836 by Pastor Theodor Fliedner and his wife. The women train to be nurses and serve for five years, receiving room and board. Can you think of someone famous who has trained with them?"

"Florence Nightingale," said Iris.

"Yes, Florence Nightingale got her training in Germany. And do you know what Nightingale teaches today at the St. Thomas Hospital in London?"

No one said a word.

"She teaches nursing, ladies. Just like we do here. She wrote a book entitled *Notes About Nursing,* which describes the five essential elements that create a favorable environment for healing: pure air, pure water, efficient drainage, cleanliness, and light. Patients also need nutritious food. They need to practice personal hygiene. They need to be treated with dignity and kindness. Where did she learn these things?"

"In Crimea, Doctor," said a young Boston nurse.

"Yes, she did. Nightingale is famous for leading a group of thirty-eight volunteer nurses to care for British soldiers wounded during the Crimean War in 1854. Her nurses were shocked by the lack of medicines and low standard of hygiene in the camps. The first thing they did was clean every room and wash their hands. Nightingale's priorities have always been cleanliness and hygiene; ours must be the same. You must learn to wash your hands often during the day and to keep as clean as possible for your work in the hospital."

Let's take a moment today to talk about your commitment to your work here. You have been working long hours for almost two months. We know it's hard, working days and then being on call at night, but this has been our way of initiating our nursing staff since we opened the hospital. Nurses have to learn to put their patients first. Your first months here are a test, if you like, to separate the wheat from the chaff. You will soon be getting more free time, with afternoons and nights off during the week. In a few months, you will be on a day shift and won't have to work nights."

There was a sigh of relief from the exhausted women.

"Do you have any questions?" Dr. Sewall asked.

"I was wondering what is in these bottles of medicine that we give our patients, Dr. Sewall?" asked the nurse from New York. "There are only numbers on the bottles, no labels. Why don't they put a name on the label?"

"That's a very good question, miss. I've never understood why we don't put the name of the medicine on the bottle. There are, of course, all kinds of medicine. Pain relievers, antipyretics, cathartics, camphor, disinfectants, etc. There are a lot of different ingredients that go into those medicines. Pain relievers can contain opium, morphine, phenacetine, and acetanilid. Anti-pyretics contain willow bark and meadowsweet. Only the doctor prescribing them knows what they contain."

"I was wondering," said Iris, "whether we could have more light in the ward at night. We're only allowed two candles per week."

"The gas is turned down after 9 p.m.," Sewall told her. "That is the rule and the candles are there to help out in case of an emergency."

"Well, that may be the case, Doctor," Iris said tartly, "but we can't do our jobs properly if we can't see what we're doing. Often there isn't even enough light to properly dress a wound."

I like this girl, Sewall thought. *She is very young, but isn't afraid to ask questions and contest the rules.*

"I have to agree with you, miss. I will talk to the captain of the night watch and have him increase the gas flow at night."

"Thank you, Doctor."

"We don't have any textbooks," said the nurse from Rhode Island, emboldened by Iris. "I was thinking it would be helpful if we could read more about nursing."

"It is not our vision nor our aim to learn about nursing from books, miss," replied Seawall firmly. "Your training here is all about doing, about the practice of medicine. You are here to learn how to do the job, not to read about it."

A new patient had been brought in during the evening with a terrible case of the 'bloody flux' or 'camp fever', as it was called. Mrs. Donnelly was in her forties and was weak, with bloody diarrhea, stomach cramps, and nausea. Bloody flux was very common in the Boston slums and was caused by the shigella bacteria, which damages the blood vessels in the gut, kidneys, and lungs. She was one of Dr. Jones' patients and he had given clear instructions on how to take care of the poor woman. Iris sent Ida to the supply cabinet to fetch an opium pill for the woman, reckoning that if nothing else, it would help her get some rest during the night. Opiates were standard remedies for hundreds of ailments, including dysentery, cholera, malaria, pneumonia, menstrual pain, and more.

Opium was the vital ingredient in all the magical, cure-all medicines sold around town. A man could purchase a pint of beer, and for the same price, buy a quarter ounce of laudanum that contained ten grains of opium. During the war, the Union Army issued ten million opium pills to its soldiers and some three million ounces of opium powders and tinctures. After the opium pill had relieved the woman's pain, Iris took her temperature, which was over 100 degrees. They let the woman go back to sleep and returned to their quarters where they drank tea while Iris made notes in a tiny notebook she hid in her pocket. She noted the patient's name, the date of arrival, the body temperature, the medicine taken, and the time it was administered. She also noted the patient's physical appearance.

"What are you doing?" asked Ida.

"Taking notes about the patient," replied Iris.

"Why?"

"Just to remind myself so I don't forget something when I have to talk to the doctor."

"You are a good nurse, Iris," said Ida, looking at her younger colleague with a tender smile.

"Thank you, Ida," said Iris, looking up.

"Can I see your notes?"

Ida came over to have a look. She sat very close to Iris, admiring her neat script. She was small and childlike, but older than Iris by five or six years. Iris watched as Ida hesitantly ran her finger down the page, pausing at certain words before moving on.

"Ida?" Iris asked softly. "Do you know how to read?"

Ida flushed with embarrassment.

"It's all right," Iris reassured her. "I was just curious."

Ida returned to her bed and appeared to be sulking. Iris continued with her notes before Ida broke the silence.

"I know something you don't," she said with a mischievous smile.

"What?"

"I know the patient."

"You do?"

"Yes, Mrs. Donnelly comes from my neighborhood in the South End. I recognized her when they brought her in. She lives near the Gate of Heaven Church. Dr. Jones is friends with the priest there. I've seen him at Sunday mass. The area is very poor. The people have nothing."

"Do you have family in the South End?" Iris asked.

"Yes," replied Ida. "My mother and a brother."

"How are they?"

"They are fine, Iris. My mother takes in laundry and my brother works in a factory."

"Do you like working here?"

"Yes, I like it better since you came."

Iris smiled, feeling a strong sense of attraction for this angelic young woman.

"What was it like at the Codman house?"

"It was a lot of work, Ida, but the family was very nice to me."

"They liked you because you spoke French?"

"No. They were just very kind and worried about their sick daughter."

"What was she like, the daughter?"

"Emily is about your age, Ida. A very nice girl."

"The family is rich, I think."

"Yes, they are. Would you like to be rich, Ida?"

"Of course, I would. I would move my family to a better place and help my mother and brother. It is not easy where we live."

Fifty-seven

Just before sunrise, Iris got up to look at Mrs. Donnelly. She was already wide awake but very pale and had dark bags under her eyes. She would not get better unless she could hold down her food. Iris gave her some beef broth and a spoonful of castor oil, as ordered by the doctor. A half-hour later, the poor woman had thrown up the castor oil and had a watery bowel movement. Iris called Ida and together they cleaned her up and changed her bedclothes. Iris was worried. The doctor had only prescribed opium and castor oil for Mrs. Donnelly, and neither was having a positive effect. There was no real cure for the bloody flux, and it was not uncommon for patients to die from it. Iris didn't want to lose one of Dr. Jones' patients.

It was almost time for the morning bell when Iris had an idea.

"Ida, can you go down to the kitchen and see whether the cook can prepare some rice water for Mrs. Donnelly? She's worse than she was last night."

"Sure," said Ida, happy to be doing something for her friend.

"We'll try the rice water first and then see whether she can hold down the beef broth."

After the morning chamber pot brigade had passed, Elsie arrived and took charge of the patients while Iris and Ida returned to the basement to wash poultices again.

"Wet yourself, did you, Frenchie?" asked Polly, determined to pick on Iris again.

"I don't know what you're talking about," Iris snapped.

"We got you, didn't we?" Polly gloated, grinning at her mates. "See, Frenchie here doesn't want to admit she pissed herself. Too full of pride, the snotty bitch."

Polly's friends moved in closer, smirking and hoping for a fight.

"You're not making sense," said Iris dismissively.

Polly turned to her friends. "She ain't gonna admit it."

"She knows," snarled a dark-haired wisp of a girl with a thin, pox face. "We got her."

"Are you sure?" asked Polly, unconvinced.

"We got her, Polly."

Polly and her mates were still laughing when they retired to a corner of the basement.

"She's gonna come for you again, Iris," hissed Ida. "It's gonna be worse next time."

"So what?" Iris shrugged. She had work to do and didn't look the least bit concerned by the threat.

Later that morning, Dr. Dimock stepped into the ward to check on her patients. After confirming that all was well, she asked Iris to take a message to a physician in Roxbury, south of Boston proper. Iris was to take a hansom cab to the doctor's office and wait for his reply. Iris loved getting out and running errands for Dr. Dimock. She had had little time for sightseeing since arriving in the city. The hospital called a cab for her and she headed west on Tremont Street. The streets were filled with waifs and strays in rags and rough-looking working men. The surroundings began to change as the cab turned south on Warren Avenue into open country. They passed farmers driving hay wagons and men leading cattle to slaughterhouses. Iris fell asleep as the gentle movements of the cab and her fatigue got the better of her. The next thing she knew, the driver was leaning into the cab and trying to wake her.

"Wake up, sleepyhead," said the burly Southie driver in a lovely Irish brogue.

Iris instantly came awake and struggled to get out of the cab. She stood on the pavement in a daze and looked around at the small town of Roxbury.

"Please wait for me, sir. I won't be long."

The driver nodded at her as she crossed the road to a new building with a fancy brass plaque on the door. She entered the physician's office, where a young man barely older than herself asked what her business was.

"Sir, I'm here with a message from Dr. Dimock."

"Ah," said the young doctor as Iris handed him the message.

While Iris looked around the office, the doctor sat down at his desk and read the note.

"There, but for the grace of God go I," he said, shaking his head. "Tell Dr. Dimock that we tried to treat the patient's sepsis, but she died before it could take effect. We are very sorry for her loss."

He doesn't look that sorry, thought Iris.

"Sir, would you mind writing a note for the doctor?"

"Are you not an intern?" he asked Iris, surprised.

"No, sir. I'm a nurse at the hospital."

"A nurse?" snapped the doctor, looking annoyed.

She knew what he was thinking. He had mistaken Iris for an intern. *Nurses were not to be trusted with messages.* The doctor exhaled loudly and took his time composing a message for Dr. Dimock on a thick vellum prescription pad with his name at the top. He signed it, folded the sheet, and handed it to Iris.

"Go," said the pompous young doctor, waving her out of the office.

Iris left the office, her face flushed with anger at the doctor's rude behavior. She looked at the waiting cab, trying to compose herself when she had an idea.

"Give me a moment," she called to the driver. "I'll be right back."

She crossed the street to a dimly lit apothecary shop and stepped inside, returning five minutes later with a bouquet of common yarrow flowers wrapped in paper.

Back on the ward at the hospital, Iris ground up the white flowers to make a yarrow tea for Mrs. Donnelly. Ida went to the kitchen to get a pot of hot water and she poured it over the petals.

"What are you making?" asked Ida.

"Yarrow tea, Ida. It's called '*l'herbe à dinde*'."

Ida gave her a blank look.

"That's what we call it back home," said Iris, smiling. "Here they call it turkey grass."

"Turkey grass? I never heard of it."

"Let's give her the tea," Iris said briskly, reminding herself that Ida was a city girl. "This may help her keep her food down."

Ida nodded and took the cup.

"I'll be back soon," said Iris. "I need to see Dr. Dimock. After the tea, we'll try some more beef broth."

Ida went off to give Mrs. Donnelly the tea while Iris descended to Dimock's office and knocked on the door.

"Come in," said the doctor, gesturing Iris to a chair.

"Here's the message from the doctor in Roxbury," said Iris, handing her the note. "At first, he didn't want to write it out."

"Yes," said Dimock, rolling her eyes. "I know him. He's a terrible snob. He treats all his staff like they were hapless dolts, my dear, especially the women. Welcome to the masculine world of medicine in this country."

She read the note and frowned. She turned to Iris.

"That moron lost a woman patient of mine just to spite me," said Dimock sadly. "If he had treated her in time, she would have survived."

"Sorry to hear that, ma'am."

"We try to do our best," said Dimock bitterly, "but often our best is not enough."

Iris had never heard the doctor sound so discouraged.

"Yes, ma'am."

"Our patients come here in terrible shape. They can't be cured at home, so we are their place of last resort. It pains me to say this, but there often isn't much we can do."

Fifty-eight

After Elsie had left for the night, Iris and Ida were busy almost non-stop with their patients. The yarrow tea seemed to help Mrs. Donnelly. She hadn't thrown up after having taken the beef broth. Two pneumonia patients were in the ward and required poultice changes. In addition, they had to change the dressing of the woman with the amputated foot. Throughout the night, they heard the hacking cough of the diphtheria patient. There were times when she stopped and it seemed that the poor woman had expired, but suddenly she would wake up and the cough would return.

The girls had a break around 2 a.m. and sat in their room drinking tea and eating biscuits. Iris was attracted to Ida and found her to be an agreeable companion who was always direct in her questions and cheerful around patients.

"I only went to school for a few years," said Ida. "We worked in a tannery, me and my brother."

"A tannery?"

"It was a horrible place. It stank. I hated it and we were paid very little."

"Did you like going to school?"

"Sure, I did, but my ma needed me at home. So I stopped."

"You could learn to read, Ida, I could teach you."

"You don't have time for that, Iris," laughed Ida. "We barely have time to sleep in this job."

"I could get you an English grammar book. You could study the words at your own pace."

"You would teach me?"

"Yes, Ida. I'm serious."

There was a long silence as Ida thought about Iris' offer.

"So when do you think Polly will be coming around?" asked Iris.

"I don't know, but she's not gonna be happy until she gets her revenge."

"I was thinking the same thing. I can't keep changing mattresses or matron will complain to the doctors."

"We can hide your mattress and you can sleep with me," said Ida. "I don't mind. We don't get much sleep, anyway."

Iris got up and grabbed her mattress. Together, they hauled it across the ward to the supply cabinet where they left it.

They returned to their room and Iris slipped into bed with Ida, who curled into her arms.

"It's warmer sleeping together," said Ida, happily nestling in Iris' arms.

Iris said nothing, but felt wonderful, feeling the heat coming off Ida's body.

An hour later, they were up again, applying poultices and checking up on their patients. Ida smiled at Iris. She was in love with her and she knew that Iris felt the same way about her. It was a rare moment of happiness and they were almost giddy with euphoria working together on the ward. As they were finishing up, they heard heavy footsteps on the stairs. Iris and Ida looked at each other. *Who could be on the stairs at this hour?* It was unusual to see anyone on the stairs in the middle of the night. They laughed and hid behind the supply cabinet door while they watched for the intruders on the stairs.

The pox-faced maid came into the ward first, carrying a bucket of urine, followed by Polly.

"Well, feck me," said Pox Face, looking at the one mattress remaining in the room. "There's only one mattress in here. Where's the milkmaid sleeping?"

"I don't know," said Polly. "Maybe she moved out?"

"And they ain't on the floor either. They should be workin'. Something's not right."

"Yeah, let's get out of here."

At that moment, the door to the nurse's room slammed shut with a loud bang.

"What the hell was that?" asked Polly, as she grabbed the door handle and turned, but it wouldn't open. The door opened outwards and something was preventing it from opening.

On the other side of the door, Iris had wedged a heavy wooden plank that had fallen off a patient's bed frame. The door wouldn't move because the plank was pushing up against the opposing wall. Iris and Ida were having the time of their lives as they looked at each other and squealed with delight.

Polly and Pox thought they might scream, but they didn't want to wake up the captain of the night watch while holding a pail of urine. They were locked in, so they waited, silently hoping the door would open all by itself.

At 5 a.m., the hospital filled with people coming and going on each floor. The chamber pot brigade was on the move. Polly and her friend stood up, thinking they would simply step out and join up with the other women heading downstairs. They were still waiting twenty minutes later when the door opened and the matron stood in the doorway, observing them.

"Well, well. What have we here? Polly and Mary Ann."

"We got locked in here, matron. Thanks, now we're free."

"You certainly are free, both of you. You're free to find work somewhere else. I've had enough complaints about you two. And there you are, caught with the goods."

"But Matron," protested Polly.

"I'm giving you two notice," said the matron, stepping aside so the captain of the night watch could see the two miscreants. "Please escort these women out of the building."

The captain led Polly and Mary Ann out of the room and down the stairs. They passed Iris and Ida, smiling as they came up the stairs with their empty chamber pots.

At the end of the week, Mrs. Donnelly was eating solid food again and looking much better for it as was the diphtheria patient who had less swelling in her neck. She was still coughing, but seemed to be recovering. One of the pneumonia patients had died in the night while the other seemed to be improving.

Dr. Jones stepped into the ward to have a look at Mrs. Bigelow and confirmed her departure from the hospital. The doctor was astonished to see Mrs. Donnelly looking so much better. He thought her case was hopeless when the priest of his church suggested he treat the woman.

"Excellent work," said the doctor to Iris and Ida. "I had little hope for Mrs. Donnelly when I brought her in."

"Thank you, Dr. Jones," said Iris, dropping her notebook. She picked it up and put it back in her pocket.

"What have you got there, Miss Iris?"

"Just some notes, sir," said Iris.

"Let me have a look, please."

Iris gave him her notebook. He read the names of several of the patients on the floor and then located the page concerning Mrs. Donnelly.

"Well, isn't this interesting? Do you mind if I borrow your notes, miss? I will return them."

"Of course, Doctor."

"I like to write up each of my cases, you know, for posterity and also to determine whether the treatment was appropriate and the correct dosages were employed."

Iris nodded, and the doctor left to continue his round. Matron came by with the sad news that Mrs. Peters with typhus had died, along with several smallpox patients on the top floor.

Dr. Jones was on his way out of the hospital when he saw the door to Dr. Dimock's office was open. She was having tea with her colleague, Dr. Sewall, and discussing the content of an upcoming lecture for the nurses. The discussion soon turned to the rise in mortality among patients at the hospital.

"We can do better, Lucy," said Dimock.

"I don't know, Susan. If you are sick and relatively healthy, you stay at home and call the doctor. If you are beyond hope, the family sends you to us. That's the reality."

"Hello, Dr. Jones. How are you?" asked Dimock.

"I'm fine. I'm quite impressed with your nurses, Susan."

"You are?" asked Dimock.

"I want to show you something."

He flipped open Iris' notebook and dropped it on the desk.

"What do you make of this?"

"These are notes about our patients on the third floor?" asked Dr. Sewall.

"Yes, you have the details of our medical interventions, the dosage of the medication, and other observations. Look at the notes about Mrs. Donnelly, my bloody flux patient."

"This is Iris taking notes?" asked Dimock.

"Yes, it is. She notes everything, writing in a neat, legible hand," said Dr. Jones.

"She is quite amazing," said Dimock. "She is an excellent nurse."

"I've never seen a nurse take notes before," said Dr. Sewall.

Dr. Jones picked up the notebook.

"I just wanted to show you. It's going to be useful when I write up my cases. I better be on my way. I failed to mention that Mrs. Donnelly is doing well and is back on solid food. Your nurses did a great job, Dr. Dimock. Don't lose them."

The two women nodded at Jones as he left.

Fifty-nine

"Epidemics of puerperal fever are to women as war is to men.
Like war, they cut down the healthiest, bravest, and most
essential part of the population; like war, they strike their victims
in the prime of their lives."
Jacques-François-Édouard Hervieux (1818-95)

In the New Year, Iris and Ida were recruited for work in the lying-in ward in a nearby building. There were some twenty pregnant women on two floors who were there for bed rest before and after birth, the latter referred to as postpartum confinement. Iris was put in charge of the ward, which was undergoing a particularly pernicious outbreak of childbirth fever or puerperal fever. It was a bacterial infection of the female reproductive tract and produced high fevers and vaginal discharges. Childbirth disease was the single most common cause of maternal mortality, with death rates sometimes rising as high as 20% of birthing mothers.

Dr. Dimock showed Iris and Ida around the ward. Two midwives were working with a woman who was going into labor. The other women, at various stages of their own pregnancies, hovered close by, watching and waiting. Several women had come down with a fever a day or two after birth, and the doctors suspected an outbreak.

"I want cleanliness to be your priority here," said Dimock. "You can spread the disease if you aren't very careful. I want you to wash your hands in that pail of chlorinated lime solution before you even think of touching a patient."

"What about the midwives, ma'am?" asked Ida.

"The midwives have been forewarned. They are washing their hands too. Your job is to look after the patients with a fever. Try to keep them stable, but don't touch them."

"I understand, Doctor," said Iris.

"We must try to contain the outbreak or more of our patients will die."

Dr. Dimock had read Ignaz Semmelweis' seminal work on childbirth fever at the Vienna General Hospital. In 1844, Dr. Semmelweis reported that women giving birth at home had a much lower incidence of childbirth fever than those giving birth in the hospital's maternity ward. It was common for a doctor to deliver one baby after another in the maternity ward without washing his hands or changing his clothes between patients. Semmelweis suspected that it was the doctors themselves who were carrying the infection from one patient to another. The doctors' plague theory did not go over well with his distinguished colleagues. Their scorn and ridicule were so intense that Semmelweis was chased out of Vienna and eventually committed to a mental institution.

At the end of their first week, two women had died from puerperal fever after they had shown a brief improvement in their condition. Not long after that, a third patient and a fourth had also come down with the fever. As the number of patients with puerperal fever increased, most of the healthy women fled the scourge and returned home.

Dr. Dimock came in frequently but couldn't understand how the disease could propagate so quickly. The midwives appeared to follow her protocol, washing their hands frequently and avoiding unnecessary contact with the contaminated women. The midwives came and went, day and night, delivering babies. Iris and Ida assisted them from time to time but tried to keep their distance. The midwives called in Dr. Dimock when the placenta of one woman refused to come away. The doctor proceeded with the manual removal of the placenta, a procedure that unavoidably caused the woman great pain. Two days later, the same woman had an intense shivering fit and a high fever. Her condition worsened with abdominal pain, and after a week, she died in the night. Iris and Ida were shocked by her death, as was Dr. Dimock, but there was nothing they could do. The waiting women who were healthy enough were asked by the matron to make shrouds for the victims who had passed away. The rate at which the epidemic was claiming new victims made some of them wonder if they might be making shrouds for their own passing.

The American physician Oliver Wendell Holmes (Senior) summed it up in a lecture he gave in Boston on the subject of childbirth fever. He advised all physicians who had treated women who had succumbed to the fever to burn their clothing, destroy their surgical instruments, and stop seeing patients for six months on both moral and safety grounds. Holmes' advice was remarkable at the time because it predicted the contagiousness of what we now understand was a streptococcal infection.

Dr. Dimock redoubled her efforts and worked closely with the midwives and the nurses. Together they managed to prevent any further contamination of patients and after a time, the dreaded fever disappeared from the ward.

After twelve months of training, Iris graduated from the School of Nursing. She was immediately offered a nursing job at the hospital by Dr. Dimock. She loved her work, but above all she wanted to be near Ida, so she accepted the job and stayed on at the hospital. Dr. Dimock had nothing but praise for Iris, who continued her innovative practice of taking notes about the treatment of patients. It wasn't long before all the nurses were doing the same. By the end of her second year, each patient had a personal file, and the nurses were obliged to keep them up-to-date.

Sixty

September 1876
Louisville, Kentucky

The letter arrived in the morning mail. It had taken three days to arrive from Boston. It was a terrible blow to both of them. Bennett and Eliza sat in silence in the dining room of their beautiful new home on Fourth Street before Eliza spoke.

"You must go."

"I'll take the train tomorrow after the partner meeting."

"I would go with you, darling, but the morning sickness."

"I know you would, my dear."

"We can help her. I can look after her when you are at work."

Eliza reread the letter.

Dear Mr. Young,

Iris Gagnon gave me your name. She has succumbed to the worst kind of melancholia after working as a nurse at our hospital. She was among the first women to graduate from our School of Nursing. She has given us three years of excellent service. She is a kind, brilliant young woman. Her present state saddens all of us. She is suffering from severe depression and insomnia, and she refuses to talk about her condition. She cannot work and is staying with me at home. We have discussed finding treatment for her in Boston, but she only wishes to be reunited with you and your wife.

Kind regards,

Dr. Susan Dimock

New England Hospital for Women and Children.

Boston, Massachusetts

"I can hardly believe it," exclaimed Bennett. "Iris depressed? It's not like her."

"The dear girl has always been such a steady, dependable young woman."

"I don't know, but something terrible has happened to her."

"Melancholia is not so rare, Bennett. I have an aunt who had it and went mad. They had to put her in a mental asylum."

Boston

She sat immobile in the parlor, her eyes fixed and unseeing, her face a mask. She stared straight ahead, looking neither left nor right. She was unkempt, dressed in dirty rumpled clothes, with her short blond hair sticking out in all directions. Bennett had never seen her in such a state. He could hardly believe his eyes when Dr. Dimock brought him into the parlor. He had hoped for a joyful reunion, but she hardly recognized him.

Bennett sat down near her.

"Iris, it's me, Bennett. You remember me?"

Iris looked up but said nothing.

"Iris, I've come to take you home."

Iris continued to fix the wall unseeing.

"Eliza has prepared a room for you."

Bennett felt a light touch on his shoulder and looked up.

"She needs time, Mr. Young," Dr. Dimock said softly. "Time to heal."

"Yes, ma'am."

"Don't expect too much from her. Give her time."

"I was thinking of taking the train tonight, Doctor. Do you think I should wait? It might be too much for her."

"It's hard to say, Mr. Young. The distraction might be good for her."

Dimock leaned in close to Iris and smiled.

"Iris, Mr. Young has come to take you home. We are going to get you cleaned up and then pack your bags."

There was no reaction from Iris at all. Dimock straightened up and turned to Bennett.

"My housekeeper will look after Iris and get her ready. I need to go to the hospital for a few hours. Why don't you come with me and I'll show you around? We can have our supper together here at six and you can be on your way."

Iris appeared to hear the words, but her face remained a mask.

"Thank you, ma'am."

Moments later, they set off in a hansom cab for the hospital.

"It started a month ago after an outbreak of yellow fever," said Dr. Dimock. "The nurses went on a picnic together. Iris caught a mild form of it and recovered while some of her friends died. It was a huge shock for our medical staff. We do what we can to keep our people safe."

"How many died?"

"Three ward maids."

"Was there a funeral?"

"Yes, a very moving one. Iris was fine at the funeral, but several days later she just closed up like a clam. She wouldn't say a word to anyone."

"And she's been like that ever since?"

"Yes, that's why I brought her home with me. I thought I could help her," said Dr. Dimock, turning to Bennett and for just an instant he saw the faintest glisten of tears. "As you can see, I haven't succeeded. I only hope that you and your wife can."

When they got to the hospital, Bennett remained in the lobby while Dr. Dimock went upstairs to meet with her patients. He wandered into the chapel on the first floor and sat silently in a pew. He pulled out his Bible and read from Psalm 41: 'The LORD will sustain him on his sickbed and restore him from his bed of illness.' He read from the Book of Isaiah 33:22: 'For the LORD is our judge, the LORD is our lawgiver, the LORD is our king. He who will save us.' He took comfort in his readings. *Whatever had happened to Iris,* thought Bennett, *it had sucked the life out of her. It was not going to be easy to resuscitate the cheerful girl he and Eliza had known in the past.*

In the evening, Bennett and Iris took a hansom cab to the New York & New England Railway Station near Dewey Square. The housekeeper had bathed Iris and washed her hair. She was dressed in clean clothes for the long train journey. She looked better, but the mask was still there. She sat close to Bennett and held his arm, never letting him out of her sight. When they got to the station, they joined a crowd waiting to embark on the overnight train to New York and points west. After a short wait, they boarded the Pullman car and found their seats. Iris stuck close to Bennett and was uneasy in the presence of the other passengers. Bennett looked like a father accompanying an emotionally distressed daughter.

After the train left the station, Bennett pulled down their sleeping berths and helped Iris climb up to her couchette. After he kissed her good night, she closed her eyes and was soon fast asleep. Bennett sat down and thought about the day's events. *Dr. Dimock cared a lot for Iris, but it was unclear what had provoked the melancholia. Was it the death of her friends? It was going to be a long and tiring trip with his silent companion.*

It was daybreak when Iris climbed down from her berth and found Bennett wide awake in his seat, watching the countryside glide by. A porter came through the carriage announcing that breakfast was being served in the dining car.

"Are you hungry, Iris?" asked Bennett, pushing up Iris' couchette.

Iris said nothing, but her expression said that she would follow him wherever he went.

"Let's go explore the dining car."

They got up, and Iris held Bennett's hand as they marched through the train. After a leisurely breakfast, they pulled into New York and changed trains for Philadelphia and Pittsburgh.

Cincinnati, Ohio

Their trip had been long and tiring. They arrived in Cincinnati and had to change trains for Louisville, where several years before Bennett had gone into the railroad business with Jake Doyle. It had not been easy. He and Jake had taken a risky leap of faith and bought up a defunct 'short line' railway company and turned it into a profitable business. They hadn't stopped there, and the Louisville, Harrodsburg, and Virginia Railroad was later reorganized into the Louisville Southern Railroad (LS) to challenge their main rival, the Louisville & Nashville Railroad (L&N). Bennett had been named president of the company and put in charge of development in its ongoing battle for dominance in the booming coal fields of Eastern Kentucky.

The coal industry in Kentucky was growing, with production increasing at a rate of 100,000 tons per year and by the end of the decade, would reach a million tons. The race was on to build rail connections to the eastern coalfields. The LS had launched a spur from Lawrenceburg to Versailles and Lexington which would require the construction of a bridge over the Kentucky River at Tyrone. Ground was broken in February with a delivery date in August of the same year. It was a hugely expensive project and the LS alone was footing the bill. The crossing was to be the highest single-span cantilever structure in the world with a span of 551 feet.

Bennett had taken time off to collect Iris in Boston and he did not regret any of it. He had originally intended to do some paperwork on the return journey, but after seeing her condition, he knew that she would need his undivided attention. He devoted himself to giving her exactly that, although the only evidence that it had any effect was that she would hardly let him out of her sight, clinging to his hand as they watched the countryside roll by. He was acutely aware of how vulnerable she was, and his only priority was to get her safely to their destination. She had not said a word or even changed her expression through all of his attempts to engage with her, and it was difficult for Bennett not to give in to his fears that perhaps she never would.

Then, late on the second day of their journey, they were in the dining car when she suddenly smiled. It was so fleeting that he could easily have missed it, but it was a smile nonetheless, even though he had no idea what might have prompted it. All he knew was that he had been carrying on one side of a nonexistent conversation, commenting gently on anything and everything he could think of. And suddenly, out of the blue, came the smile.

They disembarked from the train and followed the crowd to the main station. Iris clung to his arm as he struggled with her bags and his own.

"Mr. Young!" a man hailed him.

Bennett looked up to see John MacLeod, the chief engineer of the bridge project, hurrying over to greet him.

"Hello, MacLeod. What a surprise! This is my daughter, Iris. We've just come from Boston."

"Hello, young lady," MacLeod smiled at her. "Did you have a nice trip?"

"Nice trip," Iris whispered, in a little girl's voice.

They were the first words she'd spoken in weeks and even if she did sound like a child, Bennett had to restrain himself from scooping her up in his arms and giving her a big hug.

"Let me help you with those, sir."

MacLeod took their bags and walked with them along the platform.

"I wanted to catch you on your return, sir. I'm afraid I have some bad news."

That's all right, Bennett thought, barely able to contain his excitement. *I've just had some wonderful news of my own.*

MAP OF WESTERN KENTUCKY

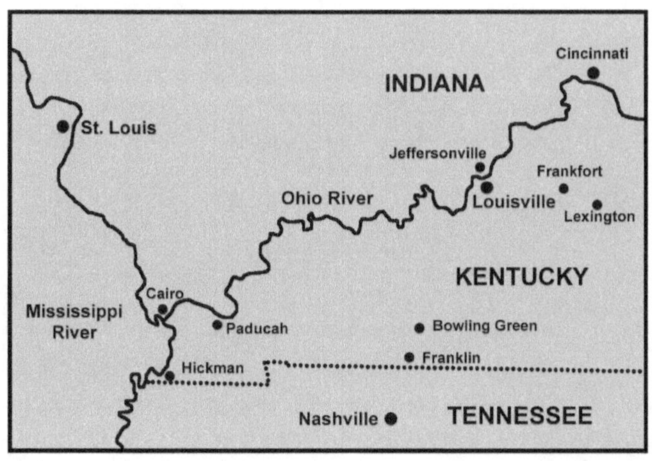

Sixty-one

Tyrone, Kentucky

Two days later, Bennett traveled with Iris and the chief engineer to the camp at Tyrone. Iris was still very withdrawn and quiet, but her fixed stare and dull expression were gone and very occasionally she would smile at something he said. Bennett reminded himself to be patient, mindful of the near-catatonic condition she had been in only a few days earlier. She still clung to him, and once, when he had to leave her for a few moments, he caught an expression on her face that was nothing less than a girlish pout. Instead of being annoyed, he laughed and hugged her, grateful she was showing signs of returning to her old self.

The trip to Tyrone had helped as well. It was, literally, a change of scenery and it brought a sparkle to her eyes. It made Bennett wonder if all the traveling and all the new places she had seen in the last few days had stimulated her recovery. MacLeod's presence had helped. It had been his question on the station platform that had prompted her first spoken words since Boston, and his easy, jovial manner made him a good traveling companion for them both. It would never have occurred to Bennett that he was the main reason Iris was showing a return to life. He was, after all, her *papa*, and for now, at least he was the center of her world. She was safe with him.

They arrived in Tyrone late in the day. The camp was situated on a high bluff above the Kentucky River. They could see parts of the cantilever span sitting on a barge moored in the river below and bits of the support structures on both banks. Nearby, there was a large tent city lodging several hundred workers spread out over a muddy field near the construction site, but no one appeared to be working. The white workers were playing cards and drinking hooch. Many were already drunk and yelled insults at their coach when it came into view.

The other workers were mostly black, many of them ex-slaves and now convicts, who had been leased from the state penitentiary. They supplied the muscle for work on plantations, large farms, quarries, and railroad construction. Convict leasing strengthened the state's dwindling budget by removing the burden of building new prisons and feeding prisoners. The Thirteenth Amendment ended slavery and involuntary servitude, but not as a punishment for a crime. It was a perverse pact between the states and their business leaders to break the power of organized labor and to exploit a loophole in the law.

The Union Bridge Company had designed the bridge, but the steel manufacturing was the work of the Detroit Bridge and Iron Works Company. The erection contractor was a rough and tumble old timer named Jim Baird of Louisville, who had a reputation for abusing his workers. MacLeod hated Baird, and the two men were in constant conflict over one thing or another. It was a tense situation made worse by the tight schedule and half a dozen Pinkerton detectives keeping an eye on the workers.

The Tyrone camp was no place for a young lady and Bennett had hated bringing Iris here, but he couldn't leave her in Cincinnati. She still clung to him like a limpet. In the coach that brought them to Tyrone, Bennett had listened to MacLeod's complaints about Baird and wondered how he could reasonably get the men back to work.

"What set this off?" asked Bennett.

"L&N, who else?" MacLeod snorted. "Baird caught one of their spies sneaking around the camp stirring up trouble. He told the men that L&N pays $2.50 a day for construction work and they shouldn't work for less. That's how it all started."

They were sitting in folding chairs in the construction office tent, drinking tea. Iris sat close to Bennett but showed no interest in the men's talk.

"How much is Baird offering?" asked Bennett.

"Whites are getting $2.00 per day, sir," said Macleod. "Baird wants to cut them back to $1.80."

"How much is he paying the state for the negroes?"

"I don't know, sir, but it's a pittance. The state saves money on their upkeep every day we keep them here."

Bennett held up a hand for silence while he took a look at the LS bridge construction accounts. It was pretty clear what was happening. He didn't mind Baird making money, but it looked like he could be playing both ends against the middle. LS had given Baird a reasonable budget to work with, and now he was trying to increase his profit margin by paying his workers less.

"How many men do we have?"

"We've got 200 whites and maybe 500 negro convicts."

"What's Baird's plan then?"

"He hasn't got a plan, sir. He wants to bring in the militia and break heads."

"Well, that won't help us one bit. We've got to deliver in August. If the whites piss off home, can we make do with the negroes?"

"There are some good workers in that bunch, sir, but a lot of them don't know a thing about railway construction. They grew up working in fields of sugar cane and tobacco. Can they go it alone? I don't know."

Bennett didn't know either.

"Get Baird in here, John. I want to talk to him."

A short while later, Jim Baird appeared in the doorway in a dusty suit coat, an open shirt and vest, and a bowler hat. He came in with a friendly air.

"Mr. Young," Baird boomed, smiling and ebullient. "You've brought along your lovely daughter? She's a sight for sore eyes, sir."

"This is Iris, Mr. Baird. We've just come from Boston," said Bennett, who remained seated and didn't extend a hand. "It seems you are in rather a pickle, old man."

"Nothing to worry about, Mr. Young." Baird waved a dismissive hand. "We'll be back at work in a day or two. The Governor is sending me the militia from Frankfort to crush the strike."

"That won't be necessary," Bennett said with a flat stare. "You can say goodbye to your contract, Mr. Baird. Construction delays are not permitted on this site and your people have been off work for a week now. As of tonight, your contract is null and void. You are no longer in charge of any bridge construction here."

"What!!!" Baird sputtered angrily.

"You heard me, sir. I want you and your men out of the camp by tomorrow morning at eight o'clock. The Louisville Southern is canceling your contract, dated the day work stopped on the site. You are finished here."

Baird lurched to his feet, red in the face, and glared at Bennett.

"You won't get away with this, Young."

"You've lost control of your men, and the project is stalled. That says it all, Baird."

Iris had been so quiet that Bennett had forgotten she was there. Now he reproached himself for inadvertently placing her in something he should have foreseen could become acrimonious. He stood up and came around the table until he was nose-to-nose with Baird.

"I would remind you, Mr. Baird, that there's a lady present. You can leave here like a gentleman or I can have you thrown out. It's your decision."

For a moment it looked like Baird might challenge him, but then he looked at Bennett's flat stare and thought better of it. He turned and stomped out of the tent. Bennett watched him go and then went to Iris, sitting in the corner. She looked up at him and his heart caught in his throat. All the progress they'd made since Boston was now at risk. *So stupid*, he told himself. *My fault for dragging her into my construction problems.*

"Iris," he whispered as he knelt beside her. "I'm so sorry for bringing you here."

"Bad...man," she replied in a tiny, little girl voice. Her face was unreadable, but at least she'd said something, however childlike. He stood up and noticed that MacLeod had entered the tent.

"Come on," he said gently to Iris, "we're going to go for a nice walk. Mr. MacLeod is going to show us around."

She stood up, clinging to his hand. He exchanged a look with MacLeod.

"Hello, Iris," MacLeod smiled. "We have a tent for you and your daddy, and I think you're going to like it. We even put some flowers in there for you, because your daddy told me you like flowers."

Bennett's heart leaped when he saw the trace of a smile on her face. The three of them set out on their walk. MacLeod, sensing Bennett's concern for his daughter, led them on a circuitous route that gave them time to become absorbed in the beauty of the Kentucky River and the surrounding woods. MacLeod waited for Bennett to speak.

"Jim Baird no longer works for us," Bennett said in a soft conversational tone. "Tomorrow morning, we will have a meeting with the men and start over."

"But, sir?" MacLeod said, hiding his alarm and keeping his tone light. "Baird's men have all the construction plans for the bridge."

"Tonight, you'll take five armed men to Baird's quarters and seize every written document you can get your hands on, including the plans. Tomorrow, I want you to find the best men for the job among the white workers. If we can employ 20-30 highly competent whites, we should be able to complete the job with 500 negroes."

Both men watched as Iris released her grip on Bennett's hand and stopped to pick wildflowers.

"Look, *Papa*," said Iris, showing him the flowers. Bennett felt a catch in his throat. Her face was the most animated he'd seen since she had left Boston. He didn't trust himself to speak.

"They're beautiful, Iris," said MacLeod, smiling. "They're even prettier than the ones in your tent."

"By the way," asked Bennett. "Where is our tent?"

"Right over there, sir," said MacLeod, pointing to a large tent visible through the trees. "We've been walking in circles around it for the last ten minutes."

It rained in the night. Bennett and Iris slept on camp beds. Around six o'clock, a knock came on the wooden upright near the entrance and MacLeod stuck his head into the tent. He invited them to breakfast and sent in a servant with a pitcher of water and a bowl for washing. Bennett produced a straight razor and shaved as Iris watched him from her camp bed. It was going to be a busy day for the president of Louisville Southern. It would take all his powers of persuasion to get his people back to work.

Bennett and Iris sat in the breakfast tent with John MacLeod. Bennett said grace as a servant brought them a full breakfast of eggs, bacon, toast, and grits.

Bennett watched as Iris tucked into the food with a gusto he hadn't seen during the train journey.

"Baird left this morning," said MacLeod. "He rode out about an hour ago, sir."

"Good. How did it go for the construction plans?"

"We got them, sir. He wasn't happy to see my men searching his tent."

Bennett picked up a fork and started to eat. He would need all the energy he could get for the day ahead.

"I have found you some excellent workers, sir. They don't look like much, but they are honest and hard-working. You can count on them to do the work."

"Very good."

"There are about twenty of them. You will need to make them an offer, sir."

"That's fine, MacLeod."

"As for the negroes, they are not bound to work for us any longer since the lease for their services came to an end last week. You will need to inform them of that fact."

"Let's gather the negroes together for a meeting at ten o'clock. Meanwhile, I want you to bring me the group of whites who are willing to continue the work. I want to see them personally before the general meeting."

An hour later, a group of rough-looking white construction workers entered the office tent. Bennett sat at a table with a leather notebook next to John MacLeod. Iris sat close behind them.

"Hello, gentlemen. I'm Bennett Young of the Louisville Southern Railroad. You know our engineer, John MacLeod. This is my daughter, Iris, who has just come from Boston."

The men smiled at Bennett and Iris, some of them whispering lewd comments to their friends. They had never met the daughter of a railway magnate.

"I'm happy to meet you all in person."

"We're happy to meet you too, sir," said an older man, followed by laughter from his cronies.

"John says you are our best workers and I believe him. He says we can count on your collaboration. We are offering you $2.50 per day for your services until the completion of the work and a bonus if you finish on time. This is a confidential one-time offer for you men alone. No one else will be getting it."

The men applauded the offer.

"Who will we be working with, sir?" asked one man. "A lot of the men have left already."

"The same negroes you worked with last week," said Bennett.

"But Mr. Baird is gone, sir? Those are his negroes."

"Not anymore, gentlemen. How good are you men at reading the construction plans?"

"I read my first plan when I was just a boy," said one man. "It ain't a problem, sir."

"Me too, but I got better eyesight than Hank over there," said another man. "He needs his spectacles to read a plan and often gets it wrong."

The men broke into a laugh.

"Good, because we're starting work right after lunch. We look forward to working with you. Thank you, gentlemen."

Bennett and MacLeod stood up and went over to shake hands with the men. The men were happy to be working again and looked cheerful as they left the tent.

"That was very generous of you, sir," said MacLeod, as they stepped out into the sunlight.

"We don't have a choice, John. We've got to get a move on or we'll never finish the bridge in time."

A small man in a military uniform approached Bennett.

"I'd like to have a word with the boss man, MacLeod."

MacLeod turned to Bennett.

"This is Jim Gates, sir. He works for the warden and is in charge of security."

"Hello, Mr. Gates. It's a pleasure to meet you, sir. Please come in," said Bennett, returning to the tent where Iris was waiting for him. "What can I do for you?"

"Well, sir. I hear my negroes ain't no longer needed on the job site."

"We're in talks."

"Yeah, well, it won't be long 'fore the warden will be pulling 'em out."

"How many guards do you have with you, Mr. Gates?"

"We are five in number, sir. We maintain the peace."

"Not a large force."

"Nope, but these negroes ain't half bad, sir. Most of 'em are serving time for vagrancy, talkin' back to their betters, and larceny—stealing food for their families. They ain't dangerous, you treat 'em right."

"Let's see how our talks go, Mr. Gates. We'll talk again after the meeting."

"Fine, sir. I'll be here."

Sixty-two

By ten o'clock, many disgruntled white workers had left the site after hearing Baird bad mouth the company on his way out of camp. The sun was out and helping to dry out the camp. Bennett and Iris sat in folding chairs on a podium with John MacLeod near the canteen where some five hundred black and white workers were gathered to hear Bennett speak. The African Americans were dressed in typical grey-striped prison garb with hobnail boots. They looked like a sorry bunch besides the whites, who wore relatively respectable civilian clothes.

MacLeod called the men to attention and introduced Bennett and his daughter. There were a lot of smiles among the men. It was not every day that they got a look at the boss's pretty offspring. Bennett stood up slowly to address the men.

"Hello, gentlemen. I am Bennett Young of the Louisville Southern Railroad. You have been loaned to us from the state penitentiary to build a bridge. A very important bridge, I might add. Your contract has been terminated. While the state decides what to do with you, we agree to hire you to continue work on the bridge. As of today, we are offering each man among you, white and negro alike, a salary of $2.00 a day until completion of the bridge. You will be paid once a week until the state comes to collect you and sends you off to do other jobs."

The white men in the crowd stood up to protest.

"These negroes are lazy, good-for-nothing convicts, sir," yelled an angry white man. "You are offering them the same rate as us whites. That ain't fair."

"I believe it is fair, sir. We fought a war against the Union not so long ago and we lost. Since then, whites and negroes are equal under the law according to the Thirteenth Amendment."

"Can we keep the money, sir?" asked a black man in the first row.

"Yes, you can keep your wages. No one can take them away from you."

The black workers looked at each other in disbelief. Some were too astonished to believe it. Their slack-jawed appearance showed how little they believed anything coming out of the mouth of a white man. They had been worked hard by Baird's men for no pay and had to put up with bad food, vermin-filled tents, and whippings. Here was a man promising them an honest wage, something that had never happened before in their experience. This was money they could send home to their families.

Gates stood on the sideline and yelled at the men.

"You fellas are goin' back to prison. Ain't nobody fool enough to pay you men for your work?"

Bennett watched the crowd's growing disbelief in his offer. If they didn't believe him, there was nothing he could do to convince them. Iris came forward and whispered in Bennett's ear.

"Ask them whether they can read, Papa?"

Bennett was overcome with joy at hearing her words. He turned back to the crowd.

"Raise your hand if you can read," Bennett asked the men. "Please show us a hand if you can read, gentlemen."

A few hands were raised among the whites and almost no hands among the African Americans. Iris looked at the poor showing of readers and again whispered in Bennett's ear. He grinned and put an arm around her.

"Go on, Iris. You tell them."

Iris looked out at the hundreds of men assembled before her and was suddenly seized by stage fright. She hesitated a long moment before daring to speak.

"It's time you men learned to read and write," she said, repeating it louder the second time. "It is time you learned to read and write, gentlemen."

There was complete silence while the men waited for her to go on.

"My father has agreed to find teachers to give you lessons in reading and writing while you work for the Louisville Southern, the best railroad in Kentucky."

There was a huge applause from the men. Iris continued,

encouraged by the applause.

"Work for us and you won't regret it. The Louisville Southern is the best railroad in Kentucky," shouted Iris. "And don't you ever forget it!"

Bennett smiled with pride. She had come out of her shell and was turning the tide of doubters. She was charming the men like only a woman could do. It was time for him to take over.

"You will return to work as free men," Bennett added. "You will be earning wages to support your families."

There was another huge applause from the crowd.

"We thank you and look forward to working with you. Work starts right after lunch, gentlemen."

The crowd broke up into small groups. There was a cheerful air among the men.

"That was quite amazing, sir," said MacLeod as Bennett sat down. "You won them over."

"Not me, MacLeod. Iris won them over."

"Your daughter was incredible, sir."

"Yes, I agree. Isn't she amazing?" said Bennett as he looked at Iris, smiling at him.

"Sir, Gates will be coming around. He isn't gonna like it one bit."

"Don't worry, John. I have an offer for Gates, which he won't be able to refuse. This should slow things down until I talk with the Governor. I know he wants this bridge built."

Bennett and Iris spent two more days on the construction site observing the work on the bridge before crossing the river by boat to the village of Tyrone and taking a coach east through Lawrenceburg and on to Louisville.

Louisville, Kentucky

Bennett and Iris arrived at the Young home on Fourth Street a week later. Eliza was overjoyed to see Iris again. She seemed older and more mature, but not quite herself. She was subdued, even shy in Eliza's presence, with a sad demeanor in her quiet moments.

Eliza's pregnancy was advancing and Iris was fascinated by all the aspects of childbirth. They spent hours together, chatting about setting up the nursery, her lying-in, baby clothes, cribs, and her choice of midwives. Iris talked about her experience at the New England Hospital for Women and Children. Eliza realized that Iris was holding something back that she didn't want to share.

One evening, Eliza got Iris to open up a little over a glass of red wine. They had spent an hour or two telling funny stories and then, out of nowhere, Iris had recited the following lines from memory:

> *"Tis better to have loved and lost*
> *Than never to have loved at all."*

"That line is from Tennyson, isn't it?" asked Eliza.

"Yes, it's in that huge work of his that he wrote in honor of his Cambridge friend, Arthur Henry Hallam, who died in Vienna. It's called *In Memoriam.*"

"Ah, yes."

"Queen Victoria liked it."

"She grieved for Albert, her dead husband, for a long time. It is a wonderful poem, my dear."

"Well, it was one of her favorites."

"You were always fascinated by the royal family, my dear."

"Yes, I was. Now it's time for bed, Eliza."

Iris gave Eliza an enigmatic smile and finished off her glass of wine. She got to her feet and said good night before going upstairs.

After a few weeks, Bennett drove Iris and Eliza to the Louisville Hospital to meet Sister Helen, the head of nursing. The hospital was a vast complex with some 400 patient beds and fifteen wards. Sister Helen was an older woman dressed in black with a white cap. She showed them around the wards and then invited them to her office.

"So, Miss Iris, what made you think of becoming a nurse?"

"Sister Helen," said Bennett. "Iris is a trained nurse. I thought I mentioned it."

"Well, I'm not sure—."

"Iris trained at the New England Hospital for Women and Children," added Eliza.

"Really. Who did you train with, Miss Iris?"

"Doctor Dimock and Doctor Sewall, ma'am. I worked there for three years."

"I'm so sorry, Miss Iris," Sister Helen's cheeks flushed with embarrassment. "I've got you mixed up with someone else. If you trained with Dr. Dimock, I have no doubt you would be a wonderful addition to our staff here. Most of our nurses have very little training."

"I know Iris is determined to start working again," Eliza said, "but as you can see, I'm with child myself and my husband has insisted that Iris also have sufficient time to care for me until the baby arrives. An ideal situation for us would be if Iris could work part-time at the hospital for the first month or two. Would an arrangement like that be agreeable to you and the hospital?"

Parents, Sister Helen thought. She was not used to such negotiations for prospective employees. *Still, I can't afford to lose her.* Young nurses as qualified as Iris were rare, if not nonexistent, and her parents were people of influence. It would not do to turn down such an offer.

"Of course," Sister Helen smiled, stifling her disappointment at not being able to put Iris to work full time. "That would be perfectly agreeable to us."

Eliza gave birth to a beautiful baby girl not long after Iris started work at the hospital. She was living at home and her work schedule allowed her time, supported by a midwife, to help Eliza during her final days. Bennett and Eliza named the baby 'Josephine'. It was shortly after the birth that Agnes decided to visit them. She had written to Dr. Dimock, who had sent the letter on to Louisville. Bennett had followed up by inviting Agnes to come out and visit her daughter. He paid for her train ticket on the Grand Trunk Railway from Stanbridge East through Chicago to Louisville.

It had been a huge surprise for Iris to see her mother in the parlor one day after she returned from work at the hospital. It had been a hot spring day and Iris was tired and perspiring in an old print skirt and bodice. She threw her bonnet down on a chair and entered the parlor to see her mother chatting with Eliza, who was breastfeeding the baby. Agnes stood up and Iris ran into a tearful embrace with her mother. She hadn't seen her daughter in over three years and worried constantly about her.

After Agnes had married Antoine, her life had changed for the better. She was now a respectable married woman, and all past slights and disrespect for her with a young child out of wedlock were long forgotten. She wanted the same thing for her daughter, who was still single and hardly looked like potential marriage material. In her opinion, Iris didn't dress properly and cared little for her looks. After two days together, Agnes flew into an angry fit over her daughter's appearance while they were having breakfast in the dining room.

"Can't you take a day off so we can go shopping, Iris?" asked Agnes.

"*Maman*, I don't like to shop," said Iris. "Ask Eliza. We never go shopping together."

"Well, Iris, my dear," Agnes sniffed, "you will never find a husband dressed like that. Look at you! That skirt and bodice are hardly presentable, my dear. You can't go out in the street dressed like that. It's disgraceful."

"It's not so bad, *Maman*."

"It is, my dear. You have no pretty dresses and you wear your hair too short. Someone might take you for a boy. You are still a lovely girl. You have a good job, so you can't keep dressing so poorly."

"It's a nice day," said Eliza, trying to keep the peace between mother and daughter. "Why don't you take the buggy and have a look around town with your *Maman*, Iris?"

"Are you sure you won't need us, Eliza?"

Quite sure, Eliza thought. *I love them both, but I need some quiet in the house for a while.*

"I'll be fine, dear. Your mother is right. You have nothing to wear. Go to the shops and buy a few things. You can charge them to Bennett's account."

Agnes stood up, followed reluctantly by Iris.

"Take your ma to that bakery," Eliza suggested, "the one with those lovely cakes and sweet things, Iris. She'll love it."

Iris nodded glumly and started for the door with her mother.

"Bye, Eliza," said Agnes, who looked supremely confident after winning the argument. *We're going to dress Iris properly with new clothes, whether she likes it or not.* Agnes allowed herself a mischievous thought. *And while we are at it, maybe we'll find a nice young man for her.*

The Fifth Street Baptist Church was well known to Bennett. He walked past it every other day. He had been surprised by the letter inviting him to meet with Reverend John Frank at the church on a Friday morning. As he entered the church, he asked for the reverend and was redirected to the basement where there were a dozen young black children amusing themselves playing games.

"Mr. Young, thank you for coming," boomed the reverend. "These kids are orphans and I am looking after them for a while 'cause their teacher is out sick."

"How many do you have?" asked Bennett.

"There are about fifty or more living down here, sir. Some are out playing in the backyard. Let's go up to my office and have a chat."

Reverend Frank turned to the oldest boy.

"Amos, keep 'em quiet for an hour. I'll be upstairs."

The boy nodded, and the reverend led Bennett up the stairs to his office. He motioned Bennett to a chair and took off the formal 'preaching robe' that covered his everyday attire.

"Would you like a coffee, Mr. Young?" asked the reverend, ringing a bell.

"Yes, I would," said Bennett. "Thank you."

A pleasant black woman appeared shortly afterward, and the reverend ordered the coffee.

"I have a member of the church who is in some trouble, sir. He's a butcher over at the slaughterhouse, and I thought you might be able to help."

"What kind of trouble, Reverend?"

"Theft, sir. He's a good man with a family and children, sir. He could go to prison."

"Has he been arrested?"

"Not yet. To be entirely honest, Mr. Young, I wanted to meet you after I heard about your generous offer to the convicts workin' on the Tyrone bridge."

"You heard about that, did you?"

"Yes, sir. I heard that you and your daughter were out there during the strike. I can't thank you enough, Mr. Young, for helping those poor men. You did the Lord's work, sir. Those men are sending money home to their families and learnin' to read and write."

"I'm happy to have been of help. The reading and writing were my daughter's idea, but it seems to be working out just fine. We recruited the teachers nearby in Versailles and Lawrenceburg, and they come in each week to teach the men during their lunch break."

"That's wonderful, Mr. Young. You know the Thirteenth Amendment is just another way of enslaving the negro. Throw a man in prison and then sell the work of the convict for next to nothing."

"I agree with you, Reverend. It's a terrible law. I needed those men to meet a deadline and they've been doing an excellent job working for the company."

"That's good to hear. You know we've been running a school here at the church since 1865. You may have known my predecessor, Henry Adams. He was a highly educated man from Georgia. He set up the school and taught here. He also opened the Colored Baptist Church in Jeffersonville across the river. You may have heard of him."

"Yes, I believe I met him. He had quite a reputation, as I remember."

"He never gave up trying to help the negro. You saw the kids downstairs. We're trying to set up a home for them in Louisville, Mr. Young. We need your help."

The war had left tens of thousands of children orphaned or 'half-orphaned', meaning the children had lost a father but still had a mother. Freed black women who traveled north with their children were met with an oppressive new reality. The families who hired them for domestic work would not allow them to keep their children, who were often abandoned and left to fend for themselves in the street or forced into servitude. Bennett had seen it all with his own eyes on the streets of Louisville. There were homeless black children everywhere. Eliza had commented how shameful it was for a town the size of Louisville.

"You've heard of the Howard Orphanage in New York City, Reverend?"

"Yes, sir. We have the same needs here in Louisville, Mr. Young."

"I agree. How much do you think it'll cost to set up a home, Reverend?"

"It's not so much."

"How much, sir?"

"For five hundred dollars, sir, we could make a start. Rent a building in the neighborhood to lodge the kids, hire a cook and a manager, and provision them."

"That's an excellent idea, Reverend."

"Our members can help with the work."

Bennett reached into his pocket and extracted some money from a wad of bills.

"Here's a hundred dollars to get you started, Reverend," said Bennett, putting the money on the desk.

"That's very generous, Mr. Young."

"I'll talk to some people. I'm a member of the Broadway Baptist Church. I'll talk to the pastor and see whether we can organize a collection for your orphanage."

As the week wore on, Iris looked more and more unnerved by the presence of her mother. She had acquired some lovely dresses and felt she had done her best to satisfy her mother's desire for respectability. Agnes was adamant that Iris should get out and court all the eligible bachelors in the town. She talked Eliza into taking Iris to the coming-out balls listed in the Louisville Society pages. The tension between mother and daughter was palpable even at the dinner table. Bennett asked Eliza what was going on between them one evening in their bedroom.

"I don't like to say this, my dear," whispered Bennett, "but Iris and her *maman* seem to be at loggerheads. What do you think?"

"It's not unusual for mothers with unmarried daughters, Bennett. There is always a lot of pressure to marry."

"I overheard an argument between them earlier," Bennett said, looking mystified. "Iris was saying that she loved her liberty too much to give it up for any man. Then her mother said something, and that set off a screaming match in French. I don't know what was said, but it was not a happy moment."

"Agnes had Iris out of wedlock, Bennett. That pretty much explains it all, you know. She's no longer the wild child of Frelighsburg, Bennett. She's a mature woman and under pressure to be like everyone else."

"Well, I hope they can make peace before Agnes goes home next week."

Eliza turned over in bed to look at Bennett.

"I love Iris. She is like a daughter to me, but she can be very willful."

"Willful?" Bennett chuckled. "She's as stubborn as a mule when she wants to be."

Sixty-three

July 1878

The story of the Haitian Revolution is tied to the terrible yellow fever epidemic that struck the island at the turn of the century and caused the death of thousands. In October 1801, after the successful slave revolt against France, Toussaint Louverture introduced a new constitution that abolished slavery on the island. The constitution prompted Napoleon Bonaparte to send General Victor-Emmanuel Charles Leclerc at the head of an expeditionary force to seize control of the island and reestablish slavery. The French did not fare well against the Haitian revolutionary forces and their soldiers were struck down in even greater numbers by yellow fever than by the bullets of the enemy. By the end of the conflict, only eight thousand French soldiers were left of the original forty-three thousand sent to the island. To cut his losses, Bonaparte sold the fever-ridden City of New Orleans and the Louisiana territory to the United States in May 1803. Yellow fever had decimated the population in New Orleans for decades. It got so bad during the summer months of July to October that the city earned the nickname 'Necropolis'—the city of the dead.

Jake Doyle looked splendid in his black frock coat, vest, and top hat as he arrived from the courts and entered the office of the prosperous law firm. After more than five years of practicing law in the state, Jake and Bennett had a sterling record of wins for their law firm and had done very well in the railroad business. Bennett was busy poring over a referral from Reverend Frank, the case of a poor black man who had killed someone in an alley after a night of drinking. It was another hopeless *pro bono* case, but Bennett felt the man deserved a defense. His secretary, Pauline, had just brought him a cup of coffee when Jake barged in, fired up by the news.

"How did it go, Jake?"

"Have you heard the news, Bennett?" asked Jake. "They've got the yellow jack down in Houston County."

Yellow fever was often called 'yellow jack' and 'bronze john' in the American South.

"Yellow jack in Tennessee?"

"Dr. Grigsby in Erin died last week after treating the first victim. It was reported in the Clarksville Weekly Chronicle. You remember we worked on a case with the doctor about a year ago?"

"Of course, I remember. The poor man."

"They say it's the malignant type, Bennett. It could be bad, real bad."

"They've got it down in Memphis and New Orleans, Mr. Doyle," said Pauline, looking alarmed. "Do you think it will make its way up here?"

"No one knows," Bennett told her.

"There are reports of yellow jack deaths in all the papers," said Jake. "I don't know how we are going to avoid it."

Newspaper reporters began referring to the yellow fever epidemic as the 'Southern Scourge'. The inability of the medical profession to explain its cause or even how it spread added to the fear. Doctors at the time were unaware of the role played by mosquitoes and could find no logical pattern for the spread of the disease. Fear was palpable throughout the South. As a result, thousands of people fled the cities of New Orleans, Vicksburg, and Memphis. By the middle of August, many river towns north of New Orleans started to enforce quarantines. Memphis was hit hard by yellow fever. All travel by boat on the Ohio River or by road into and out of Memphis was closed off. As the frightened refugees fled northward, other towns established quarantines and closed their doors to keep them out. The only exception was Louisville, the largest city in Kentucky, which refused to establish a quarantine along its section of the Ohio River. On August 2, the Louisville Board of Health met and resolved that 'any attempt at quarantine would not only be galling and detrimental to social and communal interests but also inhuman.' Dr. Luke Blackburn, a prominent Louisville physician with experience in fighting the disease, strongly opposed the Board's decision. He was ignored, and Louisville opened its gates to hundreds of refugees who lodged in the town's hotels, boardinghouses, and private homes. It wasn't long before Louisville experienced its first wave of yellow fever.

Down on the Ohio riverbank, Kathyrn Nash and her husband ran a small lunch counter for boatmen in Louisville. It was near the steamboat landing and in one of the most dangerous parts of town. You could be killed by thieves and vagrants if you dared to walk alone at night on the riverbank. Kathyrn was thirty-four years old and in the prime of life when she suddenly took sick. It felt like the flu. She had a headache, fever, and muscle aches. This lasted for two to three days and Kathryn thought she was over it, but then she entered the toxic phase as the virus attacked her kidneys and liver. Her skin became jaundiced and yellow and she started to vomit up 'black blood'. A few days later, Kathryn died of internal hemorrhaging. A physician working at the Louisville Hospital saw her before she died and noted the symptoms. His report to the authorities sparked a huge panic in town. Mrs. Nash was the first victim of yellow fever in Louisville to die.

It wasn't long before patients with yellow fever began arriving at the Louisville Hospital. Iris was summoned to the office of Sister Helen, the head of nursing.

"Miss Gagnon, I've called you in because we have a serious staffing problem at the hospital."

"Yes, ma'am. Are you talking about the yellow fever ward?"

"Yes, miss. There is a great deal of fear among our nurses. No one wants to work there."

"I understand, Sister."

"You mentioned in your file that you caught the malady in Boston two years ago. Is that exact?"

"Yes, Sister. It was in the summer. We had been on a picnic with the hospital staff. Several of us caught it that day. I was sick for a full week before I recovered. Three nurses died."

"So you think you might still have some resistance to the disease?"

"I would think so, yes."

"I would like to put you in charge of one of the wards. A new doctor is coming from Baltimore to head up the treatment of patients."

Iris accepted the promotion and was put in charge of a ward full of patients with the disease. She soon came to regret it. The doctors couldn't agree on how to treat the disease. The Baltimore doctor in charge of Iris' ward was a fervent believer in the radical medicine recommended by Benjamin Rush in 1793 during the yellow fever epidemic in Philadelphia. He had favored a treatment that involved copious bloodletting, blistering, purging, and sweating to shock the body back to health. Other doctors, however, favored Jean Devèze's gentler 'French cure', which treated patients with stimulants and quinine.

Iris had twelve sick men and women all suffering from various stages of the disease. She was assisted by two African American women who had been recruited from the cleaning staff because it was believed that black people were immune to tropical diseases. The women wore gray, long-sleeved dresses, white aprons, caps, and masks in the oppressive summer heat as they wet cupped and blistered their patients from morning to night. The bleeding was done using a spring-loaded lancet that opened a vein and used wet cupping to draw the blood to the surface. Blistering was an age-old treatment from the Georgian era used by doctors on such famous people as George Washington, Napoleon Bonaparte, and Madame Henriette Campan, a lady-in-waiting to Marie Antoinette. Physicians believed that blistering had a stimulating effect on patients. It required the application of a fine powder, composed of cantharides, pepper, mustard seed, and verdigris, which was mixed with plaster and applied to the skin. After a few hours, the skin produced a blister, which was then snipped by the nurse and dressed with a healing ointment. Iris and her colleagues employed a more efficient method, which involved dipping a polished iron covered in silk into boiling water for five minutes and then applying it to the skin to create the blister. In addition to the cupping and blistering, the doctor gave his patients large quantities of calomel, a common purgative composed of mercuric chloride, which worked as a laxative.

By the end of the first week, the three nurses were at their wits' end working under the young doctor, who they called 'Dr. Scylla' in secret. Iris' ward looked like an image from Bruegel's *Triumph of Death*, with sheets and bedclothes covered in droplets of black vomit. The Baltimore doctor was a true believer, convinced that the more you bled a patient, the better their chance of survival. His counterpart in the upstairs ward was an older doctor, nicknamed 'Dr. Charybdis', who was equally adamant that the 'French cure' was the only way to treat the dozen yellow fever patients under his care. At the end of the second week, the two doctors waited with bated breath, hoping to show their colleagues how successful they had been in fighting the disease. Neither doctor was happy with the results when it was learned that both wards had lost the same number of patients.

It was a hopeless battle against an unrelenting foe, and the medical staff felt utterly defeated. A New Orleans physician once reported seeing a patient 'mired in black vomit, with profuse hemorrhaging from the mouth, nose, eyes, and even the toes. The victim's eyes were prominent, glistening, yellow, and staring, the face with an orange and dusky red color.'

Sixty-four

As July ended, Iris demanded a transfer out of Dr. Scylla's service and was demoted to the Louisville Ambulance Service. The city had modern horse-drawn ambulances that went around the local bars at night, looking for the victims of brawls and for drunks asleep on the road. They were on call to collect shooting, stabbing, or burn victims, and to do triage on people who might be infected with the yellow fever virus. The medical equipment on board was limited to splints for broken arms and legs, a stomach pump, morphine, and a half-empty bottle of brandy.

It was a twelve-hour shift, starting at midnight and finishing at midday. When Iris arrived home one afternoon, she found Bennett and Eliza sitting on the porch in the garden drinking mint juleps with a portly, middle-aged man. Their daughter Josephine, who was nearly two years old, played with a doll nearby. As always, Iris fussed over little Josephine and then joined the adults on the porch. Their distinguished-looking guest was introduced to Iris as Dr. Luke Blackburn. His name was vaguely familiar to her. He was a man despised across the northern states for his actions during the Civil War.

"Luke, this is Iris, who I told you about," said Bennett. "She's French Canadian and works as a nurse at the Louisville Hospital."

"Yes, I believe I've seen you in the yellow fever ward, miss."

"Luke is an old friend, Iris," said Bennett. "From my days in Toronto with Colonel Thompson and the Confederate Secret Service."

"Yes," Iris said, careful to keep her tone noncommittal. "I've heard of you."

"Iris is gone from the ward," said Eliza. "She couldn't stand working there anymore. The nurses called the doctors Dr. Scylla and Dr. Charybdis."

Luke stifled a laugh, as did Bennett.

"I'm working as a nurse in the ambulance service now, sir. I couldn't work any longer with the doctors. I got tired of the constant bleeding, blistering, and purging."

"Well, miss," Blackburn smiled. "I don't blame you. I'm not a strong believer in the usual therapies. I find them to be quite ineffective."

"So you're off to Hickman, Luke?" asked Bennett.

"Yes, the situation there is very bad. The mayor of Hickman has requested our help. A paddle-wheeler from New Orleans docked there during the first week of August and brought the disease with it. The first case involved a teenager and two small children who sold apples on the wharf. All three died within four days."

"Where is this town, Doctor?" Eliza asked.

"Hickman is on the Mississippi in Fulton County, miss. It's about 200 miles due north of Memphis."

"How do you plan to get there?" asked Iris.

"We're leaving tomorrow night by steamboat."

"How many people are there in your group?" asked Iris.

"Just me and my assistant, Arthur Brady. No one wants to risk going there. They are too afraid of the disease."

In the evening, Bennett, Iris, and Eliza sat around the dining room table with little Josephine in a high chair. The black cook served the food in the kitchen and then brought in the plates. When they were all served, Bennett said grace as Eliza spoon-fed young Josephine. After the meal, Eliza took Josephine upstairs. Iris was tired but curious about Dr. Blackburn, who was known as the 'black vomit' doctor in the northern states.

"Luke's not a bad man," said Bennett. "He has treated more yellow fever patients than anyone in this country. He was our medical officer during the War."

"I heard he was a health officer in Natchez, Mississippi, during the 1853 outbreak," said Iris.

"Yeah, he was. He talks a lot about his time in Natchez. Back then, he put a quarantine around the city, which helped protect people as the fever spread north through the delta."

"What about the Bermuda outbreak? He was called a terrorist by the Union Army."

"Luke volunteered his services to the authorities after a yellow fever epidemic broke out on the island. That was in the last year of the war, Iris. The epidemic risked disrupting our blockade runners."

"So why was he collecting blood-infected bedding and shirts in Bermuda, and sending them in trunks to the Northern cities?"

"I have no idea, Iris."

"Come on, Papa. He must have told you about it?"

"He says it's preposterous to think he would do such a thing. He was set up by that bastard Godfrey Hyams. At his trial, he testified that Luke had hired him to deliver five trunks of contaminated clothing from Canada to cities across the north. Everything that man said was a lie."

Eliza returned to the table.

"I don't believe it, Bennett. Luke Blackburn was into something. You are too trusting. There was a trial in Bermuda and he was found guilty."

"I know, Eliza, but how likely is that? I've known him a long time and I can't believe a generous man like Luke would involve himself in such a diabolical plot. It doesn't make sense. We are still burning heretics in this country."

There was a long silence before Iris stood up, kissed Eliza and Bennett good night, and went upstairs to bed. Iris didn't have to go in to work because it was her day off. Eliza frowned at Bennett.

Their worst fears were realized the next day. They'd both known that Iris was tired of working for the ambulance service, but the encounter with Dr. Blackburn had lit a spark in her mercurial nature. At breakfast, she announced that she thought she would be more useful in helping Dr. Blackburn stem the epidemic in Hickman than doing triage with the ambulance service. She had no fear of the epidemic, having caught a mild case of it in Boston. Eliza thought Iris was making a terrible decision.

"You have no right to take such a risk, Iris!" Eliza was as angry as Bennett had ever seen her. "We love you and we care about you."

"Eliza is right, Iris," argued Bennett, who hated to see her go. "This epidemic is the worst we've ever seen. Too many people are dying."

"I'll take my precautions, Papa," Iris said, obviously trying to placate them both. "These people are desperate. I want to help."

Bennett and Eliza shared a look of desperation. In their mind's eye, Iris was proposing to sail up the Congo River in a tramp steamer into darkest Equatorial Africa to fight some unknown disease that was eradicating the natives. *It was a madcap adventure*, thought Bennett, *but Iris was an adult and there was nothing he could do to stop her.*

Bennett stood up and reluctantly went to his study to write a terse message to Dr. Blackburn informing him that he had a new recruit. Iris would be joining his mission to Hickman, and he was to expect her onboard. He did not doubt that Blackburn would welcome her presence. She was an experienced nurse and would be invaluable to him. *Not as invaluable to him as she is to us,* Bennett thought bitterly as he signed the note. Then he dispatched the messenger.

In the evening, Iris embraced young Josephine and shared a strained, tearful embrace with Eliza before Bennett drove her across the river to the steamboat dock in Jeffersonville. The port was located just below the Falls on the Ohio River, which made it ideal for transporting agricultural goods from Kentucky to New Orleans and beyond. The Louisville and Portland Canal had been built in the 1830s to allow boats to navigate around the falls. Steamboats from as far away as Pittsburgh made their way down to New Orleans. It cost fifty dollars to go from Pittsburgh to New Orleans and only twenty-five from Louisville. Paddle-wheelers traveled from New Orleans to Louisville in as little as four days, so the trip down to Hickman would take less than thirty hours.

They arrived at the landing and Bennett carried Iris' bag on board the paddle-wheeler. The ship was belching smoke as it got ready to cast off. Bennett hugged Iris and told her he would pray for her. *She was making the worst decision in her life,* he thought, *but there was no way to convince a headstrong woman like Iris to do otherwise. She was drawn to the most horrific of epidemics, like a moth to a flame.*

Iris stood at the rail and watched as her papa descended the gangway to the dock. She had always been so proud of his distinguished bearing and ramrod-straight military posture, but this time was different. All that seemed diminished now, his gait slower and his shoulders no longer squared, but sagging. *Turn around, Papa,* Iris thought, suddenly desperate to get his blessing for her voyage into the unknown. Bennett was watching the men releasing the mooring lines, but after a moment, he turned and saw her, waving a final goodbye. Her heart leapt at the sight of him and she waved back with tears in her eyes. The feeling of loss was poignant. She would miss her family terribly. The steamboat quickly moved away from the wharf and was whisked downstream by the current.

Iris joined Dr. Blackburn and his assistant in the bar for a drink. She was introduced to Arthur Brady, a skinny intern from Tennessee with a shy, gap-toothed smile. He wore thick spectacles and dressed in a threadbare black suit and top hat. Iris couldn't decide if he looked like an undertaker or if he was playing Sancho Panza to Dr. Blackburn's elegant Don Quixote. Considering their destination, Iris much preferred the Sancho Panza allusion.

The doctors ordered whiskey at the bar while Iris asked for a cup of tea. They found a seat with a view of the Louisville lights passing by in the night.

"Cheers," toasted Dr. Blackburn. "Let's hope we can be of some help to the people of Hickman."

"What do you expect it will be like, sir?" asked Iris.

"I have no idea, but if it is like all the other outbreaks, we will have to do everything from nursing and feeding patients to digging graves. These small towns have so few resources."

"Miss Iris, the doctor tells me you trained in Boston," said Arthur.

"Yes, sir, I did."

"Yellow jack is a terrible disease, miss. I hope you won't find it too disheartening."

"Arthur," Blackburn raised an eyebrow, "Iris worked a ward of yellow jack at the Louisville Hospital. She knows what it is and how frustrating it can be. Bennett tells me she has treated cases of typhus, smallpox, and any number of other diseases in Boston. I daresay she will be right in her element, won't you, Iris?"

Iris blushed, embarrassed but pleased by Blackburn's warm acceptance of her.

"Of course," Arthur stammered, suitably chastened.

"I want to help, Dr. Blackburn," said Iris. "I will give it all I can."

"I know you will," Blackburn smiled. "We all will. Want another drink, Arthur?"

"Yes, please," replied Arthur.

"Then we better get to bed."

Sixty-five

Hickman, Kentucky

It was a stifling, hot September morning as the town suddenly appeared out of the fog in a bend of the river, where the Mississippi flowed due west. The town rose in stages to a bluff some four hundred feet above the river. From the paddle-wheeler, the town looked abandoned. A riderless horse trotted aimlessly up and down the road near the wharf. A hay wagon was abandoned near the railway tracks. There was not a soul in sight. No women were doing their washing, and no children were playing in the streets.

The steamboat pulled in silently to the wharf and quickly put the small group of medical personnel on firm ground before hastening away. Dr. Blackburn and Arthur Brady set off ahead of Iris toward the Railway Depot and Telegraph Office, carrying their bags and those of Iris. They knocked on the door, but it was locked. They went into the adjoining waiting room while Iris remained outside. *It was eerily quiet for a town of this size,* she thought. *She had expected a busy little port town on the Mississippi, not an abandoned ghost town.*

They left their bags in the waiting room and then passed a swampy, low-lying area near the railroad tracks on Kentucky Street before marching up the road to the town. As they got closer, they spotted a scruffy-looking ten-year-old boy standing barefoot in the middle of the road.

"Don't come no closer," yelled the boy, keeping his distance. "We got the yellow jack and strangers ain't welcome."

"We're here to help," shouted Blackburn.

"You comin' from Louisville, sir?"

"Yes, we are. We've come to help."

The boy approached. He had blue eyes, a shock of red hair, and an innocent, trusting face.

"Are you doctors?" he asked.

"Yes, we're two doctors and a nurse."

"I'm Billy, sir. The mayor told us you'd be coming. He's out of town."

"So who's in charge, Billy?"

"Ain't nobody in charge, sir. People are sick, even the relief committee is down with it."

Dr. Blackburn looked at Arthur and Iris and raised an eyebrow.

"Well, Billy. We're putting you in charge of the town as of now."

"Me, sir. I ain't nobody."

"You look as good as anybody to me, son. Show us around."

"I can show you the Hendricks house, sir. Charlie and Louisa were the first to die. They were selling apples on the wharf when the Golden Crown put in."

"When was that?"

"The Golden Crown arrived in August, sir."

The doctors followed Billy, with Iris bringing up the rear. They turned onto Jackson Street and passed a closed-up hardware store before arriving at the small house on Cumberland. Billy pushed open the front door and stood back. A terrible smell of decomposing bodies assaulted them.

"God, what an awful stink!" said Arthur. "How long have they been dead?"

"I don't know, sir," said Billy. "The kids, they died first, then Mrs. Hendricks and young Annie."

"Four bodies in this heat, no wonder," Blackburn grimaced. "We're going to have to bury them. Who else lives here?"

"Mr. Hendricks and his son," Billy told him.

Blackburn glanced at Arthur, but his assistant had already pulled out a pen and was taking notes in a small leather journal.

"Gentlemen!"

Everyone froze.

"Over here."

The group turned to see a man standing at the door to a shed. He was fifty years old, bald and unshaven, with side whiskers. He wore a dirty white shirt and wool pants tied with rope.

"You must be Mr. Hendricks?" asked Blackburn.

"Yes, sir."

Hendricks gestured at the dark interior of the shed where a young man was asleep on a bale of hay.

"That's my son, John," said Hendricks. "We haven't been able to bury the children and my wife. The relief committee was supposed to send a wagon."

"Don't worry about that, sir. We'll get the bodies out as soon as possible so you can move back into your home," said Blackburn.

"When did they die?" asked Iris.

"Charlie caught it on August 12 and Louisa the next day. They died four days later. It was a terrible shock, then my wife and daughter Annie caught it around the first of September."

"Who's in charge here?" asked Blackburn.

"You should talk to Dr. Catlett or Dr. Faris. Faris is on the Relief Committee."

"Where is everybody, Mr. Hendricks?" asked Blackburn.

"A lot of people left and went north to Cairo and St. Louis. We shoulda done the same."

"How many are still living here?" asked Arthur.

"I don't know, sir. Not that many. Most of 'em are sick."

Billy led the group down Cumberland to Dr. Catlett's office on the corner. Old man Catlett was out doing house calls, so they went down the street to Holcombe's drugstore and climbed the stairs to the business office of *Faris and Brother, Physicians and Surgeons*.

Dr. Alex Faris was in and happily received them. He was a small man, thirty-eight years old, with a large bushy beard. He had lost an arm fighting for the Fifth Tennessee Infantry Regiment at the Battle of Perryville during the war.

"It's a pleasure to see you, Dr. Blackburn," said Faris. "We're in desperate need of help. We've lost three doctors already, and I don't know how many citizens have perished."

"We're here to help, whatever it takes," said Blackburn.

"There was a lull after the Hendricks family members died, but it started up again a week ago. We've had new cases every day since August 24. Even the brass band that played at the old City Hotel has been decimated. Five of the six players came down with it on the 27th."

"How many are sick?" asked Iris.

"I've lost count, miss. At least a hundred people are down with the disease."

"What about the negroes, sir?" asked Iris. "How many have caught it?"

"I've been out there. They get sick just like we do, miss."

"Look, Dr. Faris, we need to get started," said Blackburn. "Where can we set up to treat the sick and keep them away from the general population?"

"You can take over the hotel. That's probably the best place for it."

"Good. We're going to need volunteers to help out."

"Don't worry, Dr. Blackburn. I'll have the committee here in an hour to help you find volunteers."

"Billy told us the committee was down with it, too," said Iris.

"A lot of them are," Faris conceded, "but there are a few who are still active. I'll have them here in no time."

"What about burying the dead?" asked Arthur.

"Let's see about the hospital first, Arthur," said Blackburn. "Then we can worry about burying the dead."

As the men discussed the organizational aspects, Iris went out into the street and got Billy to show her around. They walked down Cumberland and up Clinton Street, past the drugstore and the Mangel Bakery.

"That's George Mangel," he said, waving to a pale, sickly looking boy sitting in the shade. He looked to be about 15 years old. "George just lost his father and mother. Dr. Catlett says he may not recover from it."

"Let's go over and say hello," Iris said, starting toward him.

"George, this lady is a nurse from Louisville."

George nodded but remained silent.

"Hello, George," Iris smiled. "My name is Iris. How are you feeling?"

"Better, ma'am."

"Did you have the black vomit?"

"No, ma'am. Just the fever."

"That's good. What are your plans now, George?"

"I'm gonna fire up the oven just as soon as I can. The people here need their bread."

"Good, but take your time, George. Get your strength up first."

"Yes, ma'am."

Billy and Iris continued their walk, passing the Samse & Son furniture store. There was a small sign in the window for customers: "CLOSED DURING EPIDEMIC."

Billy turned to Iris.

"This is my dad's store, Miss Iris. My brother Harry and my sister Augusta are down with the sickness."

"I'm sorry to hear that, Billy."

"My dad was Fritz Samse, the undertaker. He died a week ago. Ain't nobody payin' for a burial these days."

Billy had stopped and was staring at the store. *He's just a little boy,* Iris thought, *and his whole world is crashing down around him.* She knew better, but she gave in to the impulse, anyway. She hugged him and could feel his scrawny shoulders shaking with emotion.

"Did we do something wrong, Miss Iris?" He asked, his voice a whisper. "Dr. Faris says he ain't never seen so many people dyin' so fast."

"No, Billy," she told him, taking a handkerchief from her pocket to wipe the boy's tears away. "We didn't do anything wrong."

Iris stood up and tugged at his arm.

"Come on, Billy," she smiled. "I need you to show me around."

They walked along Clinton to Kentucky and met up with half a dozen ragamuffins barefoot in the street.

"Who are you, ma'am?" asked a little girl.

"She's a nurse, Mable," said Billy. "Comes from Louisville."

"Whatcha doin' in Hickman, miss?" asked a young boy.

"She came to help us out, Noah," replied Billy, proud to have all the right replies.

The small group turned right on Kentucky and headed up to the bluff to show Iris the town's best view. They passed Carroll Street and then climbed the hill. From the bluff, they could see the whole town and the crazy loop made by the Mississippi as it headed west and then south toward Memphis.

"My dad always said," Billy's voice was wistful and proud, "this was the best view in town."

"You know what, Billy," Iris smiled. "Your dad was right."

Sixty-six

"When pestilence swept through the whole known world and, notably, the Roman Empire, wiping out most of the farming community and of necessity, leaving a trail of desolation in its wake, Justinian showed no mercy towards the ruined freeholders. Even then, he did not refrain from demanding the annual tax, not only the amount at which he assessed each individual but also the amount for which his deceased neighbors were liable."
Procopius, Anecdota, Greek historian

Iris and the two doctors were put up in an empty house across from the hotel to be close to their patients. Dr. Faris hired a woman to cook and clean for the new arrivals. The next day, Dr. Blackburn took charge of transforming the hotel into an improvised hospital ward with the help of local volunteers. They knocked down several walls, cleaned and scrubbed the floors, installed beds, and disinfected the walls with lime. Dr. Faris' colleagues, Warner and Hackett, hired a crew of ten African Americans to shroud and bury the dead. They were provided with a wagon and sent around to collect the bodies and haul them out to the cemetery.

The first house to be emptied was the Hendricks' house on Cumberland. The men wore bandannas over their noses to ward off the disease as they rolled the bodies in white sheets. Then four men, working together, carefully lifted each body and carried it out to the wagon while Hendricks and his son John watched them work. It was done with great respect and solemnity and left the two surviving family members in tears. Charlie had been thirteen years old, Louisa, six, Annie, ten, and the wife in the prime of life at forty-five. As the father and son watched this sad spectacle, young John was himself starting to feel feverish and soon came down with the malady. He died six days later, leaving his father as the lone survivor of the family.

Although there was a surge of cases among black people, few of them actually succumbed to the disease. The mortality among whites was on another scale entirely. Fifty percent of whites died from the disease compared to only seven percent of blacks. In the ninety-degree heat, the bodies were transported by wagon to the cemetery, and the gravediggers set to work burying them in unmarked graves after a pastor had said a few words for each victim.

As the work at the hotel progressed, Dr. Blackburn left Arthur to supervise the workers and went down to the Railway Depot to send off a telegraph to the Kentucky Board of Health in Louisville with the news of their arrival. An hour later, he received a message of encouragement from the Louisville City Council offering their wholehearted support. He replied by sending a long list of essential items for the new hospital and for his staff:

25 mattresses,

25 blankets,

5 gallons of bourbon,

5 gallons of sherry,

1 barrel of hams,

3 barrels of bacon,

1 barrel of sugar,

100 pounds of coffee.

The supplies arrived a week later by wagon from Clinton, the nearest town some sixteen miles to the northeast. The nervous driver quickly unloaded the wagon at the hospital and took off without a word to the staff. The supplies put a smile on the faces of the volunteers and showed them that they were not alone in the world. Powerful people were lending a hand.

Dr. Faris and Dr. Catlett came around to check on the transformations at the hotel and to inform Dr. Blackburn that they had put together a list of some thirty patients ready to move into the improvised hospital. Some others were too sick to be moved and would have to remain in their homes.

"Dr. Blanton has just come down with the malady," said Catlett, who was looking old and worn at sixty-seven years old. "That's one doctor less for home visits."

"Sorry to hear that, sir," said Blackburn.

"When will you be ready to receive patients?" asked Faris.

"Tomorrow, I would think."

They looked around the enlarged room on the first floor, which could now hold a dozen beds in a long row. The interior walls had been knocked down so more beds could be squeezed into the space. The room had been swept and cleaned.

"Good, because we're getting new cases every day," said Faris. "We're going to need more help."

"Let's see how it goes on the morrow," said Blackburn. "Then we'll put together a list of people we're going to need."

The doctors followed Blackburn and Arthur up the stairs to see what the workers had accomplished on the upper floor. A wall had been ripped out and doors removed to accommodate the beds they had borrowed from the empty houses in town. Dust filled the room. The doctors gave it a cursory look and then returned downstairs. They went into the kitchen where Billy's aunt Eleanor was cleaning up the stove and kitchen counter while a teenage girl scrubbed the floor. Blackburn explained that Eleanor would be cooking meals for some thirty patients and staff. He was interrupted by a volunteer lugging a box of supplies. The young man dumped the supplies in the corner—not being very quiet about it—and then left without a word. Dr. Faris and Dr. Catlett had seen enough and left Dr. Blackburn to his work.

Meanwhile, Iris met with several local women in her new lodgings. She had gotten a couple of volunteers to deliver some chairs earlier and as the women arrived, she had asked them to sit in a circle. Iris was surprised to find that even though Hickman was such a small town, some of the women did not appear to know each other. Finally, there were a dozen women in attendance, not counting Iris herself, and when it was clear that no one else was coming, she motioned for them to be seated.

"Thank you for coming," Iris smiled. "I'll start us off, and after that, we'll go from the woman on my left to the next person, and so on. My name is Iris Gagnon. I'm a nurse. I worked until very recently in the yellow fever ward at the Louisville Hospital."

The lady to Iris' immediate left, a woman in her forties, hesitated and then began to speak.

"I'm Lily Karlach," she glanced nervously at Iris and then at the others. "I had to come here. I cain't stand sitting in my kitchen staring at the four walls and doing nothin' to help out. My husband would want me to do my part. He died recently, along with my son."

Iris smiled at Lily and nodded at an overweight woman in her fifties. She was obviously in mourning, dressed in black.

"I'm Florence, ma'am. I've lost a daughter and a husband. My son wants me to leave town and live with him in the country, but I ain't gonna flee the sickness. I want to fight it."

The next woman was in her fifties, with a tanned, heavily lined face, who spent her days out in the sun and wore an old beige Stetson.

"I'm Jennie, ma'am. I ain't from here. I live on a farm. I just buried my son. I want to do my part. I'm not scared of dying."

Iris then nodded at the two young, well-dressed women.

"I'm Alice, ma'am. My ma is at home with the sickness. I want to help. That's why I'm here. This is my sister, Agatha. She's with me, but she's real scared."

Agatha fidgeted next to her older sister and looked around the room nervously. The women finished their introductions, and then it was Iris' turn to speak again.

"As you know, yellow fever is a terrible disease," said Iris. "It's very hard on everyone, doctors and nurses included. I won't hide it from you. There is not much we can do to cure patients of the disease other than keep them comfortable and give them water. We lose faith when we can't help the sick. We become frustrated and disillusioned. What I'm saying, ladies, is try to be patient, try not to lose hope, and remain kind and cheerful at all times for the sake of those who are dying."

"I heard Dr. Blackburn was bringing some kinda miracle cure with him," said Alice. "That's what people in town are saying, ma'am."

"There's nothing of the kind, I'm afraid," said Iris. "There is no miracle cure."

"Well, why would we need you doctors and nurses from the big city if you ain't got a cure?" asked Florence impatiently. "You're sayin' you can't help people."

"We can help, but we don't have a miracle cure," replied Iris. "All we can do is wait and look for signs of improvement. A lot of patients will recover all by themselves without a lot of medicine."

Alice and her sister Agatha looked unimpressed by Iris' comments and stood up to show their discontent.

"Don't misunderstand me, we need nurses, please," said Iris to the sisters as they stood up to leave.

"I think we're juss gonna stay home and look after our ma ourselves," said Alice.

There was a long silence after the two women had left. Then Iris turned to address the others.

"It's not true that we do nothing, ladies. It is not easy to die alone in a hospital bed. We're there to accompany our patients for better or for worse. Dr. Blackburn will tell you that none of the usual remedies work with yellow fever, so we must be strong and wait to see how the sickness plays out. I'm telling you this so you know what you are getting into."

Lily raised her hand.

"Where you from, Iris?"

"I'm French Canadian, ma'am."

"You are a long way from home."

"Yes, I am."

"Well, thank you for coming, Iris," said Lily. "We'll do the best we can for our patients. Won't we, ladies?"

The women nodded with varying degrees of enthusiasm. *Who knows*, Iris thought, *whether they would still feel the same way after they'd gone home and had a chance to think about it.* For now, though, she had her nursing volunteers and was determined to keep them.

"We work as a team," said Iris. "You will not be alone."

"Thank you, Iris," said Florence.

"The patients start arriving tomorrow. It will be a hectic day," added Iris. "Remember to avoid any physical contact with them. Do not touch their hands or faces unless it is necessary for cleaning or providing food. Remember to wash your hands when you come into physical contact with a patient. So good luck and I'll see you all in the morning."

The next day, Dr. Blackburn, Arthur, and Iris waited in vain for the patients and their families to arrive. The volunteers had finished opening up the floors, but there was still some sweeping and cleaning going on in the upstairs ward. The morning dragged on and still nobody came. Dr. Blackburn and Arthur Brady sat at the table in the kitchen drinking coffee that Eleanor had prepared. At midday, Dr. Faris came around to see how they were coping and was astonished to find that no patients had come.

"You think they'll come tonight?" asked Arthur.

"I doubt it," said Faris. "Not at night. People fear the night more than the day."

"When should we expect them?" asked Blackburn.

"People are scared. They are desperate. A lot of them want to move their loved ones to safety in the country. Others are simply too sick to be moved. You should have had a few patients in here by now."

"I don't understand what's going on," said Arthur.

"Where are the women you talked to yesterday, Iris?" asked Blackburn as Iris came into the kitchen.

"I'll go talk to them," said Iris, who left the kitchen and went into the yard to find Billy sitting on a stone wall whittling a piece of wood with a knife.

"I need to find Lily Karlach, Billy. Do you know where she lives?"

"Of course I do, Miss Iris," said Billy, jumping up and putting away his pocket knife. He led the way along Clinton Street to Lily's house, where they found her washing clothes in the backyard near the water pump.

"Lily, how are you?" asked Iris.

"I'm fine, miss," said Lily, who had both hands in soapy water washing clothes in a wooden tub.

"No one came, Lily. Not a soul."

"You're going to have to go house to house, Iris."

"Why?"

"Fear, miss. They don't want to leave their homes. Many have been abandoned by their families."

Lily emptied the tub of wet clothes and went back into the house to fetch some more dirty laundry. Iris and Billy followed, walking into a cloth sheet smelling of vinegar hanging from the ceiling in the parlor. People believed that the smell of vinegar could overpower the 'putrid miasma' or bad air that was thought to cause the disease. Lily Karlach wasn't taking any chances with the sickness.

An antique world globe sat on a table in the corner near a wall full of books. There were several Roman engravings on the opposite wall, one of a mosaic depicting the Byzantine Emperor Justinian I, who tried to restore Roman imperial power in the sixth century.

"Your husband was interested in history?" asked Iris.

"Henry was a teacher, my dear," said Lily. "He was very knowledgeable. He taught mathematics, science, and history at the school."

"He was my teacher, miss," said Billy.

"Henry liked his history," said Lily. "He loved to tell stories about the past. That's a drawing of Justinian I who tried to restore the empire."

"The first plague," said Billy. "I remember Mr. Karlach talked about the first plague in our class."

"It was called the Justinian Plague 'cause it happened during his reign," added Lily.

"Wasn't it like the 'Black Death' in the fourteenth century?" asked Iris. "It swept through Europe and killed millions."

"Yes, my dear," said Lily.

"Have we got the plague here in Hickman, miss?" asked Billy.

"No, Billy, yellow jack isn't the plague," replied Lily.

"I think it's worse," ventured Billy.

Lily shrugged and collected a pile of dirty clothes before returning to the yard, followed by Billy and Iris.

"You know Henry would have enjoyed talking to you, Miss Iris."

"He sounds like an interesting man."

"He was a very dear man," said Lily as she dumped her clothes in the tub. "It's hard to believe that Henry and Robbie were taken from me just weeks ago."

"I'm so sorry, Lily."

"The patients will come just before dark, Iris. No one wants to be out and about at night for fear of catching the disease."

Sixty-seven

An hour later, Iris and Arthur set off in a wagon, following Lily and young Billy on foot to collect the sick in town and bring them to the hospital. They carried a crude stretcher to transport patients who were too sick to move by themselves. Many of their prospective patients saw the move as a death warrant and it would take time to convince them to put their trust in the doctors and the new hospital.

Lily's job was to convince them. She knew everyone. She knew how to talk to them, and they respected her. They stopped in an alley off Cumberland so Lily could speak to a woman who had the fever but didn't want to leave her house.

"How long have you worked with Dr. Blackburn, Arthur?" asked Iris as they waited.

"Going on five years now, Iris."

"So what do you know about his badly maligned reputation?"

"Oh, that was a pack of lies, Iris. Union muckrakers. They called it the Yellow Fever plot. Luke has spent much of his medical career saving lives during yellow fever epidemics. He was a medical officer in Natchez in '53 during one of the worst yellow fever outbreaks. 9,000 people died in New Orleans that year alone."

"What about those soiled bedclothes he sent home from Bermuda, Arthur?"

"Luke doesn't believe yellow jack can be transmitted by physical contact with soiled bedclothes, Iris. Back in '53, two medical students in New Orleans had a mad scheme to try to self-contaminate with the black vomit, but they couldn't contract the disease. It's not the same as with smallpox."

Lily appeared in the doorway and called to Iris in the wagon.

"We're coming, my dear."

"The reason Luke sent those trunks of contaminated clothing home was so the medical community could run tests. It was an experiment. He had no intention of contaminating the population of New York or any other city. You don't spend your entire life fighting a disease to suddenly turn around and propagate it on the innocent. It would be against your Hippocratic oath."

Lily called to them from the doorway. She had one arm around an elderly woman supporting her as best she could, making her way to the wagon. Arthur hurriedly got down to help, and once they were safely on board, they set off along Cumberland looking for new patients.

By the end of the afternoon, several patients had come in of their own accord with the help of their families. When Iris and Arthur arrived with the wagon, they brought the number to a dozen, many with high fevers. A few were already beyond hope, but they would be cared for nonetheless. The women and children were put in the first-floor ward while the men were sent upstairs.

By the first week of September, there had been over forty cases of the malady among the whites in the town, many of them fatal, with people dying within as little as four days of falling sick. After a brief lull, there had been an explosion of new cases, and the demand for space in the hospital increased rapidly. Dr. Blackburn added additional beds in the hallways but refused to do more. Patients they couldn't accommodate were asked to remain at home with regular visits from a physician. By the end of September, half of the hospital's patients had died. It wasn't a pretty way to go. Victims would experience a host of unpleasant symptoms: jaundice, chills, nausea, headaches, fever, convulsions, and delirium. Then came the blood with hemorrhaging around the mouth, the nose, and the eyes. One woman, before she died, vomited black, partially coagulated blood and horrified the nurse volunteers and the other patients on the ward.

Iris had seen it all before. She worked the day shift with Lily during the first week and they were replaced at night by Florence and Jennie. Lily was a generous, agreeable co-worker and Iris got on well with her. They followed Dr. Blackburn's remedies that he had developed during the Natchez epidemic. The patients were kept hydrated with warm lemonade, beef broth, and water. Heat-induced sweating and foot baths were employed along with blistering as a last resort if the patient was vomiting blood.

A cloth dipped in vinegar hung from the ceiling in each ward and a woman had brought in a bottle of camphor oil from home and poured it into a dish so the patients could smell its strong odor. There was also the omnipresent smell of tobacco that blanketed the wards after visiting family members smoked their pipes and cigars. People believed that the smell of tobacco, vinegar, or camphor could overpower the bad air that was thought to cause the disease.

A little girl named Mattie Gomez, only four years old, was burning up with a fever. Her mother had succumbed to the malady earlier in the week, while her father was in a bed upstairs and showing signs of bleeding. Lily had taken a shine to the child, spending a lot of time with her, to the detriment of the other patients. Iris watched as Lily put yet another cold compress on Mattie's head and decided it was time to have a word with her.

"She's still in the early stages, Lily," remarked Iris. "I want you to look after our more urgent cases. There's Max upstairs. He's starting to bleed."

"Sorry, Iris. Sure, I'll look after Max."

"I understand your attachment, Lily, but we cannot have favorites."

"The child reminds me of my niece, who is about the same age. My sister and her husband left for St. Louis before the epidemic. I don't know how they're doing."

"I know, my dear, but we've got work to do."

Lily went upstairs to the men's ward to have a look at Max Hertwick, a 42-year-old German immigrant and wagon maker with a flourishing business in Hickman. His children had all come down with the malady. Lily looked down at the unconscious man, who was bleeding from his eyes and mouth. Iris had applied a hot iron to his chest the same morning, and a blister had appeared on his skin. Lily took the scissors and snipped it, allowing the fluid to drain off. Max woke up suddenly and opened his eyes to see Lily looking down at him.

"Lily, is that you? I know your son, Robbie. My boys play with him."

Before Lily could say a word, Max closed his eyes and drifted off again.

There was a convenient myth prevalent among the white population of the South that if you were African American, you couldn't catch yellow fever. Prominent doctors spread the lie that all black people had a natural immunity to the disease. This theory—that black people could work without risk in hot, swampy areas that were prone to yellow fever—was used as an argument to justify slavery. Its validity was tested daily in the slave markets of New Orleans, where slaves with immunity were sold for 25 to 50% more than slaves from areas where yellow fever was not present. Some slaves were immune to the disease, while others were not.

At precisely six o'clock each morning, a skinny African-American boy named Nate knocked on the kitchen door. Eleanor sat him down and gave him a cup of tea while he waited to claim the bodies of the patients who had died during the night. Then two muscular black men came in and hauled the bodies out to the wagon, where they shrouded them before taking them out to the cemetery. At the end of her third week, Iris decided to enlist young Nate in her research. Dr. Blackburn had requested that she visit the poorer parts of town and get an estimate of the number of African Americans down with the fever.

Iris accompanied Nate and the men over to the cemetery to unload the bodies. Then Nate drove Iris in the wagon the long way back to town through the black community on the river. It was a swampy area with a lot of rundown shacks spread out along the river road. There were very few people around. A few women and children watched them from the shadows as the wagon passed. They stopped at a guest house near the water where most of the sick patients were staying. Nate pulled up in the wagon and Iris stepped down. She went to the front door, where she ran into a tall black pastor with a clerical collar.

"Hello, I'm Iris Gagnon, sir. I work with Dr. Blackburn in town. I'm here to find out how many people are sick with the yellow jack."

"Dr. Blackburn. He's that doctor who just arrived from Louisville?"

"Yes, sir."

"I'm Pastor Williams, miss. We've got a lot of people down with the sickness. Why don't you come in and I'll show you around."

They entered the first floor of the guest house with its vinegar-impregnated cloth hanging from the wooden beams. There were mattresses on the floor with men sleeping or playing cards in the dark recesses of the room. There was a pervasive smell of vomit and sweat coming from the unwashed bodies.

"Let's go upstairs," said the pastor. "We've had a few fatalities, miss, but most of them will be back on their feet by the end of the week."

They entered the women's ward on the second floor. A few women were asleep on the mattresses, but the place was not nearly as busy.

"The women don't catch it as much as the men," said the pastor. "When they do, they prefer to stay at home. The men get it worse and some of them die."

It was unusual to see a white woman in the house, and the kitchen staff stepped out to get a better look at Iris. They smiled at her, and the pastor offered her a cup of tea in the kitchen. They sat down at a table, watched closely by the kitchen staff.

"What's it like in town among the white folk, miss?" asked the pastor.

"It's been terrible, sir, a real disaster. Dr. Blackburn saw a lot of yellow jack in Natchez, but he says this is the worst he's ever seen it. Half of our patients are dying from the malady. We don't know why."

"That's what the boys keep tellin' me, miss. They can hardly keep up with digging all those graves."

"Do you have a nurse or any medical staff with you, Pastor?"

"Nope. Don't need it. We got the Lord on our side."

Iris looked up at the smiling women watching her.

"The four horsemen cometh, miss, just like in Revelation. The first horseman on a white steed brings the pestilence to punish the people for their sins."

The kitchen staff whispered, "Praise the Lord".

"The second horseman on a red steed brings us four years of civil war. Ain't that right?"

"Praise the lord," murmured the women.

"What else we got coming our way? The black horse and the pale horse. Famine and death. That's what's coming next. God protect us."

"Praise the Lord," repeated the women.

Young Nate drove Iris back to town. She looked forward to telling Dr. Blackburn the good news. Black people were doing much better than whites.

"My sister went to that guest house, miss," Nate told her, "when she came down with the malady. She didn't have no money, so the pastor chased her off."

"The guest house belongs to the pastor?"

"Yes, ma'am. He stole it from the owner who was dying of the yellow jack back in August. You gotta pay every day to stay there. If you don't, you're just another sinful negro, says the pastor."

"How's your sister doing now?"

"She's restin' at home, doin' better now, ma'am."

Iris remained silent and realized that human avarice didn't always hide its ugly face during epidemics and natural disasters.

When Iris returned to the hospital, she ran into Dr. Blackburn in the kitchen. He was drinking a coffee and looking at a telegram that had just arrived from Louisville.

"Sit down, Iris. How did it go?"

"It went well, sir. It's as you expected. The colored folk come down with the malady, but they have nothing like our rates of mortality."

"Well, that's good news. I have a telegram here from Bennett for you," said Blackburn, handing her a slip of paper with the name of the Western Union Telegraph Company printed on the top. Iris read:

DR. DIMOCK AND FRIENDS DROWNED.
GERMAN STEAMSHIP SS SCHILLER LOST
ON SCILLY ROCKS. SO SORRY.
WE PRAY FOR YOU. BENNETT.

Iris was shell-shocked. Dr. Dimock had drowned on her way to England. She had been a rising star in the field of medicine, and Iris had valued her friendship more than anything. She had been a role model for Iris and had taken her in when she fell ill.

"It wouldn't have been right to keep it from you, Iris," Blackburn said. "I've heard of Dr. Dimock and I know you were close."

"She was a remarkable woman, Doctor. A truly remarkable woman. She will be missed in Boston."

Sixty-eight

The next day, just before dawn, Billy took Arthur down to the landing and the two of them went fishing. Arthur had seen large white bass swimming near the shore and wanted to try his hand. Billy brought along the fishing poles and a can of worms, and they fished from the wharf-boat. It was a welcome change of pace for Arthur from the long hours in the stifling hospital ward.

"How's your brother Harry doing, Billy?"

"He's much better, sir. Dr. Blackburn came by the house yesterday and said he's gonna be all right."

"I'm real happy to hear that. And your sister Augusta?"

"Miss Iris is looking after her. I saw her yesterday, but she ain't doing too well."

"We must pray for her."

A large white bass struck Billy's line, and he happily hauled it in. He was momentarily transformed into a carefree ten-year-old, catching his first bass. Grinning from ear to ear, he quickly removed the hook and proudly dumped the fish into a wooden bucket nearby.

"How many times a year do you go fishin', Billy?"

"I fished downstream a couple of times with my pa using crawdads. The last time was in June."

There was a long silence while Billy re-baited and dropped his line back into the same sunlit spot on the river bottom where a dozen white bass had congregated.

"I lost my Pa," said Billy.

"Yes, I know. I saw his name, Billy. I'm sorry."

They fished for a while, enjoying the breeze from the river.

"What do you want to do when you grow up, Billy?" asked Arthur.

"I want to be a doctor like Dr. Faris."

"Why's that, Billy?"

"I wanna save lives, sir, like you and Dr. Blackburn. There is too much death in this town."

After another hour, they had caught half a dozen white bass. They both would have been happy to stay there all day, but Arthur had to get back. They collected their things and their catch and returned to the hospital. Their smiles said it all as they entered the kitchen with the bucket of fish. It set off a rare laugh with Eleanor and the kitchen staff. The day seemed almost normal until Arthur entered the ward and counted the number of patients who had died during the night. He had drawn a large map of the town on the wall with the names of patients in each house. He was putting together a register of those who were sick and those who had died. When a patient died, he added an 'x' after their name.

Every day, Dr. Blackburn and Dr. Faris visited patients around town, while Arthur worked in the kitchen ordering supplies and helping the nurses in the wards. When Dr. Faris fell sick, Dr. Blackburn went out on house calls with Arthur until he could find a replacement.

"How's young Mattie doing, Lily?" asked Iris.

"She's looking better, Iris. Her appetite has returned."

"Good. There is hope for her."

Iris and Lily were having lunch together in the kitchen. Eleanor had served them a plate of eggs, sausage, and grits just as an attractive young woman with hazel eyes and dark hair appeared in the doorway.

"We've got a delivery, Eleanor," she announced. "Cabbages, potatoes, carrots, peas, and corn comin' in."

A tall, muscular young man came in with three boxes of cabbages and put them in the corner.

"Let me get my Billy in here to help you unload," said Eleanor, exiting the kitchen.

"You're the nurse from Louisville?" asked the young woman.

"Yes, miss. I'm Iris Gagnon. I came with Dr. Blackburn."

"My dad told me about you. He went to the same medical school as Dr. Blackburn. His name is Dr. John Alexander."

"Of course," Iris smiled. "What's your name?"

"I'm Belle Alexander. We live on a farm in the country. My dad has been helping out in town. He comes in for a few hours every day."

They watched the young man appear in the doorway with another load of vegetables.

"Can I ask you a question, Miss Iris?"

"Certainly."

"How did you become a nurse?"

"I trained at a school in Boston, Belle."

"Is it hard being a nurse?"

Lily burst into laughter, surprised that a doctor's daughter would ask such a question.

"It's an impossible job, ain't it, Iris?" Lily managed to stifle her laughter and smiled apologetically at Belle. "I'm sorry, my dear. I couldn't help it."

They were saved from an awkward silence by the return of the young man. Billy was with him this time, carrying boxes of produce.

"That's Kevin, my boyfriend," said Belle with pride. "We were gonna get married in August and then the epidemic swept through town. Kevin's a farmer east of here."

"He's a nice-looking fella," said Iris.

"A right, handsome young buck," added Lily.

"Yep, he is," said Belle, giving Iris an appraising look. "We gotta go, ladies."

Lily and Iris shared an amused smile as Belle retrieved her young man and hustled him out of the room.

The situation in Hickman was now desperate enough that Dr. Blackburn sent a telegram to Louisville asking for additional medical staff. A week later, a contingent from Louisville arrived in town after a long train ride. All steamboat traffic had ceased in the southerly direction because of the epidemic. It had been weeks since the citizens of Hickman had seen a train pull into town. The train was not much of a train. A steam locomotive pulled one decrepit passenger car along the track. When it finally came to a stop, the medical staff quickly descended onto the platform and carried their bags toward the small crowd gathered near the railway depot. Bennett Young jumped down onto the platform with a basket and followed the others. An engineer leaned out the window of the locomotive to have a word with him.

"Ten minutes, Mr. Young," said the engineer.

Bennett nodded. It had taken all his political influence and a lot of arm-twisting by Bennett and his partner Jake to get the Kentucky Board of Health and the Louisville City Council to put pressure on the short-line rail companies in Western Kentucky to provide a locomotive and passenger car on their Elizabethtown and Paducah rail line, which had been shut down for three months due to the Yellow Fever scare. The railway company had promised to carry the volunteers to their destination, but under no circumstance were there to be any delays, and the company had categorically refused to accept any Hickman passengers who might want to make the return journey.

Dr. Blackburn and Iris shook hands with the volunteers: five young men and two women wearing traditional nursing caps. Three of the men carried Gladstone bags of the type preferred by doctors. The fourth man was obviously the druggist. He struggled with a wooden box on wheels that contained a large supply of medicines. The fifth man was the telegraph operator whom Blackburn had requested to maintain communication with the outside world.

When Iris saw Bennett on the platform, she ran to embrace him.

"Iris, my dear. We've been worried sick about you," said Bennett. "Eliza sends her love."

"I'm all right, Papa," said Iris. "Tell Eliza not to worry. I'll be back as soon as I can."

Bennett tried to hide his alarm at how thin and pale Iris looked. Even the plump and rosy-cheeked Dr. Blackburn looked haggard and had lost a good deal of weight, thought Bennett as he spotted him in the crowd.

"You could come away with me, Iris," said Bennett sadly. "You've done enough."

"I can't leave, Papa. I must see it to the end."

"Here are your volunteers, Luke," said Bennett when Blackburn came over to shake his hand.

"Thank you, Bennett. I was expecting them to arrive by wagon like last month's supplies. I never expected to see you accompanying them on the train."

"It took a while to organize, Luke, but we're happy to help."

Bennett handed Iris a wicker basket.

"Here's a present from Eliza, my dear. Fresh bread, cheese, and all the food you love."

"Eliza's a saint, Papa. Thank her for me."

The train whistle blew, and the engineer waved for Bennett to return.

"I have to go now. I'll pray for you both," said Bennett as Iris hugged him again.

Dr. Blackburn and Iris watched as Bennett waved to them as he climbed on the train.

"Bennett and Eliza miss you, Iris," said Blackburn.

"Yes," she whispered as tears welled up in her eyes.

Despite Blackburn's warnings that the volunteers should be Southerners immune to the disease, they had all come from states untouched by yellow fever, despite knowing that by doing so they were at a higher risk of catching the malady. Nevertheless, they arrived just in time. After three weeks of long days and nights, Jennie had quit her post and returned to her farm in the country, leaving Florence alone to assist Lily and Iris. Then, just as the new staff arrived for work, Florence called it quits and joined her son in the country. The three Louisville doctors soon went out on house calls and gave Dr. Blackburn some respite from the long, grueling days. The two nurses were young and eager to work in the ward.

Iris had noticed that Lily was distracted and no longer performing her duties. She would sit in a corner for long periods looking off in the distance, absorbed by her own thoughts as the other nurses called for her assistance. Lily would send them away, complaining that they were badgering her and protesting that she had other things to do. Iris pulled her aside one quiet afternoon.

"What's going on, Lily? You seem to be very moody these days."

"I'm fine, Iris, just tired. I wish we could do more. So many patients are dying. It's like nothing we do helps."

"I know," said Iris, sitting down.

"I wonder whether God even hears my prayers. I have prayed more these last few weeks than I have prayed in my entire life before."

"Think of our job as one of accompanying patients, Lily. We may not cure them, but we're here to make their last moments more endurable."

"I know, but that doesn't help much."

Iris nodded, realizing how hopeless her job as a nurse had become. There was no respite for the nurses. They worked seven days a week in the ward, and every morning, more patients passed away during the night.

"Why don't you take the day off, Lily?" Iris suggested. "Come back tomorrow."

"I hate going home, Iris. I can't sleep. I've been dreamin' about my Robbie and thinking about all the things I should have done before he got sick."

"Go home, Lily. Try to relax a bit. I'll come by later when I get off my shift and we can talk some more."

Iris didn't get off her shift until the early morning hours when she suddenly realized she had forgotten about Lily. She collected her things and hurried out of the hospital. It had been another bad night. Charlotte, one of the Louisville nurses, had complained about a terrible headache and Iris feared that she was coming down with the malady. She had given her a bed in the ward. She couldn't afford to lose a single nurse.

The dawn light was just coming up when Iris arrived at Lily's house on Clinton Street. It was a wet dawn with mist rising off the Mississippi and fog obscuring parts of the river and town. The whole neighborhood of abandoned houses was deathly quiet. She knocked on the front door and waited. It was too early for Lily to be visiting friends or going to the shops. Iris went into the yard and looked around before returning to the front step. She knocked again and waited for a moment, then she turned the knob and opened the door.

"Lily," she called. "It's Iris. I'm sorry I couldn't come by last night."

There were numerous wooden boxes full of Henry's books on the floor. The familiar cloth rags dipped in vinegar were gone, as were the drawing of Justinian on the wall and the globe in the corner. *Lily has decided to give away Henry's things, probably to the school where he had worked,* thought Iris. *She has decided to move on with her life.*

Iris entered the kitchen and noticed that there were no plates or glasses on the counter. The stove was cold, and the kitchen was tidy and spotless. *Maybe she's left town,* thought Iris. *I wouldn't blame her.* She went into the bedroom to see whether Lily had slept in her bed. As she approached the bed, she noticed the door to the wardrobe was wide open, and in the mirror, she could see her friend suspended from a beam in a corner of the room, her head at a grotesque angle, her eyes wide and staring.

"Oh, Lily. Not you," screamed Iris, as she turned and rushed over to support the body. "You're the best. You can't do this to me."

Iris came to her senses and returned to the kitchen to get a knife. She ran back to the bedroom and climbed on a chair, grasping Lily's legs while she desperately cut away at the knotted bed sheet hanging from the beam. The bed sheet finally gave way and both she and Lily tumbled to the floor.

Iris checked for signs of life and realized there was no hope. Lily had been dead for several hours. Iris collapsed back on the floor and cried. She blamed herself. If she had come earlier, she might have prevented her friend's death.

Iris didn't return to work all that day. She stayed in her bedroom in her empty house, thinking about how she was losing it. *Lily was right. They were doing nothing to save their patients. Accompanying the dying was not enough. Could she return to the job? She didn't know. She knew she was letting down the doctors by not going back to work, but she didn't have the energy to return.*

At midday, Iris reluctantly answered the knock on her door to find Dr. Blackburn standing there. He looked exhausted.

"I heard about Lily, Iris. I'm so sorry. How are you holding up?"

"I'm not, sir. Lily was a dear friend these last few weeks. I found her hanging from the rafters in her bedroom."

"I know. Why did she do it?" asked Blackburn.

"She's been depressed. I think it was all too much for her. The loss of her husband and son."

Dr. Blackburn nodded and followed Iris into the kitchen.

"Do you want some tea, sir? I just made it."

"Sure," said Blackburn.

Iris poured the tea and milk, and they sat at the table in silence for a long moment.

"Billy came by with the news about Lily," said Blackburn. "He told me that her husband had been a teacher at the school."

"Henry Karlach taught history and science," said Iris.

"Billy was in tears when he talked about Henry. He was loved by all his pupils. That's a big loss for a small town."

"Yes, it is. Henry had a passion for history and storytelling, sir."

The doctor pulled a flask of whiskey from an inside pocket and poured a good dose into his teacup.

"Iris?"

"Yes, please."

Blackburn poured her a shot of whiskey.

"I'm so tired, sir. I can't stop thinking about Lily."

"I know, Iris. Take the day off. Don't come in until you feel better."

"What are we to do, sir?"

"I don't know, my dear, but we must carry on somehow. We cannot give up."

Iris stared at the doctor, feeling hopeless.

Sixty-nine

A week after the fishing excursion, Arthur fell sick and was given a bed in the hospital. Iris took care of him, and Dr. Blackburn visited him after his long day visiting patients at home.

"How are you feeling, Arthur?" asked Blackburn.

"Hot, sir."

"I heard from Billy that you had a great time fishing for bass."

"We caught quite a few, Luke. As a kid back in Tennessee, I often fished with my daddy on the South Holston River. The best damn river for speckled trout anywhere in the country. When it rained, you could smell the trout as they broke the water. Dawn on that river was always special for my daddy and me."

"That's a wonderful memory, Arthur," said Blackburn gently as Iris interrupted him coming into the ward.

"How's Charlotte doing?" asked Blackburn.

"She's got a fever, sir."

"Yes, I thought so when I saw her this morning."

"You need anything, sir?"

"No, I'm fine, Iris," said Blackburn as he picked up a glass and poured water through Arthur's parched lips. It was going to be another long night.

Young Mattie was in the kitchen playing with a doll when Iris came in for a cup of coffee mid-morning.

"Iris, what are we to do with young Mattie?" asked Eleanor. "I took her home with me yesterday, but she has no one to look after her."

"Have you talked to Dr. Blackburn?"

"Yes, he asked me to find a family in town to look after the child, but it is not easy to find anyone to look after an orphan with the yellow jack still threatening. There are so many families grieving."

"She can stay with me for a few days, Eleanor."

"Are you sure? You are so busy, Iris."

"It's only for a few days. I should be fine."

"Mattie," Eleanor turned to the little girl, "you're going to stay with Iris for a few days."

The child looked up at Iris and smiled.

"Do you like cats, Mattie?" asked Iris.

"I love tabby cats, ma'am," said Mattie. "I had one, but it ran away."

"I've got one tabby and one cat who is black as night in my house, Mattie. We'll go have a look later. Would you like that?"

"Yes, ma'am."

The next morning at the crack of dawn, Iris was jostled awake by Mattie giggling next to her in bed. She was playing a game with the cats.

"How are you, Mattie?" asked Iris, bleary-eyed.

"You were snoring, Miss Iris."

"Snoring?" asked Iris. "Was I very loud?"

"No, but you scared the cats."

"I'm sorry. I didn't mean to."

Iris swung her legs out of bed and got up.

"We better be going, Mattie. Eleanor will prepare some breakfast for you."

Iris went outside and pumped water into a wooden bucket. When she returned, Mattie was ready to go. Iris lit the stove and put the kettle on for her morning tea.

"Come here, Mattie," said Iris. "You can't go into the hospital with a dirty face."

Iris took a cloth and dipped it into the soapy water, washing Mattie's face, arms, hands, and ears.

"That's much better, my dear," she said to Mattie, who was drying her face on a towel. "Why don't you put out some food for the cats?"

As Iris started her wash, Mattie put food in the cat's bowl.

"Dr. Faris told me that your folks came from Missouri. Is that true, Mattie?"

"I don't know, ma'am. I was born here, but my ma came from St.

Louis."

"Have you met her folks, Mattie?"

"No, they never come to visit."

"So you never met your grandparents?"

"No, ma'am."

"While I get changed, why don't you go outside and get some air? It's a nice day."

Mattie nodded and stepped outside.

When Iris came out of the house ready for work, Mattie thrust a bouquet of wildflowers into her hands that she had collected in the garden.

"They're lovely, Mattie," said Iris. "Thank you."

"My ma liked flowers."

"I'm sure she did," replied Iris, taking her hand and leading her down the road.

As soon as they arrived at the hospital, Iris put Eleanor in charge of Mattie and went on her round of the ward. Arthur was her first patient. She took his temperature and then sat down in a chair near the bed. His fever had passed, but he didn't look any better.

"How are you feeling, Arthur?" she asked.

"Better, I think."

"Good. Dr. Blackburn suggested we do some blistering today. Are you OK with that, Arthur?"

"Sure, Iris."

She noticed the worried look on his face.

"What is it, Arthur?"

"Where's Luke?"

"He's off on house calls."

"If I don't make it, Iris... I want you to tell him I never had a better boss. It's been a pleasure working with you both."

"Thank you, Arthur. He'll want to hear that. I know he will."

When Iris returned to the kitchen for a cup of coffee, she saw Mattie in front of a plate of scrambled eggs and toast. Eleanor approached Iris and whispered in her ear.

"Mattie's been asking about you, Iris."

"Really."

"She wants to know where you come from with your funny accent. I tell her you're French from Canada. She doesn't know where that is, so she figures you must be from New Orleans."

Iris looked over at the little girl having a solitary breakfast and felt a pang of guilt.

"Eleanor, you wouldn't have any games for her to play? The days are long for a girl her age stuck in the kitchen."

"I'll get Billy to bring in a game or two for her. He could also take her for a walk."

"The fresh air would do her good."

Eleanor nodded and returned to the stove.

As Dr. Alex Faris was recuperating in his hospital bed, his younger brother—also a medical doctor—traveled from Missouri to replace him at the head of the Relief Committee and to offer his services to the community. Dr. James Faris was seen with Dr. Blackburn on house calls and helped treat patients in the hospital. He was an agreeable sort and got on well with the medical staff. He had a wife and children back home but had decided to fight the disease for the sake of his brother. As Alex's health improved, James was often seen arguing with his brother in the men's ward.

"You must leave right now, James," ordered Alex with a worried look. "You must not stay here in Hickman. You have a wife and children to look after. Please go."

James listened patiently to his brother's complaints while he monitored his physical condition. Alex was a stubborn man, but so was his brother. They had worked together for years in the same office in Hickman before James had struck out on his own across the river in Missouri. Alex was married and had sent his wife and children away before the arrival of the epidemic. He felt it was his duty to remain in Hickman to help save the community, but his brother James had no such obligation, so Alex continued to hassle him about returning to his home.

"Dr. Blackburn, please," said Alex one morning when he had him alone. "You cannot allow James to work at the hospital. Sack him and send him away. Tell him it's for his own good."

"He's a very competent physician," replied Blackburn to the small, bearded man in the hospital bed. "I've observed him on numerous house calls, Dr. Faris. He knows his business. I'll try to convince him as a favor to you."

"Thank you, Doctor. James is pigheaded, always has been, but if you talk to him, he'll listen."

"I'll do my best, sir."

At the end of her day, Iris stepped out of the hospital, accompanied by Mattie. They ran into Belle, waiting for her dad in a buggy outside Dr. Corbett's house.

"How you doin', Belle?" asked Iris.

"I'm fine, Miss Iris. Who is the child?"

"My name is Mattie," the girl piped up before Iris could reply.

"She staying with me until I find her family," said Iris. "How's Kevin?"

"He's doing fine, Miss Iris."

"Any yellow jack out your way?"

"Nope."

"Kevin's family?"

"They're fine, miss. Most of them left for Cairo and St. Louis a month ago. Ain't heard nothin'."

Belle's father came out of Dr. Corbett's house.

"Dad, this is Miss Iris."

"I know who she is," Dr. Alexander smiled. "It's a pleasure to meet you finally, Miss Iris. I've heard good things about you from Dr. Blackburn. I'm the coroner of Fulton County."

"Thank you, sir. How's it going, Dr. Alexander?"

"It's hard on everyone. Belle tells me you trained in Boston."

"Yes, sir."

"We are so happy to have you. You have been a pillar of support for Dr. Blackburn."

"Thank you, sir."

"We better be on our way, Belle, if we want to make it back before dark. Nice seeing you, Miss Iris."

Dr. Alexander quickly climbed onto the wagon and sat next to his daughter. They said their goodbyes as Belle picked up the reins and whipped the horse into a trot.

Arthur's condition worsened. He was bleeding from the mouth and eyes and looked a sorry sight when Iris looked in on him one night. Dr. Blackburn had asked Iris and the other nurses to call him if they noticed any change in his condition. Iris asked a volunteer to go look for the doctor. He arrived an hour later after he returned from his house calls.

Arthur didn't seem to recognize the doctor. There was eye movement, but no recognition. Blackburn recognized the symptoms and exchanged worried looks with Iris, who got up from her chair so the doctor could sit at his friend's side. He wiped the sweat from Arthur's brows with a soft white cloth and then poured lemonade through his parched lips. As the hours went by, he held Arthur in his arms, cradling his head as he coughed, spreading droplets of black vomit across his bedclothes.

At daybreak, Iris returned to the hospital with Mattie, leaving her to have her breakfast with Eleanor. She came into the upstairs ward to find Dr. Blackburn sitting in the same chair at Arthur's bedside. He had fallen asleep and had spent the night with Arthur. Iris went to talk to young Abigail, the night shift nurse.

"Has he been there all night?" asked Iris.

"Yes, ma'am. He hasn't moved since I came on," replied Abigail.

"Let's have a look at Arthur, shall we?"

They went over to the patient, and Blackburn suddenly woke up with a start.

"Sorry to wake you, sir," said Iris.

"I fell asleep, my dear. Arthur's gone. He passed away after midnight."

Iris moved closer and laid her hand gently on Arthur's forehead. It was cold to the touch. She turned to Blackburn.

"You've been here all night, sir," said Iris, looking worried. "You need to get some rest."

"This is my fault, Iris," said Blackburn with haunted eyes. "He was not immunized. I shouldn't have asked him to come."

"You couldn't have known what would happen, sir," replied Iris.

"Arthur was a fine man, a wonderful companion. He is a huge loss to all of us."

Blackburn stood up and said nothing more before stumbling away. Iris and Abigail stared after him in shock. It was a real setback to lose Arthur, who had been at the center of their team of medical staff.

Alex Faris recovered and was sent home by Dr. Blackburn, who estimated that his condition had improved sufficiently to pursue his convalescence in his own house. He was shocked to learn that his brother James had contracted the malady and lay in a hospital bed in the same ward he had just left. James died four days later. Alex blamed himself. He had tried to send his brother away, but James had refused to go, and now he had made the ultimate sacrifice. It was a tragic denouement for Alex Faris and his family.

The town's Relief Committee members were all down with the disease, including the treasurer Frenz and the printer Thomas. They both passed away, along with a cohort of local physicians. It was a veritable hecatomb: Dr. Henry Catlett, Dr. Carter Blanton, Dr. R.C. Prather Jr., Dr. W. D. Corbett, and a Missouri physician named Dr. Hugh Prather. The town doctors had treated every family in Hickman over the years, and now they were gone. Nor was there any escape for the medical staff, who had come to Hickman from surrounding towns to help out.

When Dr. Corbett passed away in October, the family organized a funeral cortege that wound its way through town to the cemetery. A stubborn bunch of citizens who had known the good doctor from childhood lined the road and waved at the cortege, but declined to join them for fear of infection. A Methodist reverend read from the bible as Luke Blackburn, Alex Faris, and John Alexander knelt on the freshly turned earth near the doctor's corpse and prayed silently for their old friend. There were no other witnesses present other than a few solemn black gravediggers. The ceremony was short and moving, but the reverend had more work to do and he discretely signaled to the gravediggers that it was time to close this one up and move on.

It was time to go. The doctors rose from their prayers and walked to their waiting buggy while the reverend moved to the next gravesite. The corpses stacked in the wagon couldn't stay exposed to the midday heat for long and needed to be buried as quickly as possible. There were over a hundred new graves in the cemetery, but none of them had headstones, since the gravediggers could not read or write and there was no one left who could craft them.

Seventy

"We weary for these warm bright days to end,
The summer lingers at what fearful cost!
O pitying God, In mercy to us send,
The white gift of thy frost!"
An anonymous poet from Tennessee

The frost didn't come to Hickman until late November. The hot weather persisted as September turned into October. It was a lovely sunny day when Iris visited Dr. Faris at his home. She went there ostensibly to check up on his health at the request of Dr. Blackburn, but she had another reason. She was worried about what to do about young Mattie, who had been staying with her during the week. They sat on the porch with a view of the wide expanse of the Mississippi River as the doctor's old servant brought out a tea tray. Dr. Faris had made a full recovery. He looked much better but was still mourning the loss of his brother James. He asked after the hospital staff, in particular Arthur Brady.

"I'm sorry to inform you, sir, that Arthur and nurse Charlotte have both passed away. Dr. Blackburn was with them to the end."

"I'm sorry to hear that, Miss Iris. I liked Charlotte and Arthur. They were good people."

"Yes, they were."

"So many gone, Miss Iris," said Faris with a wistful smile.

They drank their tea.

"I've been looking after Mattie Gomez, sir. She's an orphan now that her parents have died."

"Yes, I know about her."

"I have become quite attached to the child," said Iris as she took a deep breath. "I wonder whether I might adopt her."

"Her folks are from Missouri. I suppose you would need to contact her grandparents."

"What do you know about the Gomez family, sir?"

"I don't know the family well. Mrs. Gomez taught at the school and I think her husband worked as a carpenter."

"I would like to take her home with me to Louisville when my work finishes here."

"I don't see how anyone in town could complain, Miss Iris. You have done so much for all of us."

As the number of people dying from the epidemic started to decline, some residents who had fled the town during the summer months heard the news and decided to risk returning home. Dr. Faris was not in a good mood when he was accosted by Alfred Walker, the owner of the City Hotel and the richest man in Hickman. Walker drove up to his house in a wagon and angrily called for Faris to step out so he could have a word.

"Faris, you son-of-a-bitch!" Walker bellowed. "You've destroyed my hotel."

"I've done no such thing," Faris said calmly, not even bothering to close the door. He was a war veteran and one of the very few people in town that Walker couldn't intimidate.

"That place belongs to me. You had no right."

"I'm sorry, Alfred. Don't they have newspapers wherever the hell you ran off to? We had to take it. It was a public health emergency. People were dying."

"You've filled it with a bunch of infected riffraff," Walker roared, "who ain't payin' nothin' to stay there, plus you've pulled down the damned walls."

"We had to confiscate the property on very short notice, Alfred. We didn't know where to find you."

"It was not yours to take, Alex."

"You better have a word with the Kentucky Board of Health in Louisville. They've been sending us people and supplies."

"I'm gonna sue your ass. You had no right."

Faris turned and entered his house. When he reappeared, he had a shotgun in the crook of his arm.

"Get the hell off my property, Walker. You heartless bastard."

"I'm going," said Walker, whose tone has softened with the threat of violence.

"Don't you understand nothin', Walker? I just buried my brother, James. I've lost colleagues—nine doctors and most of our Relief Committee. Not to mention old friends and entire families like the Hertwicks, the Samses, the Hendricks, the Sohms, and the Luttrells. Your friends, Alfred, and mine. You get the hell off my property and leave me in peace."

Walker froze for a moment, stunned by the outburst. He whipped his horse and took off.

The epidemic of yellow jack had brought death to a large swath of the population, and it continued to be utterly indiscriminate in its choice of victims. For weeks on end, the coroner, John Alexander, had driven to town in his buggy to visit patients, sometimes with Dr. Blackburn and sometimes on his own. He often stayed at Dr. Corbett's house to avoid the long drive back. The day after Corbett's funeral, Belle drove him into town to make house calls with Dr. Blackburn. It was believed that short visits during the daytime minimized the risk of catching the disease. The real danger was at night when the bad air attacked the innocent victims. On the day of his visit, the brave doctor came down with the fever, and three days later, so did his daughter Belle. The doctor died within the week while his daughter clung to life. She had postponed her plans for marriage so she could provide support for her father and the town. She died two weeks later.

Most of the medical staff who had come from Louisville to assist Dr. Blackburn came down with the malady and were treated at the hospital. They had come to Hickman to help fight the scourge, only to be struck down by the disease. Charlotte was the first to get sick, followed by two young doctors. Then in the last week of October, the third doctor was felled by the disease along with the telegraph operator. A week later, they had all passed away except for the one nurse and the druggist. It was a terrible shock for Dr. Blackburn, who felt responsible for the loss of the young doctors and nurses, even though he had warned the Louisville authorities that the volunteers needed to have immunity.

The epidemic finally abated in mid-November. Dr. Blackburn, Iris, and the surviving medical volunteers returned to Louisville on the first steamboat to stop at Hickman. They left Dr. Faris in charge of the remaining cases, but they would miss Eleanor, Billy, Nate, and all the other people who had helped them battle the pitiless scourge. The population of Hickman had been around fifteen hundred souls before the pandemic. Many people fled the area as the panic spread up the Mississippi River. 262 whites and an estimated 200 blacks became infected with yellow fever. Of that number, 131 whites and 18 blacks died.

Louisville, Kentucky

Iris looked forward to seeing Bennett and Eliza and returning to her life in Louisville. She was exhausted from the long days and nights in Hickman, but the worst of it was the emotional turmoil caused by the loss of so many friends. They arrived late at night by steamboat at the boat terminal in Jeffersonville. Iris, accompanied by young Mattie, shared a buggy with Dr. Blackburn and two members of his medical staff. Mattie fell asleep in Iris' lap as they crossed the bridge into Louisville. They were deposited on the Young family's doorstep in the early morning hours and waved goodbye to Dr. Blackburn and the others. Iris had to knock several times before a manservant came to the door. Iris and Mattie stepped inside to see Eliza rushing down the stairs in her bedclothes to greet them.

"It's Iris, Bennett, it's Iris!" cried Eliza, stopping in her tracks as she looked down at the little girl.

"And who is this?"

"This is Mattie, Eliza. You had your baby?" asked Iris.

"Yes, my dear. She's a lovely girl. I am calling her Eliza like me, or maybe it'll be Liz for short. I can't wait to show her to you. You're so thin, Iris. You look so tired."

"I am tired. It's the middle of the night, Eliza," Iris said with a laugh. "Where's Papa?"

"He's coming, my dear," said Eliza.

Bennett came down in his dressing gown and embraced Iris in the hallway.

"Iris, my dear, you have answered our prayers. We are so happy to have you home. Who is this?"

"This is Mattie, Papa. She'll be staying with us for a while."

"Of course, my dear. She can stay as long as she likes, can't she, Eliza?"

Eliza nodded and glanced at Mattie again.

"We're so happy to have both of you here with us."

"Well, we're happy to be here, aren't we, Mattie?"

The child nodded and then ran into the parlor to pet the cat.

Seventy-one

The rumors of Dr. Blackburn's Civil War crimes were soon forgotten. He was hailed as a hero for his actions during the epidemic in Hickman. Receptions were held in Louisville in his honor, and the newspapers called him the 'Hero of Hickman'. The press couldn't get enough of his story. They revealed that the good doctor made thirty or more house calls daily during the epidemic. He treated the sick and built fires, fixed coffee, prepared food, and even bathed his patients' feet. He had fought to save lives and to prevent the spread of infection and had never once admitted to fatigue. He was a saint in the making and, after the epidemic's ravages, the Kentucky citizens desperately needed one.

His reputation as a humanitarian soared across the country and overseas. He was awarded a special commendation from Queen Victoria and a prize of one hundred British pounds for his actions in Bermuda. There was so much admiration and gratitude for the man that he was nominated by acclamation for the governor's office after the epidemic. Blackburn went on to win the 1879 election for governor against the Republican rival Walter Evans and served one term in office. He balanced the budget by cutting government salaries, increasing taxes, and reforming the prisons. He was a man of few words and lacked the eloquence of previous state governors, but he got things done. His popularity waned after the party leaders complained about the number of pardons under his administration and resented that he did not favor party hacks when appointing individuals to state jobs.

It was well past midnight when Bennett got up to pee. The house was quiet, and the children were sleeping soundly in their bedrooms. Bennett was getting older, and he often had difficulty sleeping through the night. Some of it was due to the stress of running a railroad company like the Louisville Southern. He was used to that, but in recent weeks, it was his concern for Iris that kept him up. She had fought a battle with the yellow fever epidemic in faraway Hickman. He crept downstairs and poured himself a glass of milk in the kitchen before he sat down in the parlor and looked out at the backyard in the moonlight. When he couldn't sleep, he would often sit there reading for an hour or two or simply watching the sun come up.

As he sat down, he saw someone huddled under a blanket sitting on the gazebo near the fruit trees at the bottom of the garden. He stood up and approached the window to get a better look. It must be Iris or one of the girls. He stepped out the garden door in his dressing gown and slippers and walked down toward her. As he got closer, Iris sat up suddenly in her bedclothes and blanket.

"Papa!"

"Mind if I join you, my dear," said Bennett, as he climbed the stairs and sat down.

"I didn't wake you, did I?"

"No, I often get up in the night. It comes with age, Iris."

"I can't get Hickman out of my head, Papa. I came home, but sometimes I feel like I'm still there."

Bennett drank his milk and shivered in the night air. Already, there was a heavy coating of dew forming on the garden furniture. They sat in silence for a time, with only the sound of crickets and the song of mockingbirds and whip-poor-wills in the trees.

"I saw Luke the other night," Bennett said finally. "He was in town making a speech and I had a drink with him afterward. He told me how it was, Iris. He has seen a lot of things, but he says nothing compares to Hickman. That tiny hospital with sick children, mothers, and fathers all fighting for their lives, bleeding from their eyes and mouths with black vomit everywhere. He said it was a vision of horror and about the worst thing a person can experience."

"Papa, it was terrible, but the worst of it was the loss of so many friends. Lily, Arthur, Belle, and all the wonderful doctors who died. They gave everything and still they died."

"We don't choose our moment of passing, Iris. It can come at any time. I had my war, and now you've had yours. My job was to kill people, and your job was to save them."

"But I didn't!" Iris started to sob.

"You and Luke, and all the others, did everything you could when nobody else would go near the place. There are people alive today because of what you did. You know it, Luke knows it, and I know it."

"Why did they have to die? That's what I keep asking myself," said Iris, with tears in her eyes. "Mattie is a solace, Papa. Without her, I don't know what I would do. She keeps my mind off Hickman during the day, but at night it all comes right back to me."

"Of course it does," said Bennett. "It takes time to grieve, my dear. You will learn to live with it."

He stood up and put his arm around her, kissing the top of her head.

"Good night, sweetheart."

Iris watched him go.

Young Mattie Gomez succeeded in charming the Young household over that first winter, and at Iris' request, Bennett found himself searching for her grandparents in Missouri. He discovered that the grandparents had died ten years earlier from a typhus epidemic in St. Louis; nevertheless, he managed to track down a distant aunt in Chicago who could claim the child. Bennett wrote to her with the adoption request and she came in the spring.

Mrs. Walsh was a wealthy woman in her seventies. She arrived by train and stayed in one of the best Louisville hotels. She wore spectacles on a silver chain and had a harsh, unforgiving look on her face as she sat down in Bennett's office at the law firm. *She won't be a pushover,* thought Bennett, after he had welcomed her and escorted her into the room. He excused himself and moments later, Mattie was led into the room by the secretary, Pauline. She sat in a chair and looked up at the stern old woman watching her.

"This is Mattie Gomez, ma'am," said Pauline cheerfully. "She's four years old."

Mattie held up four fingers hoping to please the old woman, but Mrs Walsh's regard fixed on the child's dress, which could have been cleaner. Her hair was a mess, even though Iris and Eliza struggled daily to put a comb to it.

Pauline smiled indulgently at the woman and left them to it. For a long moment, Mrs. Walsh and the restless child silently examined each other.

"I'm sorry about your parents, Mattie," said Mrs. Walsh. "I heard you caught the malady and almost died."

Mattie said nothing. She stood up and walked around the room, ignoring the woman.

"Please sit down, Mattie," ordered the woman.

Mattie returned to her seat but remained silent. They sat observing one another before the door opened and Iris appeared. She was dressed in a grey cotton dress and blouse that belonged to Eliza. Mattie ran to her.

"Hello, ma'am. I'm Iris Gagnon. I'm a nurse at the Louisville Hospital."

She stepped forward to shake hands with Mrs. Walsh, but the woman declined. She remained seated and frowned in disapproval. Iris ignored her rudeness and withdrew her hand.

"Excuse me for a moment," Iris smiled and led Mattie out of the office, leaving her in the care of Pauline. She then returned, taking Mattie's chair.

"Did you know the parents?" asked Mrs. Walsh.

"I only met them briefly when they came down with yellow fever in Hickman," said Iris. "I was told that Mattie's mother was a teacher at the Hickman school and her husband was a carpenter."

"I met them once or twice," said Mrs. Walsh dismissively. "The husband was a worthless wagtail who couldn't get a real job in St. Louis, and the wife was no better."

"I didn't know them."

"We're Irish American, ma'am, and we don't ever mix with Mexicans. You know that her grandparents died from typhus about ten years ago. After that, the two of them left St. Louis and went to live in that jerkwater town on the Mississippi."

Iris said nothing but was shocked by the woman's words. She was a terrible snob.

"Where is your husband, ma'am?" asked Mrs. Walsh, making it sound more like an accusation than a question.

Iris hesitated a very long moment before she replied.

"I'm a widow, ma'am. My man caught the pox and died two years ago."

Iris blushed at her blatant lie. *I'm not going to let her take Mattie home with her,* she vowed, knowing that Bennett would disapprove. *There is no hope for the child if she is brought up by this pitiless old bag of a woman.*

"You ain't alone. We got lots of war widows and orphans in Chicago, too."

"Yes, ma'am."

"The child is a mess and no wonder with parents like hers. If I take her home with me," mused Mrs. Walsh, "I'm gonna have to put her in a boarding school where they'll beat some sense into her. They'll teach her how to dress properly and stay clean. Give her a life."

She lapsed into a thoughtful silence, undoubtedly weighing the pros and cons of taking such a step at her age. Iris remained silent and inwardly said a prayer. Finally, the older woman fixed her with an appraising look.

"So you think you can handle the kid?"

"Yes, ma'am," Iris said. Her heart was pounding in her chest. "I've become attached to the child ever since I got back from Hickman."

Mrs. Walsh gave her a dubious look as if Iris' emotional attachment was something alien to her.

"You be careful to bring her up right," Mrs. Walsh told her. "Naughty children need discipline, ma'am. She's gonna be in school soon and she needs to be brought up to be a lady. Spare the rod, spoil the child."

"Yes, ma'am."

Iris nodded and then stood up. She opened the door and Bennett entered.

"So Mrs. Walsh, are we agreed?"

"Yes, we are, sir."

"I'll bring the papers to your hotel tomorrow for your signature," said Bennett, leading Mrs. Walsh out of his office.

Iris had never seen her papa so angry. After meeting with Mrs Walsh, Iris had spent the rest of the day torn between her happiness at adopting Mattie and the guilt she felt at telling the lie that had made it all possible. It was not in her nature to keep it from Bennett, and she had managed to wait for a quiet moment that evening while Eliza was putting the child to bed.

"You did what?" he roared, staring at her in disbelief. Even he looked surprised by his anger, and he made a visible effort to lower his voice when he spoke again.

"You asked me to draw up the adoption papers, my dear. If you misrepresent the truth by lying about your name, date of birth, or anything else, then the papers are null and void. They will have no value in a court of law."

"I understand, Papa," said Iris, "but that woman would never agree for me, an unmarried woman, to adopt Mattie. You know it and I know it."

"By misrepresenting the basic facts of the adoption, the agreement has no force of law," said Bennett. "That's what I'm saying."

"But no one cares, Papa," pleaded Iris. "I'm doing it for Mattie, so she doesn't have to live with that old bag."

Eliza came downstairs when she heard Bennett's outburst. She was no more accustomed to Bennett raising his voice than Iris was, and she quickened her pace.

"I cannot sign off on this, Iris," Bennett said as Eliza came into the room. "I'm a lawyer. You lied, and if I sign a legal document based on that lie, I become a party to it and lose my license to practice law in this state."

"What's all this about?" Eliza asked quietly.

Iris and Bennett looked up. They had been so busy arguing that they hadn't noticed her.

"Iris made a… mistake."

"I lied," Iris corrected him. "That Walsh woman was horrible. I knew right away that if I said I was unmarried, she'd never let me adopt Mattie."

Bennett started to say something, but Eliza quieted him with a glance. She wanted to hear it from Iris.

"I see," Eliza said. "And this lie of yours? What was it you said?"

"I told her I was a widow and my husband had died from the pox. I told her I was Mrs. Iris Gagnon."

Bennett looked helplessly at his wife.

"I can't sign the document —."

"Of course, you can't," Eliza cut him off. "Just write her name in as plain Iris Gagnon, without the 'Mrs.' That will solve the problem."

It was so simple; they were surprised they hadn't thought of it themselves. Eliza always found a way to resolve an issue.

"That'll do the trick, Papa."

"It's for Mattie, Bennett," Eliza told him. "Just give Iris the adoption papers and wash your hands of it."

Bennett looked at the two women in his life and remembered why he rarely argued with them.

He almost always lost.

Iris went to the Galt Hotel the next day and met Mrs. Walsh in the lobby. They found a quiet corner and sat down in French baroque armchairs under the chandeliers to conduct their business.

"Are you enjoying your stay, Mrs. Walsh?" asked Iris, looking cheerful.

"No, I'm not," replied Walsh. "Yesterday, my room had not been cleaned properly, so I had to change floors. Can you believe that?"

"Yes, ma'am. They do have trouble with their staff. I'm sorry my lawyer couldn't make it today. Here are the adoption papers."

Iris tried to look unconcerned as Mrs. Walsh picked up the papers and looked them over. The first page traced Mattie's background with the name of her parents and their life in Hickman. The document explained that Mattie's birth certificate was lost after the death of her parents. It went on to describe the loss of Mattie's grandparents to typhus and how Mrs. Walsh was the only living relative of the child. There was no mention of Iris' marital status.

"It looks good to me, Mrs. Gagnon. Where do I sign?"

"On the last page, please."

Mrs. Walsh turned to the last page and signed her name at the bottom. She handed the document back to Iris, who looked down at her signature.

"Where do you come from, Mrs. Gagnon?"

"I'm French Canadian, ma'am."

"And your husband?"

"He was Canadian too, ma'am."

Iris picked up the pen and dipped it into the inkwell, signing her name as Iris Gagnon of Louisville, Kentucky.

True to form, Mrs. Walsh wasted no time with the usual civilities. She got up, said a chilly goodbye, and went looking for the hotel manager to lodge her complaints. For her part, Iris was only too happy to see the back of Mrs. Walsh, and she hurried out of the hotel.

Seventy-two

January 1897
Bowling Green, Kentucky

When the old lawman with his straggly beard and grimy Stetson arrived at the jailhouse with ex-slave George Dinning, he was worried about two things. A white mob might seize his prisoner out of the Warren County jail and lynch him from the nearest tree. Dinning was accused of killing a white man. The second was the prisoner's injuries. The bullet hole in Dinning's forehead was showing signs of swelling and the man was in serious pain. Sheriff Bud Clark needed to find a doctor fast to treat his wounds. After the deputy jailer had tried unsuccessfully to get a local doctor to come to the jail, Clark had hustled the prisoner over to the Wood County Infirmary in a buggy and was immediately admitted into the clinic.

Dr. W.R. Francis was in his sixties and didn't much like being in such close proximity to a man—especially a black man—who had been accused of murder. Francis nervously put on his thick spectacles and took a cursory look at the bullet wound on the man's head. He decided he had more interesting business elsewhere and ordered the nurse to look after the man.

Iris was the same vivacious woman from Lac-Brome with a wide smile and a boyish head of closely cropped grey hair. She was now in her forties and had a reputation for fearlessness when treating patients. Nothing put her off. Her mother, Agnes, had died six months earlier and Iris had returned to Quebec for her funeral. It had been a solemn affair and Iris had not got on well with Antoine, Agnes' husband, who had treated her with contempt. For the family, she was the unmarried daughter—a spinster and an outcast, who had abandoned them to live a fantasy life south of the border.

Iris was temporarily on loan to the infirmary and would return to the Louisville City Hospital the following week. She wore a blue long-sleeved dress, an apron, and a cap. She went to work, disinfecting the gash on the man's arm with a solution of water and carbolic soap. Then she had Dinning lie down flat on his back on a wooden gurney so she could disinfect the thumb-size bullet wound on his forehead.

"Somebody took a shot at you, Mr. Dinning?" asked Iris.

"Yes, more than one," said Dinning with a laugh.

"This is going to hurt a bit, I'm afraid."

Iris removed the filthy scab at the entrance to the hole with forceps so she could see the depth of the infection. She gingerly probed a little further.

"Ow," moaned Dinning.

She ignored him and went deeper, then removed the forceps and leaned in closer so she could see the path of the bullet. A small caliber ball had entered his forehead at a sharp angle and bounced off his skull, exiting three inches higher near the hairline.

"You're a very lucky man," said Iris. "The bullet bounced clean off your skull. That doesn't happen very often. You must have been shot from below?"

"Why, yes, ma'am. I was in a second-floor window and the shooter was below me."

"I'm going to clean the wound with a carbolic acid solution, sir. It will sting a bit, but will hasten the healing."

"Good, you know what's best," murmured Dinning, wincing from the pain.

Iris wrapped a towel tightly over Dinning's face and eyes before swabbing the area around the hole and along the exit wound. She then rinsed everything out with a distilled water solution. She applied a common salve over the wound to help it heal and prepared a bandage.

"You'll need to change the bandage every two days, or the infection may return," said Iris.

She wrapped the bandage in gauze and tied it several times around Dinning's head.

"Thank you, ma'am," Dinning said when she had finished.

Dinning stood up, and Iris walked him out to join Sheriff Clark and his deputy in the lobby.

"He has to change the bandage every two days or the infection may return," she said to the Sheriff, handing him some bandages and a roll of gauze. "He's going to need help to do that."

"I'll tell my deputies, ma'am," Clark gave her a wry look, passing the supplies to his deputy. He touched the brim of his Stetson and the men left. A young woman who worked at the reception desk came over.

"Iris, that man is a killer. That's George Dinning! He killed Jodie Conn, the richest farmer in Simpson County. You treated the wound of a killer."

"Well, he doesn't look like a killer to me. He just looks like any other wounded man."

Franklin, Kentucky

Three scruffy-looking horsemen had been waiting in the small town twenty miles south of Bowling Green for nearly an hour. They had a good vantage position across from the county jail, but so far, they hadn't seen any sign of Sheriff Clark and his prisoner. The group leader was Sylvester 'Sly' Waterman in his fifties, who looked like a cracker from the backwoods with his narrow foxy face and mean eyes. Sly had been a hunter all his life, growing up in Black Jack, Tennessee, and when the war came, he switched from tracking and killing animals to tracking and killing men. His specialty during the war had been tracking lost or wounded Union soldiers after a battle and then savagely killing them with the Bowie knife that he hid in his boot. He enjoyed killing, and if the men begged for mercy or tried to surrender, he killed them anyway. The war ended, but the killing didn't. People knew who he was and what he could do, and after he'd been demobilized and gone home, some veterans asked him if he couldn't help them with a family inheritance problem. That was how Sly Waterman began his new career as a hired assassin.

During the reconstruction period, a flood of 'carpetbaggers' from the Northern states had invaded the South, looking for economic opportunities and promoting get-rich schemes. There were crooked lawyers, businessmen, and veterans of the Union Army interested in buying up depressed properties at fire-sale prices. The most common of which was the sale of a farm or an estate after the owner had perished in the war. A recalcitrant relative—a brother, an aunt, an uncle—with property rights was all it took to hold up the sale of an asset, and Sly didn't mind who he was ordered to kill or disappear to facilitate the sale. Sly and his brother Ernest had worked murder into an art form across the states of Kentucky and Tennessee. They would snatch up the uncooperative relative in their wagon and cart him or her away, making the person disappear permanently. Families found it easy to hide the disappearance with the rumor that the person had signed the papers and then taken off for New Orleans or San Francisco.

Sly was in Black Jack when he heard his cousin was having trouble with an ex-slave in Simpson County. Everyone knew William S. 'Doc' Moore had been a soldier in the Confederate army and had worked as a policeman for the county. Somehow, he'd gotten himself mixed up with a bunch of night riders who had tried to chase an ex-slave off his property but had failed. The slave had fought them off, killing one of Moore's friends, and now he was in the custody of the wily old sheriff. There was going to be a trial and Moore would have to testify. He turned to his cousin Sly to make the problem go away and to keep his name out of the newspapers. Under normal circumstances, it was child's play for a man like Sly to disappear a black man in Kentucky. The problem here was that the old sheriff was guarding the man and he would need to be eliminated before they could seize him.

Sly called on his brother, Ernest, a bearded fireplug of a man who was worthless with a six-gun but knew a lot about blowing things up. Ernest had a young friend named Cyrus who was keen to show his mettle. The men were loaned several expensive firearms by the rich landowners who were friends with Moore and the Conn family. Sly got a new Browning 1897 pump-action shotgun, a Winchester 1895 rifle with lever action, and Smith & Wesson 45-caliber six-guns for his crew. Meanwhile, Ernest managed to steal enough dynamite to force the prisoner from any hole he might be hiding in. Disappearing George Dinning would go a long way to bringing peace to the county.

Sly looked around the town square and suddenly realized he'd been had. Sheriff Clark had flown the coop with the prisoner and was probably on his way north to Bowling Green. By now, he would have expected the usual mob to be gathered outside the jailhouse and yelling for blood. Instead, there were only a few people around and most of them were drunks. That damn sheriff was smarter than he'd given him credit for.

"That sonofabitch ain't here," he said to his men. "He was gone before we even got here. The only place they would take him that makes sense is Bowling Green."

"What do we do now?" Cyrus asked.

"We ride," Sly growled.

Bowling Green, Kentucky

They made it, but only just. There was an expectant crowd of people around the jailhouse. Sly got Ernest to go as close to the front door of the jailhouse as he could get. He had a shotgun hidden in a scabbard behind his saddle, and Sly figured even Ernest couldn't miss at that range. Sly and Cyrus stayed on their horses but hung back behind the crowd.

Just as they were getting into position, there was a commotion behind them, and the crowd scattered as Sheriff Clark and his deputy careened into the square in a buggy with the prisoner. It raced pell-mell toward the jail, coming from the opposite direction that Sly had expected. He saw Ernest fumbling to get his shotgun out as the buggy slowed a bit as it went through the crowd, ignoring the front door entirely and going along the side of the building before pulling to a stop in a cloud of dust. If there was an entrance back there, it had been well hidden, and in another few seconds, it didn't matter anyway. By the time the dust cleared, the buggy was empty.

Sly swore to himself as the crowd mindlessly surged toward the back of the jail. Ernest had gotten back on his horse and was coming toward him.

"They came in too fast, Sly," Ernest said sheepishly, shaking his head. "That sheriff is a crafty old bastard."

"We'll be back tonight," said Sly to his brother.

The jailer was a straight shooter by the name of Hagerman. He was clean-shaven with a scar across the cheek. He informed Sheriff Clark that he had received several urgent telegrams from Governor Bradley's office with concern for the safety of the prisoner. As Clark and Hagerman looked out the jailhouse window, they could see more people joining the crowd in the square and demanding a lynching of the prisoner. Hagerman had agreed to Bradley's plan to transfer the prisoner to Louisville, where he would be safer, but couldn't do it until the following day.

Racist lynchings were common in the deep South, and although Kentucky was not the worst state for lynchings, they were frequent enough to put fear into the souls of lawmen. Their political masters took a dim view of lawmen who couldn't defend their jails from angry mobs. While Dinning was being held in the jailhouse in Bowling Green, a mob had attacked the jail in Aberdeen, Mississippi, some 300 miles away, and abducted Perry Gilliam, a black man accused of robbing a white woman. He was hanged from a tree in open country only five miles from the jail.

All evening, the mob in the square continued to grow. Hagerman distributed firearms to his deputies and his most trustworthy prisoners in case the vigilantes broke through the front door. Then they waited with bated breath for the first shots to be fired.

It was pitch black, a good two hours before sunup, and the mob had given up for the night. Ernest tied his horse in the alley and sneaked up on the jail. The plan was simple enough: create a diversion that would force Sheriff Clark to try to hustle the prisoner out of the jail for his own safety. Sly had set up in an unoccupied house catty-corner to the front entrance to the jail, reasoning that the explosion at the back would cause Clark and his prisoner to make a run for it out the front. With the Winchester, he was confident that he could kill both Sheriff Clark and the prisoner within seconds of exiting the building. He didn't know how many guards or deputies were in the jail, so he'd given Cyrus the Browning shotgun and posted him in a parked buggy near the front door. It all depended on the effect of Ernest's diversion behind the building.

Sheriff Clark and Hagerman were fast asleep in the office when a huge explosion shook the building and all hell broke loose. Six deputies ran out the side door of the building and into the alley to see what was happening, but Ernest was already on his horse and galloping away. He opened fire with a six-gun firing over his shoulder as he turned a corner at the end of the alley. When the dust settled, the deputies examined the damage. The dynamite had blown a hole in the side of the building next door to the jail but had not damaged the jail one bit. Ernest was still learning his trade and, in the dark, he had mistaken one building for the other. Since no one else emerged from the jail, Sly and Cyrus abandoned their plans and retreated through the empty streets to collect their horses. It had all been for naught.

The next day Sheriff Clark rode out of Bowling Green, leaving the prisoner in the able hands of Sheriff Rodes of Warren County and his deputies. The instructions from Bradley were clear. Dinning was to be accompanied to the train station to catch the one o'clock train for Louisville.

Seventy-three

DINNING ESCAPES THE MOB.
KENTUCKY'S GOVERNOR PROTECTS A NEGRO.
New York Times, January, 1897

Coffee Bottom, Kentucky

It had all started after a complaint about a robbery and arson at a white man's smokehouse in Simpson County along the Tennessee border. A posse of white citizens had come together to chase the thieves and arsonists off their land. They went house to house, ordering all the black farmers in the area to leave the county. They arrived in the middle of the night at the house of George Dinning, an ex-slave who owned a 125-acre farm along the Red River.

George was a forty-year-old black man who had toiled long and hard to make ends meet. He'd never been to school and couldn't read or write, but he'd worked hard and bought the land years ago for an amount of $350. He'd built a house, added a barn and a smokehouse, and acquired numerous farm animals. He had paid off the house by growing tobacco on the fertile land near the river and got on well with his white neighbors. The house was set back a hundred yards from the road and fronted by a white picket fence.

The vigilantes ordered Dinning to leave his house, but he refused. They claimed he was a thief and arsonist. They ordered him to leave the county. They threatened to tear down his house and hang him if he didn't open the door. Dinning and his wife Mollie had several young children in the house: a four-month-old baby and six young children of different ages. They fired their guns through the front door and Dinning fired back with his shotgun from the second-floor window after he was struck in the head by a bullet.

George lost consciousness. He wasn't sure where he was when he came to. He could feel someone's hands moving a cloth across his face. Then he heard his wife's soothing voice, and it sounded like she was crying.

"They're gone, George," she told him.

"What?"

"They ran off."

He slowly opened his eyes as she pulled away the bloodstained cloth and motioned to one of their daughters for another one. The kids were arrayed behind her in a semicircle, all staring at him wide-eyed and whimpering.

"Where's Hermann?" he asked, suddenly afraid.

Hermann was their oldest son and George feared the night riders might have taken him.

"He's all right, George," Mollie said softly. "He's at your ma's tonight, remember?"

He gave a sigh of relief. Fragments of what had happened were coming back to him now, and after Mollie helped him to his feet, he went to the window to look out at the empty yard. *They're gone,* he told himself, *but they'll be back.*

George got dressed and went looking for help. He found a white neighbor, Zack Murray, at home.

"I heard the gunfire," said Zack. "Your family all right?"

"Yeah. They're fine."

"Good. The only reason that mob left your place was because of the dead man."

"Who was it?"

"The dead man was Jodie Conn."

Jodie Conn, George thought bitterly. *Conn was the son of the richest and most powerful landowner in the county.*

A familiar voice was heard outside the house. Murray opened the door to Bob Lucas, a black friend of George who lived nearby.

"They're comin' for you, George," said Bob, looking scared. "You shot Jodie Conn."

All George could remember was firing wildly into the crowd with his shotgun before he lost consciousness.

"You need to get the hell out here," said Zack.

George nodded. He realized that if the mob came back and saw them together, they'd probably kill all three of them, Zack and Bob included. He got up to leave.

Self-defense or not, George felt bad about killing Conn, who he knew personally, having worked for him from time to time. He knew his father enough to know that he wouldn't stop until he got his revenge. A mob would be out looking for him and, if they caught him, they'd hang him from the nearest tree. George decided to throw himself at the mercy of the law and hoped that would prevent the mob from going after Mollie and the children. He stayed off the main road and walked the nine miles to the Franklin County Jail.

Sheriff Clark had heard about the shooting and feared that a mob out for vengeance would soon try to attack the jail. He quickly loaded George and his deputy into a buggy and set off for Bowling Green in Warren County. As George was being spirited away, Hermann returned home from his grandmother's house and was seized by the mob looking for his father. They held the boy for several hours, thinking of using him as a bargaining chip when George returned. When George didn't come back, the men ordered Mollie to round up her eight children and leave the county. If she didn't, they threatened to hang her.

Mollie had no choice. The men had been drinking all afternoon and were angry. She knew they could change their minds at any time, so she put Hermann on a horse with young Eva behind him and then hooked several feather mattresses over the horse's neck. She climbed on a second horse with the baby in her arms, a child in front, and four of the youngest behind her. They set off at a slow pace for the Tennessee line and were greeted by their neighbors, carrying food out to the road to help sustain them on their journey as they rode south for the Tennessee line.

After Mollie and the children had gone, the mob doused the Dinning's house with kerosene and burned it to the ground, along with the barn and the smokehouse. George Dinning and his family would never return to their land. This was the harsh reality for a lot of freed slaves in the postbellum South after the Civil War.

Bowling Green, Kentucky

At the end of the day, Iris was called into Dr. Francis' office on the first floor of the Wood County Infirmary. The doctor was sitting behind a massive wooden desk and drinking whiskey as he read the newspaper. Iris waited for him to notice her presence.

"Ah, there you are, Miss Iris," he said, looking up. "We have to do a report."

"A report, sir?"

"Yes. The sheriff's department is asking for a medical report on the prisoner."

"What do you want to know, sir?"

"Tell me about the wounds."

"He had a gash and some lacerations on his arms. I cleaned them up."

"Go on," said the doctor, putting on his spectacles and writing notes in his journal.

"There was the head wound, sir. The gunshot wound."

"Ah, yes. How did that go?"

"It went fine, sir. I disinfected it."

"Anything else, Iris?"

"Well, sir, there was the angle of penetration."

"The angle of penetration?"

"Yes, sir. He was shot from below. That's why the bullet bounced off his skull."

"I don't remember hearing about that."

"Well, I asked him and he said he was shot when he looked down from a second-floor window."

"Very good, Miss Iris. Anything else?"

"That's it, sir."

"We are going to miss you when you return to Louisville."

"I've always enjoyed working here, sir."

"Well, thank you," said the doctor as he finished writing his notes. "That's all then."

Frankfort, Kentucky

With vigilantes, also known as 'whitecappers' or 'night riders' operating freely across the South, Governor William O. Bradley was concerned for the safety of Dinning and feared that another lynching in the state would be a disgrace on his record. In the last year, nine black men and one woman had been lynched in towns and cities across the state of Kentucky. It was becoming a public scandal. Even if Bradley was critical of law enforcement for not sufficiently protecting black prisoners, he felt powerless to stop the lynchings.

He sat in his lavish office in the State capital and read the letter from George Dinning. The man was desperate and had asked a notary to write down his words for the Governor. He had signed it with an 'x'. His family was homeless, living with an aunt across the line in Black Jack, Tennessee.

"I haven't seen my wife or any of my children since the night I left home. I feel confident that my life is in great peril if I am sent back to Franklin for trial. I do not feel that I have violated any law of my country; I had nothing against Mr. Conn, and regret the unfortunate circumstances which led to his death. I only acted in what I believe to be in defense of my home and my family, and I do not feel that I should suffer for it, which I know that I must do unless Your Excellency interferes on my behalf. I respectfully petition your Excellency to pardon me and not require me to go back to Franklin for trial."

The governor put down the letter and reflected on the situation. He couldn't afford another lynching in his state. That same week he had been surprised to learn that a Republican senator had introduced an anti-lynching bill at the State legislature: "An Act to prevent lynching and injury to and destruction of real and personal property in this Commonwealth." He couldn't have written a more appropriate bill himself.

The bill defined what constituted an 'unlawful mob' and fixed the penalties for whitecappers who kidnapped suspects from law enforcement and harmed or killed them. A section of the Act allowed sheriffs the right to recruit able-bodied men in the community to help protect prisoners. It even authorized a sheriff to arm other inmates to help defend a jail if it came under assault. It fixed penalties for law enforcement officers if they failed to protect prisoners and it made it possible for anyone who was injured by a mob to sue them for damages.

The governor knew that the legislation was a long shot and unlikely to pass both the Senate and the House. He would do what he could to protect Dinning and hope for the best. The legislation, to the surprise of everyone, passed both houses of government and became law in May 1897.

Seventy-four

Louisville, Kentucky

"Your honor, the shareholders of the Louisville Southern Railroad (LS) want to break up our company and harm our service to passengers on the Louisville and Nashville Railroad (L&N) line," said the sharply dressed lawyer.

"Objection," shouted Doyle. "That's a lie, your honor. There is no proof whatsoever of this man's contention."

"Overruled," said the judge.

Bennett Young sat in an oppressively hot courtroom in Louisville as his old friend and partner, Jake Doyle, argued the case. The LS was suing its rival, the L&N, over the right of way for a new rail link.

Bennett was in his fifties and wore his familiar mustache, which had gone white along with his hair. Doyle was entirely bald and wore a mustache and bushy side whiskers. They sat in court listening to the arguments of the opposing camp.

"The LS has a reputation of buying up impoverished railway companies and now they are coming after us," said the lawyer. "The rail link we are proposing has been accepted by all the parties to this judgment."

The judge sighed and rapped his gavel.

"Time for lunch, gentlemen. We'll see you back here at one o'clock."

Bennett stood up and left the courthouse with Jake. They met Eliza on the front steps and went for lunch at a nearby restaurant. During lunch, Jacob showed Bennett a copy of the Louisville Times with the headline, *HIS LIFE IS IN DANGER*, and below it, there was a likeness of George Dinning.

"Dinning doesn't stand a chance in Franklin," said Jake. "The entire town and county are against him and the trial starts in only ten days."

"I heard that Governor Bradley is sending the militia in to protect him," replied Bennett.

"The people of Franklin won't be happy seeing all those bluecoats in town," said Eliza.

"Dinning is to be escorted to Franklin by Colonel Gaither himself with some 300 troops," said Bennett.

"Gaither," said Eliza. "I've heard that name before."

"He was a Confederate soldier during the war, Eliza," said Bennett. "There's a story about him at the Battle of Brentwood in 1863. General Nathan Forrest was attacking a small Union force defending a supply depot on the Nashville and Decatur Railroad line. Gaither was just a private at the time and was ordered to fetch water for the men. Alone in the woods, he ran into six Yankee soldiers coming his way. Since he had no chance against such a force, he yelled 'surrender' to the Union soldiers, who immediately threw down their guns and raised their hands. Gaither couldn't believe it, but he kept a straight face and marched the men back to camp at gunpoint. Everybody in his company came out and cheered him."

"He was a very lucky man. He could have been shot," said Jake.

"He's a smart man. He won't leave anything to chance," added Bennett.

Franklin, Kentucky

It was the first of July and a very hot day. The Dinning trial was underway in the old courthouse. Bennett was returning to Louisville from Nashville by train when he stopped off for a couple of hours to observe the trial. As he walked over to the courthouse, he noticed two crude effigies of Governor Bradley and Lieutenant Governor William J. Worthington hanging from a tree. *Eliza was right*, he thought. *The citizens of Franklin did not appreciate the presence of bluecoats in their town.*

Bennett managed to find a seat at the back of the courtroom. He knew both attorneys involved in the case. The prosecutor for the Commonwealth was an astute criminal lawyer by the name of G.T. Finn, while the defense attorney was the very capable John Grider. Finn was just wrapping up the prosecution's case against Dinning, and Grider would soon call his first witness for the defense.

Security was tight in the courtroom, with six soldiers standing between the lawyer's tables and the public. Colonel Gaither had insisted that there be no firearms in the courtroom and everyone had been searched at the door. At the defense table, Dinning looked uneasy in his short-in-the-sleeves frock coat and vest which had been donated by Reverend Frank of the Fifth Street Baptist Church in Louisville. He had never appeared in a courtroom before and was nervous, hunched over and clutching his hat.

At the prosecution table, Finn was busy conferring with one of the white vigilante family members. There had been some twenty-five men involved in the attack on Dinning's house, and all of them sat behind the prosecution table to witness justice in the making. The day before, Finn had brought several upstanding citizens to the bar to testify to the 'peaceful' methods employed by the whitecappers. Their testimony tried to convince the jury that they had approached Dinning in a friendly manner, concerned only by the number of thefts happening in the county.

Finn called Doc Moore to the box.

"Do you know George Dinning?" asked Finn, after the witness had been sworn in.

"Yes, sir," replied Moore.

"Tell us what occurred at his house."

"We got down at the gate and walked to the house, knocking on the door."

"I called to him and he asked who it was. I said: 'George, some of your neighbors and friends want to talk to you. Get up and come to the door.'"

"He said he wouldn't come out, so I told him to stay where he was and listen to what we had to say. I told him about the stealing, the houses set on fire, and how his neighbors wanted him to leave the county within ten days. He said he hadn't done no stealing."

"And then I heard the boys shout 'Look out!' A shot was fired from the house. My back was turned, and I didn't see the boys return fire. Then we saw that Jodie Conn had been hit."

"What became of him?"

"We were supposed to carry him to Mr. Williams' house."

"Did he die there?"

"No, sir. He died as soon as we took him off his horse."

After the break, the first man to be called by the defense was a whitecapper by the name of J.M. Phelps, who lived half a mile from Dinning's house and had brought to the party a double-barreled shotgun loaded with squirrel shot.

"How far were you from Doc Moore when he was doing the talking?" asked Grider.

"Some eight or ten feet," said Phelps.

"Did you see his face?"

"Yes, sir."

"Was his face disguised in any way?"

"He had a rag over his face."

"Did he make any effort to disguise his voice?"

"Yes, sir."

"You would have hardly recognized his voice yourself?"

"No, sir."

"He told Dinning to come out?"

"Told him to come to the door."

"Did he say who you were?"

"No, sir. He told him we were his friends."

"Did you tell him he must get away?"

"Yes, sir. Within ten days."

"Did you tell him how far away he had to go?"

"Fifty miles."

After Phelps stepped down, the next man to be called was a black farmhand and laborer named Benn Conn, an ex-slave like Dinning. He had originally belonged to Jodie Conn's grandfather and taken his name.

"How old are you?" asked Grider.

"Around 65," replied Conn, who, like many ex-slaves, had no way of knowing his exact age.

"Where do you live and how far is it from Dinning's place?"

"A quarter mile to half a mile."

"Did you hear the shooting?"

"Yes, sir. They came to my house."

"Who did they ask for?"

"Alexander Conn and Bob Lucas."

"What were they doing?"

"They were in the road on their horses, and two or three of them came up to my door. One man put a pistol in my face while the other man had a gun and a white handkerchief over his face."

"One of them had a pistol?"

"Yes, sir."

"Pointed at your head?"

"Yes, sir."

"What time was this?"

"Between nine and ten o'clock."

"Did you hear the firing down at the Dinnings?"

"Yes, sir."

"How long after these men left your house?"

"Between five and ten minutes."

"How did that firing seem to you?"

"They fired three shots," said Conn. "They sounded like pistol shots."

"What happened next?"

"A shotgun."

"Then what?"

"I heard a volley of shots."

"All turned loose?"

"Yes, sir."

The next witness for the defense was Gib Hackney, a white farmer who lived half a mile away from the Dinnings.

"You heard the firing that night?" asked Grider.

"Yes, sir."

"What kind of firearms was it that you first heard?"

"I took it to be pistols. I heard three or four shots."

"Then what?"

"Then I heard a much louder report, like a shotgun."

"Then what?"

"Then a good many guns went off," said Hackney.

The audience was listening closely to the gunshot details and Bennett felt that Grider was doing an excellent job with his witnesses.

After Gib Hackney had testified, his son Claud took the stand. He was asked about his visit to the Dinning house the morning after the shooting. The men had entered the house to have a look at the damage to the door and the bedroom. Mollie had lit a lamp to light their way because the shutters were closed and it was dark inside.

"How many bullets had hit the door?" asked Grider.

"Four bullets had hit the door. Three passed through it."

"What did you see when you went upstairs?"

"When I got to the bedroom, there was a trail of blood on the floor and droplets near the bed."

Grider looked satisfied by Claud's replies and sat down as Finn stood up to cross-examine the man.

Seventy-five

The judge called a lunch break and Bennett came forward to say hello to John Grider, who was collecting his files at the defense table.

"Bennett," he smiled, extending his hand. "Nice to see you."

"I see you are doing a great job," Bennett said as they shook hands.

"I wish that were the case. It's not going to be easy with this jury," said John, turning to Dinning. "George, this is Bennett Young. He's a lawyer who works out of Louisville."

Dinning nodded at Bennett.

"A pleasure to meet you, Mr. Dinning," said Bennett, shaking his hand.

"George is testifying this afternoon, Bennett. I hope you can stay for the testimony."

"I'm returning later today, but I'll stay awhile to see how it goes."

After the jury returned to the courtroom, Dinning was sworn in. Grider stood up and approached the witness. The security was tight, with two soldiers flanking Dinning on the stand and six standing between the lawyer's tables and the public.

"How old are you, sir?" asked Grider.

"I was forty-two years old last Monday," said Dinning.

"Where did you live when the action occurred?"

"Near the State line between Tennessee and Kentucky in Simpson County."

"How long have you lived there?"

"Fourteen years last Christmas."

"Is the land yours?"

"Yes, sir."

"You lived there for fourteen years?"

"Yes, sir. The home is in my name."

"Mr. Dinning, when did this difficulty occur in which Mr. Conn was hurt?"

"In January."

"1897?"

"Yes, sir."

"Do you remember what day of the week it was on, Mr. Dinning?"

"On a Thursday."

"What time did you and your family go to bed that night?"

"Directly after sundown, about dusk."

"Tell me in your own words everything that happened that night."

"The first thing I remember," said Dinning, "was my wife waking me up. Somebody was knocking on the door."

"The voice said: 'George, get up and come out!'"

"I said: 'Who is it?'"

"The voice said: 'We're your friends.'"

"I replied: 'You ain't much friends if you won't tell me who you are.'"

"The voice said: 'Come out! I want to see you.'"

"I said: 'I ain't got no business out there.'"

"The voice asked me whether Bob Lucas was there."

"I said: 'No, he ain't here.'"

"The voice went on: 'I will give you ten days to get away from here and don't you stop within forty miles, and you tell Bob Lucas to do the same thing.'"

By then Bennett had heard enough and left the courtroom to catch the train for Bowling Green. As Bennett emerged from the courthouse, he noticed three men sitting under a shade tree in the square. The oldest was a rough-looking specimen, sitting on a bench chewing tobacco. He appeared to be watching the federal troops on the courthouse steps, while his overweight friend was sprawled on the grass having a nap. The youngest of the three was watching the pretty women coming and going, flirting with the soldiers. Bennett was sure these men were up to no good. *They're waiting for something to happen,* he thought. He stopped for a moment and stole a look back at the men. His best guess would be some kind of nefarious activity such as robbing a bank, but, of course, no one would be stupid enough to try such a thing with all the bluecoats in town for the trial.

Bowling Green, Kentucky

Bennett took the train and arrived an hour later at Iris' guest house on a leafy street in the city. It was an old Southern mansion with a wrap-around porch, a bit rundown, on a large plot of land with a garden full of flowers and fruit trees. Bennett spotted Iris on the shaded porch having tea with a group of women. Bennett tied his horse to the railing and waved to Iris before he climbed the stairs. Iris stood up in her white blouse and cotton salopettes to embrace him.

"This is my Papa, Bennett Young," Iris said proudly to her female companions, most of whom were spinsters like her. "He's a lawyer in Louisville but isn't stuck up like most of them. He even talks to the little people from time to time."

The women laughed at this.

"Please, Iris. I talk to everyone, including the ladies," said Bennett with a big smile.

"Watch out, ladies, the man is married," joked Iris and everybody laughed again.

In Southern towns, the war had decimated the number of marriageable men, and the assumption that every woman would find a man to marry and have children was no longer tenable in many parts of the country. Iris' friends worked at the Wood County Infirmary and were open-minded when it came to Iris. The other women from town disapproved of her dungarees—a French fashion that Iris liked to wear after work at the clinic—but were amused and even shocked by her behavior. In their minds, she was an odd duck indeed. They wore their fashionable skirts, bodices, and bonnets in the hope of attracting gentlemen of means, while Iris made no effort whatsoever to dress well and be respectable in the eyes of the community.

"Hot day," said Bennett as he removed his hat and wiped his brow with a handkerchief. "I just came from Franklin."

"So you saw our famous patient?" asked one nurse.

"You mean George Dinning?"

"Dinning came to us for treatment several months ago," said Iris to the women. "Dr. Francis had me clean a nasty head wound. Dinning was lucky to be alive."

"Franklin was full of federal troops and the courthouse was packed," observed Bennett.

"So what do you think are his chances of getting off?" asked Iris.

"He's a killer, he should be hanged," insisted one woman.

"Well, a lot of people share your view," replied Bennett. "I thought the defense lawyer did a good job. The facts are all there. He was attacked by a horde of whitecappers and lived to tell the tale."

"How are Eliza and Mattie?" asked Iris, as the conversation turned to clothes and the latest fashions.

"They're fine," said Bennett. "They're looking forward to your return and Mattie is starting a new job as a bookkeeper next week."

"I don't know what she finds so interesting about keeping someone's expenses in order, Papa."

"She loves math and numbers, my dear. I'm sure she'll do very well."

"I would have liked to see her in nursing," said Iris, "but the poor dear can't stand to see blood."

"How was your week?" asked Bennett.

"We were very busy, Papa. We had accidents, falls, gunshot wounds, and even a man trampled by a horse."

"You really are on the front line, my dear. All these people requiring medical assistance."

Bennett worried about Iris. She was attractive in a tomboyish way, eccentric, and very independent, but she had never shown any interest in men. Men liked her because of her natural charm and winning smile, but not one fellow had pursued her with the intention of marriage. This bothered Eliza more than it bothered him. Bennett was just proud of his unofficially adopted daughter and her successful career as a nurse.

Seventy-six

Louisville, Kentucky

Iris arrived home looking extremely agitated and perspiring in the heat. She wore her white blouse, salopettes, and bonnet, which she pulled off and threw down on a chair.

"What is it, dear?" asked Eliza from the hall.

"It's terrible, Eliza," said Iris. "The jury came in with a guilty verdict. Dinning has been condemned to seven years in the penitentiary. He's going to jail, the poor man."

Bennett appeared from the dining room with a copy of the St. Louis Daily Globe.

"It's in all the papers. They found him guilty of manslaughter for defending his own home," said Bennett.

"I saw it as I was getting off the train, Papa."

"It's a very sad case," said Eliza.

Iris embraced Eliza and Bennett and hugged her daughter, Mattie, now in her twenties.

"Who is it?" asked Mattie, who had no interest at all in current events.

"George Dinning, my dear," said Iris. "I told you about him. People on the train were saying he got off too lightly. I think he should never have been tried."

"Come and have your supper, sweetheart," said Eliza, "and tell us about your week at the clinic."

Bennett poured the glasses of water and they sat down around the dinner table. Their daughter Liz, a slim eighteen-year-old girl with Eliza's looks, arrived from the garden and took her place at the dinner table next to Mattie. The cook brought in a platter of roast beef with potatoes, green beans, and tomatoes. Bennett did the honors and carved the beef.

"I saw Dinning testify myself," said Bennett, distributing the slices of meat with a fork. "I thought he spoke very well, stating all the pertinent facts of the case. I even thought for a moment that he had a good chance of getting off. The juries in those southern counties go hard on colored men."

"We can only hope for a pardon," said Iris, as she started to eat.

"There'll be great pressure on Governor Bradley," said Eliza.

"The whole country is pushing for a pardon," said Iris. "He was defending his home and family."

"Yes, but let's talk about something more agreeable, shall we?" said Eliza.

"Well, it was another busy week," said Iris. "Dr. Francis was on holiday and we nurses were in charge of the place. Luckily, we didn't have anything too serious to deal with. Just a few fractures, no gunshot wounds or anything."

"I'm starting my new job this week, Mother," said Mattie.

"Yes, I know," said Iris. "It's a wonderful moment for someone your age starting their first job."

"I'm sure they'll be happy to have you, Mattie," added Eliza.

"Where's Larry?" asked Iris suddenly.

Larry was Bennett and Eliza's three-year-old boy and Iris doted on him.

"He's just gone to bed, my dear."

"Well, I want to see him," said Iris, jumping up and dashing out of the room.

"Mother, we're eating," Mattie said, rolling her eyes at Iris's outrageous behavior.

Eliza and Bennett smiled at Liz and Mattie as they heard Larry's squeal of delight coming from the upstairs bedroom. Iris was a joy to have around the house, and Larry loved her. Their daughter Josephine had died two years ago from pneumonia, leaving them all overwhelmed by sadness and guilt. She had been eighteen years old. Now, they had a baby boy and two young women in the house, which filled them with joy.

The girls loved Iris. She was their hero of Hickman and could do no wrong. Liz adored and worshipped her. Mattie loved her mother, but couldn't always abide by her emotional outbursts and unconventional dress style.

Bennett was in a meeting with Jake Doyle when Pauline, his secretary, appeared in the doorway with a tray holding an ornate silver coffeepot and cups.

"You gentlemen won't believe the newspaper reports about the Dinning conviction," Pauline said as she put down the coffee tray.

"Yeah, I've seen some of it," said Jake, helping himself to a cup of coffee.

"It's front-page news," Pauline told them. "The Lexington Morning Herald, the Owensboro Inquirer, the Louisville Times, the Courier-Journal. Everyone is talking about it."

"There's a huge sense of outrage in the country," Jake said.

"I think the Governor will have to act soon," Bennett said. "On Sunday, even the reverend at my church was calling for justice for the negro. That doesn't happen very often in this town."

"Dinning was sent to the Eddyville Penitentiary. He'll be doing hard labor."

"I've heard a lot of bad things about that place. Remember back in '93? Twenty inmates escaped from there."

"You should write to Governor Bradley, Bennett. I'm sure he'll listen to you."

That same evening, Bennett sat down at the desk in his study and penned the following terse lines for a telegram to the Governor:

> DINNING VIOLATED NEITHER HUMAN NOR DIVINE LAW.
> YOU WILL HONOR KENTUCKY AND YOURSELF BY
> AN IMMEDIATE PARDON. OPEN THE PRISON DOORS
> BEFORE THE SUN GOES DOWN. BENNETT H. YOUNG.

Governor Bradley would be hard-pressed to ignore Bennett's advice. The whole nation was shocked by his conviction. Bennett was hugely influential among progressive minds in the state. He was a Confederate war hero. He had marched with Morgan's men, led a raid into Vermont, raised money for blind children, served as president for twenty years on the board of the Colored Orphans' Home Society, and defended poor black men pro bono in the courts. Some of them had been innocent, some of them had not. For Bennett, that had never been the point. Everyone deserved a defense.

Eddyville, Kentucky

On July 17, 1897, George Dinning stepped out of the Kentucky State Penitentiary, known as the 'Castle on the Cumberland'. He was a free man. An hour earlier, he had been sitting in his cell with no hope of gaining his freedom when Warden Henry Smith came by with the good news. Smith had just received a telegram from the Governor's office in Frankfort, informing him that Governor Bradley had pardoned him. The warden told Dinning to be very careful. There was still a mob out there gunning for him. Smith provided him with a new suit of clothes, a train ticket for Louisville, and five dollars for his expenses. Three soldiers escorted him to the train station and provided security until he got on the train. Smith informed him that the Governor was keeping the announcement under wraps until the following day to avoid a violent reaction by the whitecappers in Logan and Simpson counties. Dinning swore to his friends that he would never feel safe in Kentucky again. He worried that his enemies would take out their vengeance on his wife and children.

Governor Bradley published a letter denouncing the conviction:

"Too long have mobs disgraced the fair name of Kentucky, and while I am Governor of the Commonwealth, no man, however obscure and friendless, shall be punished for killing a member of a mob who comes to take his life or drive him from his home."

There was widespread praise in newspapers across the country for Bradley's pardon, but not in the southern counties of the state. The people there felt that they had been cheated and justice had been denied.

Louisville, Kentucky

A large crowd awaited George Dinning at the Fifth Street Baptist Church, where he had been invited to speak. Dressed in a new three-piece suit, he arrived in a hansom cab and was introduced to the crowd by his old friend, Reverend John Frank, the same activist preacher who had provided him with a suit of clothes for his trial. Frank insisted they were not there to criticize the authorities but to allow people to express their disapproval of mob law.

Dinning told the audience that some of the jurors admitted to his lawyer that they thought he was innocent, but said they could not acquit him for fear of retribution. He said he was looking for a new home in Indiana and was putting his land in Simpson County up for sale. He added that he was thinking of filing a lawsuit for damages against the mob for destroying his property and his life. At the end of the talk, Frank called for the collection of an offering for the Dinning family. The ushers passed baskets down every pew and when the total was tallied, they had collected $37.50, a large amount of money for the period.

After giving a series of talks across the town, Dinning made a down payment on a new home in Jeffersonville, Indiana, across the river from Louisville. The city had been the first and largest Underground Railroad route for slaves escaping the South. Free black men rowed runaway slaves across the river to their friends and abolitionists in Jeffersonville. It was not long before Mollie and the children came north to live with their father again, along with his mother, Mary.

Dinning felt right at home in his new house, reported the Louisville's *Courier-Journal*:

"Dinning is a lion among the colored people, both in this city and in Jeffersonville. They follow him around as if he were a superior being, and greedily devour his slightest utterances. In fact, Dinning is living in clover. He has more money than he ever had in his life and is decidedly a gentleman of leisure."

But not everyone shared that view. Down south in Logan County, the *Russellville Ledger* reported:

"George Dinning, the brutal murderer of poor Jodie Conn in Simpson County, has now relocated to Jeffersonville. He has moved his wife and family to that city and will try to get work on one of the farms in the suburbs of the city. It is not likely he will ever return to Kentucky again."

Seventy-seven

September, 1897
Franklin, Kentucky

The passengers gave Sly and Ernest a wide berth as they climbed on board the train to Louisville. It wasn't that they wore wide-brimmed Stetsons and were armed with six-guns—neither was unusual for the time—but Sly especially had an unmistakably menacing look about him, even when he was just getting on a train. They found seats and soon fell asleep as the train slowly made its way north.

Their orders were clear. They were on a mission to kill George Dinning, who had made a laughingstock of all the good citizens of Logan and Simpson Counties. Those same citizens had agreed it was time to stamp out the 'black devil' who was getting rich off the death of one of their favorite sons. At the end of the long train ride, Sly and Ernest descended at the station in Louisville and went to meet young Cyrus, who had been sent on ahead to shadow Dinning. He was waiting for them at a rooming house near the main station.

"So what you got?" asked Sly.

"Not much, boss," said Cyrus. "Dinning ain't got no routine I can see. He never goes the same way to his speakin' engagements."

"So he comes and goes. What about the house in Jeffersonville?"

"He's got his family livin' with him. A lot of colored folks over there."

"We could attack the house and get him that way," suggested Ernest.

"Too dangerous, too many people around," said Cyrus.

"What about hitting him at night?" asked Sly.

"Those colored folk never sleep, boss. I watched that damn house 'til real late and there was always someone talking or moving about."

"Well, there must be a way," said Sly. "We just gotta find it."

Louisville, Kentucky

It was early evening and Dinning sat watching the street from his window at 706 Broadway in Jeffersonville. He could see the mighty Ohio River and the town of Louisville on the other bank, but he still felt vulnerable, even if he was living in a different state. He had a wife, a mother, and eight children to protect. Jeffersonville was safer than Louisville, but he knew the Logan and Simpson County mob had the means to send people north to kill him and his family. Although Dinning's talking engagements had fallen off in August, Reverend Frank still managed to get him the occasional invitation to churches and clubs around the River City. After these talks, he was often invited by his new friends to spend long evenings in clubs in the West End. He would frequently arrive home in the early morning hours, drunk and smelling of women's perfume. This set off Mollie, who complained about his drinking and womanizing.

On the night of September 20, Dinning was invited a second time to the Odd Fellows' Hall on the corner of Thirteenth and Walnut Street, where he had previously given a speech to some three hundred people. He looked forward to seeing his friends again, so he took the train across the river and arrived at the club around eight o'clock. It was a smaller crowd than usual, but people were still curious to meet an African-American man who had escaped a lynching. This didn't happen very often in Kentucky and the South.

Dinning was unaware that his house on Broadway was being watched. Cyrus had trailed him from Jeffersonville and saw him enter the club with a crowd of people. The kid had seen this play out several times before. Dinning would give a talk for an hour or two before going to a local bar or dance hall. Cyrus left the hall and took a hansom cab back to the rooming house. He warned Sly and his brother that Dinning was back in town.

"Where is he?" asked Ernest.

"He's at that club on Thirteenth Street," said Cyrus.

"You think we'll get him this time?" asked Ernest.

"Maybe," said Cyrus, "if we can get him alone."

"We're gonna shoot that black devil as soon as he steps out of the club," said Sly. "It'll be messy. Might have to kill a lot of negroes."

"I don't like it," protested Ernest. "We'll be makin' a lot of noise, and we'll be on foot."

"Let's just get the job done," said Sly, "so we can go home."

After the talk, the questions came hard and fast. Dinning was surprised by the number of questions about personal security. People wanted to know how to defend themselves against mobs. There had been a lot of talk across the country by black writers and speakers about taking up arms against the white man. The journalist Ida Wells had written:

"Of the many human outrages of this present year, the only case where the proposed lynching did not occur was where the men armed themselves in Jacksonville, Florida, and Paducah, Kentucky, and prevented it. The only time an Afro-American who was assaulted got away was when he had a gun and used it in self-defense. The lesson this teaches and which every Afro-American should ponder well is that a Winchester rifle should have a place of honor in every negro home and it should be used for protection which the law refuses to give."

It was after ten when Dinning was invited by his fans to a nearby bar for drinks. He was looking forward to an agreeable evening. A dozen young black men accompanied him as he came out of the club and headed across the street. Dinning noticed a large, bearded white man in a Stetson smoking a cigar near the doors, but no one else appeared out of place. He spotted another white man in a hansom cab waiting on someone, but there was nothing to alert him to any danger. A moment later, he and his group had entered the bar on the corner and any fear of the street was forgotten.

Around two a.m. Dinning stumbled out of the bar with a young black woman in a fancy dress. They walked down Thirteenth Street and then took a shortcut through a wooded area to the woman's house on Maple near the stock pens. They were laughing and carousing when Sly jumped out in front of them, blocking their passage. As they turned to reverse course, Ernest and Cyrus appeared behind them. Dinning didn't stand a chance. Sly ran at the couple and hit Dinning in the head with a brick. He was knocked unconscious and collapsed on the ground as the young woman ran off. They kicked him with their leather boots for a good minute before Sly pulled out his Bowie knife for the coup de grâce. Just as he was about to cut Dinning's throat, they heard voices approaching in the street.

Iris was on the night shift at the Louisville Hospital. She worked in the emergency room where the city ambulances pulled in. She liked the quiet hours and preferred to work alone without the day-shift matron constantly fussing around her. She was returning to work after her break when two ambulance workers brought in a badly beaten black man on a stretcher. He was unconscious and there was a terrible stench coming off his body.

"Where'd you find him?" asked the intern.

"Near the stock pens on Thirteenth Street," said the ambulance man.

"He stinks," said the intern. "Nurse!"

"Yes, sir," said Agatha, a nurse helping the ambulance men transfer the man to a gurney. Iris joined them, and they rolled the man into the surgery.

"We need to get him cleaned up," said the intern.

"What happened to him?" asked Iris.

"I have no idea," said the ambulance man as he left.

It quickly became obvious to the intern that the trauma was severe. The man's head was a bloody mess, with an eyeball attached by a thread to the socket. He had been hit by a hard object and his skull was cracked. The intern leaned in to get a better look at the wounds. He looked very young and new to the job.

"What do you think, sir?" Iris asked tactfully.

"Hard to say," said the young man. "Somebody gave him a good beating, that's for sure."

The intern stepped back so Iris could have a look. The man's head was in even worse shape than she had imagined.

"I know him," said Iris, gasping in shock.

"You do?" asked the intern. "Who is he?"

"He's George Dinning, sir. He's famous. He's been in all the papers. He's hard to recognize with his head all beat up like that. It looks like he may have a skull fracture."

"What about his eye?"

"We can't deal with that, sir. He's going to need an eye specialist. Call Dr. Cohen, sir. He'll know what to do."

"Thank you, Iris."

The doctor hurried out the door as Iris and Agatha finished cutting off the man's clothes and throwing them out. Agatha went off to prepare a carbolic soap solution, while Iris remained with the unconscious body covered in a sheet. She knew all about Dinning's courtroom battle and his pardon. Now here he was again, fighting for his life.

"Stay with us, Mr. Dinning," she whispered. "We're going to take good care of you."

Seventy-eight

Iris rushed home and arrived just as Bennett and Eliza were having breakfast. She came quietly into the house and heard young Larry's voice in the kitchen, chatting with his mother and Liz. When Iris came into the kitchen, Eliza knew something was wrong. Iris was pale and disconsolate.

"Iris, what happened?" asked Eliza.

"You won't believe it. It's George Dinning. They brought him in last night."

"George Dinning in the hospital?" asked Bennett, coming down the stairs.

"Is he all right?" asked Eliza.

"He was attacked and almost beaten to death. He's got a cracked skull and the doctors are trying to put his eyeball back in its socket. They don't know whether he'll live or die."

"Good God," said Eliza. "That poor man."

Bennett and Eliza exchanged a look. They knew how taken she was with the plight of the poor and the downtrodden. At almost the same moment, little Larry spilled his glass of milk on the kitchen floor.

"Hello, sweetheart," said Iris, quickly checking her emotions at the door. "Let me help you with that."

She wiped up the spilled milk, and Liz poured the boy another glass.

"Let's talk about this later. It's time for breakfast," said Eliza.

"We must pray for Dinning," said Bennett.

"Yes, we must," said Eliza.

"I'll go in later to see how he is," said Iris.

Iris arrived in the men's ward around eleven o'clock and found Dinning in a bed with his head wrapped in gauze.

"How is he?" she asked an intern.

"Dr. Cohen worked on him most of the morning, Iris," said the man. "He's still in a coma. They brought in an ophthalmologist who replaced the globe. It's called 'globe luxation', my dear. It's very rare."

"What are they saying about his chances of recovery?"

"No one is saying anything. He's breathing normally, so there is still hope for him."

"He's George Dinning, the man who was recently pardoned by the Governor."

"Yeah, I heard that. You were the one who recognized him."

"Yes, I did. We better keep him away from the press. They'll be coming in here, wanting to get his story, no doubt."

"I'll leave the director a note. Thanks, Iris."

At the Fifth Street Baptist Church, Reverend Frank was delivering his sermon on a Sunday morning when he turned to Bennett sitting in the front pew.

"I have invited my friend Bennett Young," he said, "to make an announcement. Bennett is a lawyer in town and is on the board of the Colored Orphans' Home Society. He has some bad news for our community."

Bennett was smartly dressed in a morning suit, vest, and ascot. He turned to face the predominantly black congregation in their Sunday best.

"Thank you, Reverend Frank. I hate to be the bearer of bad news. Our friend George Dinning is in a coma over at the Louisville Hospital after he was attacked by hoodlums last week. He was beaten up after giving a speech at the Odd Fellows' Hall. We still don't know at this time whether he will survive, but our thoughts go out to him and his family. Thank you for your time."

The audience began to murmur among themselves. Dinning was famous in Louisville, and a lot of them had followed the story of his dramatic escape from Simpson County.

"Mr. Young will be here to answer your questions after the service," said the Reverend. "Now, let us pray for George."

"Our Father, which art in heaven, hallowed be thy name. Thy kingdom come. Thy will be done on earth as it is in heaven. Give us this day our daily bread..."

There was little or no chance of catching the men who had assaulted Dinning. There were no detectives on the night shift, and crime was up two hundred percent from the previous year. The police department had thirty-five officers to cover a municipality with a population of 230,000. The city had three patrol wagons, but no mounted police officers or bicycle riders to cover the city. The officers were underpaid and sometimes not paid at all.

The *Courier-Journal* newspaper reported that George Dinning had gotten into an argument with a crowd of white men and ended up nearly beaten to death. Other papers reported that Dinning had been attacked by the same Logan and Simpson County whitecappers who had come after him before because he was planning on suing them for damages.

The Young family was at home, sitting around the dining room table, entertaining Jake Doyle and his wife. Liz was holding young Larry in her arms and playing with the child.

"You never told me about your time with Morgan's Raiders, Bennett," said Jake.

"I don't know, Jake. Maybe some other time."

"Come on, Papa," said Iris, bringing in the coffee from the kitchen. "I told Jake about our fight with Benton Wood in Quebec. Tell him what it was like charging the Union forces buck naked."

"Buck naked, you said. No, I haven't heard that one," said Jake with a laugh.

"Naked?" blurted Mattie and Liz. "You've got to be kidding, Iris."

"It was in the summer of '63, Jake," said Bennett. "Morgan had been ordered by Braxton Bragg of the Army of Tennessee to create a diversion in Kentucky to keep the Union forces away from his move into Eastern Tennessee. Morgan wanted to take us into Indiana and Ohio to disrupt the Union, but Bragg refused, so Morgan took us north into central Kentucky. When we reached the Cumberland River, we loaded our muskets and baggage on a boat to ferry them across and stripped off our clothes to keep them dry. We swam across the river with our horses, but as we came up on the far bank, we ran into a force of Union cavalry. We just had time to seize our guns from the boat and scramble up the bank to attack them."

"They must have been frightened to death by the sight of so many Confederate soldiers without a stitch of clothing," said Eliza, chuckling to herself.

"I don't know about that, but we were a pretty mean bunch," said Bennett. "We moved on the next day and fought briefly at Columbia until we reached Tebb's Bend."

"Tebb's Bend?" said Jake. "I believe I've heard that one."

Mattie and Liz had never heard the story and were all ears as Bennett recounted that terrible day.

"We attacked a fortified railroad depot manned by the 25th Michigan. It was a disaster. We lost a lot of men in a charge against the depot. There was no way we could win it. A friend of mine was killed. I didn't know his name until I came home in '68. His name was Vincent Eastham of Somerset, Company B, 8th Kentucky Cavalry."

"You carried him on your back, dear Papa," said Iris, "but you couldn't save him."

"No, I couldn't," Bennett said sadly. "I couldn't save anyone that day."

Seventy-nine

May 4, 1899
Louisville, Kentucky

There had been a huge increase in the number of lawsuits by African Americans against whites after the 1864 law passed by the U.S. Congress allowed black citizens to testify in federal courts to the same degree as whites. The number of personal injury cases brought by black litigants against whites skyrocketed during the two decades after Reconstruction from 1877 to 1897. The trial of George Dinning vs Doc Moore, et al. for personal injury and trespass was scheduled to start in the U.S. District Court on the same day as the Kentucky Derby. The lawsuit for damages by the freed ex-slave against the mob had been filed in federal court in Louisville by Bennett Young and his associates. They sought $50,000 for redress for damages against a list of thirty farmers. The judge was Walter Evans, who had served in the Kentucky House and Senate and had lost the Democratic gubernatorial race against Dr. Luke Blackburn in 1879. He had been appointed judge on the district court by President William McKinley. This would be his first trial as a federal judge.

Bennett was looking forward to the trial and felt they had a solid case. Although some thirty men had taken part in the attack on the Dinning family, the key defendants were just six men: Doc Moore, John Felts, James Flowers, Joseph Flowers, Albert Freeman, and the administrator of Jodie Conn's estate. They were to be defended by G.T. Finn, the same lawyer who had prosecuted Dinning in the Franklin criminal trial two years earlier.

The town of Louisville was already full of people celebrating the extraordinary festivities of the last few days when thousands more arrived for the Derby, the greatest horse race in the world. There had been stunning performances by Buffalo Bill's Congress of Rough Riders with their spectacular reenactments of an attack on a mail coach and the taking of San Juan Hill. Miss Annie Oakley had dazzled the crowd with her shooting skills. There had been patriotic songs and the public, young and old, had thoroughly enjoyed themselves. With all the celebrating, there had been the usual street fights among the drunken crowd and numerous accidents of all kinds.

The emergency ward at the Louisville Hospital was busy until late into the night, treating stab and gunshot wounds, as well as restoring the bruised and battered victims of domestic violence. Iris worked with three younger nurses and an intern. After midnight, the number of patients in the waiting room started to thin out. Janet and Hannah had been busy all evening treating patients. Iris was having a moment to herself around three o'clock in the morning when a young man entered the ward from the street.

"Please, miss. I need your help. My pa fell off his horse. He's got a nasty head wound."

"Let me have a look. Where is he?" she asked the young man.

"Just outside in the wagon, miss."

"Well, bring him in and we'll have a look."

"He can't walk, miss."

"Okay, give me a minute and I'll go with you."

Iris put on her coat because it was still quite chilly in the early morning hours. She followed the young man to a closed delivery wagon parked at the curb some twenty yards from the emergency ward. A sign for Malone's Groceries & Dry Goods was painted in large green letters on the side of the box. The young man opened the door for her. Iris approached to have a look at the patient inside but found it empty. She was suddenly shoved into the box from behind, and a huge ape of a man threw a tarp over her head and pinioned her arms. The young man wasted no time. He slammed the door shut and jumped up on the driver's seat, whipping the horse into motion. The wagon drove around an ambulance and a buggy parked in front of the emergency ward before it disappeared into the night.

It wasn't long before Iris' disappearance was noted by the staff. Janet went looking for her and had to ask the intern whether she had stepped out. No one knew where she had gone, and it was very unusual for Iris to leave the ward before the end of her shift.

The young man drove the wagon slowly through the crowds of celebrating townsfolk, many of them singing and falling drunk in the roadway. He was careful not to run over anyone. He had been warned not to attract attention, so he carefully threaded his way through the crowds. In the back of the wagon, Iris couldn't move an inch under the weight of the bearded man holding her down. The tarp made it impossible for her to see who had attacked her. The man sat on her legs to keep her from moving and when she cried out for help, he slammed his fist into her head. The blow stunned her, and she fought to remain conscious. She could hear the noise of traffic in the streets, but couldn't figure out where they were taking her. She thought the wagon had been pointed in a westerly direction when she'd been shoved aboard, and she'd tried counting the turns it took. The blow to the head had made her lose count. It was getting quieter, but this would be true anywhere in the city in the early morning hours when most people were asleep in their beds.

The delivery wagon finally pulled up in a stand of trees near the river. The driver jumped down from the wagon and opened the back door. The bearded man released Iris, who sat up and struggled to rid herself of the tarp. She could barely make out the faces of her kidnappers in the dim light. She had never seen either man before, but the reader would recognize them as Ernest, brother to Sly from Black Jack, Tennessee, and young Cyrus who now had a nasty scar on his face.

At first, Iris assumed that kidnapping her was all about money. Then she realized that there might be more to it than that. Her papa was not only wealthy but active both in business and politics. His name was in the papers all the time, especially now with the lawsuit. *That has to be it,* Iris thought. *They grabbed me as a way to get to papa.* It didn't make her predicament any less dangerous. Her first idea was to talk her way out of it, so she went on the offensive immediately.

"What the hell do you think you're doing?" she demanded. "I'm French Canadian! You've got the wrong person."

"What's your name, miss?" asked Ernest, confused by the question.

"I'm Iris Gagnon, sir," replied Iris. "I don't know you."

"It's her," said Cyrus. "She's the daughter."

"What are you talking about, young man?"

"You're Miss Young. I seen you around town."

"No, my name is Gagnon. Take me back to the hospital. You've mistaken me for another nurse."

"It's her," protested Cyrus. "I recognized the bitch soon as I entered the hospital."

Ernest shrugged and lit a cigarette while Cyrus roughly turned Iris around and struggled to bind her hands behind her with a piece of rope. The rope was a stiff twine, not very pliable. When he had finished, he shoved her into the dark interior of the wagon and brought her legs together, looping another length of rope around her ankles and cinching it tight. Then he clambered into the wagon after her.

"You ready to move, Cyrus?" called Ernest, banging on the side of the wagon, as he went to sit in the driver's seat.

"Yeah," Cyrus turned around and closed the doors from the inside, plunging the interior into pitch darkness.

The wagon lurched forward and Iris stayed still at first. She'd tried to bluster her way out of this, but it hadn't worked. She methodically worked on the rope binding her thin wrists. It took a few minutes, but she gradually got one hand free and then the other. *It was time to fight back*, she thought. *I've no intention of becoming a sacrificial lamb for these two morons.*

It was quiet in the streets as Ernest drove west. *Grabbing that woman had been as easy as a walk in the park*, thought Ernest. *Kidnapping was child's play compared to murder.* He figured they would be going home at the end of the day after the job was done. As the wagon rolled along, the back door suddenly swung open and Iris jumped down into the roadway. Ernest had no idea that Iris had just flown the coop. She breathed the cool night air and felt wonderful having regained her freedom. She walked in the opposite direction back towards the city lights in the distance, unaware that she was covered in blood. An hour later, around six o'clock in the morning, she entered the Young home on Fourth Street and caused a huge ruckus.

It was the first day of the civil trial and a huge panic took hold of the Young household. Iris was in a state of shock after the terrible sequence of events. She was barely coherent, mumbling something about 'killing a man and running away'. Eliza told Mattie and Liz to take her upstairs and put her to bed. If she could sleep it off, she would feel better later. Eliza met with Bennett in the breakfast room.

"Is she going to be all right?" asked Bennett.

"I think so," Eliza said to her husband. "Right now, she needs rest. You have a trial starting in a couple of hours and you have to decide what to do about it. I'll take care of Iris. You should call Jake and get ready for court."

Bennett went to the newly installed telephone on the wall and called Jake as Mattie and Liz came back down. They hovered around Eliza in a state of panic. They couldn't believe that their beloved Iris had been kidnapped. This didn't happen in the Young family.

"He's coming over," said Bennett, who returned to the table.

Jake arrived twenty minutes later while Eliza was upstairs with Mattie and Liz.

"What are we going to do, Bennett?" asked Jake.

"I'll ask the court for protection, both for my family and yours," replied Bennett. "They may try to burn down the office."

"Are these the same people who beat up George Dinning?"

"We don't know, Jake. Iris is upstairs resting. She was in such a state this morning. She was covered in blood. She thinks she might have killed one of the kidnappers."

"I'm sure Judge Evans and the Governor will provide support, Bennett, but she'll need to go in later and make a report to the police."

"I'm sure that won't be a problem."

"Are you ready for court, Bennett? We can always ask the judge for a delay."

"No thanks, Jake. I want to get started. Everything is set for today. I just need to go by the office to collect my files."

Sly was in a dirty undershirt preparing his breakfast in the safe house when Ernest arrived with the bad news. Sly looked older, with long grey hair down to his shoulders and a full beard that had gone almost white.

"You lost her. I can't believe it," screamed Sly.

"The bitch killed young Cyrus, Sly," lamented Ernest.

"Let's have a look."

The two men exited the house and went to the delivery wagon.

Ernest opened the door. It took Sly an instant to understand what he was seeing. Cyrus lay there in a pool of blood, a pair of surgical scissors still lodged in his neck and his vacant eyes staring accusingly back at them.

"Stupid kid," Sly growled, "kilt by a woman."

"I didn't hear anything," Ernest stammered.

"Course you didn't," Sly rounded on him. "That's 'cause you weren't payin' attention. That woman was nothing, you hear me? How many women have we kill't over the years? Twenty or thirty? Young and old. We strip 'em naked and tie 'em up, then we throw them down a hole. We never have a problem. All you had to do was bring her here. She beat you. She beat you bad."

Ernest wasn't scared of much, but he was terrified of the wrath of his brother.

"What we gonna do now, Sly?"

"First off, I'm gonna have a nice quiet breakfast and drink my coffee while you're goin' to grab a spade from the shed and bury young Cyrus out back along the fence line. Then we're gonna get our guns and go after that damn lawyer and his family."

An hour later, the delivery wagon rolled through the streets, heading for the center of the town. With their dirty, unkempt appearance, Sly and his brother Ernest looked like two out-of-luck peckerwoods, looking for work among the rich patrons of Louisville. They had stolen the wagon and killed the driver yesterday evening, so they weren't worried about the law coming after them. They pulled off the road into the alley behind the Front Street address of the Young family.

It was still a bit early for honest tradesmen to be offering their services to the fine people of Front Street, so they climbed down from the wagon and waited. Ernest rolled a cigarette and lit it. Then he opened the door to the wagon to check on their guns.

"What we waitin' for, Sly?" asked Ernest.

"You ready, brother?" asked Sly.

"I'm good, brother."

"We're gonna attack the house," said Sly as he wrapped the Winchester in a piece of brown tarp and tore off another piece for the shotgun. It would not do to be walking around with a long rifle in plain sight. Ernest picked up the heavy bag with the loaded six-guns, and they set off down the alley along the back fence of the Young property.

They hid behind the trees and watched a black gardener pushing a wheelbarrow between the flower beds at the back of the house. Sly took up a position with the Winchester in the bushes along the fence line. Ernest watched his brother from the alley and waited for his orders. Up at the house, the doors to the shed were open, and a horse and buggy suddenly appeared. Two well-dressed gentlemen climbed on board and headed off along Front Street, disappearing from view.

Sly realized they had arrived too late. Those lawyers were up damn early. They would have to hit the house if they wanted to send a strong message and get paid. The problem was they had no idea how many servants lived with the immediate family, and firing their six-guns in the close quarters of the house would attract a lot of unwanted attention. Sly figured that they would have to kill them silently with their 12-inch Bowie knives. The trouble with that was that lately Ernest had turned squeamish on him and didn't take to killing women and children anymore. That meant that Sly would have to do most of the hard work. He looked back at Ernest and ordered him to sneak up on the house just as the gardener stood up and returned to the shed for supplies.

Eighty

The streets of Louisville were full of carriages, buggies, hansoms, wagonettes, calashes, brakes, and traps, all heading south out to the racecourse for the twenty-fifth anniversary of the event. The racetrack was five miles from the town, but already the traffic was blocked at all the major road crossings. Jake and Bennett went first to the office and then crossed town to the courthouse, arriving just in time. The place looked deserted, but a huge crowd of reporters was already gathered inside the building.

As Bennett arrived, the reporters mobbed him before Jake could come to his assistance and lead him away to the safety of the courtroom. At the back of the room, the accused and their families glared at Bennett as he entered. He ignored them and joined the Dinning family who were waiting for him. He shook hands with George and Mollie and was saying hello to the children when Jake hurried past them on his way to Judge Evans' chambers to request federal protection.

When Judge Evans emerged from his chambers to take his place on the bench, he showed no sign that anything untoward had happened. He nodded reassuringly at Bennett and then called the courtroom to order. The reporters gathered quietly in the gallery. No one wanted to miss the first day of testimony. George Dinning was sworn in. He was well dressed and the scars on his face had healed except for his eye. He had never recovered his vision in the damaged eye and wore a patch to hide the missing eyeball. It had been a difficult winter for the family, who had all come down with the raging smallpox infection that was ravaging the country. The family had been tested in March and all ten of them had it. A yellow quarantine flag had been raised in front of their house by the Board of Health, warning passersby of the terrible disease. Miraculously, they had all survived and were no longer contagious, something George and Mollie gave thanks for every day.

Dinning took the stand, and Bennett started with questions about his life on the farm in Simpson County. Dinning explained that he made a living, growing tobacco and working for other farmers in the region. Bennett then led him through the details of that terrible night when he and his family were under attack from the whitecappers. Dinning told the same story he had at his trial in Franklin.

After Dinning had stepped down, Bennett called his 13-year-old daughter Eva to the stand.

"What was the first thing you heard?"

"I heard someone call Pappy," said Eva. "Pappy asked who it was, and they said they were friends. And then they said, 'George, you get out, and don't stop for fifty miles.' The man said Pappy had been stealing, and Pappy said he could prove he hadn't. And then the man at the door knocked and said: 'Shut up or I will tear your damn shack down.' And then I heard the shooting."

"When they said: 'Tear your damn shack down', then you heard the shot?"

"Yes, sir. And my father started up the stairs, and I heard another shot."

"Did you see your father enter the room where you were?"

"Yes, sir. He stood right at the foot of my bed."

"Was your bed near the window?"

"Yes, sir."

"Was there anybody sleeping in that room besides you?"

"Me and my sister."

"What happened next?"

"Pappy fired his gun, and then they began to shoot fast and a bullet came through my hair."

"They began to shoot fast after your father fired his gun?"

"Yes, sir."

"You felt a bullet go through your hair?"

"Yes, sir. The bullet came through my hair and Pappy went downstairs."

"What did your Pappy do when the shooting stopped?"

"He went downstairs. He went out."

Eva went on to describe how the next morning the whitecappers returned and took away her brother, Hermann. She named Pluitt,

Copeland, King, and Randolph as the men who had chased her mother and family away.

Sly and his brother moved into the garden behind the Young house. They hid behind the gazebo and the fruit trees as they watched the gardener's movements. The young man had gone to the shed and returned with a spade and garden shears. He took his time digging a hole in a flower bed. Sly stood up and simply walked right up to the man as if he owned the place. As the gardener turned to look at him, Sly smashed him in the face with the butt of his rifle. He then dragged the unconscious man behind a low hedge and waved for Ernest to move forward.

As his brother reluctantly approached the house, Sly ran up to the back wall, where he was hidden from view. A window was open upstairs and he could hear the women talking and Liz laughing at something Mattie had said. Sly wondered where the housekeeper and servants were. He moved in a counter-clockwise direction around the back of the house, looking in windows to get a better idea of the layout before he launched his attack.

After Jake had told Judge Evans of the threat to Bennett's family, the judge immediately telegraphed the governor's office to request a protection detail for the lawyers and their families. Jake knew that it would take some time, so as the judge got ready for court, Jake left the building to call on a colonel he knew at the local regimental hall. The colonel quickly mustered a dozen bluecoats to go to the address on Front Street. The men were happy to get out and show off their new uniforms and Springfield Krag carbines. They marched along Front Street as if on parade and then started to take up positions around the Young house in the streets and back alleys.

In the courtroom, the defense took over and called a dozen witnesses with the same story of a friendly visit to Dinning that turned into the murder of Jodie Conn. When Doc Moore had finished his testimony, Bennett Young got up to question him.

"Where did you meet the group of men?"

"At the New Hope mill."

"Did Jodie Conn ask you to accompany the men to the Dinning's house?"

"Yes, sir. I went there as his friend."

"Do you mean to say that you went there as the head of a band of armed men to drive Dinning away from his home and that you went there as his friend?" asked Bennett, incredulous. "Is that your idea of friendship?"

"I don't see no harm in it."

"So you marched your men in front of the house to show Dinning that you had the numbers to force him from his home?"

"I told him to look and see if there were enough of us to make him go."

"What did you do when Dinning refused to go?"

"I ordered the men to squat and fire."

"Squat and fire?" barked Bennett in shock. "That's a military order, is it not?"

"Yes, sir."

The courtroom audience could hardly believe their ears.

"My men didn't shoot to kill, sir," said Moore, realizing that he had said more than he wanted to.

The defense lawyer Finn was dismayed to see his entire case collapse in less than five minutes because of Moore's testimony. He had gone to great lengths to try to prove to the members of the jury that the whitecappers had gone as friends to Dinning's house and had no intention of hurting the man. Finn had contended that Dinning shot first and the volley of shots that followed was in response to Dinning's aggression, but to believe him, the jury would need to believe that the whole family was lying.

At the house on Front Street, Sly stopped at the door to the servants' quarters and left his rifle propped up against the wall. He removed the Bowie knife from his boot and stepped back suddenly as a young black man came out the door carrying two chamber pots, which he took down to the outhouse some fifty yards below the house in the garden. The boy didn't even bother to look at Sly and continued on his way until he saw Ernest coming up the path carrying a shotgun. The boy dropped the chamber pots and ran off after screaming for help.

Harriet, the housekeeper, heard the scream and stuck her head out the door to see what was going on when she ran into Sly with his Bowie knife coming for her. She slammed the door in his face and locked it.

"There's a man out there with a knife," she screamed.

Eliza was working on the family loom in the weave room when she heard the shout. She jumped up and ran into the kitchen.

"What was that, Harriet?"

"There's a crazy man out there, ma'am. He's got a knife."

"It could be one of those fellas who grabbed Iris!" Eliza said in a panic. "Lock the doors."

"The door's locked, ma'am," said Harriet.

"We need to defend ourselves. Find a weapon."

The cook, a large black woman named Phoebe, seized a carving knife from a drawer and held it up, ready to do battle. Eliza nodded and picked up a heavy cast iron frying pan from the stove. They joined Harriet in the hall holding a baseball bat. A moment later, they heard the glass shatter in one of the downstairs windows. Someone was coming into the kitchen through the servant's quarters.

"Hide," screamed Eliza.

Eliza hid in the pantry off the kitchen while the others found refuge in the servants' quarters. Eliza was on her knees, squeezed between the remains of a roast beef supper and a bowl of churned butter. She soon heard a man's voice coming from the servant's quarters.

"Get the hell outta here," said Sly. "I'm after the family."

"We ain't goin' nowhere," replied Phoebe.

Eliza emerged from the pantry to see Harriet and Phoebe valiantly blocking the man's passage to the rest of the house. Sly had chosen the narrow corridor through the servants' quarter instead of the kitchen door into the dining room and beyond. Phoebe was short and wide, with massive arms brandishing a very sharp carving knife, while Harriet, tall and slim, stood behind her holding the baseball bat.

"I said get the hell out of my way," growled Sly.

"You ain't comin' through here," said Harriet.

Eliza tiptoed up behind Sly in the narrow passage as he tried to slash Phoebe with his Bowie knife, but missed as Harriet swung the baseball bat at him. Sly stopped momentarily, thinking he might want to revise his plans. It was not going to be easy to get past these two women. Eliza raised the cast iron frying pan with both hands and rotated her hips, loading up for her swing. Then she heard a gunshot coming from the garden, followed by the boom of a shotgun. She swung just as Sly was starting to turn around and clocked him with a massive blow to the face, smashing his nose and flattening his features. He dropped like a stone and lay on the cement floor out cold.

"Got him," said Eliza. "That was easier than I thought."

"Nice work, Eliza," said Harriet.

Eliza, Harriet, and Phoebe ran upstairs to find Iris, Mattie, and Liz watching the battle taking place from the second-floor window. Several bluecoats were shooting at Ernest, who was hiding behind the gazebo at the bottom of the garden. The firefight raged for a short time before the bluecoats managed to flank Ernest and shoot him.

The following day, Eliza and Iris traveled with Bennett to the courthouse to support the Dinning family and hear Bennett's closing arguments. A murmur went through the families of the accused who were there to support their menfolk. They stared at Eliza and Iris as they took their seats behind the prosecution bench. The case for the accused was starting to look rather bleak after it was announced that even though there had been a firefight in the alley behind the Fourth Street home of the lawyer Bennett Young, the judge was not going to tolerate any delay or disruption of the trial.

After the bailiff had called for all to rise, Judge Evans climbed to the bench and was all smiles when he saw the Young party waiting for the hearing to begin. There had been a sigh of relief among the courtroom staff as the news of the attack on Bennett's house had made the rounds. Bennett was a popular man in Louisville courtrooms and always treated the staff with great respect. After the jury was brought in, Bennett rose to make his closing statement to the all-white jury.

"There was a great rejoicing in hell this morning," said Bennett. "When men of intelligence and high standing like the two lawyers who have spoken for the defendants in this case, stand in a court of justice and condone assassination and argue that practically a man may be murdered or driven from his home and his family by a self-constituted mob that may elect to take his life and destroy his property, all the demons smiled and applauded."

He paused for a moment to let the words work their magic. The courtroom was packed with reporters from every major newspaper in the country. He looked back at Dinning, his wife Mollie, and his daughter Eva in the audience, whose lives had been turned upside down by the mob.

"We may, in view of the brutality towards this man, his wife, and children, want to cry out. 'Is God dead?'"

The silence in the courtroom was complete. Even the usual coughing and clearing of throats from the gallery had stopped. Bennett Young was one of the finest orators of his generation and he spoke with great authority. He had the full attention of the jury, who were hanging on his every word.

"The counties of Logan and Simpson are named in honor of noble Kentuckians. Benjamin Logan defended himself against Indian attacks and Captain John Simpson was involved in the Northwest Indian War and the War of 1812. From these two counties, named for distinguished and heroic Kentuckians, came the men who are guilty of the cowardly and brutal conduct towards this poor, helpless negro and his innocent family. If they are fair representations of the present type of man Kentucky is producing, we must confess that we are the degenerate sons of noble sires."

"Far down in Simpson County on the edge of Logan and close to the Tennessee line, lived the humble, untutored negro who appears as the plaintiff in this case. By dint of industry and hard, unceasing toil, he had secured for himself 125 acres of land. It met all his wants and there in a rude, uncomfortable log cabin he lived with his wife and eight children."

"There is not in this case a single statement from any witness who has ever said that George Dinning had wronged a living being. There has been no suspicion of a crime. He has not interfered with his white neighbors; he has not disturbed their slumbers. But on the twenty-first of January, 1897, as he slept in his humble home with his children about him—the youngest four months old and the eldest 15 years of age —with one child sick and partially delirious from typhoid fever, at half-past twelve o'clock at night, he hears a rude, hard knock at his door."

"He calls to know who is there. The cowardly hypocrite responds: 'It is a friend.' This friend was a white man, backed by a gang of whitecaps and Ku Klux, armed with pistols and guns, who had come to serve notice upon this humble man."

"He must desert his fireside, filled with so many happy and pleasant memories, and depart at once from the neighborhood and put a distance of not less than forty miles between him and these marauders who in the darkness had served warning upon him."

When Bennett's appeal to the jury came to an end, there was complete silence in the courtroom. He sat down to smiles from Eliza and Iris and the reporters in the gallery. The former district attorney, W.M. Smith, stood up to make his closing statement for the defense. Smith admitted that his clients had trespassed on the Dinning property, but they had not gone there with any murderous intentions. He maintained that his clients had simply acted in self-defense after Dinning had fired from the upstairs window. His closing statement was short and to the point, and the judge gave the jury instructions and sent them on their way before adjourning for the day.

Eighty-one

Ralph Waldo Emerson

The next morning the judge called back the jury to make a special announcement. He told them that, based on the evidence, all the defendants except six would be found not guilty. The six who could be held liable would include Doc Moore, John Felts, James Flowers, Joseph Flowers, Albert Freeman, and the administrator of the Jodie Conn estate. The jury would be responsible for determining the damage caused to the Dinnings and could even impose punitive damages if they saw fit. The jury then retired to deliberate and returned one hour later with a verdict.

The jury foreman was James Breed, an assistant secretary for the Louisville Bridge and Iron Company and the son of a successful merchant. He stood up to read the verdict.

"We the jury find against the defendants and assess against them the sum of fifty thousand dollars."

This was a huge amount of money in 1899. Today, it would be worth approximately $1.8 million. The verdict was an extraordinary win for a black man suing his would-be lynch party. It was unheard of in the American South, and the newspapers lavished praise on the judge and jury.

The editor of the Daily Leader in Lexington wrote: *"Judge Evans' instructions and the verdict of the jury ought to be a warning to would-be assassins and midnight raiders that Uncle Sam will find a way to punish them when state law fails."* The editor of the Buffalo Express in New York wrote: *"This is one of the most notable triumphs of law and order ever credited to the record of Kentucky."*

A reporter in the courtroom noted that George Dinning sat immobile and had no reaction when the verdict was read. He had been wronged. He had been shot at. His home had been destroyed and he could never return. He probably couldn't believe his ears that a black man had won damages against a white mob. But the reality on the ground was not in favor of George Dinning. Five of the six farmers were poor and had no money to pay him. They preferred spending ten days in jail rather than paying Dinning.

The Jefferson Evening News reported: *"The judgment secured is not worth the paper the verdict was written on because none of the defendants have anything."*

In June of the same year, Bennett Young filed another lawsuit on behalf of George Dinning. This suit was against a group of men with money who had been dismissed from the previous lawsuit by Judge Evans because it was impossible to prove they had been there on the night of the assault. Bennett felt he could prove that they had indeed been present the next morning when the group had driven Mollie and the children away and burned down the house and barn. The new lawsuit was for $75,000, which was eventually settled out of court for a total of $3,500, half of which was paid upfront. George Dinning never received anything like the $50,000 of the first verdict, but with Bennett's help, he managed to collect small amounts over time to the amount of some $500 from Jodie Conn's father.

George wanted people to forget his controversial lawsuits and move on with his life. His last name 'Dinning', like those of many ex-slaves, had been inherited from his former owner and he felt no attachment to it. He changed the family name to 'Denning' to distance himself and his family from his past.

It was a sunny Sunday morning in the rolling countryside east of Louisville. Bennett and Iris drove the buggy to the Cave Hill Cemetery where many Confederate soldiers were buried during the Civil War. Bennett came every Decoration Day, sometimes with Iris and other times with Eliza. Iris wore her usual white blouse, salopettes, and bonnet while Bennett was dressed for a funeral in a dark suit and derby hat with a chrysanthemum in the buttonhole. They passed numerous families with colorful parasols in calashes and brakes out for a Sunday drive.

"You won big, Papa, but was it worth it?" asked Iris. "George will never get that money."

"Justice was served, Iris," said Bennett proudly. "We didn't do it so George would win a fortune in damages. We did it so whitecappers will think twice before attacking defenseless negroes and running them off their land. But I expect that George will collect a bit here and a bit there from the settlement over time."

"It was an extraordinary win, Papa. I will always be proud of you."

They drove through the gates into the cemetery and followed the long loop of Beargrass Creek.

"You never told me what happened during the kidnapping, Iris. How did you get free? I asked Eliza and she wouldn't tell me a thing."

"I'm not ashamed, Papa. It was dark. I couldn't see a thing. It was dirty in that damn wagon and the young man stank. He had bound my hands, but I managed to get free. That was when I thought about Benton Wood at *Tatie* Dorothée's house. Do you remember how he laughed at you? He was going to kill us, but I couldn't let that happen."

"He was a very dangerous man, Iris."

"I had to do something to save myself from those kidnappers. I had to get away."

They had arrived. Bennett pulled up on the reins and the buggy came to a stop.

"I had an old pair of scissors in the pocket of my nurse's apron for emergencies, for cutting gauze for bandages. I felt no fear, Papa. I didn't try to think about it. I just jumped the young man. I grabbed his head and drove the scissors into his throat. Then I opened the door and ran off. That's all I remember. It happened so fast."

Bennett put his arm around Iris and hugged her.

"You were very brave, my dear. They were evil men. You have nothing to be ashamed of. Sometimes we must do terrible things to save ourselves."

"They never found that young man. Maybe I only wounded him. I don't know. I just had to be free."

They stepped down from the buggy and collected their tools from the back. Iris carried a whisk broom and a bucket, while Bennett held a bouquet of freshly cut flowers in his hand. They walked between the gravestones to the site of Josephine's grave. Iris swept away the old flowers and dead leaves and wiped down the headstone with the wet rag. Bennett then placed the flowers on his daughter's grave and they knelt to pray. She had been eighteen years old when she died from pneumonia. The family still missed her.

After their prayers, they returned to the buggy to collect another bouquet of cut flowers, which they carried to an older section of the cemetery. There they found the grave of Bennett's old friend, Vincent Eastham, who had died at Tebb's Bend in 1863. Bennett came every year to put flowers on his grave. It was always a moving moment for Bennett, who revered the war dead, and friends who had fought for the Confederacy.

On their way back to the buggy, they wandered through the cemetery looking at headstones and Bennett pointed out the names of soldiers he'd known. They took the buggy and drove to a green park near the creek. They found a bench under the cottonwood trees. It was an idyllic setting for a picnic. They sat in the shade with their sandwich lunch, silently watching a black laborer in a wide-brimmed hat scything the tall grass along the creek. They listened to the gentle swish of the long blade cutting the grass and the songbirds in the trees. The smell of freshly cut grass wafted over them as Iris poured coffee from a thermos. They drank the coffee and ate the sandwiches.

There was a strong bond between them that had endured over the years. Iris was only ten years old when Bennett stepped into her life and told her she was named after a goddess and showed her Reuben's miraculous medal. It was a magical moment for a child without a father. The unspoken complicity was there when Iris threw the rock through the window and saved Bennett from a homicidal maniac, and again when Iris addressed the crowd of some five hundred black workers at the Tyrone bridge site. Their bond was a force to be reckoned with, a force for good and for a life filled with joy and happiness.

481

Epilogue

There is a raging debate in the American media over the monuments and military bases honoring Confederate generals in the Southern states. This has become a cultural and political flash point as people protest racial inequality and demand indemnification for the slavery of the past. American presidents such as Thomas Jefferson, Abraham Lincoln, George Washington, and Andrew Jackson all owned slaves. Jefferson Davis, Robert E. Lee, and numerous military officers in both the Confederate and Union armies owned slaves. Slave ownership went with property ownership and was never more than thirty percent in the South. Most Confederate soldiers, however, did not own slaves and fought for the cause of States' rights, or was it to preserve slavery? We'll never know. No polls were taken at the time to determine what Southerners really believed.

This fixation on the issue of slavery in the media has put blinders on our historical perspective. Americans today tend to denigrate everything and anything that ever came out of the South. Similar copycat revisionism is occurring in Canada, Australia, the UK, and some European countries. This is very detrimental to the national pride and moral fiber of a lot of democratic nations. By calling into disrepute the great men and women of the past who shaped our history, we are doing a disservice to our own history and that of upcoming generations.

The main character in this novel was a religious man who never owned slaves and was quick to accept Lincoln's emancipation of slaves. He became a successful lawyer and a philanthropist. He founded the first orphanage for black children and a school for the blind in Louisville. It is time to recognize some of the wonderful historical figures who were part of the experience of the American South and celebrate their legacy.

The Civil War saw the arrival of some deadly new weapons.

Anyone who has seen someone fire a .58-caliber Minié ball at a target will be astonished by the damage caused by the hollow, conical bullet. The minié ball knocks massive holes in cement and metal targets and is amazingly accurate. It was invented in 1847 by Claude-Étienne Minié, the inventor of the French Minié rifle. The ball was made of soft lead, and slightly smaller than the intended gun bore, so that rifle-muskets were easy to load in combat. A soldier could load and fire up to four rounds a minute with a minié rifle, and they were amazingly accurate at ranges up to 250 yards. The minié rifle made the bayonet practically obsolete and drastically reduced the role of cavalry and field artillery in battle. It was a hugely successful weapon when first used by French and British forces during the Crimean War in 1853.

The inventors of the minié ball rifle hoped to increase the firepower of the individual soldier and they succeeded, but, at the same time, they created a nightmare on the battlefield. On impact, the minié ball flattened out, causing extensive damage to the human body. It didn't just break bones; it shattered them. It shredded tissue and internal organs and left gaping exit wounds. Surgeons were soon overwhelmed by the mangled bodies and mutilated limbs. Almost three-quarters of all the surgeries performed during the Civil War were amputations and they were done in the field to prevent complications caused by gangrene. The surgeons were often accused of being 'butchers' or 'sawbones'. They amputated arms and legs as quickly as the men could be placed on their operating tables and put under with chloroform or ether, and sometimes without any anesthesia at all.

The Canadian Confederation happened as a result of the American Civil War. The political leaders of the British colonies in Canada feared an invasion by Union forces at the end of the war. In February 1865, the Canadian Parliament began debating the merits of the 72 resolutions of the proposed union of the British Colonies. Not everyone was in favor of the British North America Act, but it passed in parliament in March 1865 with 93 votes in favor and 33 against. It was then sent on to London for a vote and received royal assent by Queen Victoria in March 1867. The act divided the province of Canada into Ontario and Quebec and joined them with New Brunswick and Nova Scotia. The Canadian Confederation was born.

It is believed that the raider Charles Higbee ended up in Texas and became a successful banker with the money he stole from Quantrill's

Raiders and the banks in St. Albans. Confederate President Jefferson Davis joined his exiled family in Montreal in May 1867 after his imprisonment in a Union military jail. He stayed in a house belonging to the publishing magnate John Lovell and was very popular in Montreal. He was even cheered by the public at a showing of Richard Sheridan's comedy *The Rivals* at the *Theatre Royale*. For sixty years, a plaque commemorating Davis was affixed to the Hudson Bay store in downtown Montreal but was removed in recent years.

The story of Rose O'Neal Greenhow, the famous 'Wild Rose' as she was known in the Confederacy, and her drowning so near the shore of Fort Fisher in the Cape Fear River is based on the actual events. I don't believe that Bennett Young ever met the Wild Rose. I changed the date of her drowning, but the rest of her story is true.

Bennett Young's attempt to escape to New Brunswick after being released by Judge Coursol is based on the chronicle of the raiders' escape written by the priest Henry Casgrain in the newspapers of the time. Young and his men traveled along the North Shore in the dead of winter and got as far as Rivière-du-Loup near the New Brunswick border.

The story of the rape victim is based on the case of 33-year-old Mary Kirksey who lived in Lookout Valley, Tennessee. During the war, her house and an adjoining stable served as a temporary hospital for two Union soldiers recovering from amputations. To support herself and her fourteen-year-old son, Mary took in sewing and laundry for Union troops and sold them milk and eggs. She was raped twice by Charles Hunter, a private in the 7th Kentucky Cavalry. He was among some four hundred Union soldiers who were court-martialed for sexual crimes against white and black women and girls.

For the story of Lord Gordon stuck on a train between Montreal and Toronto, I was inspired by the March 1869 travel account of a Grand Trunk executive, Myles Pennington, who left Montreal for a 16-hour journey to Toronto that ended up taking 62 hours in a snowstorm.

Iris' year of training to become a nurse at the New England Hospital for Women and Children is based on the experiences of Linda Richards, America's first trained nurse. She arrived at the school in September 1872 and graduated in 1873. She then went on to work at the Bellevue Hospital in New York with an entirely different clientele. She went from providing care to six wealthy patients in Boston to a hundred poor patients from the slums of New York. The following year she returned to Boston to work at the Massachusetts General Hospital. I found it hard to imagine that hospitals at the time could operate effectively without trained nurses and patient notes. The ward maids working in the hospitals knew next to nothing about caring for their patients and worked long hours, often in the dark, with little or no support from doctors and the administration. So the arrival of trained nurses was a godsend for patients.

The railroad building boom in Kentucky went on for a long time. I advanced the dates of the building of the bridge at Tyrone to fit it into the story of Iris and Bennett Young. The ground was broken for the new bridge in February 1889 and the first train crossed the bridge in August of the same year. The bridge at Tyrone became known as 'Young's High Bridge'. The last passenger train crossed the bridge in 1937, but it remained in service for freight until 1985, when it was finally abandoned.

The yellow fever epidemic in Hickman, Kentucky in 1878 was an extraordinary event. I followed the facts as described in John Proctor's extraordinary *Notes on the Yellow Fever Epidemic at Hickman*, written the year after the calamity. While small towns like Hickman suffered terribly, cities like Memphis and New Orleans lost 5,000 and 4,000 citizens, respectively. New Orleans was often called the 'city of the dead' because of the deadly yellow fever epidemics that occurred there during the summer months.

The George Dinning case has been well described in Ben Montgomery's excellent book, *A Shot in the Moonlight*. This is an amazing story and well worth the read. Again, I have followed the facts with regard to Bennett Young's involvement in the events, with one exception. Iris was never kidnapped by bandits during the trial against the whitecappers and the Ku Klux Klan. Threats against lawyers representing black litigants, however, were common throughout the South during the Reconstruction era.

In his later years, Bennett Young became a well-known historian and wrote a complete history of Jessamine County, Kentucky, where he grew up. When he died in Louisville at the age of seventy-six in February 1919, there was a great outpouring of grief from his many admirers, both white and black, whose lives he had touched. The Courier-Journal reported his death on the front page:

"One of the last survivors of a memorable and heroic generation, General Young was long a conspicuous figure in the business life of Louisville and the courts of the State and Jefferson County. He was an eloquent pleader before the bar, and twenty years ago, the announcement that General Young was to argue (a case) could fill a courtroom always."

"General Young's death is a great loss to the colored people of Louisville. He was foremost in work of charity among our race," said Reverend H.C. Weedon, a black Methodist minister.

"Courageous as a lion, he had the gentle spirit of a child," wrote the editor of the Owensboro Inquirer.

The epitaph on his grave reads: *I have kept the faith.*

Acknowledgments

I would like to thank my editor Doug Sutherland, consultant Clare Dyer, wife Andrée Tousignant, son Thomas Kinsey, daughters Eve and Josée Kinsey, and my grandchildren who believed in this adventure and provided assistance.

Picture Credits

1- Cover art: "Missouri Guerillas", a painting by Andy Thomas
2- Photo, Bennett H. Young, Pewee Valley Historical Society
3- Portrait of Pvt. Philip Carper, 35th Battalion, Virginia Cavalry, C.S.A., United States, Library of Congress, https://www.loc.gov/item/2018667151/.
4- Photo of the Tremont Hotel, St. Albans, Vermont
5- Photo of the St. Lawrence Hall in Montreal, McCord Museum
6- Photo, Pied-du-Courant Prison des Patriotes, Montreal www.mndp.qc.ca,
7- Photo of St. Albans Raiders and Rev. Stephen Cameron at the Montreal Jail, December 1864, Courtesy of the William Notman Photographic Collection, McCord Museum

Other Books by the Author

Playing Rudolf Hess (2016)

An Absolute Secret (2017)

Shipwrecked Lives (2018)

Remembrance Man (2020)

White Slaves: 15 Years a Barbary Slave (2023)

See the author's blog: www.nicholaskinsey.com

One of the greatest mysteries of WWII

Cinegrafica Films and Publishing, 2016
ISBN: 978-0-9952921-0-9

After parachuting into Scotland in 1941, the German Reichsminister Rudolf Hess is revealed to be an imposter. MI5 puts together a team of intelligence officers led by Paul Cummings and his German wife Claudia to investigate the Hess double. They are sent to Camp Z where Hess is being held in relative comfort following Churchill's orders. The team soon starts to uncover the imposter's secrets involving the shadowy Herr Oberst and his secret training by the SS. But the British government decides to bury the truth and it is only in 1973 that a British doctor confronts the imposter during a medical examination in Berlin and discovers the truth.

"Makes history come alive like a thriller"

"Must read, forgotten WWII story"

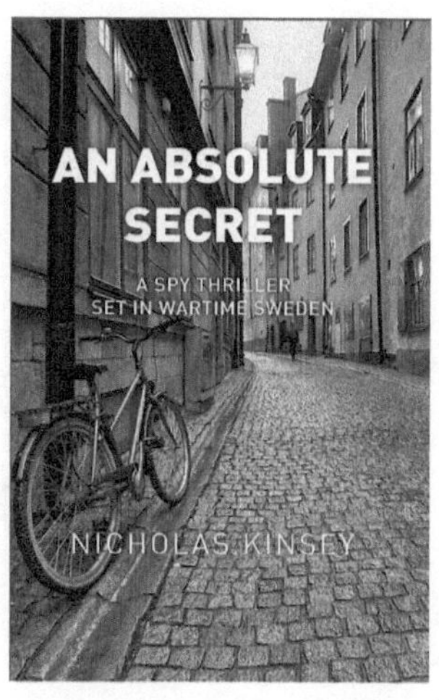

A spy thriller set in wartime Sweden
Cinegrafica Films and Publishing, 2017
ISBN 978-0-9952921-2-3

A spy thriller set in wartime Sweden when Stockholm was a bourse for foreign intelligence and German war booty. British SIS officer Peter Faye was sent to Stockholm in 1943 to spy on German Intelligence Officer Karl-Heinz Kramer. With the help of his assistant, Faye recruits an Austrian maid working for the Kramer household who manages to sneak out secret documents held by Kramer in a locked drawer. The documents are so sensitive that they cause a commotion in London. With the help of Swedish journalist Anders Berger, Faye discovers a network of Soviet moles working in British Intelligence. The novel is richly evocative, skilfully paced, and a real page-turner. Kinsey's meticulously crafted second novel is based on true wartime stories with their heroes and villains.

"A great wartime spy thriller"

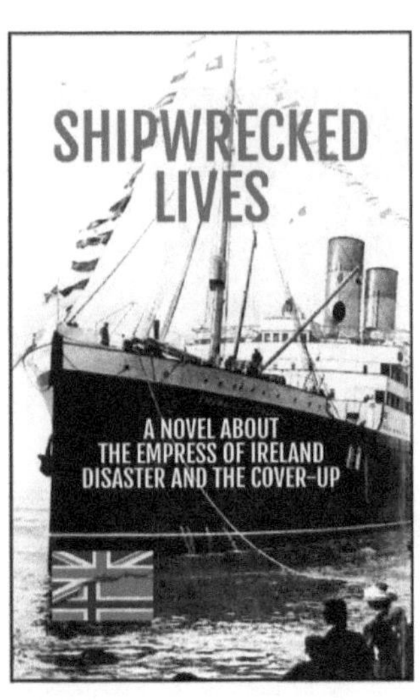

A novel about the *Empress of Ireland*
disaster and the cover-up
Cinegrafica Films and Publishing, 2018
ISBN 978-0-9952921-4-7

The *Empress of Ireland* passenger liner collided with the Norwegian collier *Storstad* in the St. Lawrence River on a foggy night in May 1914, sinking in 14 minutes and claiming the lives of 1,012 people. This is the story of the survivors and the government inquiry into Canada's worst maritime disaster. It is based on the actual testimony of witnesses at the *Commission of Inquiry*, which was presided over by Lord Mersey, the gruff and opinionated British jurist and politician.

"From the very first lines, Kinsey skillfully crafts this novel. We are drawn into the lives of the individuals on the Empress, passengers confused and frightened when loud blasts of the ship's whistle sound and the ship begins to list, then rapidly sink. He weaves the story between the disaster itself and what follows with the survivors in a courtroom as lawyers and witnesses try to unravel the cause of the collision. Kinsey has written a historical novel that is impossible to put down." Rosalie Grosch, www.norwegianamerican.com

Fear and despair during the 1832 cholera epidemic

Cinegrafica Films and Publishing, 2020
ISBN 978-0-9952921-6-1

During the 1832 cholera epidemic, Paolo works for his uncle as a gravedigger in Western Ontario. At night he earns a bonus from wealthy clients as a 'remembrance man' whose job is to watch over selected graves for signs of the undead. He discovers a young woman who has been buried alive and is drawn into a terrifying story of revenge and insanity. This is a tale of murder, greed, deceit, and the breakdown of society. Family members turn against family members, friends against friends, and soon everyone is out for themselves. Cholera victims are simply abandoned on the roads, and wagons are sent around to collect the bodies and bury them in cholera pits. During these dark days, stories spread about reopening coffins in which the dead had revived after burial, only to die in a futile attempt to escape.

"Rarely has a novelist managed to convey more vividly the breakdown of society during a cholera epidemic."

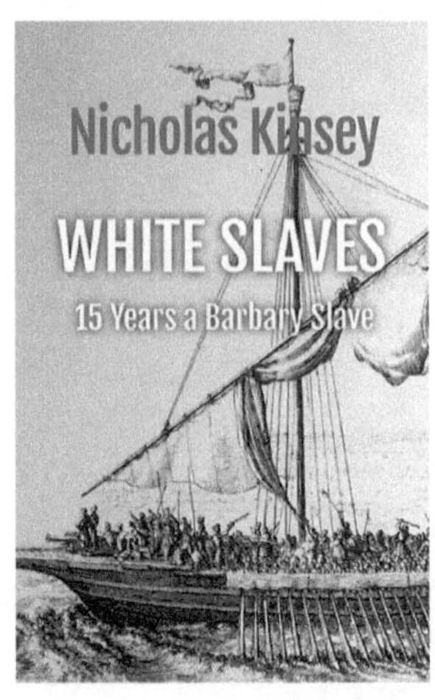

The tragic story of the Baltimore captives
Cinegrafica Films and Publishing, 2023
ISBN: 978-0-9952921-8-5

This brilliantly imagined novel tells the true story of the enslavement of the Baltimore captives and the horror of the Barbary slave trade. In the summer of 1631, the famous corsair and pirate Murad Reis attacked the peaceful fishing village of Baltimore, Ireland. They seized 109 men, women, and children subjecting them to a thirty-eight-day voyage down the coast of France and Spain to a life of slavery in Algiers. This is the story of that horrendous voyage and their new lives as slaves in North Africa before they were ransomed fifteen years later by the English Parliament.

"Raw, emotional, and gripping are the best words for me to describe it.
It was one of those "just one more chapter" scenarios
at two o'clock in the morning." BookSirens
"A wonderful read!" Shonna Froebel, Canadian Bookworm
"A skillfully rendered fictional account of an obscure
but fascinating slice of history." Kirkus Reviews